Play
for keeps

MAGGIE
WELLS

sourcebooks
casablanca

Copyright © 2018 by Maggie Wells
Cover and internal design © 2018 by Sourcebooks, Inc.
Cover design by Eileen Carey/No Fuss Design
Cover image © Dean Mitchell/Getty Images

Sourcebooks and the colophon are registered trademarks of Sourcebooks, Inc.

Published by Sourcebooks Casablanca, an imprint of Sourcebooks, Inc.
P.O. Box 4410, Naperville, Illinois 60567-4410
(630) 961-3900
Fax: (630) 961-2168
sourcebooks.com

Printed and bound in Canada.
MBP 10 9 8 7 6 5 4 3 2 1

Life is undoubtedly a contact sport, but love is the only game worth playing. This book is dedicated to all those who refuse to be benched. Play hard, play fast, and play for keeps!

Chapter 1

MILLIE JENSEN RAPPED ON THE TINTED GLASS SLIDING DOOR off Ty Ransom's patio until her knuckles ached, refusing to let up. This time, she added a threat for good measure. "Ty, if you don't open this door in the next ten seconds, I swear I'll throw a chair through the glass."

He couldn't hear her, of course. The glass was the super-duper insulated kind. The type to not only repel the elements, but also empty threats and spin doctors in the midst of mild coronary failure. She cupped her hands around her face, pressed her nose to the glass, and peered into the gloomy room. The dark, combined with a vaulted ceiling, gave the space a cavernous appearance. Caught in the flickering light of the television, oversized furniture cast hulking shadows on the walls. She peered at the screen. A pair of talking heads yammered at one another. The National Sports Network logo anchored the scrolling ticker at the bottom of the screen, but the latest scores were taking a back seat to big-time gossip this night.

She was about to call to him again when she saw the display on his phone light up with the incoming call. "Don't you answer that!" she shouted through the glass.

He didn't even check to see who was calling, much less answer. Tyrell Ransom, head coach of Wolcott University's men's basketball team, sat sprawled in a massive armchair parked in front of the screen, his long legs akimbo. The hand that held the phone dangled over the arm of the chair. Millie squinted, wishing she'd chosen high-beam night vision as her superpower when she'd clicked through the latest "Choose Your Superpower" internet quiz. The second the call clicked over to voicemail, she turned the meaty side of her fist to the glass and began to pound with all her might.

At last, the shadowy figure stirred.

Millie pounded harder, urging him to hurry up and unfurl his long, lanky frame. He rose from the chair so slowly, she almost shouted again. Instead, she held her breath as he approached. Each step he took was deliberate. His gaze never left her. A part of her—the part she liked to keep tamped down tight, because her impulses tended to get her in trouble—admired the lithe grace of his movements. No doubt this man was an athlete. Once, an elite one. He was still a man in his prime, even though his days in the spotlight were long behind him.

He narrowed those startling amber eyes and peered down at her through the glass door as if she were a specimen on display. Falling back on old habits, she snapped to full military attention before meeting his questioning gaze. Her father had been a master sergeant in the U.S. Marine Corps. It took a helluva lot more than one sulky, washed-up basketball giant to intimidate her.

"Open the damn door." She enunciated each word carefully, making lipreading possible in case her intentions were somehow lost in the shuffle. She'd slipped out of the wedding party she'd helped put together to celebrate her best friend's recent nuptials to come check on him. She wasn't about to be turned away.

"Now!" she bellowed when he didn't move fast enough for her tastes, giving the glass another thump with the side of her fist. The lock snicked, and he lifted the security bar. Before he could do the honors, she grabbed the handle and yanked the door open.

Shooting a disparaging glance at the glass in his hand, she brushed past him. "Yeah, because sitting in the dark getting drunk is always the best course of action."

"I hadn't thought about getting drunk," he mused, letting the door slide shut with a *thunk*. "Good idea." With a grace that always surprised her, he turned and walked toward the fully stocked wet bar. "Hey, aren't you supposed to be at Kate and Danny's party thing tonight?"

"It's still going on. Your absence was noted," she added pointedly.

"Yeah, well, I wasn't much up for socializing." He tossed the clear liquid he'd been drinking down the drain, then nodded to the crystal tumblers lined on a shelf. "Can I buy you a drink, Mil?"

She watched as he splashed less than a centimeter of liquid into the bottom of the highball glass he'd been carrying. This time it was amber, not clear. Crap. If he hadn't been drinking before, he was now.

Ignoring the offer, she opted to switch on a floor lamp. Warily, Millie peered down at her shoes. The nappy faux hide on her Jimmy Choo ballet flats was damp but otherwise appeared none the worse for wear in spite of her stealth approach. When Ty hadn't answered the ring of the bell, she'd had to activate plan B. Since there was no way she'd chance rolling ass over teakettle down his steeply sloped yard to get to the back door, she'd cut across the neighbor's yard to get to his split-level McMansion.

Exhaling her frustration, she shifted straight into fixer

mode. "Okay. Time to pull up your big-boy pants and make a plan."

Without taking his eyes off her, Ty tossed the drink back with a flick of his wrist. He fixed her with an oddly defiant glare as he let the tumbler slip from his fingers and drop to the floor.

"My big-boy pants?"

Millie goggled as the heavy crystal glass rolled across the wide-planked wood without shattering. She stared after it in wonder. Had it survived the fall because his arms were so long and it hadn't had far to go? Shaking her head, she thanked God she wouldn't have to add cleaning up shards of glass to her to-do list for the night.

"Right." She clapped her hands together. "Your woman has ditched you. No big deal. Happens all the time."

"Thank you for your condolences."

She let the sarcasm pass. He could expend his anger on her all he wanted. She was more worried about what he said to other people.

Moving past him into the still-shadowy great room, she spotted the remote control perched on the arm of the overstuffed armchair and made a beeline for it. She pointed the zapper at the screen and switched the power off, plunging them into thick, buzzing silence.

Feeling steadier, she faced Ty once more. "The real juicy part is she left you for one of your players."

Ty planted his big, ball-handler hands on his hips. "Thanks for clarifying," he said gruffly. "I almost missed the juice."

Millie rolled her eyes. She didn't care what her friend Kate said about an athlete's innate mental toughness.

There was nothing trickier than handling a bunch of superjocks and their touchy egos. "I *am* sorry, Ty, but you had to have seen something like this coming, right?"

"Aren't you supposed to be making me feel better or something?"

"I'm not your mommy. I'm not here to kiss the boo-boo and make everything better." A shiver ran down her spine even as she spoke the words. Awareness. Hot. Tingling. Happened every time they shared space. Which meant she'd had more than two years to get a handle on her attraction to him. Too bad being near him made her grip feel shaky. "No, my job is to help you put the best possible face on a situation that may reflect badly on the university."

He inclined his head slightly but still managed to look straight down his nose at her. "You're a real pal, Millie."

"I'm working," she reminded him. "I'll try to be a better pal when I'm off the clock."

"What do you want me to do?"

Setting her jaw, she studied him, measuring his readiness to step up to the line on this one. "First of all, we have to keep you off the phone. Then, we need to spin your marital situation: amicable split, coming for a long time, you wish her well, blah, blah, blah. When they start lobbing questions about Dante, we keep the focus on your contributions to his NBA career."

"So you don't think I should go on TV and tell the press I want to take a baseball bat to his shins?"

She blinked, surprised by even the hint of violence coming from this quiet giant of a man. "Do you?"

He shrugged one shoulder. "Kinda."

"Over her? Really?" The questions, three simple

words tinged with seven shades of disbelief, popped out before she could stop them. "I thought you two were pretty much done before all this."

The air between them sizzled and cracked with tension. At last, he ran a hand over his close-cropped hair and down to knead the muscles in his neck. "No. Not over her."

"Then why?"

The corners of his mouth curled up in a rueful smile, but she didn't see even a glimmer of happiness in his eyes. When he spoke, he enunciated each word slowly, as if he were forced to explain his reasoning to a particularly slow toddler. "Because I envy his court time. His career. His future." He flung one long arm out. "He's just starting out. No injuries. Nothing holding him back. He's going to have the career I never had."

She raised her eyebrows. "Then this could be the strangest midlife crisis ever."

He held up both hands. "Hey, I'm not having a crisis, and this is not my fault."

His palms looked to be about the size of salad plates. A fact Millie had long found intriguing. But this wasn't the time or place to speculate about how great it would feel to have those big mitts all over her. She could let her fantasies loose later. When she was alone.

Besides, the defensive note in his denial told her he wasn't quite as cool with his wife leaving him for one of his NBA-bound players as he wanted her to think. Feeling the need to do something, anything, to make him realize she was on his side, she reached out and gave his arm an awkward pat. "No. No, it's not. And I am sorry."

He looked down at her hand, a smirk curving his lips

as she yanked her fingers away a tad too quickly. "Wow. You really suck at the sympathy thing."

Millie had the good grace to grimace. "I've never been very touchy-feely."

Ty cocked his head. "I'm surprised."

"Are you?"

He took a half step closer. "You don't strike me as the kind of woman to shy away from anything."

Proved how much he knew about her. It was all she could do to hold her ground. Not because she was scared of him. More that she might not be able to keep her own impulses in check. Ty Ransom was not only tall, built, and too handsome for his own good, but he was also sweet and funny in a self-deprecating way that most successful jocks never quite mastered. A flutter of nerves tightened her belly.

Flattening her hand on her midriff to quell the internal uprising, she plastered her public-relations smile on her face. "Well, I do like a good fight."

"I've noticed."

"That's why I'm here. We don't have to let the press run this thing. Take control of your message instead of spouting off. Make the story the one you want to tell."

"I don't see what there is to control," he said with feigned nonchalance. "My wife left me for a first-round draft pick. Can hardly blame the woman for upgrading, can you?"

"Well, truthfully—"

"He's got two working knees, more vertical lift than I had on my best day, and according to our good friend Brittany at NSN"—he dropped his voice to a conspiratorial whisper as he referred to the perky, blond reporter from the sports network—"charisma." He nodded to the darkened screen, then shrugged. "God knows Brittany would know."

"Brittany doesn't know squat."

He guffawed. "You do have a way with words." He crossed to the wet bar and plucked another clean glass from the shelf. "You're hired."

"Thanks, but I already have a job."

"See? You don't even want me," he muttered as he pulled the stopper off a decanter. "Charisma," he growled. "Don't think I ever had any, even when I had game."

She hated this. Hated seeing this proud, cocky man lose his swagger over a woman who was little more than a piece of dandelion fluff. Sucking in a deep breath, she approached with caution. "Ty—"

"My game was okay one-on-one." This time, he sloshed three fingers of whiskey into the glass and sucked a few droplets from the back of his hand before replacing the stopper. "Took a lot of English classes in school, so I could quote poetry and shit." He picked up the glass and stared hard at its contents, then took a healthy slug. He didn't even gasp as the liquor went down. "Girls always liked that."

She placed a gentle hand on the center of his back. "Don't."

He stiffened, then slowly lowered the glass to the bar. "Don't what?"

"Don't downplay who you are. Don't brush off everything you've accomplished."

Ty didn't acknowledge her encouragement, but he didn't lift the glass again either. "What? What have I accomplished? An NCAA championship? Nope. Only made it to the finals. We lost. A spot in the NBA Hall of Fame?" He shook his head and gave a bitter laugh. "I didn't even have a dozen starts in the league." He picked his head up and glanced over his shoulder. "Did you know that?"

"No."

Millie knew his NBA career was roundly considered a failure, but she wasn't one to keep up with sports stats. He'd had medical issues; she knew about those. Something about fractures in his legs never healing completely. She let her hand fall to her side and curled her fingers into her palm. A part of her wanted to slug the people who called him a disappointment square in the nose. Not that violence would do much good. She was better at using her words to fight the good fight. But still, the man wanted to play. The issues he faced weren't of his making.

"Eleven starts in five years," he grumbled.

Ever the one to put the best face on things, Millie responded reflexively. "You did well overseas."

He whirled to face her, but his balance was compromised by too much strain on his bad knee and not enough sleep. Maybe a little by the booze he'd just swallowed, but Millie doubted it could hit a guy his size that fast. He staggered to the side, and she lunged to catch him—as if she could even slow his progress if he decided to face-plant. At a fit six foot eight, he was over a foot taller than she was and outweighed her by at least eighty pounds.

"Whoa, big fella," she crooned, the soles of her shoes sliding a bit as they corrected course.

He stared down at her, undeterred by their awkward little waltz. "I'm fine. My knee is messed up too."

"I know."

"I can't even get drunk," he said derisively. "Did you know that? Never have been able to catch a buzz, and believe me, I've tried."

"I believe you. You're a pretty big guy. Probably takes a couple of gallons," she speculated, eyeing him from head to toe with a comical leer.

"You know, I tried to jump-start my career when my legs strengthened, but too little, too late. No one here would touch me as a player."

Millie softened when she heard the wistfulness in his tone. "But you did good as a coach, right?"

She gave his bare forearms a squeeze to drive home her point. And yes, there might have been a little joy in handling him in a non-PR sort of way. She was still breathing, after all. Lordy, the man was beautiful. That little ditz he'd married had to be out of her mind.

"You are an awesome coach, Ty. Everyone knows you are. Even self-centered little shits like Dante Harris. Who got him where he is today? You did."

"I only want to do my job." He gestured to the television screen. "I don't want to deal with all this. I just want to do my job."

"Right. And you're great at your job. You did a good job with those kids at Eastern, and now you're doing amazing things with the program here at Wolcott. We've never had a first-round draft pick out of our men's program before."

The bit of bragging was out of her mouth before she even realized what she was saying. It was true.

Ty had produced his program's first star by coaching Dante to play up his potential. And Dante had repaid him by ditching school for the draft and stealing his coach's wife.

She bared her teeth in a quick grimace. "Probably not the best pep talk ever," she admitted as she met his gaze again. "Sorry. Now you know why I'm not allowed in locker rooms."

He gave her a lopsided smile. "Women like you aren't allowed in locker rooms because you'd incite riots."

Suddenly, the air was thick and ripe with things unspoken. The nagging hyperawareness was back. Unleashed desire crept up her spine one vertebra at a time. His breath was hot and moist. And heavily scented with scotch. Ignoring the tingle of arousal racing through her blood, Millie laughed and let go.

"See? It'd be a damn shame to let a sweet talker like you hole up here in the dark like some kind of wounded animal."

She tried to disengage, to step back out of the humming force field surrounding them, but he caught her hands before she could escape. She stared down at them, struck by how tiny and delicate her fingers looked compared to his. The contrast between the paleness of her skin and the tawny palms of his oversized hands made her breath catch in her throat.

Words. She needed words. Something to break the spell. "Make sure you're sweet when the reporters start calling," she added tartly. But Ty didn't take the bait. He just stared down at her, searching her eyes, reaching into her.

Something was about to happen. Something bad, mad,

and completely inappropriate. She should stop—she had to stop whatever this was—before they started. "Ty—"

She managed to get the syllable out before he dipped his head and gave her a taste of the smoky scotch he'd downed.

Good God, his mouth was hot. Those full lips, soft but firm. The kiss was everything she'd ever thought locking lips with him would be. More, if you counted the contact buzz from the booze.

From his first day on campus, she'd entertained a few harmless, certainly never to be acted upon, fantasies about Wolcott's most imposing Warrior. They were only something to give quality time with her vibrator some extra va-va-va-voom! She wasn't supposed to be letting him rev her engines for real. The second he came up for air, she'd put a stop to the madness. He was vulnerable. These situations had rules, right? The problem was, this opportunity, this man, was too delicious to pass up.

He shifted but didn't break the kiss. She caught his low groan as he angled his head, and she gasped when his tongue touched hers. A cannonball sailing across the bow. The second she weakened, he drove for the goal. She should have been repulsed by what she was doing. He was still technically a married man. But one masterful swipe of his tongue wiped the thought from her mind. She surely shouldn't have clung to him, her fingers pressing dents into his biceps, her own arms shaking as she fought to stand her ground.

Despite having spent years as the spokeswoman for a Division I athletic program and claiming the nation's premiere women's basketball coach as one of her best friends, Millie hadn't understood the power of a full-court press until his arms came around her. But now she did. Oh, sweet Jesus, did she ever.

The pressure was every bit as relentless as it was compelling. She tried to step up her game, take a bit of her composure back, but Ty refused to give an inch. He wound his arms around her, taking her hands with his and pinning them to the small of her back. She should have found the position uncomfortable at best, but the whole clinch was incredibly hot. Incendiary. She had to stop. And she would. Soon.

The velvet slide of his tongue over hers made her moan. Or maybe it was the way he drew lightly on her lower lip, then kissed her lingeringly. Like she was the one with the mouth dreams were made of, not him. She arched her back, pressing as much of her against as much of him as she could reach, but their heights were too damn disproportionate.

If we were horizontal, that wouldn't be a problem.

Millie banished the thought as soon as it popped into her head. This was kissing, nothing more. He was a man whose wife had just left him. His ego needed redemption, and she happened to be the nearest female. She needed to remember where she was and what was happening. If she had any sense, she'd be offended even. Employ the SING method Sandra Bullock touted in *Miss Congeniality*. But she had no desire to jab him in the solar plexus or stomp his instep. His nose was long and straight and beautiful. And the last thing she wanted to do was cause any damage to this gorgeous man's groin.

He drew back enough to press a lingering, little kiss to the corner of her mouth. She knew what the tiny, tender peck meant. Though his hold on her didn't loosen one millimeter, he was waiting for her to give him the green light. And oh, she wanted to. More than anything, she wanted to let her knees buckle and drag him down to the floor. Horizontal, she could reach every bit of him, map ever muscle, kiss every—and she meant *every*—inch of him.

But she wouldn't, damn her ever-practical nature.

She wasn't the kind of woman to allow herself to be swept along by romance, or even plain old down-and-dirty lust. No, she was the type to go in eyes open and head engaged long before she let her heart even consider entering the field of battle. She'd spent years building a reputation as the woman who could fix anything. The last thing she needed was to blow her hard work sky-high by getting entangled with a married man. No matter how much he needed her.

Ducking her chin, she dodged the next kiss. "Ty," she whispered as his too, too tempting mouth landed below her cheekbone. But neither her admonishment nor her misdirection stopped him. He chuckled softly and started trailing sweet, somewhat sloppy, but still sensuous kisses along her jawline.

"I've thought about this for so long," he murmured, almost to himself. "Thought about you."

Bad. This was the bad part. He was saying exactly what anyone with half a brain cell wanted to hear. And she had whole brain cells, and though they'd taken a short sabbatical, her synapses were starting to fire again. Wriggling her hands free from his grip, she locked her knees and came at him from underneath. She refused to take note of exactly how firm his abs felt as she slipped both hands between their bodies. She didn't even want to register the fact that his pecs were every bit as hard as the rest of him. His nipples were like chips of diamond beneath the smooth knit of his shirt—but she'd think about all these details later.

Much later.

After she'd done her job and he'd secured a divorce. Those had to be her priorities.

With a groan as heartfelt as his protest, she pushed away. They stood staring at one another, his gaze steady if a tad unfocused. His lips were wet and wonderful, but his thick, dark brows drew together in a V of confusion. Ty took several seconds to catch up, but she saw when reality clicked for him. She also saw the flash of hurt in those beautiful, golden-brown eyes.

"We can't do this now," she said, forcing a note of quiet calm she wasn't anywhere close to feeling into her voice. She wasn't rejecting him. Needing to make him understand, she risked taking one of his big hands between both of hers. "We can't, Ty. I have work to do. You have things to sort out."

He closed his eyes and blew out a breath. The force of the exhalation made him sway.

"Go home, Millie. I'm fine."

Knowing one minute could mean the difference between repair and ruin, she nodded once, then headed for the sliding door. "I wanted to check on you." The lock clicked as she released the latch. She eyed the wavering shadow in the darkness warily. "Answer your phone when I call, okay? I'm not cut out to be a cat burglar. But only answer for me," she added. "No reporters."

"Only for you."

Not knowing exactly how to respond to that or to any of the events of the previous five minutes, Millie decided to let him have the last word. She slipped out the door and slid the heavy pane of glass closed behind her. Avoiding the patio furniture, she hustled past the dimly lit swimming pool and into the safety of the darkness beyond the skirting. She waited until her Jimmy Choos touched the plush, green lawn before allowing her steps to slow. Lifting her hand to her mouth, she pressed her fingertips to her lips, trying to seal those heady kisses in.

He had a career to salvage, and it was her job to help him. A public and possibly ugly divorce was in the offing, and she had to make sure he came out smelling like a champion and not a chump. And once all her job was done, when he was stone sober and seeing her in the harsh light of day, if he still wanted a woman six years his senior as the antidote for being burned by his much younger bride, well, then, they could talk about the possibility of acting on their urges. Reasonably. Rationally. And without any crazy expectations of romance.

Because Millie Jensen didn't do romance. She didn't believe in happily ever after. Hadn't for the last twenty years, and she saw absolutely no reason to start now.

Chapter 2

THE SOUND OF THE MARCHING WARRIORS BLARING THE school's fight song, "War Cry," filled the air, and Ty's entire body went rigid. Instinctively, he reached into his pocket for his cell, but he came up empty. He groped blindly at the area around him. Nothing. Then, mercifully, the phone fell silent.

Ty felt the light pouring through the wall of glass before he even dared to crack an eyelid. It wasn't the good kind of light, the sort that welcomed and warmed a guy. No, this was diabolical light. Light determined to leech the last of his life force right out of him. He could feel his liver shriveling. The roar of his own blood in his ears. The persistent throbbing of a brain counting down the seconds to implosion. His eyes remained glued shut. If he wasn't mistaken, someone had cut out his tongue and replaced it with a swatch of suede.

The phone chirped to indicate a missed call, and he groaned. He wasn't dead.

Damn.

He winced as he peeled his cheek off the cushion. A dark patch marked the spot where he'd drooled in his sleep. *Stupor*, he corrected, pushing up on shaky arms. He hadn't been asleep; he'd been sleeping off an epic bender. One that started the minute Millie walked out his door.

Tired of women leaving him high and dry, he'd decided to get wet. Soused.

Ty swung his feet to the floor. His knees popped and creaked, as usual. His head thumped like a subwoofer. His vision swam and his stomach lurched. The second he felt the bile rise, he slammed his eyes shut again.

Funny, he'd always considered the floor-to-ceiling windows in the great room an asset. He didn't know what he'd been thinking. The massive panes of reflective glass allowed an obscene amount of light into the room. Sliding his parched tongue over cracked lips, he grunted and forced himself to sit up straighter. This injury was self-inflicted. "Man up," he whispered.

Shuffling across the room, he marveled at the fact that he'd managed the distance to the wet bar. The bottles marked *vodka* and *scotch* stood empty. Only the bourbon survived, but it had taken a hit as well.

Millie hadn't been far off in her assessment on how much it would take to get him drunk. No surprise. Millie was rarely wrong.

Ignoring the mini fridge stocked with bottles of imported water, he flipped on the tap, held a glass under the faucet, then guzzled all he managed to capture in three big gulps. Two glasses later, he started to feel reconstituted. He filled the tumbler one more time, then hazarded a look around. The television remote sat squarely on the arm of the chair. Other than the spotted sofa and the empty liquor bottles, the room didn't appear to be any worse for wear. But his phone was missing.

He stood still and listened for the chirp again. He wasn't sure if the noise was a notification or the sound of the battery's death throes. A true man of the millennium, he'd never allowed his phone to run all the way down. God forbid he risk missing something. Until this week, he might have counted his phone among his favorite possessions, and he had a lot of possessions.

But ever since a tip from one of his assistant coaches pointed him toward his soon-to-be-ex-wife's PicturSpam account, his precious phone had slipped down a few notches in the rankings. Incriminating photos. She hadn't only made a fool of him with the man she was now calling her "soul mate." Oh, no. Once people got to talking, it came out that she'd had inappropriate relationships with at least three of his former players and the assistant who'd taken a job with their biggest rival.

Mari had been restless and unhappy with his lack of high-profile success; he knew that. He just didn't know how far afield she'd strayed in the two short years they'd been at Wolcott until he saw that picture.

The phone bleeped again.

Narrowing his eyes at the oversized armchair, he approached with caution. His cell wasn't on the arm or under the cushion. He ran his fingers along the crevice between the seat and the arms and back. Nothing. Frustrated and aching, he dropped into the chair and stared up at the dark television screen. If he waited, the damn thing would beep again, and he'd get a better bead on its whereabouts. Propping his elbow on the armrest, he cradled his aching head. Two fingers pressed into his temple helped alleviate the worst of the pounding. He leaned into the relief.

He'd almost dozed off when "War Cry" blasted once more.

Hurling himself from the chair, Ty let loose with a cry of his own as his reconstructed knee hit the floor. *Bionic man my ass*, he thought as he swung his head around, desperate to find the source. He blinked as a beam of sunlight bounced off the glass screen. He lunged for the screaming device, swiping his hand across the glass as if he were a grizzly set to tear the damn thing to shreds in order to make the ringtone stop.

"Hello," he growled.

"Good morning, *friend*."

The husky rasp combined with the intimate greeting did a myriad of things to him. A flush burned deep beneath his skin. His sluggish thoughts slowed to a near halt, then jumped into hyperdrive as a series of images and remembered sensations rocketed through his brain. Millie Jensen slipping through his back door. Cherry-cola-red hair. Bright-eyed determination. Long, lithe arms. Bare but not naked. No, he hadn't gotten her naked. A realization that filled him with relief and disappointment.

Millie'd popped up at his patio door wearing some kind of silky black tank top over skinny black pants. A cat burglar in zebra-print shoes.

Cigarette pants. That's what Mari had called them. The term suited Millie. The deep, throaty timbre of her voice would lead anyone to believe the woman chain-smoked Marlboros all day. But she didn't. Millie was a distance runner. Had been since her high school days, she'd told him. Each year, she entered and completed one of the big marathons. Boston. New York. Chicago. She'd pounded the pavement in all those cities and more. And finished with impressive if not news-making time.

He wasn't surprised she would make a good showing. Everything about Wolcott's public relations guru was sleek, streamlined, and ruthlessly vetted. The lines of her clothing suited her to perfection. As did the flamboyant animal prints and outrageous colors she chose. Millie didn't do anything she didn't want to do, and what she did do, she did breathtakingly well.

Even kissing.

And Ty certainly remembered laying one on his good friend Millie the night before. Mortification mixed with a smidge of pride as he tried to figure out exactly how to respond to her greeting. As always, he did what he did best—pressed until he was forced to fall back. "Good morning, sweetheart."

"Sleep well?"

Ty didn't know how it was possible for a woman who sounded like a veteran truck-stop waitress to coo, but somehow, Millie pulled it off. "Like a baby," he grumbled.

"I bet."

Every word left unspoken sizzled and popped in the silence that followed. Weakened by dehydration and the harsh sunlight, Ty closed his eyes, then covered them with his hand for added protection. "I had the strangest dream…"

The opening hung like a buzzer beater hurled from the half-court line. He counted three full seconds off the clock before she took mercy on him and went up for the alley-oop. "Did you? Was I in it?"

"You were the star."

Millie laughed. As expected, she had few girlish giggles or glass-shattering squeals in her repertoire. Only a low, gravelly chuckle that let him know she knew exactly what had gone on in his dream. Because his fantasies had actually come to life. After nearly two years of keeping his hands shoved firmly in his pockets,

he'd given in to the impulse that had seized him the first
time he'd laid eyes on Millie. He'd seized her. Kissed
her. Finally. But the scene hadn't played out in any of
the millions of ways he'd imagined.

"I'm always the star, Ty."

Her cocky retort jolted him out of the potential
pity party. Confidence. Her self-assurance was one of
Millie's most attractive qualities. And that was saying
a lot. The woman had assets in abundance. Even if they
were the obvious ones. "I have no doubt."

Running his hand down his face, he rubbed his fingers over two-day's growth of beard. Did she leave his
house with beard burn? Did she like the way he kissed?

But of all the questions bouncing around in his head, he
only needed answers to one. "Do I owe you an apology?"

"Do you think you do?" she countered.

Ty grimaced and shielded his eyes again as he lay
back. If he stretched out on the hard, unforgiving floor
like some kind of religious martyr, would she let him off
the hook? Did he want to be let off?

Millie was a master at playing games. She'd keep
dodging and deflecting until she forced him to come
straight at her. He knew it. She knew it. This was a
dance they'd perfected over countless months of fruit-
less flirting. But soon, he'd be free. He was pretty sure
she was free too. If they wanted to, they could see if
the attraction between them continued to blossom, even
after the fruit wasn't forbidden anymore.

Exhausted by the ramblings of his own thoughts, Ty
heaved a sigh he dredged up from his toes and gave up
the struggle. "I'm sorry if I made you uncomfortable
last night."

"Well, I can tell you I'm probably not going to take up breaking and entering as a hobby. I don't have the right footwear for a life of crime."

Amused by her dry reply, he pitched his voice low and stern. "For God's sake, save the shoes."

"One must have one's priorities in line," she answered with a prim, little sniff.

"Millie, I—"

"If you're going to apologize for kissing my socks off, you can save your sorrys."

Pleased, he smiled for the first time since he woke up not-quite-dead. "You weren't wearing socks."

She snorted. "How would you know? You can't remember your own name at the moment."

"I remember kissing you," he retorted. "I remember every second."

Truth. He did remember, despite the cotton wool filling in his head. He remembered every second of it all too well. The slide of her lips. Her taut, little body pressed against his. She had small breasts and boyish hips. Her arms were toned, the muscles long and subtly cut. And they'd been bare. Silky, soft, and supple.

She wore her hair short and changed colors so often, he'd stopped being shocked by the alteration. Brusque and sharp-tongued, he'd seen her dismantle reporters piece by piece, all the while smiling as if she were having the time of her life. Taken individually, not one of these attributes should have turned him on, but wrapped up in Millie, the package worked for him.

He cleared his throat. "So you don't want me to apologize?"

"Not for kissing me, but you might consider an

apology for ignoring my instructions about not talking to reporters," she answered in her brisk, efficient
manner. "And you might consider groveling when or if
Greg Chambers calls."

Ty scowled as he searched his memory, but he
couldn't quite bring anything non-Millie-related into
focus. Dread welled in his gut. He hated the National
Sports Network's golden boy and his smug smirk, but
Ty couldn't for the life of him remember what he'd done
to owe the man an apology. "Chambers? Why? Did I
talk to Greg Chambers?"

He heard her exhale long and slow. "No, but you
talked to Jim Davenport from the *Sentinel* last night."

Jim Davenport. Greg Chambers. Millie. A mon-
tage of clips from the night before flashed through his
brain. Finally, he zoomed in on Davenport. The slimy,
sad wuss of a sports reporter worked for both the local
television station and the newspaper. Old Jim used to
date Kate Snyder, Wolcott's women's basketball coach.
Until Danny McMillan came to town and swept Kate
right out from under Davenport's nose. Good thing too.
Kate was miles too good for a jackass like Davenport.

But as a result, their once-staunch supporter had
turned against the university. In the weeks since Kate
and Danny had gotten hitched at the courthouse, old Jim
seemed to have developed an agenda. One that included
a hard-on for anything having to do with Warrior basketball. Ty's troubles with Mari had made him an easy
target. It took a second for him to connect the dots in
his head, but by the time the last line was in place, the
dread in his stomach liquefied into thick, bitter bile and
started to rise.

"I talked to Jim last night," he confessed.

"Yes, you did." Now Millie was using her patient kindergarten teacher voice, which was not a good sign. Millie wasn't known for her patience and, as far as he knew, had never stepped foot in a kindergarten classroom. "He called me bright and early this morning. Told me that while you were talking to him, you apparently cast some rather...offensive aspersions on Mr. Chambers's athletic prowess as well as his manhood. You also said you'd had him banned from the Wolcott University campus." She paused. "That is why Mr. Davenport ended up calling me. He was kind enough to ask me to verify the quote about the ban on Mr. Chambers." She paused to let the information sink in before going for the kill. "I've tried to reach you by phone a number of times this morning. I was about to come over to see if you'd put on your concrete shoes and jumped in the pool. I'm glad you didn't."

Feeling like ten thousand kinds of a fool, he wedged the phone against his ear and pressed the heels of his hands to his eye sockets. "I was angry. I didn't want to say, 'No comment.' I wanted to comment, to say... something."

"Well, you sure did," she said snidely.

He groaned again. "You left the party to check on me last night, and I kissed you."

"Yes, well, I didn't say I wasn't well rewarded."

"And now you're having to babysit me again. Millie, I'm sorry." Letting one hand fall to the floor, he took hold of the phone once more. "What story did Davenport run?"

"Well, I managed to squash the bit about the ban," she

announced. "But since the rest were direct quotes and opinions you willing gave to a member of the press…"

He didn't need to see her to know she was using the universal hand signal for "I can't fix stupid." He ran his hand over his face again, as if he could scrub the cobwebs from his brain. "Oh shit."

"The *Sentinel* doesn't have a wide circulation, and we are talking Wolcott *men's* basketball, so not a headline grabber."

The dismissive commentary didn't offend him. Everyone knew the Warriors were the whipping boys of the mighty Mid-Continental Conference. Two factors allowed the school to play with the big boys— tradition and the law of averages. Wolcott's student athletes were better known for putting up impressive grade point numbers, even if their stats lacked in athletic endeavors. As a founding member, Wolcott would have to willingly sever ties with the conference. And why would they do that when the school got a piece of the conference media pie?

"Unfortunately, one of the wire guys picked up a few of your choice comments, and word has filtered back to NSN."

Ty imagined Greg Chambers's fat head exploding on a live feed. He smiled, then groaned as the pull of facial muscles reminded him he still had his own aching head to contend with. Part of him couldn't help but wonder if cranial explosion might not be a relief. Quick, maybe somewhat messy, but painless. Not such a bad end. Had to beat the slow agony he was enduring. "You got some of those cement shoes?" he asked, his voice low and raspy.

Millie laughed, and the sharp edges of her disapproval melted away in the warmth of the sound. "You didn't say anything we haven't all thought."

"Yes, but I said them out loud. To a reporter. One with a growing vendetta to feed," he added as if she didn't already know about Jim Davenport's bruised feelings.

"Yes, you did."

Ty stared at the ceiling. For months now, he'd been spinning like a top. One whirling a little off-kilter. Now his life was careening out of control. He needed divine intervention. And he had it. He had Millie on his side.

"What do I need to do?"

She blew out a breath as if she'd been hanging out in the deep end, waiting for him to come to his senses. "First, you call Greg and apologize. It won't be enough, but it's a start. I'll sort out the rest of that mess later," she assured him, all brisk efficiency. "Then, we talk to the rest of the media."

He heard the *tap-tap-tap* of her fingernail and knew she was typing notes one-fingered into her ever-present tablet. He wished he could see her. Seeing Millie spring into action was something to behold. She was a force of nature. One of the wonders of the world. Heaven help anyone who dared to get in her way.

"So far, all the chatter has been about Mari and Dante and the morons speculating. It's time for us to step up and take control of the message."

Though he knew she was right, it still pinched to agree to the plan. After all, no guy wants to be the schmuck whose wife left him for another man. A younger man. One with the future of his choosing all stretched out in front of him. How was he supposed to make getting dumped look good?

"Ty?"

Millie's gentle prod pulled him out of his thoughts and back into the present.

And gave him the answer he needed. Millie would know how to spin this mess so he came out looking like a champion. He trusted her. Which seemed odd given what the last woman in his life had done to him. But Millie wasn't anything like Mari. He knew that right down to his bones. The two women couldn't have been more different.

Besides, what choice did he have? He was the one who had married a woman over a decade younger than he was. He'd ignored the dollar signs in Mari's eyes, hauled her off to Vegas, and tied the knot before either of them could think better of the plan. Then, when his idiocy exploded in his face, he was the fool who had holed up in his monstrosity of a house swilling scotch and spilling his guts to some reporter with an ax to grind.

Millie was right, as usual. The time had come to set things straight. He'd apologize to Chambers, let the press poke and prod at him a little, then he'd head back to Nevada to get divorced not quite as quickly as he'd gotten hitched. The wait would be shorter there, and he wouldn't have to prove anything more than irreconcilable differences. Since Mari had a kid with a multimillion-dollar contract under his belt, she was in as much of a rush as he was.

"Ty, are you still there? Snore or something if you've passed out."

"I'm here."

"You can do this. All we need is a plan."

"A plan like what?"

"Well, you could start with a shower."

Her suggestion was so on target it hurt. "Right. Shower. Getting up."

"Exactly what you need to do, Ty," she said gently. "Get up, get out, and get on with your life. I'll help you."

He huffed a little laugh, then gave in. "Okay," he said into the phone. "Let's do this thing."

Chapter 3

MILLIE CLICKED HER PEN AND PUSHED AWAY FROM HER DESK with a decisive nod. "Excellent." She flashed a stiff smile at her assistant as she snagged her tablet from the corner of the desk and rose. "Call the chancellor's office and give them the update. I'm going to run by the AD's office to get my travel lined out, drop the new press kits by the bull pen, then circle back around before I head home to pack."

"You want me to send the releases about the coaching changes in the baseball program?" Cassie asked as she stood too.

"Yes. And I'm sending you a picture Kate sent me from the island. If she asks, I'm claiming someone hacked my cell, but could you sort of…" She made a circling motion with her hand.

"Leak the photo on every social media outlet I can find?"

Millie grinned. As far as assistants went, Cassie was worth her weight in free media coverage. "Make whatever pithy caption you come up with more football related than basketball. We want to shift the focus away from all talk of basketball, so for now, Kate will have to be Mrs. Gridiron." She smirked as she pulled her phone from her pocket. "Serves her right for looking so damn good in a bikini."

"Yeah!" Cassie chirped.

Millie paused in the doorway. "Okay, maybe don't leak the photo."

"But we can still hate her for looking so awesome?" Cassie asked hopefully.

"Yes, but we have to store it deep down inside."

"Got it," her assistant chirped.

Millie held for another moment to be certain she hadn't forgotten anything. After a quick rundown of her mental checklist, she nodded and sprang into motion again. "If Chancellor Martin decides he wants to talk to me, I've moved to Mozambique."

"Do you even know where Mozambique is?" Cassie called after her, but Millie didn't break stride.

She knew exactly where Mozambique was on the map. She knew lots of things. And coastal Africa seemed as good a place to hide as any. One of the baseball coaches jumped out of her way as she swung around the corner at full speed. She smiled but didn't stop. Not when she was this close to escaping campus.

The morning after Davenport's story broke, she'd appeased the gaggle camped outside Ty's front door by sending him out to recite a brief but seemingly heartfelt statement wishing his soon-to-be-ex-wife well. Getting something slightly better than nothing worked for the majority of them. Most just wanted something to put in their sidebars. Unfortunately, the one who didn't bite was the biggest thorn in her side.

Slowing her pace, she focused on regulating her breathing before she reached the athletic director's office. The past few months had been rough on Mike Samlin. She needed to appear calm and collected. The thought made Millie smile. Not because she disliked the man, but she fancied herself the Joker to Mike's Bruce Wayne each time they stood side by side. He was everything cool, crisp, and conservative, while she liked a pop of color. Or ten. And colorful or not, she wanted to be taken seriously.

Mike landed at Wolcott in the nick of time, in Millie's opinion. The university was becoming a tad too comfortable in its role as Mid-Continental Conference's patsy, and influential alumni were getting restless. Intercollegiate athletics generated an astronomical amount of money.

Kate Snyder's unparalleled success in women's basketball was certainly a huge feather in the university's cap, but it wasn't enough. They needed to build their men's programs and fast. That's why Mike had hired Danny McMillan to revive the football program and Ty Ransom to bring men's basketball up to speed. And Ty was starting to have some success. Dante Harris was the first marquee player to come out of the men's basketball program in more than two decades. His defection was a stunning blow beyond the scandal surrounding his departure.

Millie drew to a halt and blew out a long breath, a technique she'd picked up at one of those god-awful yoga retreats her friend Avery insisted she and Kate attend semiannually. As much as Millie hated to admit buying into any part of Avery's new age crap, the breathing thing worked.

While blowing out a single measured breath, she wiped her mental slate clean. These days, her job was less about spinning Mari Ransom's infidelity and more about Ty's big mouth. Damage control had been bumped to priority one in the aftermath of Jim Davenport's scoop, and Millie hit the ground running. Ty's contract would be up in a couple of years, and the last thing Millie wanted was to give the scandal-shy university reason to look elsewhere for a basketball coach.

For nearly a week, she'd paraded Ty around to various print, web, and television outlets. As expected, interest started to wane when he opened his mouth and started speaking rationally and without rancor. He'd taken every poke, prod, and outright jab like a man... so far.

Taking it on the chin was not an easy task for a guy like Ty. He'd been born a winner. Trained to be a champion. Labeled a disappointment when he went pro. And now, after years of building his reputation as a coach and rebuilding his ego, this mess.

Their dog and pony show had kept them booked solid all week, but the next day, they'd tackle their biggest hurdle yet—the only person who hadn't succumbed to Ty's charm, NSN lead anchor, Greg Chambers.

She nodded a greeting to the grad student who acted as Mike's assistant. The girl smiled and motioned for her to go on into the inner sanctum, but she paused anyway. Millie wasn't one to open a closed door without at least tapping first. That was how a person stumbled onto unwelcome surprises.

Then again, for Millie, there was no such thing as a welcome surprise. The secret to her success was knowing exactly what cards she held versus who might possibly be hiding an ace up their sleeve. Rolling her shoulders back, she imagined an invisible string pulling the top of her head up until she stood straight and tall, then she raised her hand to knock.

The AD called for her to come in, and after making a mental note to burn Avery's newest Birkenstocks for implanting the whole string out of the top of her head thing, she twisted the knob and entered, bravado firmly in hand.

"So I have calls in to *Today* as well as *LIVE*, but word is Kelly Ripa is pretty much off the jock bandwagon since Michael Strahan jumped ship. They're both long shots, but you don't get what you don't ask—" She stopped on a dime when she spotted Ty sitting in the chair opposite the athletic director. "Oh. You're here."

Ty craned his neck to look at her. From this distance, his eyes looked like they were simply light brown. She knew they were so much more than the color of mud. Up close, she'd spotted flecks of gold and burnt caramel, sort of like a tortoiseshell. They were sheltered by thick slashes of black brows so severe they almost balanced out the lush sensuality of his full lips. Almost, but not quite. Taken as they were, the combination was arresting. Against the backdrop of his flawless, tawny skin, the individual assets packed the punch of one of those sneaky umbrella cocktails. Pretty and seemingly innocuous at first glance, but potent enough to land a woman flat on her back.

Oblivious to the turmoil clapping eyes on him stirred, he bobbed his head in a casual greeting. "Hey, Millie."

A bitter laugh rose in her throat, but she swallowed the tickle. Her brain cried a silent, *Surprise!* She wasn't supposed to see him until they left for New York. She wasn't expecting to see him. Or prepared. Damn him.

It really burned her biscuits that he had such an implacable game face. He'd kissed her, then tried to apologize for it. She didn't want an apology, but she needed at least a little time to psych herself up to be near him.

Not that she didn't want to be. On the contrary. She wanted to be near enough to him to feel his warm, damp breath on her cheek. What she wouldn't give to feel those big, broad palms slide down her back and cup her ass again. Would he pull her close and hold her so tight she might forget where he started and she ended? Or would he be more reserved in the cold, sober light of day?

This was exactly why she didn't care for the unexpected. When she was prepared, she could pretend their kiss was nothing more than impulse on the part of a friendly coworker. She could control the compulsion to stare at his mouth and make sure she spoke in a normal voice rather than the sex-kitten purr his intense gaze all but demanded she use. With a little advance notice, she could school her racing pulse and do that whole inner pep talk thing Kate was so fond of invoking. She wasn't opposed to all forms of combustion, only the spontaneous type.

"Ty." She managed to spit his name out with a cordial head bob perilously close to a curtsy. Or maybe she was feeling a bit weak in the knees. "I thought you had meetings today."

She tried to keep the observation light and casual, but the lift of his dark eyebrows told her he'd heard the hint of accusation at the edges. A glance at Mike proved he'd caught the sharpness in her tone too, so Millie did what she did best. She spun the situation to her advantage.

"I mean, you had me clear the schedule for today because you said you were booked solid." Activating the touchscreen on her tablet, she swiped the wallpaper away and punched in her security code. "If you're free now, I have a couple of bloggers I can line up for a webchat."

He rose from the chair, slowly unfolding all eighty inches of his lean, muscular frame with the grace of a man who was certain of the gifts God had given him. Ty Ransom was one of those people who appeared to be moving in slow motion, even when he was flying past in a blur. Everything he did seemed purposeful and deliberate. His wariness was one of the things she liked about him. Also the main reason the clinch they'd shared one dark, scotch-soaked night was still headlining in her dreams. She never thought he'd actually kiss her.

Like his magnificent body, his smile was slow to bloom, but when it reached its peak, the damn thing was devastating. "You know, Mike, I've gone almost twenty-four hours without being bossed around by a woman half my size. I have to admit, I was feeling sort of lost."

Mike chuckled and pulled a file off the stack on his desk. "We all live to be managed by Millie." He flipped open the folder, pulled the top sheet off the stack, and waved the paper at her. "I'm approving the trip to New York for the NSN interview, but I'm not putting you up for a week so you can make the morning show rounds." He placed the page back in order, closed the cover, and held the dossier out to her. "Your travel arrangements are in the folder. Ty's leaving from New York to head straight to Reno."

"Reno?" Her head whirled as she accepted the folder. First, she had to wrap her mind around the prospect of being alone on a trip to New York with the man, then the realization he wasn't coming back with her. "Already?"

"Takes six weeks' residency." Ty lifted a shoulder in a shrug. "If I go now, I can have the divorce finalized and be back before fall practices are in full swing."

"Right."

Six weeks in Nevada, and his divorce would be final. The plan was logical. Reasonable. And for some reason, slightly more disturbing than the prospect of Ty being free from his wife once and for all.

Ever since the night he'd bottomed out in a bottle, he'd been as calm and placid as a pond in the heat of high summer. Cool too. Not to her in particular, but to everyone and about everything. The man had his game face on, for sure. The problem was, Millie wasn't entirely certain if she was supposed to be playing offense or defense whenever she was around him.

"My lawyer and I met with Mari's. I was with my attorney all morning making sure the bases were covered. We have the plan worked out. She doesn't want to leave lover boy alone for long, so I'm going to Reno to establish residency," he explained. "The divorce will be final by Labor Day, and I can get on with things."

Something about the gleam in his eyes struck her as odd. He was wary, and his steady gaze was more than a little speculative. As if he were expecting her to react in a certain way but not quite sure she wouldn't disappoint him. Feeling as if she were tiptoeing through a field filled with land mines and all too aware of their audience, Millie gave him a small, sympathetic smile. "I see."

He laughed and took a step toward the door. Sucking in a sharp breath, Millie stood her ground as he passed too close for comfort. The little smirk tugging at the corner of his mouth told her he'd brushed past her on purpose. But she wasn't the type to be intimidated by big men. On the contrary. The bigger, the better, as far as she was concerned. The move came off as a bit adolescent, in truth. And finally, the reason why pinged on her radar. He was as off-kilter as she was. Maybe even more.

A rush of power pulsed through her veins. She tipped her chin and upped the ante with a full-on sassy-pants grin. "Well, good luck. I hope everything works out for you."

He stopped, standing way too near for either of them to be completely unaffected. "I'm going to see you later, aren't I?"

The husky, intimate timbre of his voice short-circuited her brain. "What?"

She darted a meaningful glance at Mike, seated behind his desk with his hands resting on the blotter. He studied them with narrowed eyes, like they were a couple of amoebas trapped under a microscope slide. Or worse, as if they were hooligans and he was trying to figure out which one had thrown a baseball through his window.

Clearing her throat, she arched her brows as she tried to deflect with some good old-fashioned professional detachment. "What's scheduled for later?"

Ty tapped the travel documents in her hand with one long finger. "You, me, flying to the Big Apple." He flattened his hand and mimed an airplane taking off. "You wanted a front-row seat for my beheading, remember?"

She blinked, then scrambled to recover as she threw up mental barriers in front of every naughty thought the prospect of jetting off to New York with this man spawned. "I'd never wish for any such thing," she said, pressing her hand to her heart and aiming for an accent reminiscent of a scandalized Southern belle. "The dry-cleaning bill would be horrendous."

Mike barked a laugh as he pushed his chair back. "Our Millie, the soul of sympathy." He came around the desk and extended his hand to Ty. "Be good. Do everything the boss lady tells you to do," he added with a nod in her direction.

"Yes, sir," Ty answered, his smirk growing into a smile so wide, it upgraded his face from merely handsome to breathtaking. "I always do whatever Ms. Jensen thinks is best."

"Good luck." Mike gave Ty a slap on the back, then ushered them both toward the outer office. "We'll be watching."

Before she could get another word in edgewise, the door closed behind them, and she and Ty were left facing each other. At last, Ty glanced over at the solid mahogany door. "If I didn't know he'd played football, I'd swear the guy was a point guard."

Millie nodded. "I guess there's a good reason they call them directors."

The athletic director's assistant didn't look up or even break rhythm in her typing. "I emailed copies of your itineraries to your university and personal emails as well."

Millie recovered first. Pulling the mantle of brisk efficiency around her like a cloak, she plastered a big smile onto her face and started toward the open doorway to the hall. "You're the best, SaraAnn," she called over her shoulder.

"I know!"

Millie laughed, and her stride hitched. Then, six feet eight inches of freight-train-solid man almost plowed right over her.

"Oh! Oof!"

His hands closed around her upper arms. Millie wasn't quite sure if he was trying to catch himself or keep her from falling, but she figured intention hardly mattered as long as they didn't end up on the floor of the main hall in a tangled heap.

"Sorry," he breathed as he shifted his center of balance to correct their momentum.

Ty repeated the apology under his breath while he straightened to his full height once again, but she waved the annoying little word away. "I didn't use my brake lights." Too chicken to look directly at him, she cracked open the cover and peeked at the neatly typed schedule inside as she pivoted away from him. "So I guess I'll see you at the airport this evening."

"About that." He fell into step beside her, waylaying her attempt to escape. "I was wondering what you'd think about giving me a ride."

She wasn't sure if it was his phrasing or the hopeful note in his voice, but something set off the warning bells in her head. She paid about as much attention to the clamor as a native New Yorker does a car alarm. "A ride?"

"Not that kind of ride," he said with a chuckle. "Wait. No." He drew to a sudden halt, and automatically, she stopped too. His forehead puckered as he gave the innuendo due consideration. "Yes to both kinds, if you're willing."

"Stop." She raised a hand to underscore the command.

A wicked smile curved his sculpted lips, but he ducked his head deferentially. "A ride in your car to the airport," he clarified.

She thrust her hip out, standing her ground. "You locker room jocks think everything is an opening, don't you?"

"I am a playmaker," he countered.

She rolled her eyes and directed her commentary to the trophy cases lining the deserted corridor. "Barely a week since I found him crying in his cups, and now he thinks he's a player."

His smile warmed, and his eyes crinkled at the corners. "I don't think I am. I know."

"Well, try to keep your pants zipped for the next six weeks, Romeo. I'm having enough trouble paying off the checks your mouth wrote without you adding a paternity test or two to the mix."

The winning smile disappeared, and he looked injured. "That was uncalled for," he said, his voice low and soft with disappointment.

"I'm sorry." And she was. "A joke, and a bad one."

He'd been getting too close, pushing all her buttons. She wanted to back him off a bit.

"Last week notwithstanding, I know how to handle myself both personally and professionally," he said stiffly.

"I know. I apologize."

Didn't he understand? Didn't he feel the buzz? She needed to distance herself, because having him so near was becoming too much for her to handle. Millie had spent the better part of the week reminding herself this was a dangerous situation for both of them.

Or maybe it was only dangerous for her. Maybe he wasn't actually interested in her but just…felt lonely that night.

Either way, she needed to buckle down and tough it out. She could get through the next twenty-four hours without doing something she couldn't undo. Then, once he was safely on a plane winging his way west, she could think about him.

"Aren't you on my side?"

The question surprised her. She looked up to find him searching her face as though the answer might be tattooed on her forehead. She hoped he was getting a clear read on the indignation flaring in her cheeks. "What? Why would you ask me that? Of course I am. I'm the one who's been standing right beside you all week."

"I'm not questioning your loyalty to the school or your job, Millie. I'm asking you." He paused long enough to take a deep breath. "Do you like me? As a person." He added the last part in a rush, like he felt an urgent need to sew up any loopholes she might dive through.

Torn between being mortified and affronted, she did the only thing she could do when put squarely on the spot. She fired back with the truth. "Yes. Of course I do."

"As much as I appreciate the 'of courses,' I'm well aware not everyone does like me, and I'm okay with that." He gave her a wry little smile. "I'm not okay with you not liking me though."

"I don't," she blurted.

He reared back as if she'd slapped him across the face.

Panic gripped her by the throat while she scrambled to rewind the last bit of conversation in her head. Sadly, her babbling came across every bit as muddled the second time through. "I mean, I do." He cocked his head like a quizzical spaniel, and she blew out an exasperated huff. "I like you. There. I said it, okay?"

He opened his mouth to retort, then snapped his jaw shut. Then he smiled. Not one of those broad lady-killer grins but a small, pleased smile that made her feel fluttery inside. Which was disconcerting. She wasn't a fluttery sort of woman. In fact, she prided herself on her logical, if not surgical, approach to life. She was strong. Decisive. Independent and opinionated. Millie liked to say she was a leader, not a lemming.

Her ex-husband simply called her a ballbuster.

Millie gave her head a hard shake. No sense in dwelling on ancient history. She needed to focus on the present. They were standing mere feet from their boss's office, acting like a couple of junior high kids trying to decide if they were going to be an item. She needed to make it crystal clear that they couldn't be one. Ty was still married.

Besides, he hadn't said he liked her. He'd only asked if she liked him.

The whole thing was nuts. She should be focusing on ways to parlay the media attention into positive press for the university. Instead, here she was, breathing harder than she did in mile seventeen and wondering if he was going to kiss her again. His lips parted as if he'd read her mind. Her gaze zoomed in on his mouth like she was the director of some low-budget porn flick. The ridiculousness of the situation wasn't lost on her, but she had a hard time mustering a laugh. Acting out of impulse and a healthy dose of self-preservation, she pressed her fingertips to his mouth and tried not to think about how impossibly soft his lips were.

Tried and failed.

"This is neither the time nor the place," she managed in a desperate whisper.

He nodded almost imperceptibly, the movement so slight he didn't even dislodge her hand. Millie's breath caught in a snarl when he pursed his lips and kissed the pads of her fingertips. Curling her fingers into her palm, she let her hand fall to her side.

"Pick me up at six," he ordered in a low, gruff voice. When she was slow to respond, he quirked a challenging brow. "You remember where I live, right?"

A strangled laugh escaped her, and she ducked her head, amused by his audacity. The drunk and discombobulated man was long gone. No sight of him all week. Thank God. In his place stood this quiet warrior, committed to doing what he needed to do to reclaim his life. And damn if his determination wasn't as attractive as all get-out.

Chapter 4

THE SEATS IN FIRST CLASS WERE ROOMY, BUT THEY WEREN'T spacious enough for Ty. And he wasn't bitching about the legroom. Hell, a court's length of space could stretch between them, and his skin would still prickle every time Millie moved.

"I can't believe they booked us first class," she said for the tenth time.

They didn't, he thought, pressing himself into the corner of his leather seat so he could watch her. *I did*. With her wild-cherry hair and ruthlessly coordinated cream-and-gold outfit, she looked like some kind of exotic butterfly. One who wore stiletto heels to tramp through the airport and pulled a pink-and-purple polka dot wheelie bag. She looked up to be sure he was still an active participant in her one-sided conversation, then returned to rummaging through the enormous tote bag she called a purse.

"Every time I've flown before, they booked me in coach."

He stretched his legs out as far as the high-dollar seating would allow, then shrugged. "I can't sit in coach." She looked up, her eyes bright and inquisitive over the rims of the cheetah-print half-glasses perched on the end of her nose. "Well, I can, but I'd have to buy the whole row to have enough leg room. It's actually cheaper for me to fly first class."

She blinked and cocked her head to the side. "You know, I never thought about that," she confessed.

Pleased to have found a topic other than his upcoming appearance as Greg Chambers's whipping boy, he nodded. "I order my furniture custom too. Particularly couches and beds." He tried to focus more on the relief he felt when his drool stain came out of the Ultrasuede sofa than the thought of chasing Millie around his outsized bed. The best way to do so was to talk about the elephant between them. "I would have had the kitchen and bath counters lifted, but that wouldn't have worked for Mari."

"I never thought about that either. What a pain."

He chuckled. "I should have stopped eating my Wheaties, huh?"

Millie laughed and extracted a pack of chewing gum from her bag of tricks and offered him a stick. "I bet you cost your poor parents a fortune to feed."

"Most of the time it was only me and my dad. And yeah, I remember the grocery bill being pretty outrageous." Ty smiled as he waved her offering away. The memory of his father standing at the stove in his work pants, the sleeves of his shirt rolled back to avoid catching splatters as he stirred, filled Ty's head. "God, he was a horrible cook. It's a wonder we didn't both starve."

She laughed and unwrapped a stick of gum for herself. "He never got better?"

Ty stared, transfixed by the way she bent the pliant piece into an accordion against her tongue. A waft of fruity sweetness tickled his nostrils. He glanced down at the pack she'd tossed back into the cavernous bag, shaking his head as he noted she preferred watermelon gum to anything as boring as mint or cinnamon.

"No," he whispered with an affectionate smile.

"Is he still with us?"

The cautious note in her voice snapped him out of his stupor. He wasn't exactly sure what they were supposed to be talking about, so he responded with a noncommittal, "Hmm?"

She flipped her reading glasses up onto her head and met his eyes. "Your dad. Is he still alive?"

"Oh!" He grasped the thread of the conversation and held on tight, tucking his chin to his chest as he chuckled at his own distractibility. "Yes. He's good. Lives south of Sarasota. Plays golf three hundred days a year, likes to brag he has all his original manufacturer parts, and keeps a string of girlfriends who cook for him."

"Good for him!"

Millie's eyes crinkled when she smiled, and an attractive pair of brackets creased her cheeks when she grinned. Of all the things he liked about her, these two features were near the top of his list. And the great thing about Millie was that the list of her assets was long and not strictly physical. She was real. Completely without filler. Or filter, for that matter.

Mari couldn't match his dad's brag in terms of original parts. Ty had paid for the porcelain veneers and impressive rack himself. But what irked him more than external artifice was the way she embraced her "fake it till you make it" attitude. Hell, she'd even had a little sign on her bathroom wall saying that exact thing. Mari wasn't one to work on improving herself. She preferred to pretend she was already all the things she wanted to be.

"My dad is actually flying out to Reno with some of his buddies. We'll play a few rounds."

It hadn't taken him long to discover the charm and bravado Mari had displayed during their courtship was an act, but his father had figured it out right away. He and Mari never clicked, and Ty had been too oblivious to figure out why.

"That'll be nice."

"He's a good man," Ty said gruffly. "A smart one too—he's letting me foot the bill." Millie laughed, and Ty allowed his head to fall back as he wondered how the apple had fallen so far from the proverbial tree.

Behind the facade, his Mari was possibly the most insecure woman he'd ever met. Once, before one of the chancellor's dinner parties, he'd found Mari standing in front of the mirror, practicing which smile she'd use with each conversational tidbit she'd memorized from that day's news. At the time, he'd felt bad for her. In truth, it broke his heart a little. But when he tried to engage her in conversation about the same topics, she waved them off as boring and started rambling about her next redecorating project.

He smiled back at Millie, wishing their time alone could last. From the time she'd shown up at his sliding door, Millie had taken charge. Bullied him, really, but he didn't mind too much. She was beautiful when she was bossy. Plus she seemed completely relaxed with him. He liked her ease. And he found her confidence intoxicating.

Though he was ashamed to admit how lonely he'd been in his marriage, Ty hadn't realized exactly how much his and Millie's easy camaraderie meant to him until he'd kissed her and all thoughts of comfort went flying out the door.

She'd been the first person to befriend him when he

came to work at Wolcott. She'd helped smooth the way
to a cordial relationship with Kate Snyder, the women's
basketball coach—a minor miracle, considering Ty's
hiring probably cost Kate her first marriage. Her ex had
been considered the heir apparent for the job, and when
he didn't get the spot, he'd blamed Kate for not using
her pull to make his promotion happen. Such bullshit.
Still, Kate was happy now.

He was poised on the verge of telling Millie how
much he loved the lines around her mouth, and her
laugh, and the sharp tongue she wielded like a weapon,
when the flight attendant appeared in the aisle.

"Excuse me, ma'am?" The young woman spared him
a conspiratorial glance, then placed a perfectly manicured hand on Millie's shoulder. "I'm going to need you
to stow your bag. Would you like me to lift it for you?"

Millie looked up, incredulity written all over her face.
Without taking her eyes off the woman, she gathered
the long leather handles and made a show of trying to
lift the tote from her lap. "Oh, no, thank you, dear," she
crooned. "I have this big, strong man to help me." Ty
barely had a chance to process what she'd said before
she settled an imploring gaze on him. "What do you say,
sweetie? Help your hot mama out, will you?"

The flight attendant split a perplexed look between
them, then recovered her wide smile as she straightened.
As if Millie had somehow disappeared, the girl turned
her limpid gaze on Ty. "Wonderful. Well, if you or your
mother need anything, you let me know."

Millie gaped after the girl as she swayed toward the
front of the cabin, astonishment shining in her wide eyes.
Knowing there was nothing he could say to recover the

situation, Ty simply took the tote bag from her grasp and placed it in the overhead compartment. Settling back in his seat, he buckled his seat belt low and snug across his hips, then rolled his head to look at her.

"I think I get my coloring from you, Ma."

She huffed a laugh, then tugged on the end of her own seat belt. "Too bad you didn't get my smarts, kiddo."

They shared a smile, and he watched the last of her pique fade away. Not for the first time, he wondered if she truly was a redhead. She had the flash-fire temper of one, for sure. Mesmerized by the gleam of humor in her eyes, the question slipped out before he could censor himself. "What color's your hair?"

One perfectly shaped eyebrow rose. "I think it's called Strawberry Crushed."

His ears burned with embarrassment, but he was in too deep to back out now. "I mean, for real."

"I have a thousand inappropriate remarks running through my head right now, but I promised myself I wouldn't work blue for the cheap laughs."

He chuckled and glanced away, the heat traveling from his ears into his cheeks. "Sorry. I was curious."

"Brown," she said with a smirky little smile. "Plain old brown."

"Nothing about you is plain." He shifted a few precious inches closer to her as the clueless attendant took her place for their preflight instructions. He waited until the girl looked directly at him, then reached over and took Millie's hand from her lap. "Or old," he added. "Unless you were one of those medical miracles and gave birth at six."

She looked down at their clasped hands. "I'm good, but I'm not that good."

"I bet you are."

The quick response coaxed another smile from her. She started to extricate her hand, but he held firm. "Ty, this isn't a good idea—"

"It's the best idea." When she attempted another escape, he pulled her hand over to rest on his thigh. "Takeoff scares me witless." He held her gaze, unrelenting. "I need you to hold my hand so I don't cry like a baby."

Millie blew out a breath and let her head fall back. "Bullshit."

Ty just grinned in response. She made it through the part about seat cushion flotation devices before she glanced at him again. "What happened to your mom?"

He tossed the question off with a weak shrug. "She left when I was four."

A small gasp escaped her, and he squeezed her fingers to show both his appreciation and to reassure her. "We were fine." He chuckled. "That's what my dad kept telling me. 'We're fine. We're gonna be fine.'"

"You never heard from her?"

He answered with a bitter little laugh. "Oh yeah. She showed up when I was playing college ball. The second the press dubbed me the next Michael Jordan, she came flitting around doing the old 'that's my boy' routine, but I shut her down."

"How?"

He gave her a sad shadow of a smile. "Distract, deflect, deny. You'd have been proud of how well I handled her. Eventually, she went away."

"How long did it take?"

"She hung in for a couple of seasons after the draft.

When she realized she wasn't getting a slice of the pie, she tried manufacturing stories for the tabloids." He looked up to find the attendants stowing their props. The plane began to taxi toward the runway, but his heart slowed to almost a stop when he saw the stark outrage on Millie's face. "What?"

She narrowed her eyes, not the least bit put off by his inane question. "Nothing. I hate when people fumble planting a fake story. It's so damn easy, a child could do it."

Ty laughed. "Yeah, well, I wasn't quite Kobe Bryant and nowhere near M.J. in terms of success. I think Kris Humphries ended up with a better Q score than I ever did, but I didn't have to get hitched on TV either. Why bother with a headline about a guy no one cares about?"

Twisting in her seat, Millie crossed her slim runner's legs and angled toward him. "I love that you know about Q scores."

"I think I peaked when I was twenty-two."

She shrugged. "Most men do."

He grinned. "A myth."

"So you would have me believe," she retorted without missing a beat.

She gave his hand a gentle squeeze as the plane started down the runway with a roar of engines. Enthralled by the contrast of her skin against his, he traced the lines of her long, slender fingers with his free hand. "I'd like nothing more than to prove my...stamina to you over and over."

"You're a married man." She uttered the reminder as the nose of the plane lifted. The moment they were wheels up, Millie straightened her fingers in an unspoken demand he release her. "I've spent the last week telling the world what an upright kind of guy you are. Don't make me a hypocrite."

Reluctantly, he let her go. But she didn't put the expected distance between them. Instead, she loosened her seat belt a little, pushed the button to recline, and shifted fully onto her side.

"It isn't that I'm not interested," she said bluntly. "I think we both know I am. I know you are. We like each other, which is both a bonus and an obstacle—"

"How do you figure?"

"Bonus, because, hey, we like each other," she said, throwing up her hands. "It's also an obstacle because, hey, we like each other."

Her delivery on the second part held a note of warning that rang too true to suit his purposes, so he ignored it. The crew moved through the dimly lit cabin, working with the kind of hushed efficiency he equated with hospital waiting rooms and the lobbies of funeral homes. But he wasn't anyplace so morose. He was on a plane winging his way to the most vibrant city in the country with a woman he'd found fascinating since the day they were introduced. He didn't want to be hushed or quiet or, heaven forbid, circumspect. For the first time in years, he wanted to draw attention to himself. To her. To the fact that he was the guy she chose to sit beside.

But of course, she hadn't really chosen to run away to New York with him. She was going because leading him through the press steeplechase was her job. He was her project. The pathetic part of this whole mess wasn't his wife leaving him for another guy. No, he worried more

Millie could be playing him with this whole "we like each other" spiel, and he was falling for her line. She might be humoring him. Or worse, babysitting to be sure he didn't go off the deep end live on the National Sports Network. And the only defense he had was to play his kind of up-tempo offense.

"And your folks?" he asked, pretending their conversation hadn't taken a sharp left turn at sexual hypocrisy.

She blinked, and her forehead creased. "What?"

Pressing his shoulder into the seat, he mimicked the intimacy of her body language as much as the space would allow. "Your parents. Tell me about them."

The lines of her brow smoothed, and the wariness in her eyes melted into something close to gratitude but not nearly as standoffish. "What about them?"

"Anything."

She smiled, and he could have sworn she set the whole cabin ablaze. Or maybe only him. Either way, heat pumped through him with every thud of his heart.

"Nothing much to tell. Still alive. Still married to the first taker. My mom was a teacher, and my dad worked for a small appliance company. They were bought out by General Electric about twenty years ago, and he took an early retirement."

"Golf?"

She shook her head. "He plays poker. Tournament level. She spends whatever he makes at the tables on crafting supplies."

He grinned, wondering if Mrs. Jensen had passed the creative gene on to her daughter. "Do you do crafty things?"

"Well, some people would say I'm pretty clever with

a press release, but other than knitting, I leave the crafty stuff to Mom."

"And Mr. and Mrs. Jensen live…where?"

She laughed softly, then gave his attempt to draw her out a pitying, little head shake. "Well, last I heard, they were in Phoenix, but Mr. and Mrs. Piotrawski live outside Atlanta."

He peered at her, confused. "What? Who?"

"My maiden name was Piotrawski. Jensen is my ex-husband's name."

"Ex-husband's? You were married?"

This time she actually scoffed. "So hard to believe?"

"Yes. I mean, no!" He tripped over his tongue, then tried again. "No. Not hard to believe. I mean, I didn't know."

She looked him in the eye. "Why would you?" she asked with a bluntness so characteristically Millie she could trademark it. Still, the question felt like an accusation. He opened his mouth to reply, but she shut him down with an airy wave. "Ancient history. I haven't seen or heard from John in, God, almost twenty years."

"Right." Ty digested the information. "No kids?"

"Not a one."

He nodded. "But you kept his name?"

"Jensen is a helluva lot easier to spell than Piotrawski. Makes ordering pizza a snap." She snapped her fingers to punctuate her assertion.

Taken off guard, he frowned at her. "It never occurred to me you might have been married before."

Millie gasped softly, then pressed her hand to her throat in mock dismay. "You mean you thought I was a virgin?"

"No, I just…"

He didn't complete the thought, so she jumped right into the gap. "…thought I was an old maid?"

"No!"

"…hoped maybe I was saving myself for the love of a good man?"

"Hardly," he retorted dryly.

"…never dreamed I'd be the type to host orgies on the weekends?"

He sighed. "Nothing I can say to stop this now, is there?"

"Not much," she agreed amicably.

"I suppose an invite to one of those orgies is out of the question?"

"I'll put you on the waiting list."

Never one to pass up an opening, he charged down the lane. "Think maybe a space will become available in about six weeks?"

"It's possible," she said with a coy smile.

He returned the playful curl of her lips with the broad grin of a man who'd scored on the first drive to the hoop.

"I do tire of them so quickly," she mused, almost to herself.

Ty barked a laugh so compelling, the sound drew the attention of the businessman across the aisle. Shaking his head in awed dismay, he straightened his cramping muscles and sprawled as far as a first-class ticket would allow. "And his shot was blocked, folks," he murmured to the crowd of air vents and reading lamps above their seats.

Following his lead, Millie rolled onto her back, a grin spreading across her face as she joined in on his color commentary. "And the crowd goes wild."

He shrugged. "I'm known for coming from behind to win."

"Again, so many dirty things I could say, but I'd have to take a shower, and this isn't one of those fancy planes." She heaved a heavy sigh, placed her hands on her lap, then pointed her stiletto-clad toes as she stretched. "Only plain old first class."

"Spoiled brat." Closing his eyes, he tried to remember the last time he'd smiled so much in such a small amount of time. Had he ever laughed like that with Mari? Probably not. In the beginning, she'd been all sweetness and charm, and he'd wanted nothing more than to be her man. Her protector. But Millie didn't need any man stepping in to take care of her. Hell, she'd probably knee any guy who tried. And Ty liked that about her. Liked her independence.

She was right: he liked her. But that didn't mean he couldn't want her too.

~~~

"So, Ty, you spent five years in the NBA, not playing most of the time, but you still collected a check. Then you spent some time playing in the EuroLeague, trying to prove you had legs under you, but not much came of your time in the league."

Ty wanted nothing more than to smack the smug smirk off Greg Chambers's face, but his clenched fists weren't the optic he was instructed to present. Swallowing his pride for the fifth time in as many minutes, he leaned forward and propped his elbows on the very legs that had let him down all those years ago. Genial smile plastered on his face, he waited for the question. As usual,

Chambers was slow on the trigger, so Ty lobbed a pass. "Well, I did get to see a lot of Russia. Not many guys who grew up in Memphis can say the same."

"Do you think the fact you couldn't cut it has given you some kind of edge in grooming talent to play at a higher level?"

He had to laugh at the guy's chutzpah. An English professor would need an hour to parse the question enough to determine whether he'd been complimented or insulted, but Ty didn't need the time. He knew the source. Greg Chambers had been an above-average but not-quite-great player on a team with three consecutive Final Four finishes.

Ty's Eastern Panthers had blocked Greg's path to undefeated seasons more than once. There'd been more than one strategically thrown elbow whenever they'd matched up. But Ty wasn't the only enemy the guy had made along the way. Hot-tempered and unable to break through to the next level, Greg Chambers was quickly overshadowed by more talented, less controversial players.

He came back for his senior year and could have been drafted in the end. But in the final weeks of the season, Chambers managed to have an on-court meltdown of such epic proportions, he'd become a verb. A part of the lexicon of the game. And virtually untouchable.

Chamber (Chambered, Chambering): To miss eighty-five percent of shots attempted, then proceed to have a very public breakdown. Involves blaming everyone from the referees and hoop manufacturers, to the pope for one's lack of skill.

Ty did his best to keep his expression neutral as he gave the answer he and Millie had cobbled together for questions such as these. "I don't think playing and coaching are as closely related as people think. A great player may not be a very good coach. I know plenty of coaches in a variety of sports who never distinguished themselves as players."

"But you were able to use your success as a player as a springboard into coaching," Chambers fired back, his body language making the statement an accusation.

Once again, Ty chuckled. "Well, I'm hardly the first to go the coaching route." Before Greg could spur his high horse on, he continued. "And it's not like I jumped over a line of guys angling for a head coaching job. I started as a second assistant."

"At Eastern University, your alma mater."

He nodded, acknowledging the connection. "Right. I'm grateful to Coach Washington and Athletic Director Wisnowski for the chance. I learned a lot working beside my former coach. I can tell you, watching the game from his end of the bench was…an enlightenment."

"Grateful but not grateful enough to stop you from jumping ship when the Wolcott Warriors came knocking." Greg stared straight into the camera's lens and treated the viewing audience to his smiley sneer.

Ty watched with a sort of detached amusement, wondering if the man had the semiconstipated expression patented or something. "I didn't have to do some kind of interpretive dance for them to know the Wolcott offer was the chance of a lifetime. Not only did both Coach and the AD give their blessing, but they practically packed the U-Haul."

"Were they the ones who encouraged you to take a cheerleader with you as a parting gift?"

Despite everything happening between them, it irked Ty to hear Mari spoken of so dismissively. "Mari and I had been married for some time when the first rumblings of an offer from Wolcott came through."

Unfortunately, he hadn't spent as long planning his wedding as he had considering the offer from Wolcott. The trip to Vegas had been a spur-of-the-moment idea. They were married less than thirty hours after their plane had landed.

"And her cheerleading days were behind her. I may have been older, but Mari wasn't a student when we married. She was twenty-three."

"Now, a few years later, she's left you for a young man who seems to be carrying the mantle you let slip."

Greg's expression was so solemn; Ty could only assume this was his version of a mocking face. For one wild and woolly moment, Ty fantasized about letting his snark off the leash.

He could smash Greg Chambers like a bug, expose him as a bitter wannabe. Ty was tempted. So tempted. Then he caught a flash of firecracker-red out of the corner of his eye and squashed the thought. He wouldn't.

Doing so would only be a Band-Aid slapped on his wounded pride. It certainly wouldn't help the university or his program. And going off half-cocked would only hurt Millie.

Poor Millie. Spinning this mess was an impossible task. Like the guy from Greek mythology who had to keep pushing a boulder up a hill. Did the chancellor and the AD appreciate how hard her job must be? She was one slick, savvy woman charged with wrangling more than a half dozen superjock–sized egos. Hell, he knew guys twice her size who'd crumble under the weight she shouldered. But not Millie.

His Millie.

Well, maybe not his yet, but she would be. Once he got this mess pushed to the back burner and his divorce was a done deal. The minute all the pieces fell into place, he'd be making his play. Resolved, he straightened his already straight tie as he focused his attention on Greg Chambers.

"Yes, well, I'm sure we'll work things out to everyone's satisfaction. As for Dante Harris, any mantle he has to carry was put on him by the people who sit and talk, not by the people who are actually working with these young athletes." He drew a deep breath and ran his hand the length of his tie. "The problem is, you all forget that fact. They are *young* athletes. Sure, they have God-given talent. Those who play at the collegiate level are both built to excel and driven to succeed, but they are still young enough to need and seek direction."

Pausing to collect his thoughts, he slid his damp palms over his thighs. "If anything, I've learned we fail as coaches when we allow these athletes to start believing their own press. I didn't shield Dante Harris from you and every other media mouthpiece who'd crowned him king before the season had even ended. Every coach has to put forth the effort to reach a player who seems to be unreachable. Because of my personal situation…the suspicions I had about my marriage, I couldn't see beyond my own admittedly healthy ego. I didn't do everything I could do as a coach and as a mentor to help him review all his options before he put the play into motion."

Ty nodded, almost to himself. "I failed him." But before Chambers could launch his celebration dance, Ty beat him to the punch. "So, yeah. As you pointed out earlier, my career as a professional player was a bust, and I think we all know I pretty much tanked as a husband too. Maybe I'll turn out to be a failure as a coach. We'll see. But I believe only one thing makes a person a true success—conquering the fear of failure."

He smiled wanly for the camera.

"Someone once said success was going from failure to failure without loss of enthusiasm, and I can tell you I am every bit as enthusiastic about the Wolcott Warrior basketball program as I was the day I started the job. And I can guarantee you I will be every bit as enthusiastic about the game of basketball tomorrow as I am today. These past few weeks have been a setback both personally and professionally, but that's all failure is—a temporary state before we try again."

Having said what he needed to say, he nodded to Greg, then began to unhook his microphone. Holding the tiny clip pinched between his fingers, he paused to speak directly into the mic. "Thanks for letting me have the chance to talk to you here tonight, but I have to keep on schedule. Always a treat to see you, Greg."

Chapter 5

TEMPTATION, THY NAME IS ACQUA DI GIÒ. MILLIE SLID CLOSER to the door of the town car. The distance wasn't nearly enough. Ty seemed to take up every single cubic inch of space. She knew it wasn't a purposeful thing. The guy was more than six and a half feet tall and, according to the crazy basketball junkie website she'd bookmarked, boasted a wingspan measuring seven feet across. He also wore a size sixteen shoe—the kind of stat she couldn't help but memorize.

"I think the interview went well."

She shook off the haze of attraction and looked directly at him for the first time since the driver closed the door. Bad idea. Meticulously groomed to be camera ready, the man looked even better than he smelled. "Yes. Very well, until you cut it short at the end."

"Not too short," he argued. "Just enough to reduce the risk of me punching the guy on national TV."

Needing to shift the balance of power and keep his mood light, she swung her legs toward him, knocking her knees into the side of his thigh. "What's the deal with you and Greg Chambers?"

Ty looked out the window. The neon lights of Times Square danced across his face, highlighting the smooth curve of his high forehead and a jaw chiseled enough to make a statue jealous. "No deal. He's a jerk-off, and I'm a failure." He curled his index finger over his upper lip, but a tiny muscle jumped in his jaw. "No breaking news here. I just wish we could stop rehashing it."

"So what's the old news?" she asked. He blew out a breath, and her suspicions were confirmed. Ty and Chambers had a history. A past that might prove to be more dangerous than a few insults mumbled to a small-time reporter. Knotting her fingers together, she kept her gaze steady, refusing to be shut down by his non-answer. "Tell me the story."

Without so much as a glance, he waved her off. "Nothing." A beat passed. "Everything."

He shrugged those wide shoulders, and Millie grabbed hold of the armrest to keep from launching herself across the car at him. A week of intermittent bouts of sexual tension was one thing. Six straight hours of sizzle was enough to frazzle a nun. And she'd never been a particularly religious woman. Though at the moment, hearing Ty's confession seemed to be the best way to keep her mind off the fact that this too-small town car was heading for her hotel, and if the itinerary SaraAnn had printed for her wasn't lying, she had a king-sized bed in her room. "Tell me what 'everything' is."

At last, he looked at her. "It's stupid. Kid stuff some-one never outgrew."

"After you tell me what's behind this grudge match, we'll mock him mercilessly. Now, go," she prompted with a nod. He heaved another one of those whole-body sighs, and her hormones kicked into overdrive. Pressing her fingernails into the soft leather of the armrest, she forced a fake smile. "Unless you're the one who never outgrew it."

He rolled his eyes at her tactics but gave in with grace.

"We played against each other a few times in school. I won. We both declared for the draft. I got picked; he didn't. I had the chance he thought he should have had, and I couldn't deliver. Plain and simple."

"Doesn't look plain and simple."

"You'd think at some point he'd let it go." He shook his head and made a show of studying the blur of lights whizzing past his window. "It's been twenty years. Why can't he find another yardstick?"

She had no answer and didn't feel inclined to make one up. As far as she was concerned, it was better to let these testosterone-fueled flares burn themselves out. No sense in getting scorched when they got their drawers in a twist over the stupidest things. The male ego was a strange, indecipherable mystery, one she had given up trying to sort out years ago. So she changed the subject.

"When do you leave for Reno?"

He twisted his wrist and pulled back his cuff to check the time. She liked the way the chunky wristwatch looked on him. Usually, he wore a utilitarian sports watch, but this was one of those sleek stainless-steel deals that probably cost more than her first car. Hell, maybe even her current car. "Eleven forty. Plenty of time."

Millie's jaw dropped as realization sank in. She'd made a general note of the flight time when she scanned the itinerary, but she didn't think to check which side of the meridian they'd be on when he left. "Tonight?"

He nodded. "Might as well get started on my residency."

"Oh. Wow." A nervous laugh escaped her. She ran a hand through her hair, then quickly shook the layers back into place. No sense in scaring the man off for good with the Cruella de Vil look. "Yeah, right. Good plan."

She gulped down a lump of disappointment. In the back of her mind, she'd been playing out a variety of scenarios for the evening. Drinks. Dinner. An interview postmortem designed to slide right into playful flirtation. A chance to see if he liked her enough, wanted her enough to push past the playful part and try to make a play. She'd have to shut him down, of course. He was a married man, and while she claimed to have few scruples, vows were one of them. But it would be nice if he tried...

"I'm following your advice."

She looked up, taken aback by the assertion. "Mine?"

"Divorce her as quickly as I can." He stretched his arm across the back of the seat as he leaned toward her. "Get up, get out, and get on with life. That's what you said."

She gave him a wry smile. "Pretty easy to say."

"Surprisingly easy to do," he countered. "Once the hangover wore off, I mean."

Tilting her head, she studied him in the not-so-subtle glow of Manhattan at twilight. "You're not sad?"

"I wouldn't say I'm not, but I will say I'm not as sad as I think I ought to be."

Millie pondered his statement. When David left her, her whole world imploded. For years, she felt fragmented and cast adrift. Then they'd run into each other and...nothing.

"Aren't you going to ask me why I'm not as sad as I should be?"

She wet her own parched lips, then softly cleared her throat. "Uh, no. Your feelings are your own business."

"You're not curious?"

Millie pondered his question for a moment, then shook her head. "You know, I didn't see my ex-husband for over a decade after we signed our divorce papers," she said quietly. "We met when I was sixteen, divorced when I was twenty-six." She cast a glance in his direction, trying to gauge his reception as she clarified her stance on the end of her marriage. "He divorced me."

"The man had to be a fool."

Millie chuckled. "I thought so too. But that didn't mean I wasn't heartbroken for a long, long time."

"I'm sorry," he said, so sincerely, her heart gave a dull thud of gratitude. "But you bounced back. I mean, look at you."

"Took me a while to—as you say it—bounce back." She smiled as she recalled her metamorphosis. "When I hit my midthirties, I started dating again. With a vengeance," she added with some relish.

"I'm almost scared for the guys," he said gruffly. "Or I would be, if I didn't feel so damn jealous of them."

"Bought my first vibrator for my fortieth birthday," she said as if he hadn't spoken.

"The gift that keeps on giving."

"Then I ran into David again, and I wondered what the hell I'd been thinking, wasting all that time between him and...anyone else." She turned to look him directly in the eye. "My point is that I know how you feel, being sad about not feeling more sad."

"I'm sorry that you do," he said, enveloping her hand in his much larger one.

The gentleness in his tone almost broke her resolve to keep her distance. Almost, but not quite.

She wasn't the gullible girl with stars in her eyes, nor was she the desperate parody of the panicked divorcée any longer. Millie knew who she was and what she liked. Cocktails with umbrellas and skewers of fruit she refused to eat, outrageously expensive dark chocolates, and shoes topped the list. A nice, hard fuck came in somewhere in the top five, but depending on the pickings, a hot bath with a good book topped it in the pecking order. She eyed the man sitting beside her, trying to slot where he might rank. As if reading her mind, his eyebrows rose, and his mouth curved into a panty-dampening smile.

The driver hooked a sharp right onto a cross street, and Ty used the change in momentum to his advantage. A shiver zinged down her spine as his arm slipped from the seat to her shoulders. He curled one hand around her upper arm and pulled her closer as he slid across the soft leather seat. She looked up to find him lowering his head.

"Don't." She pulled back, making it clear she wasn't being coy. Darting a glance at the front seat, she ignored the persistent ache low in her belly and forced a tremulous smile. "The driver."

"I don't give a damn."

"He might recognize you," she insisted in a low whisper.

"You really overestimate my public appeal."

Millie was about to say she could write a press release highlighting all the ways she found him appealing, but he pulled away. A pout threatened. Her upper arm tingled, demanding she take back whatever she'd said to deprive it of his warm caress. Her libido was working itself up to rage level when he leaned forward between the headrests.

"Hey. How're things going…Manny?" he asked the driver.

For a split second, she wondered how he knew the guy's name, but then she saw he had his credentials prominently displayed on the dash.

The man barely flicked a peek at the rearview mirror. "Going better up here than back there, buddy."

Ty chuckled and hung his head in mock shame. "I'm trying, Manny. I'm trying."

Clearly, the driver had seen such situations before. Heaving a sigh, he craned his neck and eyeballed the traffic ahead of them. As usual, cars sat bumper to bumper as they waited for the light to change. Anywhere else in the world, this would be called gridlock. In Manhattan, this was the usual flow.

"You've only got about six blocks. Try harder," the man said gruffly.

Ty leaned forward. "Do you know who I am?"

"No." The answer came swiftly enough to be the truth, but Manny gazed long and hard into the mirror, his eyes narrowing. "Should I? What are you, some kind of big deal?"

Ty shook his head. "Not at all."

"Then why are you askin'?"

"My girl—" Ty shrugged as he cast a sidelong glance at Millie, then stared out the windshield. "She's kind of shy." The descriptor made Millie snort, but Ty seemed to gain confidence from her disbelief. "So I'm gonna kiss her and stuff for the next six blocks, and you're gonna keep your eyes on the road. We get her to the hotel happy and in one piece, I'll make it worth your while."

"You've got a deal." Eyes forward, the driver lifted his hand from the wheel and held it over his shoulder for Ty to shake. "Not too much of the 'and stuff' stuff, okay? I'm not one of those *voyeur* people or anything."

"Gotcha."

Negotiations concluded, Ty fell back, planting one hand on her door and the other on the back of the seat beside her head. "We struck a deal."

"So I heard." Her smile faded as she planted a hand on his chest, needing to establish at least a minimal barrier between them. "Ty, I don't think—"

"Good. Don't think."

"I want to," she whispered, her lips hovering over his. "But now—"

"Is the perfect time," he finished for her. "Just one kiss, Mil. It's going to be a long six weeks."

And God help her, he was right. "Okay. One," she said, knowing they had a snowball's chance in hell of stopping at one kiss, but too far beyond temptation to care.

He captured her protest with a long, sweet kiss. Her teeth ached with the sweetness. Her toes curled in her shoes—no easy feat in a pair of extra-pointy Louboutins. She slid her hand under his jacket and clutched the front of his shirt. She didn't have to worry about wrinkles now. She wanted to muss him. Muss him badly. Muss him so hard, he'd be a marked man. He must have picked up on the tenor of her thoughts, or perhaps she'd pulled a handful of chest hair, but either way, Ty angled his head and added a smidge more pressure to the kiss.

Parting her lips, she encouraged him to take what they both wanted.

She slipped her tongue out to meet his, and he groaned deep in his throat. The car lurched and surged as Manny urged them toward their destination. Ty's hand slid down her side, his thumb grazing the side of her breast in the time-honored tradition learned by teen-age boys everywhere.

"Nice move," she panted when they broke for air.

He stared deep into her eyes. "I have more."

Wiping a smear of lipstick from his mouth with the pad of her thumb, she held his gaze and gave his ethics a nice, hard prod. "You've got an hour or two before you have to be at the airport. Come up to my room." A slow smile overtook her as she fell back on her usual blunt-force seduction gambit. "I'm sure we can find a way to pass the time."

He gave his head a gratifyingly slow shake. "You're the devil."

"I don't have a blue dress on," she pointed out.

"If you had a dress on, Manny'd be giving me hell right now, because I'd be in it too."

"So sure of yourself," she chided.

"You're the one trying to tempt me to come up to your room." He kissed her again, a lingering kiss packed with promise but lacking the sharp licks of heat she craved.

Before she could bend him to her will, he broke away, his breath coming fast and shallow as he pressed his forehead to hers. "I won't. And I hope to God I don't have to tell you it's not you, it's totally me. I don't want to be that guy, Millie."

"I understand."

"I've resisted this…us in my head for so long. I'm not sure I can resist the reality of us, you know…"

"In the flesh?" she offered with a helpful smile.

He groaned and flung himself back into his seat, draping his forearm over his eyes. "You *are* the devil."

Millie gave a quiet laugh. "I'm not sure the 'in the flesh' thing is a good idea anyhow. You're used to women a few boy bands younger than me."

"Don't." He jerked his head sharply. "Don't say that kind of thing."

"Truth."

"You're beautiful, Millie. Desirable. I desire you," he added for emphasis.

"Thank you." She gave him a smile that edged toward wicked. "I desire you too."

"Your confidence is one of the sexiest things about you."

She inclined her head, pleased to have evolved to a point where others recognized and appreciated her independence. "Thank you again." A flush warmed her cheeks, then burst into flame the second she told herself she was too old to blush when a man paid her a compliment.

"One of the many things about you that I find irresistible," he murmured. To her delight and mortification, he ran a knuckle over the curve of her cheek.

"And I find your moral fiber very attractive, even if I am cussing you in my head right now," she said in a husky tone.

"The Merryton Hotel," Manny announced. Without another word, he darted into the drop-off lane and jerked to a stop. He popped the trunk and threw open his door. A uniformed bellman reached for the back door, and Millie jerked upright.

Fear, unwelcome and irrational, gripped her as she eyed Ty. He was leaving. Getting on a plane and heading to the other side of the country for six long weeks. Desperate to hang on to the quasi-intimacy of the past week, she searched his face, eagerly cataloging each feature as she drank in the overall effect. "I don't want you to go yet."

He gave her hand a reassuring squeeze. "The last thing I want to do is leave now, but I can't stay here. This past week has been heaven and hell."

She gave a mirthless laugh. "I know exactly what you mean."

Lifting her hand to his lips, he kissed her knuckles as Manny tapped on the lid of the trunk to spur things along. "I'll call you. I'll wanna get the scoop on the Wolcott water polo team's plans for making a splash this season."

This time, she blushed deeply, but more with pleasure than embarrassment. Swallowing a sigh, she accepted the doorman's gloved hand and swung her legs from the car. "You have to admit, that was a good headline."

"Damn straight it was."

They shared a long look. "Safe travels, Ty."

"See you soon, Millie."

Unwinding the towel she'd wrapped around her hair, Millie tossed the heap of wet terry cloth onto the lip of the tub. She padded into the bedroom wearing nothing but boy-cut panties and a pair of rainbow-striped, fuzzy socks Kate said were supposed to be infused with shea butter.

The socks were nice but not exactly the kind of infusion a girl thinks about when she's been burning through the double-A batteries a lot faster than she'd like. Reaching into her bag, she extracted a washed-thin Warrior tank top three sizes too big and slipped the soft cotton over her head.

Pulling her phone off the charger, she checked to see what she'd missed in the forty minutes since she plugged the darn thing in. A dozen or more media outlet apps boasted alert notifications, but she only clicked on the icon for National Sports Network headlines. A quick glance at NSN showed nothing to send her rushing to check the other sites. The scandal of the week had pretty much petered out. Greg Chambers hadn't managed to bait Ty into a fight, so the gist of the interview had been boiled down to a few sound bites and a still of Ty smiling broadly and looking far too fit and handsome to be anyone's cuckold.

She found a couple of emails in her inbox, the most important one a sale notification from ShoeIn. A text from Avery confirmed the date and time for Kate's post-honeymoon debriefing at Calhoun's Bar and Grill the following week. And one missed call from Tyrell Ransom.

Her thumb tapped the callback option before she even had a chance to check the clock. Three minutes after eleven. He'd be boarding soon. One little phone call should be safe enough.

"Hello."

His voice was warm and deep and put her in the mood

for Barry White music and lamps draped with gauzy scarves. "Plan on visiting any brothels while you're in the great state of Nevada?"

He laughed. A full, rumbling laugh that did little to dispel the red-wallpapered room she'd conjured in her head. "You never know. If the casinos don't have any good headliners…"

She could see the whole setup perfectly. Of course, her version was highly romanticized and most likely television inspired. Reality was no doubt a fairly businesslike concern, but this was her trip down the rabbit hole. If she wanted piles of pillows, sheets made of satin, and heavy velvet drapes on the four-poster bed she had him tied to in her head, who could tell her no?

"Boarding soon?"

"Let's get back to the brothel thing," he teased.

"Not the kind of headline I want to spin. Besides, it's been done. Promise me you won't do anything reckless."

Ty sobered instantly. "My dad is flying out, remember? I'll probably be playing thirty-six holes of golf each day and listening to the old man heckle me about my slice."

Dropping onto the bed, she leaned back against the headboard and pulled her knees up under her shirt. "Shift your weight before you start your downswing."

"You golf?"

"Some," she replied, relishing his pleased surprise.

"What's your handicap?"

"The shoes," she said without hesitation. He laughed again, and she beamed, delighted to have found their easy rhythm once again. "Pick up any good trinkets in the gift shops?"

"I've been hanging out in the Captain's Club."

"Free drinks?"

"Coffee."

She nodded. "Good boy."

"I'm no boy."

"Man," she corrected, allowing a sly smile to color the words. "Big, strong, handsome man."

"Much better."

"So your dad will be keeping an eye on you. That makes me feel much better."

"Were you really worried?"

Millie caught a hint of injury in his question and hurried to correct course. "Well, not really, but I wanted to make you feel all badass and loose cannon, because I know guys like to think they are."

His chuckle told her she'd hit the right note. "Yes, well, I think I perfected my badass loose cannon act last week."

They lapsed into silence but not the uncomfortable kind. This was easy. Companionable. The quiet was unusual for Millie but not unwelcome. She spent so many hours of the day pitching and talking and promoting, she sometimes found it hard to switch off the ticker in her head. But Ty made the quiet she'd dedicated her life to filling seem almost natural. Almost but not entirely. Nature abhorred a vacuum and all that.

Plucking at the hem of her tank, she asked the question that had niggled at her all day. "Are things really going to be this easy with Mari?"

There was a beat of hesitation so brief, she wasn't sure anyone else would have noticed, but she did. Her job hinged on her ability to pick up on cues, verbal and nonverbal. Millie only wished she could see him. Pauses were so much more eloquent when one could see the body language accompanying them.

"She's the one who wants this," he reminded her.

"You don't?"

"I didn't say that," he corrected with heartening speed. "I'll admit I wouldn't be zipping out to Reno for the quick fix if this hadn't happened, but I think we both knew we weren't going to last much longer."

Genuinely curious, Millie felt compelled to pry. After all, the man had left his taste in her mouth, then kicked her to the curb. Almost literally. She figured she was entitled to a little nonprofessionally motivated probing if she wasn't going to get the kind of probing that made spending a night in a hotel room so much more enjoyable. "Why do you think?"

His laugh rang hollow, even over the phone. "Oh, I don't know…a lack of any common ground, maybe?"

"You had to have something in common at one time. You married her."

Ty paused, then said, "I'd like to exercise my rights under the Fifth Amendment."

"Ah." She grinned, pleased by the surprising candor of his nonanswer. "Com*bust*ible, huh?" She waited a beat. "Did I put enough emphasis on the bust part? I hate when I fall…flat."

This time, his chuckle was for real. "You crack me up."

Sinking into the pillows, she stared at the muted television without really seeing the screen. "How'd you meet her? Your typical sideline romance? You made up a play, and she let you touch her pom-poms?"

"Actually, we met in class."

The answer would have shocked her right out of her smarty-pants, if she had been wearing any pants. "Class?"

"Yes. When I wasn't busy populating the world with illegitimate children or buying another set of ten-carat studs for my ears, I was in class."

"And here I thought I had you pigeonholed. Go ahead, shatter more of my illusions."

"When I went back to Eastern to work with Coach Washington, I decided to finish my undergrad degree."

"Because you went into the NBA early."

"Not that early compared to some, but I did need to complete my senior year."

"I think it's great you did. Let me guess, kinesiology major?"

"Funny," he deadpanned.

The entire athletic department knew Millie loved making jabs at the jocks and their preferred fields of study, but she was no longer surprised when football players told her about their biochemistry classes. Acknowledging the scope of study the degree entailed didn't stop her from making fun of those who chose the major, but it did change the tenor of her teasing.

"When I left school, it might have been something along those lines," Ty admitted, jerking her from her ruminations. "But when I finished, I ended up with a degree in psychology."

"Huh."

"Then I went on to do some postgraduate work in psychology. Emphasis in sports psychology, of course," he added with a self-deprecating chuckle.

"Brains, beauty, and brawn," she murmured. "I guess you had to screw up somewhere."

"I'm not particularly lucky in love." The gruff admission sent a shiver racing through her. "But thanks for saying I'm pretty. I feel so much better now."

"You met in class," she prompted.

"I was doing a little time as a teaching assistant. Psych 101. She was making up a couple of missed general studies courses before graduation." The words were cut off by a too-perky-for-the-hour voice making a flight announcement. "The professor and the coed. A tale as old as time," he said brusquely. "I have to go. We're boarding."

Reluctant to give in to the demands of the airlines, she blurted out the one thought running through her brain like a hamster on a wheel. "This isn't at all how I envisioned tonight."

She heard his breath hitch. "I think we can save some conversations for another night."

A hot blush scalded her cheeks and set the tips of her ears aflame. Between the tomato face, the decidedly unsexy nightwear, and her now air-dried and uncombed hair, she was damn glad he hadn't thought to try a video chat. "No."

"Yes," he countered. The background noise became more pronounced, and she figured he'd left the VIP lounge. His breathing became choppy. "Good night, Millie. Think about me."

She closed her eyes and tried not to groan. Those huffy, little puffs in her ear were doing something to her. Something she hadn't packed the equipment to handle, even though she knew his sense of honor wouldn't allow anything to happen between them. Yet. Damn wishful thinking. "A pretty good bet."

"I'll be thinking about you too. Probably too much."

"Good night, Ty."

"Sweet dreams."

She ended the call and, out of habit, double-checked to make sure the screen showed they had disconnected. Tossing the phone aside, she reached for the remote and zapped the television as well. Flopping back on the bed, she stared at the ceiling, waiting for her body to give her the go/no-go. Of course, her engines were revving. Sliding her hand under the thin cotton of her shirt, she closed her eyes and pictured Ty sprawled in his seat, ready for takeoff. If she was going to have the kinds of sweet dreams she wanted to have, she'd have to make them happen on her own.

Chapter 6

THE FIRST WEEK, HE ONLY CALLED HER THREE TIMES. PROOF of his near-Herculean strength of will. Each of those occasions, he was careful to make contact during business hours and to have a media-related question ready as an excuse. Even if the ploy was one so lame a child could see through it. He also timed the calls to be sure they didn't last any longer than ten minutes, though he really wanted to talk to her for hours.

At the end of the third call, she said simply, "You don't need to make up excuses to call me, Ty. If you want to talk, we can talk."

Her candor was both a comfort and catalyst. Before he could stop himself, he was calling her daily. Sometimes more. He hoped his father's arrival the following week would prove to be a distraction, but he wasn't counting on it curbing the urge altogether. The casual intimacy of their conversations on the plane and over the phone was a revelation. Though Millie's questions weren't particularly probing, he'd given her more information than he'd given anyone. He'd never had anything like this openness with Mari, even when things were fresh and new. When his marriage started to flounder, he'd tried to recapture the closeness they'd shared only to discover he and Mari had never had a tight connection.

Talking to Millie made him realize he'd never really had a confidante. Oh, he was close with his father, and they had a good, solid relationship, but delving deep wasn't their forte. He was lonely. And like a bad tooth or a partially healed bruise, he couldn't help pushing on the sensitive spot. Acknowledging his loneliness left a dull ache in his gut only the sound of Millie's voice seemed to soothe.

Feeling something, even the sharp sting of regret, was better than the numbness he'd been living with for too long.

He wanted someone in his life. Not an arm charm or a warm body in his bed, but someone who wouldn't hesitate to call him on his bullshit. A woman he could talk to without having to parse his words. Someone to guard his back and maybe set a few picks for him in life. A partner. Millie.

He wanted Millie.

The second week he was in Reno, he played a lot of golf. Staying active kept him off the phone, but working up a sweat didn't stop him from thinking about Millie. Incessantly. And oddly enough, those thoughts weren't entirely salacious. Mostly but not entirely.

After long days on the course, his father crashed early, leaving Ty with too much alone time after business hours. Every night, he played a little game with himself. How long could he go before he cracked and placed the call? Some nights, his will was pathetically weak. Others, he held strong.

The first time he delayed his gratification as late as eight o'clock, he'd caught her in bed. Stupid time difference. The mental image he conjured played havoc with his swing for the next few days, but the husky welcome in her voice was consolation enough. They talked about everything and nothing. What she had for lunch. His dad's outlandish golf pants. Whether he could blame his sad performance on the back nine on his custom Pings or if he needed to man up and admit he sucked at the game.

He always ended the call with a smile on his face, even if Millie had been prickly with him. Glutton that he was, he discovered he liked her salty side almost as much as the sweet she tried so hard to hide. Every night, he ticked off another day on his mental calendar. With every conversation, Ty realized he'd thought about hanging around Millie more than any married man should over the years. Still, when he searched his conscience for a hint of guilt, he came up clean. He never acted on the impulse, and if his marriage hadn't gone south in such a spectacular way, that kiss might never have happened.

All jokes about players being players aside, he simply wasn't built to be a dog with women. Sure, he'd dated a lot in his younger days, but he'd never been one to juggle relationships. He claimed he didn't have the skills for keeping multiple women happy, but in reality, he didn't have the interest. Even in his globe-trotting days playing EuroLeague ball, he'd known he wanted to come home to the States, meet a nice woman, and try to build a family complete with both a dad and a mom.

Lust. He'd been blinded by lust when he met Mari. And she'd been the starry-eyed girl who hung on his stories from his playing days. He never really gave her curiosity much thought. People liked knowing pro athletes whether they were retired or not. Hell, his own father still took great pleasure in holding court with his golf cronies, bragging as if Ty'd dunked a game-winning shot the night before.

By the time his third week in Reno rolled around, he and Millie were on a semiregular schedule. Ty found himself looking forward to their nightly calls more than anything. They hardly consisted of anything earth-shattering. Mostly day-to-day stuff. Millie dished what little gossip she could scrape up on a college campus in the summer session. He told funny stories about his dad and the guys they golfed with each day.

They laughed and teased, keeping the conversation light, but all the while, he was mining for information. Small pieces of Millie he could pretend he alone knew. Like her inexplicable aversion to seeded hamburger buns or the fact that she enjoyed knitting. One night, she'd talked about how devastated she'd been when she lost her grandmother. He told her about the magical inlet in the Greek islands where he'd found peace with the end of his career as a ballplayer.

When things got too deep or too heavy, Millie got them back on track with a quick quip or Sahara-dry observation, but he didn't let her deflections bother him. Stories were exchanged. The connection was deepening.

At least on his end.

Ty had a hard time figuring out exactly what Millie was thinking or feeling. She was a woman trained to hold her cards close to her vest. Not one to air her every grievance or frustration aloud. If Millie didn't like something, she found a way to shape what troubled her into something more palatable. Her restraint and deter-mination were qualities Ty found both admirable and frustrating as all hell.

Of course, the juxtaposition between Millie and Mari cut both ways. If Mari had chosen to end their marriage in a more circumspect way, he wouldn't have gone through all the upheaval that gave him opportunity to spend more time with Millie. Maybe they would have found their way to each other eventually, but if his wife hadn't publicly humiliated him, he'd have moved slower. He would have gone through the formalities and let a decent interval go by before he even thought about dating.

But his relationship with Mari hadn't ended with grace and decorum. He'd ignored the snarky tweets she posted with a hashtag #TydDown whenever he dragged her away from her online life to attend one of the many university and booster functions a coach's wife was expected to attend. He'd also tried to ignore the PicturSpam images of his wife and other men. They'd been popping up here and there for months, but he chose to turn a blind eye. To pretend he didn't know she was making a chump out of him. But they both knew the jig was up long before Mari packed her bags and loaded them into her car the night before the NBA draft.

She claimed to be in love with Dante Harris. Since Ty couldn't, in all honesty, make the same declaration concerning his feelings for her, he didn't try to stop her. When Dante's name was called in the draft, the first person Dante kissed was his mama—and the second was Ty Ransom's wife. If ever there was a film clip guaranteed to make the sports world hum with speculation, it was a star player planting one square on his coach's spouse.

Ty's quiet life became a circus, and Mari was its scantily clad social media ringmaster. That night, she changed her favorite hashtag to #NotTydDown and proceeded to post photos and video of all the ways she and Dante celebrated, some of them featuring bits and pieces the sports media was required to blur when they aired them.

Part of the agreement their lawyers had made included a cease and desist on all public commentary about their split following the NSN interview with Greg Chambers. As far as Ty knew, Mari had stuck to the bargain, and he certainly wasn't interested in stirring things up, so all was quiet on the Ransom front. Just the way he liked it.

He could go on with his life. Choose his own furniture. Eat Chinese food straight out of the container while standing there with the refrigerator door wide open. Drink milk from the carton. Leave the toilet seat up. His life was his own again, and he liked having control. Ty considered himself an essentially private man. On leaving the league, he learned to appreciate the simplicity of life outside the limelight. This past month had reminded him how much happier he was when people minded their own business. Therefore, he saw no reason to announce his desire to have private relations with the university's public relations guru to the world. He was content with the way things were.

Mostly.

Wrapping one of the thin, rough towels that came with the short-term rental around his hips, he stepped from the shower. Water beaded on his shoulders and rolled in tickly rivulets down his back, but he paid the tickling streams no mind. Goose bumps pebbled his skin. He tried to blame his shiver and the subsequent goose bumps on the air-conditioning, but he knew all too well it was more likely caused by the message alert on his phone.

Millie had called.

In all the weeks since he'd dropped her off in front of the Merryton Hotel, he'd been the one to do the dialing. A hot rush of pleasure heated his skin. He could almost hear the droplets of water sizzling as he reached for the phone and scanned the missed call notification. A part of him wanted to curse the old man for strong-arming him into going to one of the casinos for dinner. The other part was glad he'd been the one to be unavailable for once. He liked calling her later in the evening. Bedtime.

At least, bedtime for her.

For him, they were prime time. Which meant he usually showered later. Better to wash all evidence of his pent-up frustration away before hitting the hay. But tonight, after a couple of hours in the trenches, he needed to wash the stench of slots, smoke, and the all-you-can-eat snow crab off before he could settle in. Peering into the mirror, he ruffled the water from his close-cropped hair. He saw more gray hairs creeping in on the sides, and the other day, the old man had teased him about the silver stubble in his beard. He rubbed his hand over his cheek, trying to decide if he wanted to shave before calling her back or wait for morning.

He opted to play it smooth and hard to get. Pulling his razor and a can of cream from the cabinet above the sink, he smirked at his reflection, feeling smug. She could wait. At least a few more minutes. Millie certainly had no compunction about postponing their chats to a time more convenient for her.

Clean-shaven, minty fresh, and unable to stand waiting a second longer, he snatched up the phone and padded into the condo's master bedroom. The furnishings were comfortable if not a bit generic. The bed was a standard king, which meant he slept diagonally most nights, but the pillows were firm and plentiful. Hitting the recall button with his thumb, he propped a couple against the headboard, then dropped onto the bed. The knot at his waist loosened a bit but held the ends of the towel together enough to keep him decent.

"Hi, Ty."

The throaty rasp of her greeting did things to him. Stirred thoughts and urges he'd bank for later. For now, he had to set the jumble aside and form coherent sentences. "Hey, sorry I missed your call."

His lack of explanation might have been a bit of payback. Millie never gave excuses for why she would need to call him back or accounted for her time in any way, so he followed her lead. He didn't want her thinking he counted down the hours until he could talk to her again. Even if he did.

Playing by the unwritten conversational rules, he opened with an inane yet remarkably telling question. "How was your day?"

She sighed. "Boring. I hate summer session. Campus is like a ghost town in the afternoons. Kate has banned me from her office because I told her I was tempted to release the bikini picture from her honeymoon. I have no idea why she's being such a pill. If I were built like her, I'd dance a bikini-clad flamenco on top of every swimsuit edition in the athletic department's secret archive."

Ty wasn't sure how he was supposed to respond, so he stretched his legs out in front of him, crossed one ankle over the other, and started in what seemed like the safest place. "Secret archive?"

She guffawed. "Don't play innocent. I know what's in the file cabinet at the back of the bull pen."

He smiled, the image of Millie rifling through the battered metal drawers in search of contraband forming in his mind's eye. She wasn't wrong. When the university's human resources director cracked down on "potentially offensive" materials displayed in the workplace, the warren of cubicles housing the coaching assistants was hardest hit. All calendars, posters, and, yes, a nearly exhaustive collection of *Sports Illustrated* swimsuit editions were deemed too dangerous for public display. But instead of taking the stuff home, some smarty-pants locked all the loot in a filing cabinet no one bothered to use once departmental records became computerized. A limited number of duplicate keys were made, and being awarded one had become a departmental rite of passage.

At least now Ty had a pretty good idea who'd planted a copy of Burt Reynolds's *Cosmopolitan* centerfold in the mix.

"Are you the one who keeps slipping issues of *GQ* and *Esquire* in?"

"Not me," she said in a singsong voice. "But I can tell you people really are crazy about a sharp-dressed fella."

"Sadly, I don't think they're having any impact on Mack's or Beau's wardrobe choices," he said gravely.

Mack and Beau were the elder statesmen of the Warrior coaching staff. They were known for their love of polyester shorts, snow-white athletic shoes, and, in Beau's case, striped tube socks color coordinated with whichever polo-collared shirt his wife of over forty years had pressed for him. They were also two of the handful of coaches who'd willingly relinquished their keys to the cabinet. As far as Ty knew, the head coaches declined their copies. He knew far better ways to get shit-canned in professional coaching than ogling two-dimensional versions of scantily clad women. The three-dimensional ones caused enough trouble.

"I'd run away with Mr. Beau if he'd ditch that hussy."

"Watch yourself. She may look all sweet and charming, but I'm pretty sure Mrs. Beau would claw your eyes out if you put the moves on her man."

Millie heaved a heavy sigh. "No use. I can't get the guy to look twice at me anyhow."

"I have fifty that says he's looked more than twice."

Her delighted laugh made the prospect of coughing up fifty bucks on a bet he couldn't prove one way or another totally worthwhile. "You're so good for my ego."

"Is that why you keep talking to me?" he asked, knowing the question was shameless enough to border on pathetic but beyond caring.

"No, I keep talking to you because your voice gets me hot."

Stupefied by her bluntness, he stared at the ceiling for about ten beats too long to be cool, then pulled the phone away from his ear, not certain he'd heard her correctly. "I, uh… Did you just say—"

She didn't let him finish. "So Danny told Kate I was ogling him when I went to the fitness center."

Reeling and desperate to catch up, he blurted. "Were you?"

"Have you ever seen me step foot in the fitness center?"

Ty blinked, his whirling thoughts stopped cold. "No."

"If the little shit thinks he can bully me by fueling Katie's fire, he's going to be in for a rude awakening."

Several parts of her statement leaped out at him. First, Danny McMillan was about as far from a "little shit" as a man could be. Sure, the guy had toned and trimmed his physique from the height of his NFL playing days, but he was still built like a bull. Second, she wasn't wrong about her "Katie" calling her new husband on his bullshit if she saw fit to. If any person was qualified to deliver a master class on gamesmanship, it was Coach Kate Snyder. And last…he had no fucking idea. He'd lost the handle on the entire conversation when she'd said his voice made her hot.

"My voice makes you hot?"

"Yeah. Sure it does."

Her confession was glib. Completely offhand. As if he'd asked what color the sky was, and she'd reminded him it was dark outside. A bark of a laugh escaped him. "You're a piece of work, Millie."

"About time you noticed," she answered without missing a beat.

Catching on to the tempo, he grinned as he adjusted his grip on the phone. "You want me to list all the things I've noticed about you?"

"Would you?"

This time, he was better prepared for her no-nonsense volley. "Do you play tennis?"

"God, no. What's the point of doing all that running and never getting anywhere?"

"But you ran track in school?"

"Cross-country," she corrected. "I've never been good at staying inside the lines."

"I can believe that," he said. She laughed, and his dick perked up and took notice. "You're awfully good at this."

"At what?" she asked, all innocence.

"Keeping the conversation moving, never lighting for very long on one subject. Particularly not when the subject is you."

He'd swear it wasn't possible, but her voice dropped even deeper. "Oh, you're wrong. I'm my favorite subject. Ask me anything."

Emboldened by her straightforward play, he drove straight to the goal. "What do you do about it?"

"About what?" Her voice rose on a coy note, letting him know she wasn't the least bit confused by his line of questioning.

"You said my voice makes you hot. When we hang up, do you…handle things?"

"Sometimes I don't wait until we hang up."

Zero to one hundred in a split second, he was feeling turbo-charged. "Christ almighty, woman."

"You asked."

She lobbed those two little words back at him. A chance and a dare. Now, after weeks of keeping things friendly, comfortable, and strictly aboveboard, she was changing the game and challenging him to play along. Without allowing himself a chance to think better of his actions, he opened the knot on his towel and tossed the now-stifling terry cloth open wide. Blessed cool gusted from the vent above the bed, but the conditioned air offered little relief. Every ounce of restraint he'd cultivated dried up. His body pulsed as if he hadn't jerked himself raw nearly every night since he'd left her. He was melting down at the core, and he was help-less to resist.

"Millie."

Her soft sigh wafted through the phone. "You know, I've always hated my name."

He swallowed hard, trying to come up with enough spit to form at least one more syllable. "Why?" he managed to croak.

"Well, it's not exactly sexy," she said with a husky laugh. "I'm named after my grandmother. Not much of a surprise. Aren't too many women my age called Millicent."

"I like your name. It suits you."

This time, her laughter carried a sharp edge. "Wow. I know I'm a little older than you, but I'm not that old."

"You aren't old at all." Whoa. The comment didn't come out sounding like the compliment he intended. He took a breath and tried again. "I mean it suits your personality—a sharpshooter who's not afraid to be flirty."

"Like Annie Oakley."

"Like you," he retorted. "All woman. And a little all-knowing."

He could almost hear the smile in her voice. "You mean Cassandra?"

"Stop trying to distract me."

"As I said, you can ask me anything you want." The unmistakable sound of bedsheets rustling sent his heart rate soaring, but her breathy chuckle kicked down the last of his defenses. "Make sure you ask me in your superhot voice though. Oh, and say my name. A lot," she added as if he'd need the extra coaching. "I like the way you say it."

"Do you want me, Millie?"

"I think we both already know the answer."

"No deflecting," he admonished. "I want to hear you say you do."

"You've heard me say so before. I like you. I want you. When you come back with those precious divorce papers in hand, I'm going to do things to you. I'm gonna make you cross-eyed."

"You're a big talker."

"The biggest," she boasted. "Now, ask what you really want to ask."

"Are you touching yourself?"

"Of course." She panted softly. "Are you?"

Her unabashed answer coupled with the hitch in her voice turned his dick hard as titanium. He wrapped his hand around the stiff length and groaned out loud. "God, I haven't let myself. Not while we were talking." He ran his palm lightly over the head of his cock, then gave himself a hard stroke. "I wanted to, but I didn't want to make things…weird."

"But you are now," she coaxed.

"Yes."

He hissed the word, torn between pleasure and the strange impulse to deny himself, just to prove he could withstand the force of wanting her.

"You remember when you were telling me about going to Greece?"

His stroke faltered. For the love of everything holy, he had no idea why she would bring this up now. Closing his eyes, he moved his hand faster, setting the ruthless pace he liked. "Yes, I remember telling you about Greece."

"I came when you were telling me about the lagoon," she whispered. "I kept picturing you swimming. The clear turquoise water. White sand. You, brown as a nut and bare naked. All long and lean and…wet."

"Jesus." He gritted his teeth and slowed his strokes as he searched his lust-hazed memory. "I never told you I swam naked."

"Hey, my fantasy. I want you naked, I get you naked."

He'd also told her about the day he'd tried to outswim his grief over the end of his career, and she winnowed it down to him frolicking naked in the ocean. "Swimming naked. That's what you took from that story?"

"I understood the larger picture, but I have to admit, the image stuck with me."

"I was. I did." Frustrated by his stammering, he cleared his throat and tried again. "I did swim naked."

"Were you alone?"

"Yes."

The shush of fabric brushing over the phone muffled her voice. "Too bad. I was hoping for pictures."

Her brassy response coaxed another laugh out of him. One night, he'd keep count, but not tonight. Tonight, after weeks of toeing the imaginary line, they were jumping right over it. "I know this might be hard to believe, given my ex-wife's tendency toward exhibitionism, but I've always been a pretty private person."

"Skinny-dipping in the Greek isles aside," she interrupted.

Ignoring the bait, he continued as if she hadn't spoken. "I'm also pretty low tech. I think I've taken maybe a dozen pictures with a phone in my whole life." He paused, watching his hand glide over his stiff dick as though the parts didn't belong to him. "And I've never used one for…this."

"Phone sex," she clarified.

Heat raced through him, but he was hard-pressed to determine if the increase in tempo was arousal or embarrassment. "Yeah."

"Relax," she cooed into the phone. "I haven't either."

Her confession stilled his hand. He squeezed his dick hard, torn between the need to hold off the mounting pressure building inside him or to hold on to his hardon. Suddenly, he was in the midst of a situation with the potential to top Mari's defection on the humiliation meter. "You said you did," he accused.

"I said I got off while talking to you," Millie clarified. "I don't think it counts as phone sex if the other person doesn't know what's happening."

Still gripping his dick in one hand, he smashed the phone to his ear with his bicep and covered his eyes with his forearm. "Is this happening?"

"Ty?"

"Hmm?"

"I meant what I said earlier. I'm going to climb you like a damn tree. Now, talk to me in your sexy seducer voice," she demanded. "Tell me what you think about when you think about me."

The sultry promise in her tone assuaged any qualms he had. He began to stroke himself again, his palm growing damp with sweat as he picked up speed. "Everything. I think of everything."

Her breath whispered through the phone. Soft, swift pants. She was every bit as worked up as he was. "Can you be a little more specific?"

"I wanna see you naked," he growled.

"Do better."

"Is your skin pale all over?"

"Yes. Some places even more."

"God, I want to see me on you. You on me." He licked his palm, then started to fuck his fist in earnest. "I want to wrap myself around you. You know the necklace thing your friend Avery always wears? The black-and-white one?"

"Yin and yang," she whispered.

"Sounds stupid and corny, but that's how I see us. You and me." Closing his eyes, he confessed the one thing he'd tried to keep locked down since the day he first set eyes on Millie Jensen. "The first time I saw you, I recognized you. Not your face, but you. All I could think was, 'Yes, there you are.'"

She moaned so softly, he might have missed it if he wasn't pressing the phone to his ear hard enough to make it ache. He knew she came because something in the silence clicked for him. The same comfortable intimacy enveloped them when he'd spoken of his trip to Greece all those years ago. They'd found the silence of acceptance. And as much as he relished that millisecond of blank space, something primal stirred deep inside him. Something that demanded he make her declare her release. Own it. And acknowledge the man who'd helped get her off.

"Did you come, sweet Millie?"

His own breathing grew rough and ragged, filling the heavy air between them. She gave a moan he interpreted as a yes. The smallness of her climax tore at him with a force equal to the eruption building inside him. He hated the thought of her holding back anything. Not with him. Not when they had come so far.

"When I see you, I'm gonna make you scream." Tightening the ring of his thumb and forefinger, he thrust his hips up to meet each punishing stroke. "I'm going to make love to you so slow and sweet, you'll beg me for more. I'll fuck you so hard, the neighbors will wonder if they should call 911."

Millie laughed at the last bit, but he was beyond serious.

"Are you listening to me? I'm gonna…arruh." He gasped as the climax ripped through him, drawing up from his balls and bursting from the head of his dick with a force he hadn't known in years. "Coming," he growled into the phone. "Oh, fuck me, I'm…"

"I'd love to," she purred.

Her whisper kicked him the over the cliff. For the next minute, he was in free fall. His hand, slick with his own spunk, moved of its own accord. He stared down at his dick in wonder. Like he was twelve and enamored with beating off all over again. His thoughts tumbled over one another. Only two things kept him grounded—the smooth face of his phone practically implanted in his ear and the joyous ease of Millie's soft exhalations.

He grimaced with a mixture of pride and distaste as he released his dick and groped for the towel trapped beneath him. Gaze locked on the ceiling over the bed. Not his bed. Not his place. And Millie wasn't his woman. Yet.

Grabbing the discarded towel, he cleaned himself up as much as he could be bothered. His heart thrummed against his breastbone, beating harder than when he ran wind sprints with his team. A smile curved his mouth as he pulled the phone away from his ear, switched to speaker, and lowered the volume to minimize the chances of his father overhearing through the condo's paper-thin walls.

Resting his hand over his heart, he drew in a bracing breath. "This was great, but let's not do it again."

"No?"

He caught her disappointment, but her reluctance strengthened his resolve. Sort of. "It's not that I don't want you. Trust me, my right hand and I have been spending a lot of quality time together lately." He forced a laugh but sobered quickly. "But as much as I want you, I don't want our every call to be some kind of…" He trailed off, searching for the right word.

"Foreplay?"

"Yes." The second the word was out, he realized he'd chosen incorrectly. "No. I mean, this is all sort of foreplay, right?"

"I guess one could call whatever this is foreplay," she conceded.

"I don't want to make our conversations all about sex, because I don't think our relationship is all about sex."

A long silence followed. This time, he was pretty sure she wasn't pausing for pleasure.

"Ty, you're in a really weird place right now, and I—"

He had to cut her off. "Don't." He took a shaky breath. "Can't we just…let it be for now?"

She laughed softly. "Yeah, Ty, we can let it be."

"I feel good. Incredible."

"But you don't want to do this again."

"I wanna do it again so bad I can taste it." She laughed, and he managed a lazy, "Wasso funny?" His words were slurred with lazy satisfaction.

"I think we know which of us is gonna be the screamer."

Chapter 7

Ty was steadfast in his determination to nip any further phone antics in the bud, much to Millie's frustration. She also found him a little more appealing for his sexual scruples. Talk about annoying ironies. Tipping the paper umbrella out of her way with a flick of her fingernail, Millie didn't even bother lifting the glass to take a long pull from the double straws Bartender Bill always put in her drinks. Icy shards of strawberry daiquiri slid down her throat but didn't quell the searing heat inside her.

The fire burning inside her started as an ember. A single unextinguished spark leftover from the holocaust of one indulgent phone call. As the days passed, the glow reignited. She did her best to play along, dampening her expectations each time the phone rang, but every time they hung up, she was aflame again.

Twice, she'd tried to tempt him into dumping his misguided moral code, and twice, she had been gently refused. Unaccustomed to being rebuffed, Millie found herself growing edgier and edgier with each passing day. Three nights ago, she had snapped and told him not to bother calling her until he was a free man.

Ty, of course, ignored her hissy fit. He called every night, right on time. And when she refused to answer, he proceeded to have charming conversations with her voicemail. Though she wasn't a fan of his impression of her voice, she had to admit his knack for exchanging flirty banter with himself nearly made her crack a couple of smiles. Giving her slushy drink a desultory stir, she indulged in the one big sigh she allowed herself each day, then took a healthy gulp of the rum-laced cocktail.

"Who repressed your First Amendment rights?"

Millie rolled her eyes as she released the double barrels of her straws and grimaced when she caught sight of her friend Avery's latest thrift-shop getup. The other woman was three inches shorter and a damn sight curvier than a porn star, but the population at large would never know. Wolcott's one and only women's literature and feminist studies professor covered herself from head to toe in a mishmash of fabrics that would have made Joseph's coat of a kazillion colors look drab.

Though Millie liked to rib her friend about her boho-chic fashion choices, in her deepest, innermost thoughts, she envied Avery a little. Not that she wanted to swap closets, necessarily, but because she'd never once heard the other woman apologize or even appear uncomfortable with the way she looked. Avery's utter self-possession twanged one of the few threads of insecurity Millie would admit to owning. So she covered with sharp-edged commentary.

Cocking an eyebrow at the ancient army jacket Avery wore, she shook her head. "What? The Che Guevara look is back, and no one told me?"

Avery simply smirked as she lifted her usual glass of neat scotch in mock salute. "Power to the people."

Millie didn't bother to hide her smile as she watched her friend's smirk slide to a grimace as she swallowed. Avery had started drinking scotch because she was all about tearing down gender barriers—real or perceived—regardless of her own personal preferences. Millie admired her friend's tenacity but refused to feed Avery's already healthy ego by saying so. She enjoyed the slightly contentious byplay the two of them had developed over the years, even if Kate got tired of playing the peacemaker.

"What's our cause of the week?" Millie asked, looking forward to the distraction of one of Avery's tirades. "We've worn out equal pay."

Avery quirked a brow. "Oh? Are you getting paid the same as a man?"

"A man wouldn't have the balls to do my job."

Laughing, Avery toasted her again. "True. Too true."

Millie took another sip of her drink, tapping her nail against the side of her glass. "I'm bored with equal pay. Let's save some for the next time Kate's contract is up for renewal."

"Domestic violence? Maternity leave?" Avery visibly perked, her already bright eyes gleaming with the zeal of a crusader ready to rush into battle. "Genital mutilation?"

Thankfully, Kate arrived in time to intercept the conversational grenade. "Not today, thanks." The queen of women's collegiate basketball dropped a gym bag beside the table then a kiss hello on each of their cheeks. "Danny says I'm perfect just the way I am."

Millie pointed an accusing finger at the willowy brunette as she settled on the high stool. "He steals his lines from Colin Firth."

"I don't care where he gets his dialogue. It worked." Lifting her hand, Kate signaled to the older gentleman behind the bar. Less than a minute passed before a frosty mug of beer appeared at her elbow. Hoisting the glass in a wordless toast, she took a deep gulp before setting the heavy mug down with an exaggerated, "Ahh."

"Refreshing?" Avery asked with a pointed look.

"I worked up a thirst," Kate replied.

Millie nudged the heavy gym bag with the toe of her shoe. "Dragging your anvil around again?"

"Never know when I'll need to fire some iron." Kate took another drink, then twisted the handle of the mug from one hand to the other. "I wonder how Danny'd look in a wet white shirt."

"If you hose him down when you get home, we want pictures," Millie instructed.

"I was thinking of making him go for a swim in the campus pond. If we're doing Firth, I want it done right."

"I'd love to do Firth," Avery said with a wistful sigh.

"Speaking of doing Firth, when is Coach Handsome coming back?" Kate asked with an oh-so-innocent lift of her eyebrows.

Millie dropped her straws back into the hurricane glass and gaped at her friend, astounded by the lack of subtlety from a woman known for her finesse. "What? How is that…" She sputtered to a stop, then narrowed her eyes as she caught sight of the sly smile curving Kate's lips. "Nice segue."

The smile morphed into a grin, and Avery let loose with a giggle-like noise she immediately covered with a snort.

"I thought it was a real attention-grabber," Kate said, preening on her stool. "Must be about time, right?"

The six-week mark had passed the previous Thursday.

Classes had started, and Ty's assistants were holding conditioning workouts. To Millie, they looked suspiciously like full practices. But she couldn't tell him about them, because she'd stopped taking his calls. Then, when she finally broke down and tried to reach him, she went directly to voicemail. Apparently, Ty was done taking it on the chin, and she couldn't really blame him.

Still, she hadn't expected him to go completely radio silent. No talking, no texting, not even any responses to business-related emails. Like he was punishing her for their telephonic transgressions. Or the lack of finesse in her gamesmanship. Either way, she was the one in the doghouse, and she hadn't a clue when to expect him back on campus.

Taking a stab at studied nonchalance, Millie reached for her purse and pulled a tube of lip gloss from the inner pocket.

"Errrrrrgh!" Avery made an obnoxious nasal sound reminiscent of a scoreboard buzzer.

Millie froze, her gaze darting from one friend to another, her fingers clutching the tube like a lifeline. "What the hell?"

"The lipstick defense won't work." Kate reached over and snatched the gloss from her hand. "And don't even bother with your phone. I'm onto the bit where you email yourself from one account to another to make it buzz."

Avery gave her a slow, pitying shake of her frizzy head. "Almost as bad as the bit where a woman sends herself flowers to make herself look desirable." Millie glared, but Avery simply shrugged the pointed look off. "I saw someone do that in a movie. Or maybe it was a rerun of *Cheers*."

Seeing her opening, Millie dove through. "I loved that show. Sam was hot, but I think I would have done Woody instead. The name, you know."

"Of course." Kate nodded. "So, are you going to spill, or do I need to get Gloria Steinem"—she gestured to Avery—"to remind you the solidarity of sisterhood is the only thing that separates us from the animals?"

"I thought we were superior due to our ability to accessorize," Millie quipped, lunging for another pop culture lifeboat in hopes of distracting her friends from this line of questioning. "Did I tell you about the handbag I scored? Kate Spade. Well, a fake Spade, because university salary and all."

She tossed in an airy wave of her hand but quickly tucked it back into her lap when she saw the women across from her were as entrenched as CNN reporters. Sucking in a breath, she exhaled in a huff strong enough to stir the stack of paper napkins tucked into the condiment caddy on the table. Crossing her arms over her chest, she leveled a stern stare on one, then the other before owning up. "No, I don't know when he's coming back."

Kate grinned like a cat covered in canary feathers as she sat up even taller on her stool. "I do."

Millie squinted at the woman who, up until three minutes before, she would have called her best friend. And she kept her narrowed gaze locked on her on the off chance her laser-like focus might cut through the barroom gloom and extract the data directly from Kate's brain. When the mind meld failed, she cocked a brow and reclaimed her daiquiri.

"Good for you." She lifted the glass and latched on to the straws with a vengeance.

"Tell me you're sorry about wanting to leak my honeymoon pictures to the press."

"But I'm not," Millie countered. "If anything, it would have given you an opportunity to be the first collegiate coach with a legitimate shot at making the swimwear editions."

"Exactly what I've been aiming for my entire career," Kate muttered.

"I'd never let them exploit our Katie." Avery's response was automatic but a bit distracted. "How much do they pay for those things anyway?"

Millie looked over and found Avery staring intently at the scotch in her glass. She smirked. "I hear you get some decent moolah. Should we call a modeling agency?" Millie asked with exaggerated sweetness.

"I think between me and Danny, we'll be able to cover the light bill." Kate laughed, but an edge of sharpness undercut the effect. Wetting her lips, Kate dismissed her moodiness with a short shake of her head. "Sorry. Just a little tired of being talked about like a commodity."

Millie grimaced an apology. Kate's contract negotiations had taken on new dimensions when the university had tried to dismiss Danny due to their personal involvement. All of Kate's future happiness, personal and professional, had boiled down to what essentially became a game of chicken played out in the media. As her friend, Millie couldn't blame her for wanting to shy away from the spotlight, but professionally, she had an obligation to the university and to Kate herself to be certain she was positioned to grab all the best possible opportunities for publicity. It was a constant struggle for balance but one she was supremely adept at handling. The high-wire act was part of what Millie loved about her job, and Kate knew and understood. The dichotomy kept their friendship interesting, if not always harmonious.

Avery set her glass on the table and, with her trademark single-mindedness, followed her thoughts straight down the rabbit hole. "I bet they pay well though, and if you were to put the money toward—"

"I don't want to be anybody's poster girl." Kate paused, then split a look between them. "Like everyone else, I want to be left alone to do my job."

Millie nodded, swallowing any smart-assery she might have spewed a couple of months before as she remembered Ty expressing the same sentiment nearly word for word the night Mari's defection became public. She gave her friend the same canned answer she spewed at him. "No one lives in a vacuum," she said instead.

"I know," Kate murmured, staring at the scarred tabletop.

Then she lifted her head, tossing back a fall of smooth, chestnut hair that always made Millie think of the sleek, glossy mane on a thoroughbred horse. That's exactly what her friend was—a thoroughbred. Beautiful but skittish. Born to run like the wind but kept carefully corralled.

The increase in revenues generated by college athletic programs meant the system had become a gilded cage. Deep-pocketed alumni or enthusiastic boosters still mattered, but they weren't where the big money came in. No, the networks supplied the grease to make the wheels turn. The public had staked a claim on inter-collegiate athletics, elevating some of the programs and their players to a level many professional franchises aspired to reach. And a run of bad publicity had brought down more than one legendary program.

Coaching was the one area where the pay for perfor-mance was entirely legal. Fail to live up to potential, and the press would take great joy in helping to dismantle a career. It had happened to Danny and a good many football coaches before him.

Now, the spotlight was shining brighter on the hardwood court. The men's programs, like Ty's, were destined to take the heat, but high-profile women like Kate were becoming a bigger target. Avery considered this progress, from a detached, feminist point of view. But both Millie and Avery were attached to Kate, and the strongest argument for the advancement of women either of them could make was to help her bargain from a position of power. In all things.

"What's happening, Mil?" Kate asked, her voice gentle with concern. "For a couple of weeks, you were all coy and enigmatic whenever we talked about Ty—"

"Apparently not too enigmatic," Millie grumbled.

Avery chuckled, then reached over to pat Millie's hand. "More the giddy kind of enigmatic. Gives you away every time."

Kate nodded and tapped the thick handle of her mug. "For the last couple of weeks, you haven't said anything at all, which leads us to speculate."

"Right now, the leading theories are Mari had him killed, and someone's making a hole in the desert," Avery said, holding up one finger.

"Holes in the desert would be Las Vegas. Ty's in Reno," Millie corrected. "Besides, Mari's getting her divorce. Why would she kill him?"

Avery shrugged. "Quicker?"

"Messy," Kate interjected.

"I'm pretty sure he's not dead." Flicking up a second finger, Avery moved on. "Okay, possibility number two is Ty met one of those chorus girls, and you discovered they're busy trying to repopulate the earth with freakishly tall children."

"Wow. Talk about fast work," Millie commented, raising both brows.

"Personally, I think that's your long shot," Kate chimed in. "I think we all know Ty prefers the vertically challenged types to those of us with loftier aspirations."

"I may not qualify as freakishly tall, but I'm not exactly petite," Millie reminded her.

Avery sat up taller on her stool, but the adjustment didn't do much good. "As one of the vertically challenged, I find this line of reasoning offensive."

"It was Kate's reasoning," Millie hurled back.

"And in the absence of any other information." Avery made a circling motion with her hand, prompting her to be more forthcoming.

Millie inhaled deeply and closed her eyes, savoring the familiar and not-at-all-sexy scents of Calhoun's — stale beer, industrial cleansers, and postadolescent pheromones run amok. God, she wanted to talk to them. She'd always thought she could tell her best friends anything, but this was hard. How did a woman admit she failed as miserably at long-distance relationships as she did the ones up close and personal?

"No one lives in a vacuum," Kate whispered sotto voce.

Millie narrowed her eyes at Kate, annoyed her friend had the balls to throw her words back at her, but even more irked she wasn't big enough to kick Coach Snidely-Snyder in the ass.

"Fine." She pushed her drink to the center of the table and clasped her hands primly on the sticky surface. "You want to know what happened?"

Avery rolled her eyes so hard, she almost toppled off the stool. "We're mildly curious."

"And if you answer with 'nothing,' we'll know you're lying." Kate tucked her hair behind her ear and focused her full attention on Millie. "Something happened. We've been trying to wait for you to come around to telling us, but you've lost the giddy, and now we want to know why and how badly we need to hurt Ty."

"We had phone sex," Millie blurted.

Avery gripped the edge of the table as she reared back. "Whoa. So not what I expected."

Kate barked a laugh, fluttered her eyelashes in disbelief, then knocked her ear against her open palm a couple of times as if to knock some water out. "I'm sorry, I don't think I heard you clearly."

"We. Had. Phone. Sex." Arching her eyebrows, Millie eyed each of them challengingly.

Avery's bright, inquisitive eyes narrowed with suspicion. "Has to be more than that."

"Obviously," Kate said, bobbing her head. "You had phone sex, and his head exploded?"

"As far as I know, Coach Tyrell Ransom was last known to be alive, well, and unexploded in Reno,

Nevada." Millie looked from one woman to the other but found only the bafflement she'd been feeling for the last two weeks written in their expressions.

Kate shook her head. "I'm still processing the leap from phone sex to no phone."

Swallowing what was left of her pride, Millie gave up the tough-girl act and leaned in close. "Everything was going so well. He kissed me the night he spouted off to Jim Davenport on the phone," she said in a hushed rush.

"He owed you at least a kiss for shooting his mouth off," Avery said in an officious tone.

"Before, not after," Millie clarified.

"Either way, I'm not surprised," Kate interjected. "You two have been throwing off more sparks than a soldering iron since the day he came here. Of course he kissed you."

"Again when we went to New York…" She paused, not sure how to explain how conflicted she'd been about the events of that night. "We kissed, but nothing else has happened."

"Until now," Kate concluded.

"Nothing's really happening now. I'm here, and he's there," Millie sputtered. But her friends knew her too well to buy into the spin.

Avery definitely wasn't buying. "Other than the phone sex."

Kate cocked her head, her face open and curious but not condemning. "Did you want something to happen? Then, I mean. Knowing he was still married."

"Technically," Avery interjected. When both heads swiveled in her direction, she lifted a shoulder in a defensive shrug. "I think we can all agree the marriage pretty much had a fork sticking out of it."

"Still, he was married." Kate's voice was firm and uncompromising.

Millie's cheeks burned as she recalled the ambivalence she'd felt about his marital status as they'd jolted through the New York streets in a darkened town car. She might have slept with him. She wanted to—a fact she wasn't exactly raring to admit to her newly married friend. Millie had long ago given up any illusions she might have had about the matrimonial state. The old saw about taking two to make a relationship work was heartbreakingly true. No one person could love another enough for the both of them.

Bypassing the moral quagmire, she steered the conversation back to the facts. "We kissed. Things were said. Certain…implications were made," she said, choosing her words as carefully as she would for a press release.

Avery ran a fingertip around the rim of her highball glass. "Dirty implications?"

Millie considered her answer carefully. "Somewhat."

"Errrrrrgh!" Avery made the buzzer noise again, then glanced at Kate. "I'm going to need a ruling on this."

Kate pulled back in surprise. "A ruling on what?"

"Can an implication be somewhat dirty?" Avery persisted.

Kate's brow creased as she gave the concept consideration. "Well, yeah. I think so. I mean, an implication is by nature vague, so the connotation of an implication can be vague as well, can't it?"

When Kate looked to Millie for backup, she held up both hands in self-defense. "I'm not the professor here."

The two of them zeroed in on Avery, and Millie drew a calming breath as they joined forces to bounce her request for a ruling back at her. But Avery, being Avery, threw her head back and laughed, accepting the parry with grace. The younger woman could be bold to the point of aggressive, but she wasn't the least bit cowed by being proved wrong or reluctant to admit when caught out.

"Fine. Implications, connotations, and ambiguities," she chanted.

"Oh my!" Kate grinned, tickled by the verbal byplay. But simple amusement wasn't enough to knock Kate Snyder off her game. The unwavering intensity Kate brought onto the court zoomed in on Millie. "Be as vague as you want, but anything you don't tell us, we'll fill in with our own versions."

Resigned, Millie gave up the struggle. "We kissed. He called. Things were said," she recapped.

"Can we get a little clarification on the 'things' bit?" Avery signaled the waitress for another round of drinks, then drained her own glass. "Not the dirty things, the other stuff. The general tenor, so we can better parse the subtext."

Millie treated her friend to her own version of the impatient eye roll. "Okay. We discussed some of the finer points of the attraction between us—"

"Saw this coming from the get-go," Kate interjected.

"From the start," Millie conceded with a regal dip of her head. "I wasn't alone in indulging some less-than-professional thoughts about him."

"God, I love it when she gets all choosy with the words," Avery murmured.

Millie paused as a perky coed in short shorts and a skintight shirt emblazoned with Greek letters delivered their drinks. To buy a little more time, she plucked the umbrella and uneaten fruit garnishes from glass number one and added them to the second before allowing the girl to take the melted dregs of her daiquiri away.

"Tell me, in any of these 'less-than-professional thoughts,' was Ty perhaps wearing those tight shorts like Magic Johnson used to wear?" Kate raised hopeful eyebrows. "I bet he'd look great in them."

Avery cast a wistful sigh. "Ah, the days of guy thighs. I miss tight baseball pants too. I swear, they're killing all the eye candy in sports. Then again, I don't have a lot of luck with the baseball players."

"Since when do you know anything about baseball players?" Kate demanded.

"Since the night of your wedding party," Millie supplied, filling their friend in on what she'd missed while romping around on the beach. "Miss Avery made a play for Dominic Mann."

"No," Kate gasped, her gaze shooting to Avery, then back to Millie for confirmation.

"She's been tight-lipped about it," Millie said pointedly.

Avery shrugged. "Nothing to tell. I struck out." She blinked beguilingly at her friends. "See what I did there? I sports-talked."

"Very good," Kate commended warmly.

"I'm into soccer now," Avery added. "Did you know soccer guys wear knee-highs?"

Millie blinked in surprise. "You think those are sexy?"

"I've found a way to twist it into some variation of the Catholic-school-girl thing."

"You are twisted," Millie declared.

"Sauce for the gander." Avery toasted her with the scotch, took a sip, then shuddered as she gulped the alcohol down. "But back to the thighs at hand. I mean, the guy we're talking about," she corrected with a smirk. "Tyrell Ransom, Coach Handsome, the fella about to be divorced and man voted most likely to tear up Ms. Millie Jensen's sheets." She planted an elbow on the table and rested her chin in her palm. "Tell us about the phone sex. You can go word for word with that. Maybe we can help figure out where you went off the rails."

Tiring of interrogation cloaked in conversation, Millie decided to charge right into the fray. "One night he called, the conversation went to a…more intimate place, and we backed our words up with deeds. But then Ty told me he didn't want to do it again. He babbled something about saving things until he got back, and then the phone calls became a little too tense, so I backed off on talking to him, then…nothing."

"Bupkus," Avery added with a sad wag of her head.

Kate sighed. "Shut down."

"Yeah," Millie and Avery said on the same breathy sigh.

"So sad, to have the sex shut off like a spigot," Avery said morosely.

Touched and more than a little suspicious of the depth of her friend's empathy, Millie eyed Avery closely before stating the obvious. "You're drunk."

Avery's unpainted lips ticked up in a wry smile. "A

little." She swirled the whiskey in her glass. "This stuff is strong."

Kate removed the glass from Avery's clutches and set the highball on the far side of the table. "Now you know why the big boys all call it firewater."

As if to controvert the accusation of impeding inebriation, Avery straightened her spine. "I'm sorry you were clit-blocked on the phone sex, Mil."

Kate opened her mouth to say something, but Millie held up a hand to stop her. Millie appreciated the sentiment. "Thanks, Ave."

"Clit-blocked," Kate muttered under her breath as she lifted her beer.

Unable and unwilling to dance around the topic anymore and desperate for the reassurance only her closest friends could offer, Millie blurted her biggest fear. "But what if he didn't want to because I was bad?"

The question seemed to jolt Avery from her stupor. "Bad? What do you mean bad? Like God is going to strike you down, bad?"

"No, bad as in I sucked at phone sex," Millie corrected.

Kate was quick to shake her head. "I highly doubt you were bad."

"How do you know? You and I have never had regular sex, much less phone sex."

"And we're going to keep that little bonding activity in the never column," Kate said firmly. "But come on. I can't even imagine how bad a woman would have to be for a guy, any guy, to be all, 'No, that's okay, don't talk dirty to me,' you know?"

"Men are not verbal," Avery added, nodding sagely.

"Right, I know, but come on." Millie practically wailed the last part. "We go from 'I've thought about you for years' to 'I want you so bad, I can't take it anymore' to 'We're never doing this again' in, like, a split second."

"God, I must be drunk," Avery said, her eyes fixed on a point beyond Millie's shoulder.

Desperate for input, insight, a little female compassion, Millie cast a baleful look at Kate. "Hell, I was still basking in the self-induced afterglow and the sonuvabitch was deleting my phone number. Can I really be *that bad* at phone sex?"

But Kate didn't seem to have the words to give her the reassurance she needed. As a matter of fact, her attention appeared to be locked on whatever Avery had been staring at across the bar. Peeved, Millie twisted on her seat, anger rising inside of her as she sought out what could possibly have snagged their interest.

And there stood Ty. Live. In person. Gorgeous as ever and standing not two feet away from her, clearly surprised by her outburst.

He cleared his throat, then nodded greetings to Avery and Kate before taking the single step to close the distance between them. "The answer to your question would be a resounding no."

"Hi." The word came out in a mortifyingly girlish whisper, but she had no way to take it back and reissue the greeting in a more controlled tone.

"Hello." As if to punctuate the greeting, he dropped a bundle of papers creased in a loose trifold onto the table.

Ears burning, she spared the papers a sidelong glance. "What are those?"

"My divorce papers."

She looked up at him. "Why are you here?"

"Danny said there was a meeting of the minds at Calhoun's this evening, and he wasn't sure when you'd be done. I couldn't wait any longer." He held out his hand palm up. "I've come to take you home."

"Oh, Firth me, he's good," Avery whispered.

"Mm-hmm." Kate jabbed an elbow straight into Millie's ribs. "See you later, Mil. Nice to have you home, Ty."

"Ladies." Ty inclined his head slightly, then lifted his brow as he darted a meaningful glance at his proffered hand. "Ms. Jensen?"

Millie stared down at his hand, fascinated by the map of dark creases webbing his palm. She'd been to a bridal shower one time where the bride insisted they all have their palms read. She'd thought palmistry was a bunch of hooey then, but now she wished she'd paid more attention. Life, heart, and head lines. She knew that was what they called them, but for the life of her, she couldn't remember which was which. May have been something about fate too, but Millie didn't put a lot of stock in destiny. People make their own luck, either by seizing opportunity or by chasing after their goals. Ty's fingers twitched, then started to curl in, a clear signal her chance was slipping away.

Sliding her fingers into his broad, strong palm, she slid from the stool. She covered her wobbly knees by stooping to scoop her leather tote from the floor, then swept the bundle of legal papers into the bag. "Been a treat, girls, but Coach Ransom and I have a few things to talk about."

She kissed them each on the cheek, closing her eyes in silent appreciation when Avery gave her arm a gentle squeeze to buck her up. "Make him grovel. At least a little," Avery whispered in her ear.

Millie laughed and cast Ty a pointed look as she followed him toward the door. "Oh, I plan to make him grovel…a lot."

Chapter 8

THEY EXCHANGED NO GREETINGS. NO "HEY, HOW'S IT going?" No air kiss. Not even a nice professional handshake. With her hand tucked firmly in his warm, strong grasp, they came close on the last one. But she felt nothing businesslike in the way he wove his fingers through hers and held on. She followed him through the murky bar. The crowd had thickened in the time since she'd camped out at their regular table. When they didn't have serious matters to discuss, Millie, Kate, and Avery usually indulged in one round of drinks, then skedaddled before the students started to take over the bar. But given the angle their conversation had taken, this evening was proving to be anything but the usual.

Millie tried to keep up as they plunged into the knot of patrons near the door. A muscle-bound bouncer in a snug Calhoun's T-shirt checked IDs. He hadn't been at his post when she came in, but Millie chose to believe he would have carded her too. Young men liked to flirt with her, and she saw no reason not to encourage them.

Ty zigged, then zagged. Her tote bag hit a guy in an oversized rugby shirt and sagging jeans right in the solar plexus. "Hey, watch out, lady," the kid groused.

Embarrassed, she ducked her head and mumbled an apology she didn't really mean. If she'd known he was going to call her "lady" in front of God and everyone, she would have whacked him with the bag on purpose.

The bouncer smiled broadly as she passed. He dropped a wink, and her confidence shot straight through the stratosphere. Ty was here. He came for her. She didn't care what pimply-faced little shits in ill-fitting clothes thought of her. The cute bouncer would have checked her age and maybe even checked her out. She was viable, damn it. Hell, she was beyond viable. She was vital!

Before she could finish her internal pep talk, Ty threw open the exterior door and pulled her out into the balmy, late-summer evening. The sun sank steadily closer to the tree line to the west, but the glowing orb wasn't going down without a fight. Hazy rays of golden sunlight bathed the trees and student rental homes lining the street. To their right lay the campus quadrangle, with its brick walkways, manicured flower beds, and center-piece fountain. If they went left, she'd be only seven blocks from home.

But Ty kept moving straight ahead.

Twisting his large frame, he sidestepped between the bumpers of parked cars. Millie tried to haul the straps of her bag up to her shoulder as she trotted to keep up. "Where are we going?"

A sharp chirp and flashing lights drew her attention to a low-slung luxury sedan parked on the opposite curb. She let out an appreciative whistle as he led her directly to the passenger door. "How'd you score front-row parking?"

Ty opened the door wide and gestured for her to take a seat. "Convinced a kid in a jacked-up four-by-four the walk would do him good."

Millie laughed as she pictured innately elegant Ty Ransom negotiating with the local rednecks. Taking her time, she tossed her tote over the seat, then lowered herself onto the creamy glove leather, swinging her legs in last, like some kind of Hollywood film star. "Did you now?"

"I might have thrown in an invite to sit courtside at the Green-Gold scrimmage next week," he admitted, then let the door swing shut.

By the time he reached the driver's side, she'd composed herself enough to start putting a bit of her own spin on the situation. He dropped into the seat with a low groan, then leaned back to maneuver his long legs into the cabin. Fascinated, she watched him unfurl. "Why don't you have the driver's seat removed? You could be an actual back-seat driver."

He slanted her a pained look. "But the rear seat isn't heated and cooled."

She smiled, tickled by his practical, if a bit spoiled, rationale. "Oh, well, butt warmers make all the difference." Millie found herself feeling a bit miffed when he twisted the key in the ignition without saying another word. Or giving her a kiss hello. "Aren't you forgetting something?" she asked as he began to work the car out of the tight parking space.

Without taking his eyes off the mirrors, he asked, "Is your car parked nearby?"

She blinked. "No. I walk to work if it's not raining."

When he was satisfied with the angle, he peeled out of the spot. "Good." He hit her with another one of those skimming glances that took in everything. "You walk in those shoes?"

Millie looked down at the high-heeled gladiator sandals strapped onto her feet. "I've been known to," she said, tipping her chin up with feminine pride.

"You really are an iron woman."

A blush flooded her skin with heat. She couldn't help but revel in his admiration. But she wouldn't give in to his silent treatment and caveman tactics because he knew exactly how to compliment her.

"Actually, I've never done a triathlon. I prefer to do my swimming in cement ponds. Preferably on a raft. With an umbrella drink close at hand," she added with a sniff. She didn't tell him she carried a pair of running shoes in her bag at all times.

After all, who was she to shatter his illusions?

She scanned the houses and apartments surrounding the campus dispassionately, all the while trying to get a handle on her erratic heartbeat. She should have been lambasting him about the high-handed way he'd walked into the bar, stolen her away from her friends, then hauled her out of the place like she was some kind of wayward woman who needed to get her mind right. But much to her dismay, her feminist sensibilities were no match for a passel of frustrated hormones.

This was probably the closest she would ever come to an honest-to-goodness *An Officer and a Gentleman* moment, and if she didn't get a grip on herself, she might swoon. She mustered up a few scraps of indignation by the time he slowed for the stoplight at University Street. "You didn't ask if I wanted to come with you."

Ty tensed, then flexed his jaw. He didn't look at her. Not even a peek. Instead, he wound those long fingers tighter around the steering wheel and stared at the signal suspended over the intersection. She could almost hear him willing the signal to change.

She looked up at the red light. The lens glowed bright

and insistent. As if it were hung at this intersection for the express purpose of keeping them from taking a step they couldn't take back. Pursing her lips, she glowered back at the light. "I do, of course. But it's polite to ask."

He loosened his grip on the wheel, and the skin over his knuckles creased once more. She stared at his hands, fascinated. His blood was as red as hers, but instead of flushing a mottled pink, his skin glowed soft and tawny in the pastel-painted twilight. Wasn't that just like a man? Not only did the jerk earn a full one hundred pennies on the dollar, but he also scored mile-long eyelashes that curled up at the tips and somehow managed to score the best possible lighting, even when sulking.

It wasn't fair. She'd worked a full day in the office, coached a couple of Danny's football players on how to speak in complete sentences when talking to the press, and put the finishing touches on the alumni meet-and-greet set to follow Ty's precious Green-Gold scrimmage. Her mascara had flaked off by midmorning thanks to a rebellious contact lens, she'd trickled salsa on her top at lunch, and her feet ached more than she would ever admit to any man wearing faded jeans and what appeared to be well-loved sneakers.

The light switched to green, but Ty didn't step on the gas. No, Mr. Clock Management decided to take the opportunity to check in with her on her wishes. "Would you like me to drop you off at your place?"

"No, you idiot," she snapped.

One corner of his mouth ticked up, and his size sixteen landed hard on the pedal. The car lurched forward, tires squealing so sharply, a driver in the opposite lane honked in annoyance. "My place it is."

Her smile spread, slow and knowing. "Missed me?"

"I'm done talking."

The pronouncement made her laugh. Twisting in her seat, she faced him. "Done talking? We haven't talked for almost two weeks."

He tightened his grip on the wheel again. "I told you why."

"And you get to call all the plays?" Shifting to face forward, she pooched her lips as she stared through the windshield. She wasn't sure if she was pleased or pissed. In the end, pleased won out. By a hair. "The only reason I'm going along with this is I'm a little het up and I think it's time you put out."

He drove fast and sure. She let her gaze travel down to the pulse throbbing in his throat. The telltale thrum beneath smooth, brown skin was too delicious to resist. She'd taste him soon. Rev his engine and wind him up. She'd been primed since the night they first kissed. Aching to put the pedal to the metal on this relationship. Now, she was ready for the rush.

Ty reached up and pressed a button on a control panel above the rearview mirror, then he hooked a sharp left into a wide drive paved in sand-colored stone. Ahead, one of the doors on a three-bay garage slid up into the rafters. She barely had time to note the sleek, black motorcycle parked in the center stall of the showroom-like interior before Ty killed the engine. In one smooth move, he pulled the key from the ignition and threw open his door. "Stay put."

The command jumped all over her last nerve. Fed up with being bossed, she looped her arm through the straps of her bag and reached for the handle. The second her fingertips grazed the lever, the door swung open wide. She looked down to see his gunboat feet planted in a wide stance and an open palm hovering mere inches from her face. She wanted to slap his hand away, but she saw something so vulnerable in the gesture.

He wasn't simply offering to help her from the car. It was a request. A silent plea for her to take this step. This was more than a red-hot rendezvous. Ty was asking her to pick him.

She took his hand on pure instinct, not caring about what he might think her acquiescence meant or, for that matter, what she wanted in terms of their future. They only had now. This night. Her long-delayed, built-up-in-high-definition dreams seemed paler. Here was an opportunity to take what she wanted.

And she was certainly not a woman to let opportunity pass her by.

Two mildly grimy concrete stairs led from the garage to the door of the house. Millie chuckled under her breath as she mentally compared them to the intricately laid flagstone patio and the dressed-to-impress front entrance. These steps showed signs of life. They were a part of a home. Ty's home.

She followed him down a short corridor and into the great room, where she'd found him wallowing that fateful night. Until then, she never registered the fact that this architecturally homogenized monstrosity was actually Ty's place and not just another overpriced accessory chosen by his wife.

Ex-wife, she corrected herself quickly.

Here, all the things he'd comically complained about in his Reno rental would be a nonissue. He'd fit in the bed. With room to spare, if he hadn't been exaggerating. Thanks to the vaulted ceilings, Ty didn't have to worry about hitting his head on a ceiling fan or light fixture. A sad smile curved her lips as she recalled the creative cursing he employed on such occasions.

All thoughts of interior design fled when he took a sharp right into what had to be the master suite. Here, the miles of beige blandness were broken up with shades of chocolate-brown and deep ocean-blue. The room itself was enormous. Panes of tinted glass extended the wall of glass from the great room to the roofline. Streamlined lamps graced a set of cherrywood nightstands. He flipped a switch, and circles of mellow gold gilded the dust-sheened tables. One stood empty. The other was cluttered. Peering around his arm, she eyed the detritus. A couple of hardback books anchored a spiral-bound notebook like the students used. She liked the stylistic analog clock. He kept his charger cords coiled in neat loops. She noted a tube of lip balm and a pair of rectangular reading glasses nudged up against the lamp.

"I, uh…" He made a helpless motion toward the bedside table. "I came straight to campus."

His eagerness pleased her. Stepping into his space, she pressed against his arm and craned her neck to look up at him. "Do not pass 'Go,' do not dust the bedroom?"

He wound his arms around her and pulled her closer still, fitting her to his long, lean frame like they were pieces of a puzzle.

"Something like that." He lowered his head and brushed the barest of kisses across her lips. "Do you mind, or should I go get one of those mop-cloth things from the kitchen?"

She smiled, tickled by his terminology. "I'm not afraid of a little dust, but I am a teensy bit worried about rust."

His brow puckered. "Rust?"

She stared straight ahead, focusing on the tantalizingly smooth skin revealed by the open collar of his shirt. "Been a while since we talked. Even longer since you left me high and dry in a limo."

He raised one perfectly shaped brow. "Dry?"

"Don't even start with the innuendo." A thirst for revenge gave her the leeway to indulge her impulses. She pressed a soft, open-mouthed kiss to the hollow of his throat. His skin was warm, his aftershave cool and citrusy. "You wouldn't even talk to me on the phone." She smiled when he swallowed hard. She was getting to him. Like his silent treatment got to her. "What were you so scared of, big guy?"

"You," he said without hesitation or apology. "Besides, you were the one who started playing the not-talking game. I only saw it through to the end."

Ty gripped her hips, his thumbs pressing into the dip of her pelvis to emphasize his point. He tipped his chin up even though she'd have to shimmy up him to risk bumping into his jaw. His luscious mouth curved into a smile. Amber eyes glimmered with deviltry. He was enjoying every second of this torture.

The sadist.

Millie opened her mouth to zing him, but once again, he was too fast for her. She yelped as those big hands clamped around her waist and her feet left the ground. Grabbing hold of his arms, she proved she wasn't above copping a feel when his biceps bulged and flexed. She'd give herself points for holding her own later. When it came to putting a cocky man in his place, she might have come up a bit short, but she had an unerring sense of where to put her hands.

When they were finally face-to-face, she closed her eyes and leaned in for his kiss. A kiss that didn't happen. Her eyes snapped open, and she pulled back as far as she could, desperate for some distance and the ability to actually focus on him. "What?"

His expression sobered. "I wasn't kidding. You terrify me."

"Well, if you don't shut up and start kissing me in the next three seconds, I'm going to become your worst damn nightmare."

In a flash, his pirate's smile was back. She scarcely had time to draw her next breath before her back hit the mattress. A low, throaty moan escaped her when he covered her body with his. The laws of physics said she should have felt crushed or smothered by his weight, but those paltry theories didn't hold up against the red-hot reality of him. Vertically, they were as mismatched as a gym sock and a thigh-high stocking. Horizontally, they were a perfect fit.

Ty peppered her face and throat with fervent kisses, letting her feel every ounce of his desire with each maddening little peck. He found the sensitive spot behind her ear, and she arched beneath him. "Kiss me," she whispered urgently.

"I am."

"My lips." Cradling the curve of his skull in her palm, she tried to steer him back to her mouth, but the man had an agenda of his own. "Kiss me."

"I can't yet." The ragged edge in his voice was supremely satisfying. He ran one of those big hands down her body, the spread of his fingers teasing her breasts and tickling her ribs. His fingers closed around the side zip of her skirt with an accuracy she might have found disturbing if she didn't want him so badly. "You wanna know why I didn't call?" His breathing was nearly as rough as his voice. "Because of your mouth."

Taken aback, she gave a wiggle. The movement did nothing to dislodge him but did help inch the pesky zip down a centimeter or so. "My mouth? What's that mean?"

He chuckled against her ear. "I'm obsessed with your mouth, Millie. The things I want to hear from you. The places I want you to put those lips. What I want to do to your mouth."

This time, her squirm had nothing to do with protest. She had wants of her own, and it was high time the man started filling them. "Tell me."

"Oh, I'm gonna."

A threat. A promise. The best possible harbinger of things to come. He'd drawled the words, infusing each one with a deep, dark menace that made her want to giggle with maniacal glee.

"Tell me," she urged again. As added incentive, she ran her hands down his back, her fingertips trailing along the crevice of his spine. His ass rose up out of the small of his back, tight mounds of pure muscle. He was big and broad and long and lean, but damn, if the sweet curve of his ass didn't fit perfectly in the palm of her hand. "Tell me everything you thought, every place you wanted me, every way."

At last, he pulled the zipper down. "I can't right now."

"Why not?" She smiled when he lifted his weight enough to start working the fabric down over her hips. "Chicken?"

"Plenty of time for finesse later." He plucked open the first two buttons on her blouse, then ducked his head to nuzzle the top of her breast. "We'll play all those games after."

He was putting her off. Something niggled at the back of her mind. A nagging voice insisted she should be put out by his bossy behavior. But she found herself not paying that pesky, little cricket chirping in her brain any mind. Not when she was so turned on by Ty's commanding tactics. "But now?"

Ty lowered his body into the cradle of her hips, then peeled back enough to look her straight in the eye. "Now? Well, right now, you and I are going to play a little one-on-one."

"We are?"

"Hot. Fast. Messy."

"No blood, no foul?" she asked.

A slow smile spread across his face. "Where'd you learn that?"

"You forget, I hang out with you jockstraps all the time."

"No blood, no foul," he repeated, his incandescent smile lighting the dim room.

She held his gaze for the span of a heartbeat, then gave a brief nod. "Ready? Go!"

Lips. Teeth. Hands. Oh Lord, those hands!

He palmed her ass and lifted her off the mattress,

grinding against the thin fabric barriers between them until she prayed they'd disintegrate into dust. His mouth was hot, his kisses sweet and sultry one minute, all-consuming the next. She was pretty sure she felt one of the buttons on her blouse pop off. He broke the kiss long enough to sit back and yank the collar of his shirt over his head with one hand. His smooth, muscled chest rose and fell at a flattering rate as he tossed the wadded shirt aside. The patch of dark, curling hair between his pecs beckoned to her. She answered the call, running greedy fingers through the tight spirals, then skimming the heels of her hands over the hard ridges and planes she'd fantasized about night after night.

"I watched you and Kate go at each other one-on-one," she told him in a breathless voice. "Not like this. On the court."

"You did?"

"Last spring. She was working off a little Danny frustration."

"I remember." One corner of his mouth kicked up. "She kicked my ass."

Millie's smile was smug on her friend's behalf. "She did."

"Wasn't fair." He pressed into his palms and lowered himself onto her once more, leaving room for her to explore but giving them both the proximity they ached for. His lips grazed her ear. Hot breath tickled her neck. "She has a bionic knee."

"Use whatever excuse makes you feel better, big guy, but she had you on *your* knees," she countered. "She also got the shirt off your back. The spectators in the stands will be forever grateful."

He jerked, then pulled up to look at her. "Spectators?"

"Me, Cassie, SaraAnn from Mike Samlin's office." She punctuated each attendance entry with a lingering kiss along the column of his throat. "A couple of the trainers." She brushed the pads of her thumbs over flat nipples, then squirmed as she felt his flesh pebble and bead. "I bet Kate didn't buy her own lunch for a month. Grateful public and all."

She felt the heat rise in his skin. A flush darkened his cheeks, but it had nothing to do with lust. The man was blushing, and it made him look good enough to eat. Scissoring her legs, she clamped them tight around his thigh. His eyes widened in surprise, and she smiled. All the miles she'd run over the years paid off in more than shin splints and free bananas. Her legs weren't only shapely and supple; they were powerful. She could crush this big, strong man between her thighs and make him thank her for the punishment.

"On your back," she ordered.

To his credit, Ty hesitated only for a second. A smile worthy of the Cheshire Cat lit his face as he rolled, dragging her along with him for the ride. "Please be gentle," he teased.

His gruff acquiescence told her he was hoping she'd be anything but easy on him, which was good. He'd said hot, fast, and messy. Magic words.

Ignoring the fact that her skirt was already unzipped, she grabbed the hem and gathered the fabric up over her hips. She had to shimmy a bit, but he didn't seem to mind the show. The fabric bunched at her waist, she hooked a finger under the button of his jeans and yanked. It opened with well-worn ease. She was about

to grope for his zipper when four more buttons gave way
with satisfying pops.

Millie grinned. "Thank you, Lord, for button flies."

A moan that sounded more like a purr rose from her
throat as she slipped her hand into the V. The hard,
hot length of his cock strained against the confines
of his boxer briefs. Unable to resist, she stroked him
through the thin fabric. The cotton was silky smooth
against her fingertips. She hummed with appreciation
when she felt the wet patch dampening the fabric near
the wide waistband.

"Condoms?" she asked.

He nodded eagerly. "I bought some."

"Where are they?"

He stared at her blankly, then his handsome face contorted into a grimace. "In my suitcase."

Her eyebrows rose. "Please tell me the airline didn't
lose your luggage."

Ty wet his lips and shook his head. "The car. I'll go."

As much as she wanted to watch him streak through
the house with his pants around his ankles, Millie wasn't
about to let him out of her clutches. Not when she finally
had him where she wanted him.

"Lucky for you, Avery pilfers free rubbers from health
services and hands them out to anyone and everyone."

Scrambling off the bed, she spotted her tote where
she'd dropped it inside the door and made a beeline for
it. She didn't care if her blouse flew behind her like a
cape and her skirt was rucked up around her middle like
a damn tutu. Frankly, if she had to walk around naked
in front of the man, she preferred a little camouflage.
Unlike his last lover, she hadn't been anywhere close to

twenty in a long, long time. She plunged her hand into the bag, found the tab for the zipper compartment, and within seconds closed her hand around the foil square.

"Usually, I'd be better prepared myself," she said, rolling her shoulders as she sauntered back to the bed, triumphant. "If I'd known you were coming home, I would have stockpiled." She waved the condom at him, then tore the wrapper in two. "Lucky for us, I have what Avery likes to call 'a little packet of hope.'"

She waited until she saw his gaze drop to her satin bikini panties. Once she was sure she had his full attention, she hooked her thumbs into the band and shucked them. Crawling up onto the bed, she shed the shirt as well, glad she'd chosen to wear a semipretty lace-edged bra that day rather than the jog bra she sometimes wore under her clothes for convenience. The lingerie wasn't from her top drawer, but thankfully, it wasn't laundry day stuff either.

"Do this for me?" she asked, handing over the condom.

Ty snatched the coil of latex from her fingers with one hand and pushed at his jeans and briefs with the other. She took over, curling her fingers into the double waistbands and drawing them down. The reveal was at once too slow and way too fast. She stared openly at the length of him as he set to work with the condom. While he was busy, she pulled his worn jeans down over taut thighs and below his knees.

"I say we go for hot and fast first, work on messy later."

"Good plan," he agreed. "But, Mil, I'm gonna get you messy. Every way I can."

The creak in his voice nearly set her off. Abandoning his pants, she crawled up to straddle him. Ty rose to meet her, his hand sliding slowly up her spine and coming to settle at her nape. He drew her down and kissed her. Slow. Deep. The tip of his tongue teased the seam of her lips before plunging in to take what she so desperately wanted to give. His cock pressed against the curve of her stomach. He moved his hips, each undulation timed to match the swirl of his tongue and the thrum of his heart.

They broke apart, breathless, panting, and damn near feral with want. Even with her seated on his thighs, they were still eye to eye. Looking directly at him was too much. She wanted him too badly. And having him only for a little while would certainly bring her heartache. Needing to claim a modicum of control, she pressed the heel of her hand into his shoulder and created some distance between them.

He stared back at her, sleepy-eyed and too gorgeous to be real. He must have seen something in her face. A flash of apprehension, a hint of fear, some chink in her armor. She knew that stare all too well. He wore the look of a warrior. A champion. Someone born to win at all costs.

"You still game, Millie?"

The challenge was unmistakable and irresistible. She hadn't backed down from a dare in over twenty years, and she wasn't about to start now. Not when she wanted this every bit as badly as he did. If he broke her heart, she'd survive. She had before. She would again.

Sliding her hand to the center of his chest, she lifted

her hips as she pressed him back into the mattress and positioned herself over him. "You bet, Coach. You watch how game I am."

Chapter 9

Ty knew of nothing better than watching a mostly naked woman climbing on top of him. Okay, maybe a *totally* naked woman swinging a leg over would top the list, but this was good. For now, he was content with the visual. He'd make sure they had time for totally naked later.

High, small breasts curved over the top of her bra. Her lingerie wasn't porn-star quality, like the stuff Mari preferred, but the bra and panties were pretty and feminine. No one would ever accuse her of being a Barbie doll. Her figure was slim and subtle, her waist a trim indention and her hips rounded enough to give him something to hang on to. So he did.

His eyes closed of their own accord as she lowered herself onto him. Christ, was there any better feeling on earth than the give of a woman's body? He felt her hand on his shoulder and forced his eyes open. Millie leaned down over him, her wild, red hair tousled and her eyes bright with arousal.

"You ready for this?" she whispered.

Any words he might have conjured tangled in his chest. The only thing that escaped was a strangled groan. She moved. Up. Down. Lord, she was hot. Tight. He clenched his teeth, his fingertips pressing into the soft curve of her ass. How could anyone possibly be prepared for this? "God yes."

She rode him, holding him to every promise he'd made concerning speed and intention but spinning them higher than he'd pictured in his fantasies. She was a Technicolor dream. Vivid hair. Flashing eyes. Her black skirt was bunched around her waist. Pale-blue lace obscured but failed to contain her breasts. He could see her nipples pressed against the peekaboo fabric, hard and red as ripe berries. Could almost taste them. Damn, he needed to taste them.

Ty tried to rise, but she planted both hands on his shoulders and slowed, her eyes narrowing in unspoken challenge. Wetting his parched lips, he gave in. Plenty of time to make good on the laundry list of things he planned to do with her. To her. In her. Later.

Holding her hips as she stepped up the pace once more, he sank back into the pillow, prepared to enjoy the show. If she wanted to call the shots for now, that was okay by him. This wasn't a one-sided thing. And certainly not a one-time chance either. He'd have to work at getting to her, but he would. Soon.

He blinked hard, willing his mind to stay sharp despite the fuzzy edges of pleasure threatening to encroach. He needed to stay with her. In her. Holy hell. He tensed his abdominals, trying to hold back the surge rising inside him. He needed to think about something other than the sultry pull of her body.

Baseball. Trite but true. The national pastime was, after all, the world's most boring sport. Aside from tele-vised golf. Or curling. He wasn't a big NASCAR fan—

"I wanted to climb up in your lap and do you like this on national television."

The breathy confession jolted him straight out of

the wide world of sports and plunged him right back in the here and now. Heat. Friction. Her hot, slick pussy clenched tightly around him. Her breaths coming fast and shallow. His voice came out so rough and deep he almost didn't recognize himself. "You what?"

"When that tight-ass Chambers had you in his hot seat, I wanted to do this," she said, holding his gaze. "When he was talking to you like he could ever be half the man you are, I wanted to hike my skirt up, straddle you in that hideous chair, and show the whole damn world how fuckable you are."

"Jesus Christ." He groaned the words, acutely aware they were half prayer, half blasphemy, and entirely necessary. If she kept on saying shit like that, he was going to need some divine intervention on his side.

Warming to the subject, Millie leaned down. "I wanted you in the car. Hell, I'd have given old Manny a show that would have ruined him for Broadway." Her face hovering above his, she pumped him like a piston. "Might have reminded him of Times Square before the facelift."

She huffed and puffed, but her pace never slackened. The muscles in her thighs tensed and flexed beneath his roaming hands, but he didn't feel even a tremble of exertion.

Not on her part at least. Hell, he was straining so hard not to come he was pretty sure his fucking lips were quivering. Not above cheating a little to keep the playing field even, he slid a hand between their bodies. Her clit was swollen and slick. The damp curls of her pubic hair were thrillingly exotic. He wanted to bury his face between her legs and smother himself in those damp curls.

Millie moaned when he pinched the sensitive flesh between his thumb and middle finger. Thrilled by her responsiveness, he slid his other hand over her ass and ran his fingers slowly along the crevice. As far as he was concerned, her bold talk gave license to test her boundaries. Millie was a woman who wasn't afraid to use her words. He pressed the pad of his index finger to the tight pucker of her anus, and she let loose with a sharp cry.

Ty tucked his chin to his chest, frantically scanning her face for a hint as to whether the squeal was one of ecstasy or revulsion. He needn't have bothered. With the next thrust, she pressed back against the invasive finger and came completely unspooled.

Watching Millie climax was a revelation. No artifice or enhancement. No overly theatrical moans or exaggerated head thrashing. She didn't claw, bite, or even scream. She just…came. Beautifully. With abandon. And he wanted to go there with her.

He pushed back against her restraining hand and rolled up to meet each rise and fall of her body. He gripped her ass and started to thrust up into her, each jerk of his hips awkward and a little sloppy, but he was beyond caring about style points. "God, you're beautiful." He panted the words, his gaze locked on her heavy-lidded eyes. "I wanna watch you come over and over again."

The sentiment was accompanied by a particularly sharp push into her tight, pulsing heat. Whether the thrust or his near-orgasm confession shook her from her trance, he didn't know, but she threw her head back and laughed the husky laugh that zinged straight to his balls every time.

Helpless, he tucked his face into the sweet curve of

her neck and let go. His teeth scraped tender, fragrant skin. He roared long and loud, not caring if the whole damn neighborhood heard him. Grasping the soft, round cheeks of her ass, he spread her wide, bucking like a fired-up bronco as the first pulses ripped through him. At last, he gave in and let his eyelids slide shut. For the first time in a long time, he loosened his hold on his impulses and let momentum carry him.

Their bodies slowed long before their ragged breathing. Gradually, Ty became aware he was wrapped around her like a cartoon coyote who'd run face-first into a telephone pole, but he didn't move. Couldn't. She smelled like perfume and powder and a half dozen other delicate feminine fragrances. He wanted to stay right where he was until he identified every one of them.

Millie ran her hand over his hair. The gentleness in her caress was almost too much but, at the same time, not nearly enough. She was soothing him, all the while stoking the embers of his need again. Embers, hell. The woman ignited him. Smiling, he nipped playfully at the curve of her neck, then roused himself enough to lift his head.

Her sleepy-eyed gaze made him want to pull her down, tuck her into the curve of his body, and drift off. But he couldn't. They had the logistics of the condom disposal to contend with and various other nuts and bolts to discuss. And now, the warmth in her eyes was tempered with more than a little wariness. The tension in her supple thighs wasn't only from exertion. He got the feeling Millie would bolt from his bed the minute he gave her the opening. And he had no intention of leaving the lane open for her.

He kissed her. It started as a simple covering of her mouth with his but soon melted into temptation. They fit together so well. His lips. Hers. Their teeth touched once, but rather than jarring, the collision sent a bolt of lightning zipping through his body. Her tongue was velvet soft but strong and every bit as sly as the woman in his arms. Christ, he wanted to kiss her crazy and keep right on kissing her until he'd tasted every flavor of her. Like one of those desperation-fueled teenage make-out sessions that left a guy aching and antsy, willing to promise the moon and the stars for one glimpse of the heaven between her legs.

He let his lips cling to hers as he tried to find the power to extricate himself. If he didn't take care of some business, things would get messy. And that wouldn't be good, because when things got messy, Millie went into fixer mode. Ty didn't want her to start spinning what happened between them. He liked her right where she was.

Still, the condom situation had to be handled. With a grumble of frustration, he broke the kiss. "Up."

Millie looked down at him, lingering hunger glowing in her eyes. "Hmm?"

Lord, he wanted to snap a picture. Her riotous hair was even more tousled than usual. Her skin flushed a pearly pink. She looked sleepy, sated, and yet, stirred. And he'd been the one to wreck her. Pride gave him the strength he needed to disengage. If he'd made her go boneless once, he could certainly do it again. And better. Practice led to perfection.

He slid a hand between them to hold the base of the condom, then gave her bottom a playful tap. "Up. I need to get rid of this thing."

Heaving a put-upon sigh, Millie rose up on her knees. They both groaned when his dick slipped out of her. She swung her leg over and fell back onto the bed with a huff.

Flashing her a reassuring smile, he leaned down to plant a firm kiss on her mouth, then rolled to the edge of the bed. Pausing only long enough to free his feet from his shoes and his ankles from the fabric binding them, he strode toward the adjoining bath. "Be right back."

Disposing of the condom took about thirty seconds. He chanced another few seconds checking his reflection in the mirror and making sure he had no reason to suck in his stomach. His usual regimen didn't include six weeks of steak, scotch, and golf, but not too much damage had been done. Other than a farmer's tan.

Shrugging, he turned away from the vanity. He wanted to get back before Millie's mind started to whir and click. When he opened the door, he regretted taking those precious minutes to spruce up. He was too late.

Millie glanced up as she tugged the hem of her skirt into place, and his heart flipped over in his chest. She still wore only the bra on top but held a crumpled wad of fabric in one hand. On closer inspection, he concluded they were her panties. Panic morphed into determination.

"What do you think you're doing?" he asked.

She looked him square in the eye, then arched one brow. "Hoping to avoid awkward conversation?"

He took the panties from her hand and tossed them over his shoulder. "Fine. We won't talk."

Millie laughed, then gave her head a rueful shake. "Listen, I appreciate your enthusiasm, and I definitely look forward to a rematch, but neither of us are kids. I don't need you to cuddle me and make pretty promises you can't keep, Ty. Let's not make this more than what it is."

Her tough talk coupled with the challenging set of her jaw both amused and annoyed him. Winding an arm around her waist, he hauled her up against him. "What if I need you to cuddle me? What if I'm the one who wants pretty promises?"

She tipped her head back. The expression in her eyes was flat and serious. "I don't make promises." She gave his arm a consoling pat. The caress was a clear signal for him to release her, but he chose to ignore the cue. If she truly wanted him to let her go, she was going to have to use her words. "I'm also not very cuddly."

"Why don't you let me be the judge?"

She smiled and leaned in enough to press a conciliatory kiss to the base of his throat. "We can plan a sleepover another time. A girl likes to pack her toothbrush and PJs, you know."

"You don't need any PJs." He raked his fingers through her hair, marveling at the extraordinary color and wondering how the hell some women knew exactly what to do to make them unforgettable. "Stay, Millie. I'll unpack my suitcase and keep you happy."

"Sounds suspiciously like a pretty promise to me. Besides, I'm scheduled to get ten in before work tomorrow, and I don't have my gear."

"Ten?"

"Miles. I'm doing a half marathon next month. I'm in training, Coach."

She bit her lip as she placed her hands on his chest and made a show of trying to push away, but they both knew she didn't want to go. She wanted to be convinced.

"I saw your shoes in that suitcase you carry around. Stay, and I'll give you a complimentary membership to the home gym downstairs. I'll even loan you a T-shirt." Her smirk telegraphed her intention to shoot him down, so he went in for the kill. "I'll throw in hot tub time and breakfast at no additional fee."

The tips of her ears flushed pink. She ducked her head, but the curve of her cheek gave her away. He almost had her. All he had to do was sink the last couple of shots, and victory would be his.

Lowering his head, he pitched his voice low and soft. "Want me to tell you what all's included in hot tub time?"

She trailed the tip of one nail through his chest hair. "I was more concerned about the breakfast menu."

Ty threw his head back and laughed, but he didn't let his amusement get in the way of his ultimate goal. Sliding his hand up her back, he found the clasp of her bra.

Millie gasped, her eyes widening with surprise, then frank admiration as the elastic band opened. "Wow. You're good."

"When I was in junior high, my friend Mike stole one of his sister's bras so we could practice." He let his own smile spread as he drew the straps down her arms. "I can tell you, you look much prettier in yours than he did."

She barked a laugh and let the bra fall to their feet. "I'd be willing to wager you haven't seen a pair as small as mine since his."

Her cupped one subtle mound. She barely filled the palm of his hand, but size didn't matter one bit. He'd touched a lot of boobs since those days he and Mike spent mastering the hook and eye, and every time, the soft curve of a woman's breast was a fresh wonder to him. Millie wouldn't believe him if he said as much, so he didn't bother with anything more than the unvarnished truth. "I think you're beautiful."

To prove he meant what he said, he folded his body nearly in half and took the tightly furled nipple into his mouth. Millie moaned and clutched at his head, arching her back and pressing into him in silent command, an order he was more than happy to obey. He sucked deep, relishing her soft gasp. Her hips rolled, instinctively seeking him out. Cursing their height difference, he released her with a loud pop, then staggered back a step.

"Take your skirt off. Stay awhile."

Her eyes locked on his as she withdrew another couple of steps, granting him full view of her as she drew the zipper down over her hip again. A shove and a shimmy later, the skirt lay puddled around her feet.

"On the bed," he ordered.

Her eyebrows popped up, and she hesitated a beat. He countered with a blank stare, hoping he could convince her he was willing to wait all night for her compliance, but playing it cool was next to impossible when his dick was hard and practically dancing with joy at the prospect of another go with her. Her gaze dropped to his crotch, and her mouth curled into a knowing smile.

"Impressive recovery time, Coach."

Ty didn't dare admit he was impressed with himself. Clutching this scrap of pride, he shrugged. "I'm highly motivated."

Millie backed up until her thighs hit the edge of the mattress. Without breaking eye contact, she sat down, hooked a heel on the rail, then pushed back until she lay stretched out atop his comforter in all her cream and pink glory, her hands resting on the pillows above her head. "Like this?" she asked in a throaty whisper.

"Just like that." Unwilling to be sidetracked again, he held up one finger in a stern motion for her to stay put. "Don't move. I'll be right back."

He booked out the door and down the hall, her laughter chasing him as he hurtled down the stairs bare-assed naked. He nearly tore the door to the garage off its hinges in his haste. His foot barely skimmed the cool concrete step. His left shinbone sang out in protest when he hit the concrete floor at full stride. The right joined the chorus when he drew to an abrupt halt.

The overhead door was wide open, and Mrs. Westlake's Yorkshire terrier was taking a leak in his flower bed. More specifically, on the Wolcott Warrior garden gnome Mari had won in some booster club auction. And he was naked. Stark naked. For a few endless seconds, he and his neighbor across the street, Mrs. Westlake, stared at one another, frozen in shock.

The thought clicked, and he lunged for the button to lower the door. Then he crouched behind his car, taking what cover he could get as the damn thing lowered at a snail's pace. Squeezing his eyes shut, he did his level best to pretend what had happened hadn't happened, and by the time the door touched the sealed concrete floor, he might have convinced himself if he hadn't heard Mrs. Westlake call out a mocking "Go Tigers!" through the paneled steel.

Ty narrowed his eyes at the door as he rose. He'd seen the orange-and-blue logo of Wolcott's in-state rivals on his neighbor's car, but he hadn't realized the Westlakes were rabid fans. Nor had he suspected their

overgrown guinea pig of trashing his landscaping. Now
he knew better.

Glancing down at his nearly deflated dick, he hoped
the nosy neighbor had gotten a good eyeful of him at
his best. He wanted her to remember this moment well,
because as of two minutes ago, there was no team Ty
was more devoted to defeating than Mrs. Westlake's
beloved freaking Tigers.

He moved to the driver's door and reached in to press
the button to release the latch on the trunk. Between his
luggage and the new set of Ping golf clubs he'd treated
himself to as a divorce present, the compartment was
cram-packed. But the last thing Ty wanted to do was
haul his bags into the house like he was the bellman at
a nudist resort. Unzipping his suitcase, he groped inside
until he felt his shaving kit and yanked the bag free.

Tucking the small bag under his arm, he slammed the
trunk lid, tossed one more scowl in the direction of the
garage door, and stomped back into the house. He was
still grumbling under his breath when he walked into the
great room to find Millie perched on the edge of the red
suede sofa. Every bit as naked as he was.

"Wha—"

"I heard the garage door and a dog barking." She
gave him a slow once-over, and Ty had to resist the urge
to cover his junk with his toiletry bag. "Tell me you hit
the button before you made your mad dash."

He paused for a second, trying to gather what dignity
a naked man with a semisoftie could before answering.
"Let's say the show was more impressive when Mrs.
Westlake caught the opening act."

Her eyes crinkled, and she covered her mouth with

her hand, but the preventative measures came too late. Laughter flowed out around the edges of her fingers like hot lava, deep and rich and terrifyingly beautiful. He moved toward her, drawn by the siren song of those husky chuckles. The shaving kit hit the floor near her feet with a dull thud.

Her wrist looked so delicate and fine. Half-scared he'd crush her with his big, clumsy hands, he gently drew her hand away, allowing the full-bodied joy of her laugh to wash over him unimpeded. The mortification he'd been feeling drifted away as he drew her hand to his mouth. Hungry for the taste of her skin, he pressed a lingering, open-mouthed kiss to the center of her palm. Triumph and remorse wrestled in his chest when her laughter faded into a breathy sigh. Her bright eyes fixed on him. He felt her pulse quicken beneath his fingertips.

"Ty—"

His life was a mess. He was freshly divorced, publicly humiliated, and facing a make-or-break season in terms of his career. Shit, he'd barely undressed enough to make love to the woman he'd been lusting over for longer than he'd care to admit, but he managed to give his neighbor a flash of full-frontal. If that didn't prove some kind of talent for getting things ass-backward, he didn't know what would. But he knew one thing with absolute certainty. He wasn't ready for the night to end.

"Lie back."

"What?"

"You look like some kind of surrealistic porn star on that couch."

She blinked like an owl. "Is that a compliment?"

"God yes." He took her hand, pressed her palm to

his chest, then slowly slid it southward. The sight of her waiting for him had managed to erase the lingering effects of getting caught flagranting his delictos in front of Mrs. Westlake. He inhaled deeply through his nose as he wrapped her hand around his reviving erection. "You look so pretty when you get all flushed and flustered."

She gave his cock a firm squeeze, then stroked him teasingly. "Who's flustered?"

"Lie back."

Millie let her hand fall away. A feline smile curved her mouth as she spared the oversized sofa a glance. "Here? You want me to lie back here?" She was teasing, but the underlying challenge was serious. She ran her hand over the subtle nap of the fabric. "You want to defile this pretty red couch?"

Ty thought back to all the times Mari had thrown a damn conniption over him sipping a beer while on the stupid sofa and let his smile spread. "Oh yeah."

Without another word, Millie pressed into her hands and scooted back until she was perfectly centered. Smiling her smug smile, she lifted her hands over her head as she'd done on his bed, her red-raspberry nipples hard and reaching for the sky. She reclined, arranging her legs to accord the scene a tantalizing hint of modesty. "Like this?"

"Perfect."

And she was. Distracted by the mere sight of her laid out for his taking, he sat down on the edge of the sofa near her hip.

Surrealistic porn star.

He wanted to kick himself for ever thinking the words, much less saying them out loud. The curve of her belly was a work of art. Soft. Utterly feminine. Welcoming.

Everything about the two of them being together rang true for him. Natural. Sure, the hair color wasn't something a person saw out in the wild, but it suited her. She didn't have the body of a twenty-year-old, but her curves and angles had been engineered by God and hard work. He loved the long, lean muscles of her legs. Those runner's legs. Wanted to feel them wrapped tight around his hips.

"Did you want me to pose for you?" she asked.

The question shook him from his musings. Chuckling at himself more than her bold prompting, he gave his head a rueful shake and reached down to reclaim the leather toiletry kit. "I thought I'd come home, clean up, maybe cook some dinner for you," he said as he unzipped the case. "But the minute I hit town, I couldn't get to you fast enough."

"You cook?"

"I like to eat, so yeah, I cook," he countered.

She let out a low, sultry moan as she rubbed the top of her shin with the sole of her other foot. "Stop, or I'll be tempted to keep you on a permanent basis."

Ty paused, his gaze zooming in on her face as he freed the box of condoms from the bag. "Would keeping me be a bad thing?"

"You know I'm a go-with-the-flow girl," she said in a husky tease.

This time, he had no hope of holding back his snort of disbelief. "Bull. You're the ultimate control freak."

She raised those perfectly shaped eyebrows and eyed him with unconcealed impatience. "Yes, well, I was giving you a shot. Don't make me put you on your back again."

Tearing into the box, he fixed her with his sternest stare. "As much as I enjoyed letting you…" He yanked a string of rubbers from the box. "It's my turn."

Chapter 10

SHE WISHED SHE HAD THE STRENGTH TO PRETEND SHE DIDN'T want him. Not wanting him would be safer. Easier. After a lifetime spent cleaning up other people's messes, the last thing she wanted was complications in her own private life. And this man was the most magnificent complication that ever existed.

Millie let her eyelids drift shut as Ty wrapped one of those deliciously enormous hands around her ankle. She looked to see if his fingertips overlapped, but she already knew they would. She'd been memorizing bits and pieces of Ty Ransom since the day they'd met. His big hands topped her list of things she liked about him.

Like a squirrel gathering nuts, she oh-so-casually picked up a hint here and a factoid there, then stashed them away in her private hidey-hole. The man was a study in contrasts. Strong but unfailingly gentle. Large but born with a grace nonathletes could never emulate. She could stare at him all day. Would think about him night after night. And tonight…this night would live on in fantasy for years to come.

The second he'd walked into the bar to claim her, she'd started taking a greedy inventory of their time together. She'd gathered every tidbit she could. The deep furrow between his brows. His freakishly long legs. Every bit of his Stretch Armstrong body. Then she noticed the tan lines. He had the faint lines of a golfer's tan on his arms and legs. She was a fairly uniform pasty pale from top to bottom, but Ty was a veritable Pantone study in browns. The knowledge that he'd earned those tan lines while freeing himself to be with her made every shade of him even more irresistible. He ran his hand up her leg, his fingers loosening to fit the curve of her calf, his palm hot along her shinbone. Thank God she'd shaved her legs.

"Millie, look at me."

He spoke so softly she had no choice but to obey. With superhuman effort, she opened her eyes and waited for his handsome face to swim into focus. Almost immediately, she wished she hadn't. The way he looked at her. So intent. So absorbed. His unabashed desire for her was almost too much to bear. Not when she had so little to offer him.

Desperate to deflect his rapt attention, she forced a flash of a smile. "Wanna tie me up with your ties, Ty?"

Astonishment wiped his face clean. He blinked once, then gave his head a sharp shake. "Huh?"

A fierce blush scalded her cheeks. "It's a line from an old movie," she explained. When she saw he wasn't catching on, she shifted straight into babble mode. "*Caddyshack*. Chevy Chase's name was Ty and this girl… Never mind. Kate, Avery, and I do that a lot. Use movie quotes, I mean. Not tie each other up with ties."

He cocked his head to the side, then let his hand slide higher up her thigh. "I've spent the last six weeks doing two things—playing golf against the septuagenarian hustler who calls himself my father and thinking about all the ways I want to crawl inside you. You ask if I want to tie you up with my ties, and you think I'm gonna cop to a quote from a golf movie?"

"I'm a little nervous."

She wished she could take the words back. Millie wasn't the kind of woman who let any man get the better of her. She never got nervous, even with dozens of cameras pointed in her direction, and she didn't babble, for God's sake. Words were her weapons. A strong offense was always the best defense. She needed to get ahold of herself.

"You?" Ty's surprised expression went a long way to soothing her nerves.

She covered with a wry twist of her lips and a pointed look at the wall of windows. The last rays of summer sunlight streamed through the panes, washing the entire room in a golden glow. While she was thankful the room wasn't lit with banks of harsh fluorescents, bright light from any source was rarely kind to a woman her age. Making a show of shielding her eyes from the brightness, she squinted. "I don't suppose you have any shades on those things?"

Ty barked a laugh, then rolled onto his side, effectively blocking her from the light. "How's this?"

Blinking up at him, the first thing she noticed was the halo. He ran an appreciative hand up her thigh, over her hip, waist, and rib cage. His wandering hand stopped beneath her breast, but his thumb had gone rogue. The rough pad teased the shallow valley between her breasts. Golden glow or not, the wicked grin he wore was sure to disqualify him as a model for one of those old portraits of saints they used to print on funeral cards.

"I keep thinking I should make some crack about throwing shade, but I'm a little distracted." He cupped her breast gently, then lowered his head. "Quick, think of something quippy while I do this."

His mouth closed on her nipple, and any chance she had at concocting anything clever flew right out one of those massive windows. She bucked and bowed, her body responding to the heated pull of his mouth. He squeezed her, shaping her to fit his palm. The sharp edges of those toothpaste-white teeth abraded the sensitive flesh. Millie could almost feel the debate going on inside her nerve endings. Part of her softened like melted butter with each swipe of his velvet tongue. Another part stiffened against the sharp edge of want he unleashed in her.

She wanted him, and she couldn't think of one logical reason in the world she shouldn't have him. They were colleagues of a sort, but he wasn't her boss, nor she his. Unlike his ex-wife, people would consider her an age-appropriate match. Of course, she could come up with dozens of illogical ones. Number one being the very high probability of falling hard for him. As a newly divorced man, he wouldn't be looking to her for anything serious. She had to keep things light. Easy. Physical, not emotional. All she had to do was concentrate on the feel of his hands on her body, the tug of his lips and hot slash of his tongue.

"Harder," she panted.

He complied without hesitation, sucking her deep into his mouth, then teasing the hypersensitive skin with each retreat. His body moved against hers. Funny how well they fit when they were horizontal. Each hard plane of muscle matched up to her softer counterparts. She vowed not to think about the roll of excess flesh no amount of jogging could budge. Didn't matter. The long, hard length of his cock pressed insistently against her thigh. She felt invincible. Like a goddess. She was Atalanta, the great huntress from Greek mythology. The woman no man could outrace.

Unless she chose to let him catch her.

Which she wouldn't. Couldn't. When the time came, he'd pick someone younger. A better prospect for a future. And a family. This was a fling. One she could enjoy for as long as it lasted.

He moved down her body, mapping the curve of her rib cage with tiny kisses, murmuring sweet, sexy words of praise and appreciation. She drank them in, letting them fill her up. He didn't know their relationship had already sprung a slow leak. And though she should, Millie couldn't quite bring herself to tell him the pale skin he seemed to like so much was a hint as to who she really was—a ghost of a woman. Translucent on the outside, hollow within.

As if following the trail of her thoughts, he kissed his way down to the scar that traced the curve of her lower belly. His tongue highlighted the long-healed wound. He looked up. Questioningly. She could feel the heat of his stare on her face, but she couldn't meet his gaze. Instead, she gave the briefest, bluntest explanation she could. The kind designed to stop any further questions cold.

"I had cervical cancer in my thirties and had a hysterectomy." She nodded to the condom box. "We don't have to worry about any late-in-life babies, but safety first, right?"

He gave her a puzzled look, then nodded. "I'm sorry—"

Millie pressed her finger to his lips and fixed him with an unwavering stare. "It was a long time ago. I'm fine."

In an effort to obliterate any other notions of sympathy—or worse, pity—he might be harboring, she removed her finger and slid her hand around to cup the back of his head. Ty hummed his approval when she exerted the barest bit of pressure. Nuzzling and kissing his way, he slipped down farther and pressed his full, wet lips to the apex of her pussy.

"Here? Is this where you want me?"

His breath was hot and damp. The words spoken in a feverish hush made her toes curl. "Exactly."

He ran the tip of his nose teasingly along her sex, then gave her clit a nudge that nearly made her sit bolt upright. She felt the curve of his smile against her heated flesh. Heard his pleasure in the sultry timbre of his voice. "And what did you want me to do while I'm hanging out down here?"

"Lick," she answered at once. He complied but with only a solitary swipe of his hot tongue. One that didn't go nearly far enough, or deep enough, to do anything but add fuel to the fire. "Suck."

She barely uttered the command out before his mouth closed on her clit. The first pull yanked a gasp right out of her. The second stole her breath entirely. They had no need for words, which was a good thing, because Millie wasn't certain she could form them. His mouth was hot, his appetite for her voracious. If the delicious sensations of his slick, wet flesh sliding over hers weren't enough to send her sailing, the enthusiasm with which he applied himself might have been.

The storm gathered inside of her once more, her climax building with shocking speed. She was a one-and-done kind of girl. Usually, she found second orgasms overrated when one weighed effort exerted in the balance. This seemed to be barreling down on her like a bullet train.

"Oh!" Her cheeks burned, and her muscles coiled. She lifted her hips higher. All the better to meet the thrusts of the fingers he'd slipped into her.

And then she broke.

Waves of heat pulsed through her. Yes, they were gentler than the minor explosions he evoked before but no less intense. Each fresh wash of pleasure rippled through her whole body. This wasn't a tsunami or even the kind of arcing crests people in 1950s beach movies boast of riding. Every stroke of his tongue unleashed another round of shudders. At the last, she lay quaking beneath him, her skin so tight she felt like she might burst straight out of her own birthday suit. If only she had the energy for bursting.

Before she could draw a deep breath, he was looming over her. Crowding her. Giving her the thrilling weight of his body pressing her into the cushion. Staring deep into her eyes, he hooked his arm under her knee, settled himself into the cradle of her hips, and thrust home in one stroke.

She gasped again. This time, the pleasure was tinged with shock—and a healthy dose of feminine *rawr*. She raked her nails up his back, signaling her approval of his actions and hoping to spur him to greater heights. Then she drew back enough to watch the show. After all, who didn't like a man who knew when to take charge?

"Did you think about this?" She tried to make her voice low and taunting, but to her own ears, she sounded more like an oxygen-impaired bullfrog. Determined to goad him a little, she cleared her throat and tried again. "Fucking me here...on this pretty red couch?" She raised one arm above her head and stroked the fine nap of the fabric. "Did Mari pick this out?"

He grunted, and his jaw tightened. The question seemed to throw him off for a beat, but he quickly recovered. "Yeah, she did."

Moving with the languid laziness of a bumblebee drunk on nectar, Millie lifted her hand and cupped his face. She ran her thumb over the high arcing crest of his cheekbone, down to the rough of his incoming beard. "Funny how a woman can have such questionable taste in men and such good taste in decorating." Ty's only response was a sharp increase in tempo. "What? You don't wanna talk about your ex-wife while you're fucking me on her sofa?"

"Filthy mouth." He ground the words out from between clenched teeth, but his lips were curved up at the corners.

Her answering smile stretched wide as she slipped into the groove. Literally and figuratively. The angle of Ty's thrusts set her body tingling again, but she dismissed the notion of going for the three-peat. Twice was very nice, and she wasn't feeling overly greedy. Just smug. "Like that, don't you? You like my dirty mouth."

"Keep going."

Running her thumb over his jaw, she narrowed her eyes in challenge. "What if I don't?"

Ty shifted his weight, the hard ridge of his hip bone biting into hers as he grappled for the arm of the couch. The next flex of his hips made her vision blur ever so slightly, but she couldn't be bothered thinking about possible blindness now. Not when this new position granted her new access to his chest and the defined contours of his abs.

"This is a crime, you know," she murmured.

He paused midthrust, every muscle in his body going rigid. "What?"

"A man your age looking like this." She softened her chide by sliding her palm over the subtle bands of muscle. "No wonder all the teenyboppers want you to do them."

He gripped one side of her ass and spread her even farther as he lifted her bodily off the couch to meet his next thrust. "I'm not interested in girls."

She blinked, then let a sly smile come. "Wow. One night with me, and he becomes a switch-hitter."

"Women," he managed to grunt, his lip curling in a snarl. His gaze locked on her. He gulped visibly, then corrected himself. "Woman. One woman."

Gratified to discover she'd robbed him of his ability to string words together, she reached down, grabbed the taut globes of his finely sculpted ass, pulled him deep inside her, and held him close. His breath caught. His arms trembled with exertion. Until she ran her hand over one bulging bicep, it hadn't occurred to her that he still held the lion's share of his weight off her. And she wanted that weight. All of it. All of him.

"Come," she ordered, staring straight into his eyes.

"Huh."

The grunt was a question, a refusal, and a fervent prayer all wrapped up in a single syllable. Her smile softened as she basked in the glow of the need lighting those amber eyes. She wet her lips, then repeated her request. "I want you to come. Don't hold back, Ty. Stop fighting."

"But…"

She squeezed him tight, and he groaned long and loud, proving all the Kegels she'd done to strengthen her pelvic wall were not for nothing. He seemed to lose the thread on his protest, so she decided to goad him along a little. "Butt? On the first date?"

A laugh boomed from him like a cannon blast. Then his hips jerked, and his entire body seemed to bow and flex as he unleashed a rough, ragged groan. His eyes closed, and his face contorted. Gorgeous, white teeth gleamed in the fading light of the day, but Ty wasn't smiling as he pumped into her. His handsome face was twisted into a grimace as he lowered his head into the crook of her neck. Full, soft lips sought and found the tender spot beneath her ear. She shivered at the contact, but she wasn't the least bit cold.

Heat radiated from his skin. She imagined waves rising off him the way they wafted from overbaked asphalt. His chest heaved as he blew like billows, each breath fiery and moist. He groaned again, but she heard little pleasure in the throaty surrender.

"What?" She ran comforting hands up over the planes of his back. "Did you throw your back out? Pull a muscle? Charlie horse?"

His only response was a huffy chuckle and weak shake of his head.

"You're not some kind of shape-shifting animal that breaks its yoohoo off in the female, are you?"

"Wha?"

The question was muffled and loaded with enough

disbelief to give her an answer. "Never mind." She slid one hand up into the downy soft curls at his nape. "You just…you don't seem happy."

The observation earned her another soundless laugh and a half-hearted version of his earlier groan. He drew a breath deep enough to make her think of birthday cakes loaded with those candy-striped candles, but instead of a hearty gust, he let go slow and soft. "I'm not happy that I can't seem to manage to make love to you naked in a bed like a normal human being with reasonable impulse control. Maybe I am some kind of animal."

Millie grinned at the apex of the vaulted ceiling. "I hear being a normal human is boring. Never saw the point in being average."

He lifted his head, holding her gaze, and slowly peeled himself off her. His feet found the floor, and he canted his body away from her. Broad shoulders hunched as he dealt with the condom. She smiled. If he was an animal, he was a cautious and considerate one, even if their encounters hadn't quite lived up to whatever standard he had set in his head.

Sated as she was, she still felt a little…squirmy. Millie raised her arms over her head and pointed her toes, twisting to one side then the other as she indulged in a long, luxurious stretch. Letting her muscles go slack, she opened her eyes to find Ty staring down at her. Unrepentant, she gave him a lazy smile. "I like this couch."

"I slept here the night you came creeping across my back lawn."

The image of him passed out in this exact spot pleased her for some reason. Like this overstuffed, overused sofa was somehow destined to be tangled up in their affair.

She ran her hand over the fine grain of the upholstery. "You got drunk after I left."

"Yes, I did." Ty held up one finger to ask her to hold her thought, then pivoted on his heel, headed for the narrow hallway, and opened one of the doors.

A light flicked on, and a second later, she heard the toilet flush and water run in the sink. She let her head fall back and blinked up at the ceiling, willing her bladder not to give in to the siren song of water rushing through the pipes.

Too late.

Cursing the daiquiris she'd downed earlier in the evening, she heaved a sigh and rolled up off the couch. She hadn't thought to grab a shirt or something when she followed the sounds of the commotion in the garage. Now, she cursed her lack of forethought. Straightening her shoulders, Millie forced herself to walk across the room as unselfconsciously nude as he had. After all, she looked pretty damn good in the buff. For a woman of any age. Besides, the sunlight was waning, and he'd seen all she had to see. No point in playing shy.

Ty opened the door to the powder room, then drew up short. "Oh. Sorry. I needed to get rid of the…"

He waved in the general direction of his crotch, and she bit back a laugh. "Evidence?"

"Encumbrance," he countered.

Millie ducked her head as a prickle of heat danced through her. "Have I ever told you how hot it is when you jock types show your smarts?"

He smirked. "Is that what the kids call them now?"

"I need a minute." Placing her hand on his chest, she pushed him back enough to give her room to slip past him into the half bath and close the door behind her. "I wouldn't mind a glass of water, if you feel like treating a girl."

"I'll treat you to anything you want," he called through the door. "Water, wine, beer, booze?"

"Water is good," she answered, hoping he'd go away. Her muscle control wasn't as absolute as it used to be.

"How about dinner?"

Millie dropped onto the commode and let her face fall into her hands.

"I don't think I have much here other than stuff in the freezer," he continued as if they didn't have a door between them. "I could order in."

She scrubbed lightly, then gave her cheeks a light pat, gathering the strength to hold on a few seconds longer. A whimper rose in her throat, but she managed to squeak out a weak, "Sounds great."

"Do you like Chinese? Pizza? Hey, do you like Thai? I know a good place that delivers—"

"Go away, Ty."

"Huh?"

"I can't pee until you go away. Now, will you go away before I explode?"

The door rattled slightly, and she realized he'd been leaning against it. "Oh. Yeah. Sorry."

She closed her eyes and counted to ten, praying he'd actually walked away. Satisfied he had, she blew out a breath and let go.

A few minutes later, she'd washed her hands with the Midnight Magnolia–scented hand soap and finger-combed her hair into some semblance of style, wishing she had a tube of lip gloss at hand. Her lips were swollen from kissing and a bit chapped. She spotted patches of pink beard burn on her chin and cheeks, but she didn't mind. Her eyes looked bright and shiny. Almost feverish. All these added up to proof that getting laid could do things for a girl a vibrator simply could not.

Taking a bracing breath, she spun away from the mirror before her attention strayed below the neck. No sense in undermining her self-confidence.

She reentered the great room to find Ty standing at the wet bar in almost the exact spot he stood the first time they kissed. Except now he was naked. Two tall glasses of water waited on the granite countertop. One with ice, one without. She offered a helpless shrug as she approached. "Sorry. Shy bladder."

He gave her a nervous smile. "No, I'm sorry. I wasn't thinking."

She nodded to the glasses. "One of those for me?"

Again, a flush darkened his cheeks. "I didn't know if you liked ice or not."

The small smile tugging at her lips stretched into a grin as she reached for the ice water. "I can take it any way you want to give it to me."

"Stop."

He practically growled the word at her as he took the other and began to drain the contents in big, noisy gulps. Millie paused midsip, then slowly lowered her glass as she watched his Adam's apple bob. The skin below the line of his beard was smooth and tan. A deeper brown than his chest. Her gaze fell to the line of demarcation spanning his narrow hips and she swallowed hard. "You know, I've never thought about whether African Americans tan."

His dark brows arched as he lowered the glass. "I don't need to ask if you do. You're the same shade all over."

"Milkmaid Millie," she said, saluting him with her glass. "Wasn't easy being so pasty in the tanning bed era of the eighties, let me tell you, but Halloween costumes were a breeze."

"You're beautiful."

The cubes in her glass clinked as she took another sip. "You're blinded by the white. Blink a few times."

"Millie."

With a single word, he sliced right through the smokescreen she was trying to set up. But she wasn't subject to his intuitive skills. She had to give in to the pull. Placing the glass on the counter, she tipped her chin up to meet his gaze. "Tyrell."

He smiled. "What would you like for dinner?"

The question gave her pause. He sounded so easy, but the question was more complicated than he could imagine. Asking what was for dinner was a couple question. Almost homey. Hell, the guy was barely back in town, the ink still wet on his divorce decree, and he was acting like the two of them hanging around in his house — naked — discussing their next meal was an everyday thing. And it wasn't. Wouldn't be. Not forever. This was some kind of fantasy land. Not the X-rated kind but more like the two of them were operating on separate levels. A parallel universe.

Pushing away from the bar, she tossed a throwaway smile in his direction and headed for the stairs. "You're sweet, but I have a Lean Cuisine and a ton of work to do tonight."

Her foot had barely touched the bottom step when he caught up to her. "Wow. Well, I can see how it would be hard for a guy to compete, but…come on, Millie. Why are you jerking my chain?"

She froze, her hand wrapped tightly around the polished wood banister. She couldn't stand being accused of emotional gamesmanship. She might spin things in her professional life, but in her personal relationships, she made it her policy to be strictly forthcoming. Pivoting to look directly at him, she drew a calming breath. She told herself going off on him wouldn't be fair. Ty didn't know any better. But now the time had come to lay out the ground rules.

"I think we need to talk."

He didn't move or even flinch. The tension stretched between them to the point where the silence was almost funny, given the fact that they were both completely naked. Almost but not quite. "I guess I should tell you right up front I'm probably one of the few guys in the world who isn't terrified by that sentence."

"And I think I should tell you I won't be bullied into having a relationship with you." She tried to soften the statement with a smile, but the shock on his face told her she missed the mark. Still, she had a point to make, whether he liked what she had to say or not. "I get really touchy when people make presumptions on my time."

His eyes narrowed. "I wasn't aware you felt you were being bullied. I apologize." He inclined his head in a sort of old-fashioned show of deference. A lump rose in her throat, and her chest ached. He gestured to the stairs. "If you aren't interested in having dinner with me, then we'll get dressed, and I'll drop you at home."

Her grip on the rail tightened. So did the knot in her stomach. Deep down inside, she didn't want to go home to a frozen dinner and her laptop. She wanted him to ask. Nicely. Ask her out like a real date, not pick her up at a bar, take her home, and make her see stars. "You didn't ask if I wanted to," she pointed out.

"Wanted to?" He looked truly perplexed, then completely panicked. "I didn't ask if you wanted to what?"

Millie saw the flash of horror in his eyes and raised her hand to his cheek. "No, not that. I fully consented to the sex, Ty. What I'm saying is, you didn't *ask* if I wanted to have dinner with you."

"Would you like to have dinner with me?" he asked with cautious precision.

She leaned in and caught his mouth in a soft, lingering kiss. His eyes were hooded as she pulled back, but the embers in them flared. "Yes to the food," she said, nipping any other ideas he might have in the bud. Taking his hand, she curled her arm until their clasped palms rested square in the small of her back. "Funny. Suddenly, I have the worst craving for Thai…Ty."

Chapter 11

TY MADE A POINT OF FOCUSING ON THE WINEGLASS HE'D placed on the countertop in front of her. If his gaze strayed a few inches down, he'd get an eyeful of long, lean thigh. If he looked up, he'd start obsessing about how few buttons Millie closed on the shirt she'd commandeered from his closet. She'd picked a bottle of white from the cooler built into the bar setup. Ty wasn't a big fan of sweet wines, but Millie insisted the Riesling would be the perfect complement to the spicy duck and shrimp pad Thai they'd ordered, and he wasn't about to argue with her. The woman had one toe on the starting line, and she was waiting for him to slip up so she could beat a path on out the door.

He filled another glass for himself, then toasted her. "To ground rules."

Millie looked up from the array of cartons she was opening. Her eyes widened with appreciation, then narrowed as she wound her fingers around the stem of her own glass. "You're awfully gung ho about these rules." She touched her glass to his, then quirked an eyebrow. "How do you know you'll like them?"

He fell back against the opposite counter as she dished up their dinner. Squelching the urge to yelp when the cool granite made contact with the bare skin above his waistband, he crossed one leg over the other and drank in the details of her. Smiling into his glass, he took the obligatory sip to seal the toast. "I don't have to like a rule to play by it."

He'd already proven his willingness to adapt, so Millie suggested they shower while they waited for supper. Unfortunately, she also insisted they do so separately for the sake of expedience. A waste of time and water, as far as he was concerned, but she obviously wanted a little space, and he wasn't about to push her.

Looking at her now, he was glad she'd suggested the short hiatus. The breather had allowed him time to gather his wits before facing her again. Good thing, because she looked so damn good he was about to take a bite out of her. Her skin was rosy. He caught a whiff of his soap on her skin each time she moved. Her hair was damp. Dime-sized splotches darkened the fabric where water had dripped on her shoulders, and one intrepid streak pointed the way to the crest of her right breast. Lucky drop.

Of course, all he could do the whole time he was in the guest bath was picture her in his shower, her hands splayed on the tile wall as water spewed from the multiple jets to rush over her slender curves. He could picture her nipples—red, ripe, and hard as cherry pits. Soap suds running down the shallow valley between her breasts and tangling in the tight curls between her legs. Yeah. He spent a fast three minutes under a cool spray getting the cleanup job done as fast as he possibly could without resorting to jacking off.

Now, he was scrubbed up and partially clad in a pair of sweats, but his thoughts were anything but clean. He wanted to get whatever was bothering her out in the open so he could take her back to his room and mess her up again as soon as possible.

"I think the occasional hand check is an important part of any effective defense," he said. "No one wants to play zone all the time."

Millie smirked and pushed an empty plate across to him. "I'm not your mama. You know what that means?" She didn't bother giving him a chance to answer. "Two things. I don't have to fill your plate, and I don't have to pretend I know what your sports talk means."

Ty laughed and pushed away from the counter with his hips. "If you're not my mama, why do I have to call you ma'am?"

She grinned as she twirled a fork in a bed of noodles. "Because I like when you do. Makes me feel extra naughty, and you like when I feel extra naughty, don't you?"

Setting his glass aside, he set to the task of filling his plate with singular efficiency. "Yes, ma'am."

He felt her eyes on him but studiously avoided looking up. She was the one who wanted to talk. If Ty knew one thing, it was strategy. No point in initiating a conversation that wasn't going to give him the result he wanted, so he hung back. He was okay with waiting her out. He hadn't expected to get everything he wanted from Millie right away. He'd woo her with plenty of sex and wine over the stretch of a few weeks, months, or even years if time was the deciding factor. He'd always been good at working the game clock.

Millie shoveled the tightly wound forkful into her mouth and chewed, a tiny frown appearing between her brows. "This can't be a relationship."

Picking up his plate, he fell back against the counter once more, needing the time and distance to put the lid on the slow simmer starting to bubble inside him. "I thought it already was."

"Not a *relationship* relationship," she said, as if repeating the word clarified everything.

"Okay." He drew the word out, but he figured he was entitled to a little dramatic effect if she was going to be issuing proclamations. "Let me ask this… Why not? I have no morals clause like Danny's in my contract, and even if I did, we both know ways around those pesky clauses."

The reference to the morals clause that gave the football coach such a hard time in establishing his relationship with Kate Snyder made Millie stiffen. Kate and Danny had circumvented disaster with a marriage license and a quick trip to the courthouse. The abject horror in her expression told him Millie wasn't itching to be a loophole bride.

"Not even up for discussion," she said dismissively, but her posture remained stiff.

"I'm involved too, and I say we open the debate." Impervious to her glare, Ty plowed ahead. "Why can't this be a relationship?"

Millie stopped, the tines of her fork buried in the pile of noodles but unmoving. At last, she lifted her head and met his gaze. "Because I don't want one."

Her bluntness shouldn't have shocked him, but it did. Her answer landed like an elbow to the solar plexus, but he'd been a pro for too long to let any sign of weakness show. He nodded as he processed her declaration. "Okay."

"But we can have sex."

Boy, she was quick to toss sex out as a consolation prize. Needing to buy some time, he fished a shrimp out of the mountain of food he'd dumped on the plate and popped the morsel into his mouth. Shifting the spicy tidbit around as he chewed, he nodded as if he understood. Which he didn't. What kind of person wanted to hook up with someone for sex but nothing more?

Then it hit him.

Men.

Righteous indignation and shame weren't the best chasers for overspiced shellfish, but he swallowed them along with the shrimp. If Millie's militant friend Avery were privy to his inner thoughts, she'd be doing a feminazi goose step all over him. And he'd deserve every bruise. If not for the initial reaction, then for using the term *feminazi*.

He hated knee-jerk labels. His whole life, he'd had to fight his own battles with people who wanted to put him in a box. Now, he was doing the same damn thing. If Millie wanted their relationship to be purely physical, she had every right to say so. Just as he had dozens of times through his twenty and thirties. And he had the right to say no. As if he would. "You're saying you only wanna have sex?" The question was out, his tone a bit too incredulous. "No strings attached?"

Millie's pointed stare was loaded with challenge. "If having sex is okay with you."

Her manner was so patronizing he had to set his plate on the counter before he smashed the ceramic to bits on the tile floor he'd so painstakingly chosen. When he didn't answer, she flashed a patently insincere smile. This was a woman who dealt with the media sharks on a daily basis. She wasn't going to be bullied into anything, but neither was he.

As expected, she didn't back down. "I don't want you to feel used or anything."

There was nothing he could do. He knew he was at her mercy. She did too. If he objected, he'd not only look like a big, fat jerk, but he'd also be denying them both what they desperately wanted. And maybe if he agreed, he might be able to win her over.

"Oh no. Feel free." Holding his hands out like some kind of religious martyr, he tried to play the whole thing off with a shrug. "Use as much as you want."

She smirked at him, but it softened into a smile. "Of course, there are strings. We're friends. Colleagues. We'll have to set some boundaries for work and stuff, but we can figure those out." She glanced down at her own plate. "I don't want any unrealistic expectations popping up," she said, attacking her food with renewed vigor. "We're having fun, enjoying each other's company—"

"And the sex."

Ty cringed and wished the words back with all his might. Something about being this close to this particular woman robbed him of any control over his tongue. Ironic, considering she was the one person he trusted implicitly to help him find the right words. Being near her was enough to fill him with an overwhelming urge to claim the title of biggest, neediest moron who ever threw himself at a woman's feet. Hell, he hadn't even made this big of an ass of himself with Mari.

Cool as a cucumber, Millie sucked up the ends of her noodles, then wiped the corner of her mouth with her pinkie. "Yes, the sex. We like the sex."

He saw no reason to argue the statement, so he inclined his head in acknowledgment. "Yes, we do."

"I like it a lot." She speared some duck with her fork, then shoved it in her mouth. He couldn't help but stare as she chewed. She swallowed the bite, and he jerked his attention away from her lips. Millie was watching him, a knowing gleam in her eyes. "Wanna have some more, or are we done for the night?"

"Oh, I wanna have more."

She nodded. "Good. I thought so, but I wanted to be sure we were on the same page."

"Yeah, we're on the same page."

Her smile blossomed into the real deal, and suddenly the thought of dropping to his knees in front of her didn't seem like such a bad idea. Still, if they were going to play this game, he wanted to know all the rules.

"Where do we fall on sleeping together?"

She snickered but avoided his gaze. "I thought we covered that. Weren't you paying attention?"

Her evasion told him she was torn on the topic. The realization pleased him. He had some leverage after all. He could fall back a little and let her come at him. "I wasn't speaking euphemistically."

"Ooh, using the vocabulary words, are we?"

All thought of dinner abandoned, he crossed his arms over his chest, hoping he struck a pose of casual nonchalance. "I can drive you home after, if you want, but I'd like to know up front so I don't get too comfortable."

"And here I was thinking about what remarkable powers of recovery you seem to have."

"Stamina too," he said without missing a beat. "If you decide to stay the night, I'll prove how remarkable my powers are."

"Oh, I don't doubt them or you."

He watched carefully as she pushed the food around on her plate. The conversation seemed to have robbed her of her appetite. But then, Millie looked up, and the heated hunger he saw in her eyes forced him to amend the thought. She'd lost any appetite for food, but she was still interested in him. Thank God.

"Why don't we plan on you taking me home tonight? I don't have a change of clothes with me, and I prefer to avoid doing the walk of shame." She wrinkled her nose, then flashed a weak smile as she set her plate aside. "The dean of the English department lives next door, and that old fart gossips more than my great-aunt Maude."

Skirting the edge of the island, he kept his gaze locked on her. "Do you really have a great-aunt Maude?"

She bobbed her head. "Yep. She's ninety-four, has three boyfriends, and cheats at canasta."

He stepped within reach, hooked a hand around her waist, and pulled her up against him. "So you're a chip off the old block."

She swatted his chest. "Don't let her hear you call her old."

She smiled down at the hand resting on his arm. The inexplicable urge to make her swat him again swept over him with such ferocity he almost laughed out loud. It was a feeble move unworthy of the hellcat in his arms, and he loved it. His smile was irrepressible.

"I'm calling you trouble."

Millie beamed up at him. "Well, I think we both know you're probably right."

"I'm feeling the need to try to teach you a lesson."

Finely arched brows rose. "You can try."

The words were scarcely out of her mouth before he bent down and hoisted her up over his shoulder. Formidable as she was, the woman hardly weighed more than his father's overburdened golf bag. Delighting in her squeal and squirms, he stalked toward the master bedroom. By the time they crossed the threshold, Millie had stopped writhing and started cooing.

"Oh, you're so big and strong, Coach Handsome. Promise you won't hurt me. I'm only a girl," she added with a phony giggle.

She'd pitched her voice high and tried for breathy. The effect was something between a defective foghorn and his ex-wife in a wheedling mood. The combination set his teeth on edge. "Stop."

The order made her laugh, but it was her real laugh. Throaty and full. Pure pleasure rolled over him like summer thunder, low and rumbly. The sound reverberated through him, making the hairs on his arms stand on end and his dick harden. He stepped up the pace, hoping to get to the bed before his desire for this obstinate woman hobbled him. He made it in the nick of time.

Ty dropped her onto the bed, and she spread her arms wide across the mattress as she scuttled to find a more dignified position, laughing the whole time. The sound of her happiness bounced off his bedroom walls and cut his legs out from under him. He fell on her with a grin and a growl, hoping to sustain the carefree, playful air between them. His fingers skimmed over her rib cage, and she wriggled beneath him. He planted a loud, sucking kiss to the side of her neck. She yelped another laugh, this one accompanied by a protest so absurdly lacking in vehemence, it might as well have been an invitation. He teased the tender flesh with the tip of his tongue, and her giggle segued into a gasp.

Millie planted both hands on his shoulders and pushed. His mouth curved into a smile, and he gave enough resistance to make her increase her efforts. He wanted her giving one hundred and ten percent this time around. No rush to the finish line. This time, he wanted their lovemaking to be more on pace with a marathon than a sprint.

"Tell me you want me," he ordered.

She pursed her pink lips and gave him a pitying look. "Aw, are you feeling a little needy?"

He shifted to one side and slid his leg up until the meat of his thigh pressed hard against her pussy. Her hips rose off the mattress, her body straining to meet his demands. "I have a lot of needs, but ego-stroking isn't one of them."

Her smile heated as she let her hand slip between their bodies and start its teasing slide down to his cock. "How about I stroke something else?"

"Yes, please."

"So polite." She cooed the words, but the grip she took on his dick was anything but sweet and playful. "How do you want me?" she asked, her breath hitching as she gave him a hard stroke. "Slow? Fast? Soft and gentle, or do you like things a little…rough?"

He kissed her. Partly to shut her up long enough for his brain to engage again, but mostly because he loved the taste of her. Sweet. Spicy. Hot. Kissing Millie was something like shoving an entire pack of cinnamon gum into his mouth. The heat and flavor nearly unbearable, the sugary shock of her addictive.

"I want you to suck me."

Her hand stilled, and her gaze flicked up to meet his. The words, stark and unadorned with any of his usual niceties, seemed to jolt her. Truth was, the simple statement shocked him as well. He hadn't been so blunt with a woman since his days of banging groupies. An apology sprang to the tip of his tongue, but he swallowed it at the last second.

Millie's mouth—the mobile mouth that drove him to distraction—curved up at the corners. "Do you?"

Her saucy smile erased all thoughts of apologies and rescinding the request. He'd told her what he wanted, and he didn't want to back down. Excitement pulsed through his veins. But unlike the short, sharp strobes pushing him too quickly to the brink, this surge of desire made his blood run slow and sluggish. As if he had all the time in the world, and she was his to command.

"Yes, ma'am."

Still smiling, she wet her lips, then popped the collar on his shirt so the tips stood up around her ears. "I didn't hear the magic word."

The games they'd played on the phone came rushing back in time to keep him from making a huge tactical error. Of all the teases and taunts they'd exchanged, this was one he would not lose. Whether he had what she wanted or needed was for her to decide. He'd be damned if he forfeited his pride to a woman again. Particularly not one who'd been clawing his back a short time before.

"I won't beg you."

"You will if you want me bad enough," she taunted.

The lilt in her voice told him she issued the challenge with the same gravity as a playground double-dog dare.

He smirked in response, then bent to nuzzle the creamy skin exposed by the open collar. Her back arched when his teeth scraped the rise of one breast. "Never mind. I can find other ways of entertaining myself."

"No, I want to," she said, grappling for a hold on him as he slid down her body.

"Nah, that's okay." Ducking under the shirttail, he pressed a lingering kiss to the juncture of her hip and thigh. Then he let his tongue trace the tender crevice leading to the sweet folds of her pussy. "I'll just…" He inhaled deeply, taking in the scent of his soap mixed with her arousal. Then he buried his nose in the downy nest of curls. "This seems as good a place as any to hang around a bit."

"Oh, it's a great place," she answered with a husky laugh. And Millie, being Millie, spread her legs wider in blatant invitation. "Stay as long as you like."

He brushed a kiss across the curve of her belly, a chuckle rolling through him. "So generous." Clasping the insides of her thighs, he spread her wider still. "Accommodating."

She moaned as his breath ruffled those damp curls. Millie pressed her heels into the mattress and lifted her hips off the bed, offering her pussy up like a trophy. "That's me. Putty in your hands."

Oh, yes. She'd be wet. And hot. And so fucking tight, he could lose his mind. If he hadn't been raised believing without pain, he'd achieve no gain, he might have broken. But Ty was a professional athlete. A team player. She didn't realize she was trying to toy with a man long accustomed to finding triumph through hard work, self-denial, and the ingrained notion that no single player could carry the day every day.

He glanced down at his hands. She might be putty, but he was hard as granite. The tips of his fingers sank into pliant flesh. His palms curved to fit the bend of her knees. He was more than twice her size and more stubborn than she could ever imagine. Raising his head, he waited until their eyes met and held. "Maybe I should wait for *you* to say the magic word."

Her laugh came fast and breathless. "I'm not that easy."

"All evidence to the contrary."

"I'm being polite."

She added a smirk to the prim statement, which only served to increase his determination. Releasing his hold on one leg, he trailed the very tips of his fingers along the seam of her pussy. He wasn't wrong. She was wet. And impossibly hot. Without breaking eye contact, he thrust one finger into her wet welcome.

Millie gasped, but he withdrew before she could get a word out. Planting his other hand on the mattress, he stretched up over her again. Her eyes widened with shock, then darkened with arousal when he traced her lower lip with his wet finger, coating the pillowy softness with the evidence of her own arousal.

"Suck me," he whispered, his voice hoarse and raspy.

And God help him, she did.

Eyes open but heavy-lidded, she drew the digit into her mouth. Her tongue curled around his finger, the very tip barely grazing his knuckle. She pulled him deep, sucking hard enough to make his eyes cross. He closed them, unwilling to give her even that small concession. Not until she gave up something of herself.

But of course, she wouldn't. Not easily. Millie sucked

his finger the way he dreamed of her working his dick. Fast, hard, relentless. He felt each pull down to the soles of his feet. Her mouth was hot and plush. He wanted to swap appendages. Demand she do the little flicker thing she was doing with her tongue to his dick instead.

His mind clouded, but he didn't have to be a genius to realize Millie was as turned on by this game of brinks-manship as he was. She moved beneath him, her hips bucking and her legs restless. At last, she hooked a foot behind his knee and pressed his leg down so she could grind against his thigh. She rode him like a rodeo queen, her body gyrating in every possible direction, but she kept her seat. The heat of her pussy emanated through the thin nylon of his sweats.

"Huh-uh." He wasn't about to let her push him to the brink again. Not like this. Not so fast. He yanked his finger from her mouth and raised himself, holding his body up and away from hers. "You're not gonna rush me."

"What if I have a curfew?"

"You'll miss it." Pressing into his hands, he lowered to kiss her. Her hands closed around his biceps. He smiled against her mouth when she gave him an appreciative squeeze and purr. "Like that?" he asked, lifting onto his toes and following through until his arms were fully extended.

Never one to miss an opportunity, Millie flashed a million-watt smile, hooked her thumbs into his waistband, and promptly pantsed him. "Do it again," she cooed, running the flats of her palms over his stomach.

He did as she asked. Her mouth was wet and eager, each swipe of her velvet tongue pure temptation. When he pushed up again, the tip of his cock caught the tail of the shirt she still wore. He tucked his chin to his chest and stared, captivated by every nuance of the sight. The glowing translucence of her skin against the deep blue of his shirt. Her sleek, willowy frame smothered in the voluminous fabric. Three tiny, plastic buttons kept her breasts hidden from view, but the bottom of the shirt fell open, exposing the riot of dark curls and the place he most wanted to be.

"The red hair suits you," he said as he dipped down again. "But I have to say the brown is pretty hot too."

"I've always felt like more of a redhead." Her lips curved into an inviting smile. "Took me a while to find the right shade. I'm not really the carrot type."

He kissed her slow and deep, their tongues circling in a sensuous, hands-in-each-other's-back-pockets kind of dance. He felt her wriggle her hands between their bodies. She got one button open before her intention registered. Breaking the kiss, he shook his head and growled. "No. Leave the shirt on."

A huffy laugh escaped her, but those busy hands fell to her sides. "Okay."

"I like the way you look in my clothes." He kissed his way down the taut tendon in her neck, then allowed himself the luxury of licking a path along her collarbone to the hollow of her throat. "I like how you look in my bed." Hoisting his weight one more time, he rolled to the side and reached for the nightstand. "But what I like best is being inside you."

He tore open the condom wrapper, mentally congratulating himself for not using the word that sprang to mind first. *Love*. He loved being inside her. But he didn't dare use the big l-word in any context. Not when he had her right where she belonged.

Millie's breath hitched when he pushed into her wet heat. Her pussy closed around him, swollen tight from their previous encounters. Conscious she might be a little sore—hell, *he* was—Ty moved slowly, sinking into her inch by mind-blowing inch. When he was seated deep inside her, he paused to catch his own breath. Millie made a soft mewling noise in the back of her throat and squirmed. Somewhere in the depths of his sex-addled brain, he recognized the noise, but he couldn't quite put a finger on why. All he knew was the squeak had about the same effect as a ref's whistle on him.

He moved cautiously at first, gliding in and out of her snug pussy with excruciating care. Biting the inside of his cheek, he watched and waited while she adjusted, wriggling her hips until they met at the right angle. Then she wound those long, lean legs around him, tilted up to meet his thrust, and smiled beatifically.

"Ten bucks says you can't make me come again," she whispered.

The challenge made him stumble, but he soon caught up to pace. Bracing his weight on his forearm, he wedged his hand into the nonexistent space between them. "I'll take that bet."

"Nuh-uh." She clamped a hand around his arm and yanked. "No hands, sport."

Growling deep in his throat, he acquiesced to her request. "Fine. Game on."

Shifting his weight forward, he pressed into his knees and changed the angle. Pushing into her from above, the shaft of his dick trailed along her slick clit with every stroke. "Like this? Will this get you off, Mil?"

She made the squawky noise again, and Ty knew he'd hit the right spot.

"Gonna get me too, but I can wait. Oh, I can wait." His breath came harder. He was pretty much lying his ass off about the waiting thing. Thankfully, her pussy was getting tighter still with every stroke, and those maddening gasps and grunts were coming fast and furious now. Greedy for more of them, he picked up the tempo. "I'll wait, Millie. I can hold off. As long as it takes. I'm gonna win."

And win he did. Big. Her fingernails bit into his back as the first shudder rolled through her. If he wasn't mistaken, the last gasp sounded a lot like his name. And then she screamed. Not long or loud. Barely more than a yelp, really, but Ty couldn't hold back. Those slippery, sweet walls clamped tightly around him, and the next thing he knew, he was coming again. This time, his climax was far more feeling than force, but Ty couldn't give less of a damn if he tried.

She owed him ten bucks.

Chapter 12

MILLIE WAS EXHAUSTED, AND NOT BECAUSE SHE'D SPENT THE night being worked over by her lusty new lover. No. For the first time in her life, she had gone and fallen into bed with a man of his word. The minute their breathing slowed, Ty had rolled off the edge of the mattress and began stalking around the room, moving with the lithe grace of a panther. He'd gathered her discarded clothing and placed the pile on the end of the bed before disappearing into the attached bath.

He'd returned as promised, plucked up the jeans she'd peeled him out of earlier that evening, and thrust his long legs into the tangled denim. "Come on. I'll take you home."

But it didn't matter if she slept in her own bed or not; the man was responsible for the dark circles under her eyes. She'd tossed and turned all night. Thoughts of Ty and their romp in bed chased her through her morning run. She'd even dressed for him. Slim cigarette pants and a crisp, white shirt. She'd slicked her mouth with her favorite lipstick, Rapscallion Red, and then left her house, determined to make him pay for her lack of sleep.

Thirty minutes later, she breezed through the door of the Warrior Center with her tote swinging from the crook of her elbow and enough swagger to do a sailor proud. She nodded to a couple of students hauling massive equipment duffels, floated a flirty smile at one of Danny's assistant coaches as he wandered past with his phone pressed to his ear, and waved to the athletics editor of the *Warrior Weekly*. Without breaking stride, she hooked a sharp right into Kate's office.

"I'm thinking we should hit the mall tonight," she announced. "I have need for new lingerie."

"I'm sorry, think I have a colonic scheduled this evening," Kate replied without missing a beat.

Millie stopped short when she spotted the hot hunk of man sprawled in the guest chair across from her best friend. The tablet perched on Ty's knee was dark and smudged with fingerprints. He craned his neck to look back at her. The smile he wore stretched from ear to ear. "Hey, Millie."

Not one to back down from anyone or anything, she leveled a blank stare on him. "Hello, lover."

Kate choked on a laugh. Slapping a hand to her chest, she threw her head back and let loose. "Wow. Okay, well, I guess I don't have to ask what you kids did last night."

"We played Monopoly." Millie strolled the rest of the way into the office, hoping they couldn't hear the thudding of her heart. "I bankrupted him with my hotels." She smirked at Ty. "Are you in here begging for a little lunch money? Our Katie isn't just a winner. She's carrying cash around in those bags with the dollar signs now."

Ty inclined his head, acknowledging the hit. "I've got lunch covered, thanks." He picked up the tablet and rose to his full height, inch by spectacular inch. "I was dropping off a jersey for the Kids Kare auction, but I'd be happy to make a donation to the lingerie fund if you're accepting contributions."

She cocked an eyebrow. "Maybe you'd like to go with me?"

Ty chuckled. "Well, luckily, I do not have an enema scheduled, but I do have a practice to run." He lifted a hand in farewell to Kate, then sidled past Millie. "But if you're looking for input, I like the pretty, lacy things more than the hooker stuff."

"Hooker stuff?" Kate and Millie asked in unison.

Ty shrugged and started toward the door, unfazed by their questioning. "If you see something you think my ex-wife would have picked out, you'll know what I mean."

He took off before either of them could respond.

Millie watched until he disappeared, then swallowed a sigh as she leveled a pointed look at Kate. "Sadly, I know exactly what he means."

Kate nodded. "I do too." Her smile shone a shade too eager as she said, "Take a seat."

Shaking her head, Millie hiked her tote a little higher on her arm. "I really need to get—"

"Take a seat." This time, Kate used her coach voice, and as if her good friend held a set of marionette strings, Millie found herself moving toward the chair Ty had vacated. "Avery had a lecture first thing this morning, so I promised her I'd get the scoop and report back while she's doing office hours."

Affixing her patented camera-neutral expression, Millie let her bag drop to the floor beside her feet. "No big scoop. We had sex." She treated her inquisitor to a lopsided smirk. "Bet you girls didn't see that coming."

"Only thing that might have made the scene better would have been Ty in dress whites carrying you out of the bar."

Millie's heart fluttered as she recalled exactly how giddy she'd been as she slipped her hand into his and hopped down off her bar stool. Determined to get a grip on herself and the spin, she rolled her eyes. "Let's not over-romanticize this."

"Looked pretty damn romanticized all on its own."

"The ink isn't even set on those divorce papers. The man wants a fling. I love being flung." The pro that she was, she brushed the most intense sex of her life aside with a flick of her hand. "I'm hoping he'll fling me again. Soon."

"I think you can bet on it."

"But it's nothing more," Millie asserted firmly. "Do not make this a big deal, or you'll make us all uncomfortable."

"I love how you can turn pretty much anything around and point the finger at someone else."

She heard no rancor behind Kate's words. If anything, she may have detected a note of admiration in the commentary. Millie took the compliment at face value. "Everyone has a talent," Millie said, plastering on a smile.

"If it makes you feel better to think you're all cool with a casual affair, fine." Kate looked straight at her, her expression intense and solemn. "But be sure you're being honest with yourself from the get-go. Nothing more embarrassing than getting slam-dunked by an arrow-shooting cherub."

Without deigning to reply, Millie bent and scooped

up her bag. As far as she was concerned, the conversation was over the second someone introduced naked angels into what was essentially a straightforward conversation. She told her best friend she and Ty were lovers. She'd made no allusions to anything more, nor did she indicate she had any such designs.

Millie steeled herself against the temptation to buy in. She'd already spent half the night haunted by the guy. She wasn't going to spend her waking hours mooning as well. If Kate wanted to get all touchy-feely about a night of screwing, that was her problem.

"I'll tell you what made me feel pretty damn fantastic," Millie said as she rose. Holding up three fingers, she waggled them proudly. "Three orgasms." Pausing inside the door, she looked back at Kate with a puzzled frown. "Or was it four?"

"I know." Kate grinned and kicked back in her chair, planting her grasshopper-green high-top sneaker on the corner of the desk and crossing one blindingly clunky foot over the other. "I had five this morning."

The boast halted Millie's retreat faster than a battalion of G.I. Joes wielding assault rifles. Flaunting the advice given by the town's best and only plastic surgeon, she frowned at her friend, trying to gauge her level of veracity. "Liar."

Kate raised her hands palm up. "My pants aren't on fire, but that might be because I wasn't wearing any at the time."

Ninety-nine-point-nine percent certain the woman was lying, Millie scoffed. "You are so full of crap."

Then Kate started ticking things off on her fingers. "Two in bed. Technically, one was before we went to sleep, but it was after midnight, so I'm counting it. One in the shower. Another while I was applying my lotion." She paused, a dreamy smile ghosting across her face. "I swear, the man has a thing for the scent of lanolin."

Millie squeezed her eyes shut, torn between imagining Danny McMillan splashing about in a vat of moisturizer, and…not. "Stop."

"Then the toaster got jammed, and he had to use tools and electricity and strawberry jam, and, well, one thing led to another."

Flashbacks of Ty lounging against his kitchen counter dressed only in low-riding running pants flooded her brain. The scent of food and sex pervaded every last molecule of oxygen. The potent aftertaste of spicy shrimp and hot man had tingled on her tongue hours after he'd kissed her goodbye. "I hate you very much."

Kate laughed and dropped her feet to the floor. "No, you don't. And no matter what you try to tell yourself, I also know you're dying to spill all the gory details, Mil."

"No, I'm not."

"But I can wait," Kate continued as if she hadn't spoken.

Millie stiffened. Did Kate know she'd echoed the exact sentiment Ty expressed the night before? Had she given something away? Was there a chink in her armor she hadn't realized the rest of the world could see? Apparently, people figured if they waited long enough, she'd cave. Well, she'd prove them wrong on that point. She'd sleep in Ty's bed when she was damn good and ready to sleep in his bed, and not one minute before. And she'd give Kate the gory details of her dealings with Coach Ransom when and if Millie thought she might have reason to do so.

"Take a number," Millie called over her shoulder, then took off down the hall at a pace brisk enough to make seasoned power walkers breathless.

Let them wait. Jocks like Ty and Kate—Danny too—were so damn cocky. They played the glory sports. They were used to the scrutiny of rabid fans and waves of adulation hurtling toward them each time they tied their laces. They didn't know about strength born from silence, the power one gathered from competing against only their personal best. They might be champions in those sports ruled by whistles and buzzers. They might excel in arenas where success was measured only in points. But they didn't know true endurance came with only the sound of one's own breathing.

Millie had never jumped the starting gun in her life. If they thought they could get her to do so now, they were going to have a damn long wait.

She bought a pair of the prettiest, pasteliest panties she could find—with a split crotch.

Millie also had an assortment of low-cut demi bras in a rainbow of sherbets, matching lace boy shorts because she refused to wear a string of floss up her ass, and one almost puritanically demure satin teddy in her shopping bag. Of course, she chose a retina-searing shade of streetwalker red for the last one. She figured she needed at least a splash of red if she wanted to ignite sparks in the bedroom.

While she was out shopping for this recent uptick in

her sex life, Millie also made a stop at the one and only adult store in town. As far as sex shops went, Fantasia's was pretty tame. The storefront was a tiny space in an ancient strip mall. The neon-red lips and a sign warning the underage away were the only hint of what lay behind the tinted glass.

Millie had been patronizing the shop for years. The way she figured, any woman over thirty and without a regular partner in her life had better be well versed in seeing to her own pleasure. She considered the judicious use of her vibrator a simple matter of public safety.

"Hey, Stase," she called as the bell above the door heralded her arrival.

Anastasia Wallace popped up from behind one of the locked display cases, a giant glass dildo in hand. "Millie! Where've you been?" Vivid blue eyes narrowed into laser beams. "You haven't been ordering online, have you?"

Millie snorted and shook her head. "Never. You know I like to touch the merchandise." Tilting her chin up, she slid her glasses down from her head and placed them on the end of her nose. "What's new?"

"Got a whole batch of these in from this guy living up in the Poconos." She beamed at the dong approvingly. "Beautiful, aren't they?"

Nodding, Millie admired the craftsmanship, even though they both knew she wasn't about to buy one. She had a strict policy against putting anything that could shatter in her snatch. Anastasia swore up and down such a thing couldn't happen, but Millie didn't see the point in tempting fate. "Lovely, but I really stopped by to pick up some lube."

"Got a shipment of flavoreds in the other day."

Millie smirked, gave some serious thought to buying a tube of vanilla to go with the nonhooker lingerie. "Plain is fine."

"You're in a rut," Anastasia announced as she unlocked a display cabinet. "When was the last time you tried something new?"

Tipping her head like a spaniel, Millie gave the older woman her sweetest smile. "Last night, and his flavor was all natural."

Anastasia barked a laugh and plucked a bottle of Millie's preferred brand from the case. "Good for you!" She eyed the array of supposedly homeopathic stimulants arrayed near the cash register. "Older or younger?"

"Younger," Millie replied, her smile a shade more smug. "Not by much, but yeah, younger."

Anastasia chuckled again and nodded appreciatively. "Maybe two bottles of lube, then?"

"Always the upsell." Millie tsked but took a spin around the tiny store. There wasn't much to see. A wall of toys, a few racks of the kind of lingerie Ty Ransom didn't find appealing, and a sagging shelf stocked with collections of erotica.

She knew Anastasia struggled to make ends meet even in the low-rent space she leased and wanted to buy something more, but Ty's commentary on the lingerie tempered her willingness to test his boundaries. Letting her gaze rove over the selection once more, she backtracked to the shelf of books. What could a naughty bedtime story or two hurt? If Ty didn't like them, well, she couldn't think of a reason why she shouldn't have a nice collection for her own edification.

"What's good to read?" she asked, jerking her chin toward the bookshelf.

"Ooh! Got a new one." Anastasia left the lube next to the register, then made her way toward the books. "Not the raunchiest stuff I've ever read, but good." She wrinkled her nose as she extracted a slim volume. "Sometimes I get a little tired of the really kinky stuff. This one is different. Very sexy but more on the sensuous end of the scale. Almost hedonistic, which is probably why I liked the stories so much. Goes well with a big glass of wine."

"Sold!" Millie raised a fist and lowered it as if she were banging a gavel. "Ring it up. I have to get home. Got mind games to play with a certain young whippersnapper."

"That's my girl," Anastasia crowed and started punching prices into her ancient cash register.

Lipstick-red bag in hand, Millie waved goodbye a few minutes later. The clock on her dashboard told her the men's basketball team had likely wrapped up practice for the night. She pulled her phone from her purse and checked the notifications. Two missed calls and a text from Ty that simply read, Answer your phone.

"Oopsie," she singsonged as she switched on her ringer. Grinning at her screen, she made no move to swipe the redial option. "Did you call and I didn't answer? Poor baby."

The pad of her finger barely grazed the power button, and the phone went dark. Feeling inordinately pleased with herself and the productive evening, she dropped her cell back into her bag and twisted the key in the ignition. She'd barely left the lot before the blare of her ringtone amplified by hands-free technology overpowered the soulful ballad on the radio.

A glance at the dashboard display reinforced Ty's persistence. She pressed the button on her steering wheel to ignore the call, then started to hum, picking up the tune as the stereo came to life again. Two blocks down, a pulsing buzz indicated an incoming text. Her smile widened, but she didn't bother to look until she'd parked the car in the narrow garage sandwiched between her bungalow and the next. For a guy who like to brag on his ability to wait, the man needed to learn a lesson in patience.

Her cell buzzed again as she dropped her shopping bags in the hall. More amused than annoyed by his persistence, she looped the strap of her bag over the back of a kitchen chair and sashayed to the fridge. She uncapped and took a deep drink from a bottle of water and swayed rhythmically from side to side, keeping time with the song playing on the radio.

Letting her eyes close, she pictured Ty as he'd appeared in Kate's office that morning—relaxed, gorgeous, of course, and…happy. Until he'd smiled up at her, she hadn't realized she'd never really seen him so kicked back. The night before, he'd been intense. Focused. Determined. As a matter of fact, those were the exact words she might have chosen to describe him in any situation.

She was starting to truly know him.

Know him well enough to understand that his ease was a momentary thing. The man was a born competitor. He wanted her attention, but she wasn't about to run to him whenever he called.

Her pulse jumped at the thought, but her mind was racing about ten steps ahead. She'd have to watch herself. Falling for the guy would be too damn easy.

Though she hadn't planned on a simple one-night stand, carrying on with Ty for any extended period of time was out of the question. This was why she wasn't answering her phone. If she did, he'd want to see her. And if he wanted to see her, she'd say yes, because she wanted to see him every bit as badly. Wanted to be with him enough to stay the night in his bed or even wedge him into hers, though his feet would poke through the iron bedstead she'd unearthed at a flea market years before.

She could have him here. All she had to do was hit the redial and say, "Come over," and he'd come. She knew he would. And so would she. Over and over again. And before she knew what was happening, they'd blow through his box of condoms. Too fast. Far too fast. And then their affair would be over.

Water bottle clutched to her chest, Millie wandered out of the kitchen, her mind clicking through scenarios and discarding them with every step. She needed to come up with an alternative plan. One that would involve a minimum of condom usage but still leave all barriers to emotional entanglement in place.

The shopping bags on the floor caught her eye, and a plan started to form. She snatched the bags from the floor and started toward her bedroom. Millie smiled as she dumped the lot onto her bed and yanked the book of erotica out of the sack. Kicking the rest of her purchases aside, she propped herself against the headboard and started to skim. His stint in Reno proved a safe distance could make a world of difference. With the right

material, they could both be in the same town, enjoy a highly satisfactory sexual relationship without any messy entanglements, and hopefully circumvent a run on the latex industry. She read until she hit a passage that made her cross one leg over the other, thumbed the button to recall the last number, and lifted the phone to her ear.

He answered, and her mouth curved into an involuntary smile. At the same time, her heart started to race, but her blood slowed, arousal flowing like warm honey through her veins. "Hello, Ty. Were you looking for me?"

His chuckle unleashed a ripple of gooseflesh. "I figured you'd get back to me sooner or later."

Sliding down into her pillows, she set the book aside and cradled the phone. "You settled in for the night?"

"I'm at your beck and call."

Millie grinned, knowing if she let him in the door, they'd be going toe-to-toe for control. "Get comfortable, big guy. I'm going to read you a bedtime story."

Chapter 13

TY'S LAUGHTER TRAILED OFF AS THE SILENCE ON MILLIE'S end drew taut. She was waiting for his response, but he had no idea how he was supposed to react. Every nerve ending in his body went on high alert when the phone rang. But her mention of a bedtime story made the jumpy little buggers stand down.

Ty eyed the glass he'd pulled off a shelf and the decanter of scotch he'd unstoppered. A bedtime story? What about some bed time? Was she saying she wouldn't see him? The thought was enough to spur him into lifting the cut-glass bottle and tipping a couple of slugs into the glass.

Had he spent the whole day drowning in nothing but wishful thinking?

Given how things went the night before, he figured she might be a little wary, but he never anticipated not seeing her. His ego wouldn't let him believe she didn't want to see him. She was into him. He knew that as sure as he knew the pattern of his hook shot.

She'd said she was going lingerie shopping. He might not be any expert on female behavior, but he'd been married long enough to know some women kept a whole hierarchy of bras and panties stashed away. Certain bits and pieces for everyday wear, another whole category dedicated to special circumstances like jogging or strapless dresses, and finally, the ones designed to make someone sit up and howl.

Millie wanted him. He was sure she did. The problem was, she seemed to want him only on her terms. Too bad he had no earthly idea what those terms were. She was using her no-nonsense voice. The one she used with nagging reporters and other pesky annoyances. It galled him to hear it. The last thing he wanted was to be another necessary evil in her world.

"Did I lose you?" she asked, her voice sultry and teasing.

Perhaps he was overthinking things. She might not be rejecting him. This tease about a bedtime story might be a ploy to get the upper hand. Which he'd give her gladly, as long as he could get his hands on her. He weighed and discarded a couple of possible moves she might be setting up and chose the obvious option. Home-court advantage. She probably wanted him to come over to her place. "How about I come over and get settled in?"

"Not tonight."

Her answer was short and delivered with a quiet firmness that marked the decision as final. But he wasn't one to give up without hurling one last miracle shot at the goal. "Why not? I could pick up ice cream. We could eat it in bed."

Millie hummed appreciatively. "Ooh, ice cream. Tempting, but no. Not tonight," she repeated.

This time, he caught a ragged edge of impatience in her voice, so he eased up. Taking the tumbler of scotch from the bar, he crossed the room to the oversized chair positioned directly in front of the television. The screen glowed in the darkened room. He dropped into the seat like his ass was weighted down with concrete and took a gulp of his drink.

Fire ran down his throat. He gripped the glass tightly. A growl of disgust rose in his chest when Greg Chambers's stupid, smug face filled the center of the screen. Without even looking, he jabbed the power button with his index finger and smacked his lips as the room sank into further darkness. "Why not tonight?"

Millie didn't miss a beat. "I like the anticipation."

Well, hell. How was a guy supposed to argue with that kind of logic? "Do you?"

"Oh yeah."

Her voice was rich and deep. Each syllable crashed over him like an ocean wave. Drawing a bracing breath, he let his arm swing down. He set the glass on the floor beside the chair, then carefully placed his hand on his leg. "Okay, fine. Tell me this bedtime story of yours."

"You comfy?"

Ty glanced at the dark-wash jeans and custom-tailored shirt he'd put on in expectation of seeing her. They weren't nearly as "comfy" as the sweats he'd ditched when he got home. Hearing her voice made him semihard. Listening to her dictate the way his evening would go left him torn between wresting control of the situation from her pretty little hands and surrendering to her every demand. But Millie had a point. These were early days for them. No need to push until she shoved.

"I'm comfy enough," he replied at last. "How about you? You...comfy?"

"I'm completely naked."

The promptness of her reply coupled with the purr in her voice marked the statement a bald-faced lie, but he figured her fib was the kind of untruth a man could get behind. "Oh yeah?"

"Naked and hot. So hot," she said, letting her voice go wispy at the end.

Acting or not, the image she invoked worked for him. In the blink of an eye, he went from mildly aroused to hard enough to bust a zipper. "What got you so hot?"

He half expected her to come up with some phone sex hotline BS about him and how she'd been thinking about him all night, but as usual, Millie was full of surprises.

"I bought a book of erotica."

He took a full minute to absorb what she was saying. Not only had his brain short-circuited, but the synapses still firing had also immediately zeroed in on the possibility she hadn't been teasing when she'd said she was naked. And hot.

"You, uh…" He paused to swallow the boulder lodged in his throat. "You did?"

"Yes, and I have to tell you, this might be the best thing I've ever read."

He blinked, then blew out the breath trapped in his lungs. As he exhaled, Ty slumped in the chair, tugging at the snug denim of his jeans in an effort to make his situation a tad more comfortable. "Is it?"

"Well, I've only just started reading," she confessed. "But when I got to this one story, I thought you might enjoy hearing it."

"Yeah?"

"The title is 'One on One' and stars a woman who likes big, tall basketball players."

"She does?"

"Mm-hmm."

He heard a rustling noise, and the throb in his groin area picked up pace. He knew the sound. She was in bed. Or on the bed. Somewhere near a bed. Location didn't matter. "Let me come over, and you can read your story to me live and in person."

"No, it's more fun this way."

"I could argue otherwise."

"Don't." She spoke with enough decisiveness to make him snap his mouth shut. "Do you want me to read you this story?"

He hesitated long enough to swallow his disappointment and sink down lower into the chair, stretching his legs out wide in front of him. "Yes. Please."

His phone beeped to indicate an incoming call, and he pulled it from his ear to check the caller. Mari's face filled the screen. Instinctively, he dismissed the call. The last thing he wanted at this moment was his ex-wife intruding on his time with Millie, even if it was only over the phone.

"Still with me?" Millie asked.

"Yes."

"Good."

In the lull, he heard the distinct sound of pages being flipped. Frowning at the ceiling, he wondered if Millie had taken the time to write down whatever dirty little ditty she wanted to share with him.

"Mind if I pick up where I left off?"

He chuckled. She could start wherever she wanted as long as she kept talking to him. "Not at all."

"Okay. Here goes."

She cleared her throat so officiously he had to smile.

"Sweaty. Beads of perspiration dotted his brow. Occasionally, one made a fast break, the tiny droplet of exertion coursing down his temple, over the rise of his cheekbone, then sliding along the sharp angle of his chiseled jaw."

"Sure, always the guys with the chiseled jawlines," he murmured.

"You're no slouch in the sculpted department, so stop moaning," she said derisively.

Thrilled by the zing of her sharp wit, he sat up straighter, if for no other reason than to prove he was no slouch in any department. "Ma'am. Yes, ma'am."

"God, I love the way that sounds." He laughed, but she picked up right where he'd interrupted. "Celeste wanted to lick him. Taste the salty tang of his skin, feel his heat against her tongue. But he was in the zone, and there was nothing more mesmerizing than watching Beck take down his faceless foes. The flex of his calf muscles as he pivoted was a thing of beauty. Stepping onto the asphalt court, Celeste beamed an incendiary glare at the long, baggy shorts he wore. She used to mock the pictures of those hoopsters from days gone by in their snug, tight shorts. Now, she yearned to see him in a pair."

"Never gonna happen," he muttered.

"Hush." The command was crisp, but he heard the smile in her voice.

"Sorry. Hushing."

"Celeste never considered herself a gambling woman, but she'd bet his quads were a thing of beauty. And to run her hands up those taut hamstrings as she took him deep—'*You playing?*' At first, she didn't realize that Beck was talking to her. He didn't look at her. Nor did he miss a step in his charge to the basket. The chink of the metal link net made her nipples tighten to hard, aching buds. The ball fell into Beck's outstretched hands as soft and silent as a leaf drifting to the ground. His chest heaved as he shifted his weight onto his right foot. He tucked the ball snug against his side and squared up to face her head-on."

Millie paused to catch her breath, but Ty didn't dare interrupt. She'd said one of the magic words — nipples — and now she, Celeste, and Beck of the chiseled jaw officially had his undivided attention.

"Emboldened by the challenge in his stance, Celeste stepped out of the shadows and into the pool of orange-gold glow shed by the playground's lone security light. Adding a sway to her step as she approached, she smiled. '*A little late to be playing ball all by yourself.*'

"He raised an eyebrow, rolled the ball out from under his arm, and held it aloft on the very tips of his fingers. '*I was hoping someone would come out for a pickup game.*'

"'*Aren't you lucky I came along?*' When she was within striking distance, she nudged the ball from its perch. He didn't stop her.

"'*What do you want, Ce?*'

"Unintimidated by his gruff question, she stepped up, stopping only when they stood toe-to-toe. '*Same thing I've always wanted, B. You.*'"

"Christ, I want you," Ty said, his voice much rougher and deeper than Millie's imitation of a man teetering on the edge.

"Do you want to hear this story or not?"

"Tell me your story," he countered. "Tell me what you'd want to do if you were Celeste."

His voice cracked at the last, but he was beyond

caring. His jeans were too tight. The shirt felt like a goddamn straitjacket. He'd go full-on Bruce Banner if he didn't get out of them soon.

He popped the button on his pants for comfort's sake, then set to work on getting out of the shirt. His breathing was ragged, big gusts of air blown directly into the phone as he yanked the tails of the shirt from his waistband. He made short work of the last buttons. The phone dropped into his lap as he yanked his arms from the sleeves, oblivious to the fancy cuff links he'd chosen to impress her. A growl of frustration rose from his throat when his arms got stuck. Fumbling through the bunched fabric for the fasteners, he spoke loudly enough to carry through the speaker.

"Does he have a shirt on? Or is good old Beck playing skins against himself?" One hand free, he grabbed the phone and tucked it back under his ear before setting to work on the other. "Because I'm almost out of my shirt, and soon I'll be down to my skin too. Tell me what you'd do, Millie."

"I'd have to touch you," she said, her voice quiet and almost quivery. "Your chest. Damp and slick. Celeste has the right idea. I want to lick you like a lollipop every time I see you running around on the court."

"Do you?"

"God yes."

"And if we were all alone on a dark playground court? What do you think's gonna happen, Mil? Is she going to take him home? Is he going to fuck her on the playground?"

"Oh yes."

She moaned the words. But she couldn't give in so

easily. If she wanted to hold him off, then he'd play along. For now. As long as she told him the whole story. Her way.

"What happens? What do they do?" he prompted.

She drew a shaky breath, then exhaled in a rush. "Do? What else can she do? She's gonna push him up against the fence."

His chest tightened, and his heart skipped a beat. "And?" he managed to ask, expelling the last bit of oxygen he had left.

Millie didn't answer right away. Damn if she wasn't right. Anticipation crackled between them like a live wire. The wait was…unbearable. And unbelievably hot. He'd never figured he'd go for the delayed gratification thing, but then again, he never anticipated resorting to phone sex to get his rocks off.

While he was in Reno, sex by proxy seemed like a reasonable means to an end. Now that he was back and Millie was a scant few miles away, it felt like an exhibition game. Each move was meant to get them primed and ready for the real deal. Frustrating but sexy as hell.

"She'd pin him against the wires, using her body to press him into the shadow outside the ring of light."

She hesitated, and he was quick to jump in with an encouraging, "Mm-hmm." The last thing he needed was for her to leave him alone in the dark. Waiting. Wanting. He unzipped and hooked his thumbs into the waistband, waiting for her to toss the ball into the air so the game could begin for real. As expected, Millie didn't disappoint.

"Then she'd sink to her knees, dragging those hideously baggy shorts down as she went."

"You like the short shorts too, huh?" He shoved his jeans and boxers down, wincing when his painfully hard dick sprang loose. He'd have to hold off on touching himself. This woman set him off like a damn bottle rocket.

"Of course I do. What could be better than watching a bunch of guys with tight asses and long, muscular legs running and jumping?"

"Women's beach volleyball."

His prompt answer earned him a laugh. One of those husky, rumbling laughs that hit him low in his gut and reverberated through his entire body.

"To each his own," she said, a chuckle coloring her words.

Time to stop pretending to be other people. He pressed on with only a subtle, but important, change in pronoun. "I'm up against the fence," he reminded her as he pushed his jeans and briefs past his knees. "My baggy pants around my ankles."

"Your fingers tangled up in the wires, your bare ass pressed against the cool metal," she added.

"Ah, chain link. Anyone could see us, Millie." He wrapped his hand around the base of his dick and squeezed. Hard. "Is that what you want? You want people to watch?"

"I'd get down on my knees," she whispered. "The ground would be hard. Your cock too. But your skin is so soft."

She trailed off into a whisper, but now his hand was moving up and down. Too damn late. There'd be no stopping now. "Take me in your mouth." He heard Millie moan. He was so distracted he almost missed the buzzing hum. "Do I hear a vibrator?"

"Mm-hmm." Millie's confirmation was more a purr than a proper response. "My favorite one."

"Jesus." He groaned and covered his eyes with his free hand. "You have more than one?"

She laughed, but he didn't care. She could laugh all she wanted. He would sit and fuck his fist while he pictured her sliding a rubber dick in and out of her sweet, tight pussy.

"I have about a half dozen, but some aren't as...satisfying as others." Her breath hitched, then she sighed softly. "This one is almost as good as the real deal."

"You're fucking killing me," he ground out.

"I'd like to suck you."

The rasp in her voice only amped him up more.

"Outside. In the dark. With your skin all hot and damp, and the breeze cool on my neck."

He could picture her so perfectly. Feel the sweet tug of her mouth. Her heat. The plush velvet of her tongue. He'd push deeper, dragging the head of his cock over the vulnerable spot at the back of her mouth.

"Hard and deep," she continued, insinuating her point of view into the vivid images he'd conjured in his head. "My hands on your thighs. Celeste had the right idea. I'd squeeze your quads, feeling them bunch and flex as you pumped into my mouth. I'd stroke your hamstrings and drag my nails lightly, so lightly, under your balls..."

He groaned then, loud and proud. Literally the only response he could manage.

"I'd press you deeper into the fence. The links would give some under the pressure, then bite into your ass. I'd like to bite your ass," she added, almost as an afterthought.

"Do it." Hell, he'd let her shred him limb from limb if he could only be inside her.

"I wanna suck you, Ty. Outside. In a place where it's dark but not pitch-black. Where anyone or everyone could see us. See me. On my knees, bringing you to yours."

"I'm there," he panted. And his warning was no lie. His cock pulsed with the need to let go. He clenched his teeth hard, and he wished he had the stamina to hold back indefinitely. Make her keep going. Never stop.

Her breathing caught again, then she gave a maddening half squeak, half moan that told him she was teetering right on the edge with him. "I want to suck you so hard you'll think I turned you inside out."

"And I'm gonna fill you up." Words burst out of him with the first pulse of his climax. He went wild. Hot, wet lashes of release streaked his stomach, thighs, and hand, but his orgasm didn't stop him. He pumped away, fisting his cock in perfect syncopation with the quick puffs of breath exploding in his ear. "I'm gonna come in your mouth. In your pussy. On your tits, your belly, your ass. I'm gonna cover you in me, because you've already got me crazy for you."

She came with a cry she didn't even bother to stifle. One of the things he liked about Millie—she was a woman who knew how to take her pleasure and revel in it.

But she never let emotion overtake her.

He needed to remember she wasn't the type to be swept away. And as much as he hated to admit as much, he kind of was.

When he was young, he had dived headfirst into the sea of willing women that surrounded professional athletes. In Europe, he'd seen and done a few things he couldn't imagine asking an American girl to do. A couple of sophisticated French girls had laughed at what he'd called his "American prudery."

He'd fucked a Russian dancer with a pierced clit for a while. The sex had been great and the girl nearly insatiable, but he'd bailed when she suggested he poke a hole through his dick. He'd been relieved when his contract was up and he had an excuse to pull up his good old American underpants and run back to the United States with all his parts intact.

He'd thrown himself into coaching and his postgraduate studies with the same single-minded focus he'd brought to the court. And the day Mari first walked into his lecture hall, he'd made up his mind to have her. She'd been so beautiful. So fresh-faced. At least in those days. She was no virgin, of course, but after the excesses he'd seen as a player, her Midwestern sensibilities were a balm. But everything changed not long after they started seeing one another exclusively.

Letting his head fall back, he listened to the sound of Millie's ragged breathing as he tried to pinpoint exactly when he'd lost the handle on his marriage. First, he had bought her a pair of perfect tits. Mari was self-conscious about the size of her small breasts. While he'd been perfectly satisfied with them, he had wanted her to be happy and comfortable in her own skin, so he'd paid for the augmentation.

The wedding had been a circus. He blamed Kim Kardashian and Kris Humphries. Mari'd watched their whole wedding fiasco with rapt attention and figured since she was marrying a basketball player too, she should have the same. Ty hadn't had the heart to point out he was a somewhat failed and now-retired ball-player. He also didn't have a bevy of television executives bankrolling their nuptials. The wedding should have been a big, fat red flag, but he'd been neck deep before reason made even the slightest bit of headway.

After the honeymoon—two weeks at an exclusive Bora Bora resort she'd seen on some celebrity gossip show—she'd moved into his small house off Eastern University's campus and started her relocation campaign. The offer from Wolcott had given Mari the perfect opportunity to buy and furnish her dream home.

But no matter how much he gave, nothing was ever enough. Between the weight of her demands and the resentment building inside him, their marriage had started to show the first stress fractures. And he'd let those go as well, took the path of least resistance. Each wave of discontent had pushed his relationship with Mari closer to the breakers. He hadn't done anything to hold off the inevitable. Frankly, he hadn't cared enough to try. When he'd first heard the rumblings about her infidelities, he'd even been a little relieved. He hadn't expected his star player, the kid he'd helped groom for greatness, to betray him as well.

"Ty?"

He jolted at the sound of Millie's voice in his ear. Pulling the phone away, he gave his head a sharp shake to disperse any lingering reveries and glanced down at himself. He was a mess. The liquid fire that jetted out of him minutes before was now a cool, sticky reminder that he was alone. Again. Jacking off in his living room because the woman he was seeing thought she should call all the shots. A flash fire of anger ignited inside him. He scowled at the sad, sorry shambles he'd made of himself and cursed under his breath.

"You okay?" she asked.

No. He was far from okay. He was righteously pissed. He'd wanted to do right by her, and she wanted to toy with him. Yes, he'd told himself he could wait. He'd be patient and let her come around to seeing things his way in her own time. But he wasn't going to play these games for long.

"I'm fine," he answered, clipping the words off short. "Thanks for the story, Mil. I have to go get cleaned up. See you tomorrow."

Without waiting for her response, he ended the call and dropped the phone to the floor beside his glass of scotch. "Why do I bother?" he muttered as he used the tail of his once perfectly pressed shirt to clean himself up.

Apparently, reminiscence and bitterness were two main ingredients in whatever witchcraft were needed to conjure up the ghosts of big mistakes barely past. His phone rang, and the screen lit up. Mari's smiling face beamed up at him. He shoved himself up out of the chair, wincing as he yanked his shorts and jeans up over his hips. "That's all I need," he grumbled.

Ty stepped carefully around the abandoned drink and the shimmying phone. He made it two steps before the anger gripped him by the throat again, and he whirled to glare at the photo on the phone's display. He'd snapped the picture here, in this room. The couch and chair had just been delivered, and Mari'd been so proud of her decorating skills. And he'd been happy to see her happy.

"Ain't nobody happy now," he said, directing the pronouncement toward the phone.

As if the damn thing heard him, it fell silent, and the call kicked over to voicemail. Swooping down, Ty dragged his hand along the floor until he scooped up the glass. No message alert chimed, so he bolted the drink, welcoming the burn of liquid fire scorching its way through his chest and down into his belly.

His mouth twisted into a grimace, he eyed the now-silent phone with trepidation. He wasn't interested in anything Mari had to say. She had gotten what she wanted—a hotshot star in the making and a chunk of Ty's nest egg. He had gotten his freedom. They had nothing left to say to each other. They'd said all that needed to be said in her lawyer's office.

Shuffling his feet, he set the glass on an end table as he passed, then wandered into the powder room off the hall. The sight that greeted him wasn't pretty. The lines between his eyebrows and around his mouth cut grooves into his skin. His eyes looked dull and tired. He needed a haircut. Leaning heavily on the pedestal sink, he peered into the mirror. "Get a grip. Tell her you're not playing these games."

He blinked, then snorted at his own theatrics. Flipping on the tap, he ran cool water over his right hand, washing away the residue of the evening's activities. He was right. He knew he was. He had things he needed to say to Millie. Things that had nothing to do with naughty stories, yanking his own chain, and this power struggle they had going on. He needed to figure out a way to tell her he'd give her whatever she needed without coming off sounding like a pushover.

"Yeah, good luck, buddy."

Chapter 14

TY FOUND FEW THINGS AS SOOTHING AS THE THRUM OF A ball bouncing off hardwood. Eyes locked on the rim, he bent his knees and sent the ball arcing through the air. The previous year, their team trainer told him he figured Ty to be somewhere between fifty and five hundred jump shots away from total knee replacement. From that day on, Ty stayed well within the arc, and he made damn sure his feet never left the floor.

Palming the ball, he tucked it firmly against his hip and trudged to the foul line. He was on number forty-three of the hundred free throws he'd assigned himself.

His day had been chock-full. Wall-to-wall meetings, videos to review, phone calls, and a particularly excruciating staff meeting that included the public relations director, who'd been avoiding him for days. For a woman who prided herself on being conspicuous, she had a maddening way of disappearing each time she happened to catch sight of him.

Practice seemed to drag. The season was about to start, and the team was still off tempo. His assistant coaches were short-tempered, the players in turns petulant and belligerent. Fifteen minutes into a forty-minute scrimmage, his head throbbed from the cacophony of squeaking shoes, screeching whistles, and shouts from the sidelines.

Smooth as silk. Smooth as silk.

The mantra had started as a playground brag back in middle school, became his lucky bit of braggadocio in high school, then an integral part of his ritual with his introduction to Division I ball. *Smooth as silk*.

The words ran through his mind as he cocked his arm. *Smooth as silk*.

Bend. Extend. Release. The ball sailed through the still air. Number forty-three's trajectory appeared to be spot-on.

Retrieving the ball, he dribbled as he walked back to the line. How many nights had he spent shooting hoops rather than going home to Mari? Too many. Especially at the end. He'd been stupid enough to think things would even out in his life with Mari gone. He hadn't counted on Hurricane Millie blowing through.

Placing his finger over the tiny valve hole on the ball, he stared down at the gleaming hardwood. He didn't want to think about Millie now. He wanted to clear his head. A twisted part of him wished his love life had been this crappy back in his playing days, because his free throw average had never been higher.

Smooth as silk. Bounce, bounce, bounce.

Smooth as silk. Spin and settle.

Smooth as silk. Sight the shot.

Smooth as silk. Bend, extend, release.

"Forty-four."

He stiffened as her throaty voice filled the small practice gym. Snagging the ball, he propped it against his hip. Without looking toward the door, he sauntered back to the foul line to prepare for number forty-five. "How long have you been watching?"

"Since I saw everyone leave but you."

He nodded but kept his eyes locked on the goal. "Getting a few in."

"Looking good."

The click of her heels echoed off cinder-block walls. He didn't dare look, but in his mind, he saw the shiny, red stiletto she'd swung off the tip of her toes through the whole damn meeting. The very stilettos he'd been fantasizing about all evening.

He ran through his ritual without missing a dribble. His mantra bounced around in his head, but this time, the words had little to do with tossing a ball through a hoop.

Smooth as silk.

Smooth as silk.

Smooth as silk.

He growled long and loud when he overshot. The ball hit the back of the rim with a sickening thud, then caromed toward the foldaway bleachers. Millie sat on the lowest row, her long legs crossed, that damn shoe dangling off the end of her foot again.

"What do you want?" Ty cringed even as the words left his mouth, but goddamn, the woman was making him crazy. One minute, she was hiding from him; the next, she was invading his sacred space. If he couldn't escape her here, then no place was safe.

"I want you to make the next one."

He slid her a side-eye known to make guys who stood more than six foot six tremble, but she only gave him the kind of encouraging smile one saved for toddlers refusing to eat peas. Collecting the ball, he stalked over to her.

"I don't get the game, Millie."

She looked taken aback for a moment, then lifted one shoulder in a half shrug. "Well, I don't pretend to know all the nuances, but I think you have five people on each team, and they run up and down the court bouncing a ball and throw it into the basket thingy." She waved a hand at the goal like some kind of game show hostess. "Whoever has the most points at the end of playtime wins."

He fought the urge to smile at her blatant oversimplification of the sport he'd built his life around. "Funny."

She sent him a look so wide-eyed and guileless he momentarily doubted his skepticism. "Did I not get it right? I get this one mixed up with the kicking one all the time."

But he wasn't buying. "The game with you and me, Millie. I don't get this…whatever we're doing."

She took the time to uncross her legs, wiggle her shoe back onto her foot, then restart the entire process with the other leg topping and the other shoe dangling. "We're having a torrid affair," she whispered in a conspiratorial tone. "Complete with hot sex and various forms of takeout foods."

"Yeah, well, not tonight. I have a headache." No lie. The pounding was back with a vengeance. And so was the need to finish taking his foul shots.

He'd lined up number forty-six and chanted through two rounds of "smooth as silk" before he heard the click of her heels again. But instead of retreating, she was coming closer. Gripping the ball so hard, his fingers dimpled the rubber, he glanced over his shoulder to find her standing on the three-point line.

"No hard-soled shoes on the court," he snapped.

Without taking her eyes off him, Millie stepped out

of the sky-high heels. Her toes were polished the purple of grape jelly. She shifted her weight from one foot to the other, then covered the insole of her left foot with her right. He met her disconcertingly direct gaze and blew out a long breath. She obviously wasn't going anywhere until she was damn good and ready. "What?" he prompted.

"I like my life, Ty. I live exactly the way I want to."

"Good for you."

She ignored his snide commentary. "I like my house, my stuff, my friends, my time." She paused, searching for words. "I have no plans to change anytime soon."

"Did I ask you to change anything?"

Millie gave him a small, sad smile. "No, you'd never ask me to, but they would change. I'm not sure I want them to."

"So…" He groped for comprehension, but it remained inches out of reach. Giving his head a shake, he held up a hand in defeat. "Yeah, I don't know what you're saying."

"I'm saying I need to do this in my own way. In my own time," she said quietly. "But I like you. Did I mention that?"

The weight inside him lifted, but he approached her confession with caution. "No. I don't think you did."

"I do." She spoke firmly enough to chase his doubts away. At least for the moment.

"I'm glad. I like you too."

She smiled, then bent to scoop up her shoes. "I'm happy we got that settled." Jerking her head toward the bleachers, she quirked an eyebrow. "Mind if I watch? I'm kind of a team sports voyeur."

"I don't know if you noticed, but I don't really have a team out here."

Her smile spread wide enough to light her eyes with mischief. "I don't know if you noticed, but you're really the only one I like watching."

———∿∿∿———

She woke up in his bed. Millie tried not to think of her presence there as anything more than an inevitable outcome fulfilled. As she suspected, once she got comfortable in his place, she didn't want to leave. After the night they spent tearing up the sheets, she'd claimed she was too exhausted to be roused for breakfast. He'd insisted they share the most important meal of the day. They compromised by eating in bed. She knew she would spend the rest of the day thinking about how incredibly hot Ty Ransom looked when he was hand-feeding her bits of buttered toast.

They'd lolled around naked all morning, leaving a sprinkle of crumbs to add to the torn condom wrappers on his nightstand. Three wrappers. By her calculations, he had maybe five or six. That is if he'd started off with a new box. A half dozen in his arsenal, exactly eleven in hers. She figured at this rate of consumption, they had approximately five more nights together. Longer, if she could come up with more creative delay tactics. Or if Avery happened to make another commando run on health services.

Minutes before noon, he'd kissed her on the mouth, slapped her on the ass, and rolled out of bed. "Up. Up."

Millie sighed and groaned, muscles she'd forgotten

she had protesting as she flipped over. "Smack my ass again, and I might bite you."

"Gotta get up," he said, leveling a stern look at her. "We'll play your kinky games later."

She snorted. "If you're lucky."

"Gotten lucky once already this morning. If you hurry, we can take an extra lucky shower together."

Millie bit her lip, genuinely torn. She wanted nothing more than to slip into his big glassed-in shower and lather him up, but water play might lead to the use of condom number four, and she wasn't sure about stretching her game plan yet.

"You go ahead. I'll laze around here, then shower when I get home."

Ty scowled, displeased by her answer. "You sure?"

She nodded, then treated him to her slyest smile. "While you're getting all hot and sweaty in a not-so-fun way, I may take a bubble bath and read my naughty book."

His eyes narrowed to slits. "You know, you have a cruel streak a mile wide."

"I know." She rolled over as he rose, immediately claiming the spot warmed by his body heat. "It's one of the things you like about me."

Completely unselfconscious, he strolled to his dresser and pulled out a pair of boxer briefs. "You know, I thought you were making the story thing up."

"Nope." She chuckled to cover the low internal purr the sight of his taut ass spurred. "Maybe one day I'll loan you my book."

He cocked an eyebrow as he stepped into the adjoining bath. "I like it better when you read to me."

"Okay, but next time, no going off the rails," she called after him.

He leaned back enough to poke his head around the doorframe and flashed a wicked grin "Going off the rails is the best part."

Seconds later, she heard the rush of water spraying from the shower jets and fell back against the flattened pillows. He had a practice to run. The last Saturday practice before the tournaments leading into the regular season began. The one and only Saturday morning Millie might get to spend with him. And it had been perfect. Damn him.

He wasn't going to go for the phone sex thing anymore. She got that. She admitted it was a little weird, considering they weren't thousands of miles apart now. But maybe he'd go for sexting. Fun and flirty, and sexting wouldn't cost any condoms.

As if sensing the direction of her thoughts, his cell began to vibrate. Millie watched the phone skitter along the top of the nightstand but made no move to answer the call. Ty had silenced more than one since he'd kidnapped her the night before. This one could wait as well. She wasn't his secretary.

Sighing, Millie fixated on a spot on the ceiling and let her vision grow fuzzy as she tried to make heads or tails of her situation. They'd had too much time and distance at first, and now she couldn't get enough. Ty was pushing, and he was pushing hard. Admittedly, a part of her liked his persistence. But the other part, the one she relied on more than her mutinous heart, was wary.

He'd swooped before she could escape the previous night and blown right through her token resistance.

She'd managed to buy a little time when Danny McMillan caught them in the hall and invited them to join him and Kate for dinner. All Millie could do was smother her smile as she watched Ty weigh the pros and cons of declining the invitation. In the end, he accepted on their behalf but made up for lost time when he got her alone. In truth, she hadn't been any better than he was at hiding his impatience. The second they were ensconced in his car, she practically climbed into his lap.

Millie was still mentally recapping some of the highlights of the previous evening when he appeared a scant few minutes later.

"So I figure I'll come by about six to pick you up," he announced, strolling into the room in boxer briefs molded to every contour of his narrow ass and thick thighs. "I'm in the mood for a steak. All this strenuous activity makes me crave red meat."

His presumptuousness inflamed her. It also made her stomach do a squiggly dance that left her feeling weak and vaguely ashamed. She wanted a steak too, but if she didn't hold out at least enough to make him ask her properly, she'd be hearing Avery's lecture on feminine self-determination in her head for the rest of the night.

"I don't recall agreeing to have dinner tonight."

"You'll probably get hungry at some point. I'm good with toast, but buttered bread isn't going to hold you."

"I don't recall agreeing to have dinner with *you* tonight," she reiterated.

He shrugged and pulled a pair of dark-green nylon track pants from a hanger. "I think we should have dinner together tonight. If steak doesn't appeal to you, I'm open to negotiation." Undeterred, he carried his fistfuls of clothing back to the bed. "Maybe we can rent a movie or something. I see the kids getting DVDs out of those box things all the time."

His phone began to buzz again, but he paid it no mind as he patiently waited for her response.

She glanced at the screen, saw Mari's face, then eyeballed him. He stood in the middle of the room wearing nothing but briefs that left little to the imagination, holding the pants as if he needed her say-so to put them on. Looking past him, she spotted a dozen pairs exactly like them hanging in an orderly row in the closet. A flash flood of feminine resentment rose in her.

Life seemed so easy for them. *I'm a man. I don't have to think about what to wear, but I do think I want a steak. I'm picking you up at six. We'll have dinner, then sex. Lots of sex. So much sex you won't be able to walk right or think right or keep a decent stash of rubbers on hand.*

He might as well have said, *I'm going to pick you up, fill you up, use you up, and then I'll shrug and hike up my pants and go on home to my freaking McMansion and watch sports and drink scotch.*

Then I'll make you fall in love with me.

And in the end, I'll leave you when someone shinier comes along.

"No, thanks," she answered tersely, barely aware the last bit of conversation had taken place entirely in her head. Swinging her legs over the edge of the bed, she started to gather the clothes she'd discarded with such fervor the night before.

Like an animal scenting danger, Ty stood stockstill before starting a cautious approach. "No thanks to the steak?"

"To all of it. I'm busy tonight," she said, stepping into the pale-peach panties he hadn't even bothered to admire.

"Busy."

He repeated the word as if the syllables were entirely new to his vocabulary. In all fairness, rejection was probably an unfamiliar concept. After all, he'd been married for a few years, and she'd bet he hadn't struck out often on the dating scene when he was single. But she wasn't the kind of woman who invited assumptions on her time or her person. If he wanted to spend time with her, the man was going to have to figure that out sooner rather than later. She spotted her bra half-hidden under the bench at the foot of the giant bed and stooped to retrieve it.

"I'm sorry. Did something happen?" Ty took another step in her direction but stopped when she popped up, the expensive bits of lace and satin crushed in her hand. He cocked his head, a look of baffled bewilderment overtaking his expression. "Are you mad at me?"

"Nope."

He blew out a breath. "Well, that was convincing."

Shrugging into the bra, she avoided his gaze as she untwisted the straps. "We've had the conversation about presumptions before. You don't dictate my time, Ty. You don't get to assume I want to have dinner with you tonight."

He let loose with another exasperated breath. "Sorry."

He bit the word off. The fixer in her wanted to stop him before he went a word further and point out all the tactical errors he was making, but the woman in her wasn't about to buy the man a clue if he didn't already own one. A teeny part of her felt sorry for the oblivious creature when he went on in a manner several shades short of placating.

"Would you like to have dinner with me tonight, Millicent?"

"No. Thank you." She added the last bit with a saccharine-sweet smile. "I have other plans."

"Other plans to do what?" he persisted.

All shreds of sympathy gone, she pulled on her blouse and started buttoning. "Well, first I plan to make a list of all the things I do that are none of your damn business."

He was beside her in three long strides. His hand closed around her elbow, stilling her motions.

Her gaze flew to his. "Okay, so presumption, sarcasm, and effrontery haven't been effective tools. Are we resorting to physical intimidation now?"

As expected, he released her before she could draw her next breath, but he didn't step away. Millie added a point to the deficit he'd been running. She admired a man who stood his ground.

"I'm not trying to intimidate you, nor do I mean to make presumptions."

"God, it's sexy when you look all muscly jock guy, but then you use your fifty-cent words," she said, fluttering her eyelashes at him in a way that could only be construed as mocking.

"They were your vocabulary words, Mil. I was only trying to explain myself," he retorted.

"And doing a really crappy job."

"I don't know why I have to explain at all," he cried. Throwing his hands in the air, he spun away from her and stalked to the dresser. "All I wanted to do was have dinner with you."

She watched as he yanked a gray athletic department T-shirt from the drawer and shook the wrinkles from the fabric. "Are you afraid of being alone or something?" she asked.

His head snapped back as if she'd slapped him. "What?"

Millie shrugged, then bent to grab her pants from the floor. Without pausing to give the wrinkles a second thought, she plunged one foot into a twisted leg opening. Beyond caring about how graceless she might look, she stumbled around until she got the other leg lined up and then gave a couple of good hops to yank them into place.

"Look at you. You've been divorced less than a week, and you're trying to line up a date for every night."

"I'm not lining up dates. I'm trying to be with you."

"Right, because I am the date du jour," she said, fastening the waistband.

He paused, the sleeves wrapped around his thick biceps but the body of the shirt suspended above his head. He blinked, then gave his head a dismissive shake before he pulled the shirt down over his head. "Christ, you must really have a low opinion of yourself."

The commentary was muffled, but his meaning was unmistakable. Millie smirked at the implication. Fully clothed, she felt more prepared to see this battle through to its inevitable end. She opened her mouth to blast him, and his phone went off again. Annoyed, she crossed her arms over her chest and jerked her chin toward the nightstand. "Your ex-wife is calling again. Why don't you answer? Maybe you can get her to go for a nice, juicy steak with you."

He spared the phone a quick glance, then grimaced. "No."

His too-quick answer made her realize he knew exactly who was calling. She kept the smirk firmly in place as she strolled toward the bedroom door where her shoes lay cast aside, but only because she was worried her chin might wobble if she didn't. "Ah, been there, done that?"

"Got the divorce papers as a souvenir."

Millie blinked in surprise, then frowned at the phone. "Why is Mari calling you?"

"Damned if I know." He stepped into the track pants and settled the waistband low on his hips. "She's been calling for the last couple of days."

"What does she want?"

He let one shoulder rise and fall as he pulled a pair of athletic socks from a drawer. "No idea."

"You aren't answering?"

He shook his head. "Don't see the point. Mari and I are done. So done," he added, dropping onto the bench at the foot of the bed. "Papers are signed, she got the settlement she wanted but didn't deserve, and I have nothing else to say."

She eyed him as she wriggled her toes into her shoes. "Aren't you the least bit curious?"

At last, Ty looked up and met her gaze. "No. Not at all."

"I hear she and Dante may be on the downhill slide."

"I don't care," he replied stubbornly.

"You just cut her out of your life? Easy as that?"

Bending over, he slipped a sock over his toes. "I didn't cut her out. She left."

"Right, but you're not even a little curious about what she wants?"

He turned his attention to the other foot. "No. I'm really not." He snorted softly. "But maybe later on, when I'm all alone and so scared, I might be tempted."

Millie frowned as she tried to puzzle the last part out. "Was that some kind of threat or something?"

"No, it was more of that sarcasm you like so much," he said, placing both feet square on the floor before looking up at her again. "But if threats work for you, I might be able to muster one."

"No, they don't."

He nodded as if digesting the information, then pressed his hands to his knees and stood. "Well, then. I should get you home so I can get to practice and you can start on that list of yours." He slid his sock-clad feet into a pair of athletic sandals, snatched up a duffel bag he had packed and waiting beside the dresser, and swung the strap over his shoulder. "Later on, I'll try to get some practice in on being alone. But, Millie, there are only certain games I like to play. Don't tempt me into proving your theory about not being alone.

"Now, that was a threat," he added as he sauntered past her, the bag bumping against his hip with each step. Pausing outside the bedroom door, he looked back at her. "How'd I do?"

Though she wasn't quite done being indignant, Millie also knew Ty had every right to be pissy with her. She was disgusted with herself. She, Millie Jensen, was spewing so much unmitigated bullshit in the poor man's direction, she was half-amazed he hadn't bolted already. This wasn't like her. She was a woman who prided herself on living a life of no spin. And now, she was spiraling out of control.

She drummed her fingernails on the sticky bar top and waited as a blond bartender dressed in short shorts and a Warriors basketball tank top chopped off below her perky breasts mixed her daiquiri. Avery sat at a tall table in the corner, holding their spot and grimacing into her scotch. Kate was running her own practice tonight, so she was unavailable for the intervention Millie called for herself. Her lips thinned into a straight line as she watched the bartender add a skewer of fruit to the tall glass. This was an emergency. Avery and her new age BS would have to do.

A couple of beery undergrads jostled for position behind her. One of them caught her on the arm as she was pushing away from the bar, drink in hand. Sticky, icy sludge sloshed over her knuckles. She gave the culprit her best "drop dead" look. The kid straightened up fast, swallowed hard, and mumbled a gruff, "Sorry, ma'am."

Millie huffed as she pushed past them, her sights set on the tiny table. When had she gotten used to being called *ma'am*? Why was she such an ungodly mess these days? Wasn't sex supposed to make a person feel all upbeat and whistle-y? Where the hell did Avery find those god-awful patchwork skirts?

Millie voiced the last question, and Avery treated her to a surprisingly sharp-edged smile. "I'd say you need to get laid, but the sex doesn't seem to be doing you any good." She swirled the amber liquid in her glass, then placed it carefully on the cardboard coaster without taking a sip. "What's the matter? Ty not living up to his hype?"

"No," Millie snapped, instantly defensive. "Ty's great." In the next second, Avery's choice of words sank in. "Hype? You've heard hype about how good Ty is in bed?"

"Should I have?"

"You said it," Millie pointed out.

They both paused, and Millie could see Avery playing the exchange back in her head. Finally, Avery shrugged. "A turn of phrase."

Millie eyed her friend closely. Creative phrasing was a possibility. As an associate professor in the English department, Avery loved words and wordplay. Therefore, word choice was important to her. She wouldn't have said *hype* unless she'd heard some hint of hype. Taking a sip of her drink, Millie pondered the possible outlets for said hype. Media? Whispers in the student body? Were faculty members speculating about Ty's member?

"What hype, Avery?"

Pushing her wild curls back from her face, Avery settled a startlingly direct gaze on her. "The hype you built up in your head."

"My head?"

"The guy was gone for six weeks. First, the two of you were burning up the mobile minutes, then not talking at all. I have to tell you, this is the weirdest game of cat and mouse I've ever seen." She paused long enough to lift her glass in a mocking salute. "Including in cartoons."

"Ha-ha."

Avery took a sip of the scotch, grimaced, then set

the glass down. "Seriously. I'm not sure which of you is the cat and which the mouse. I figure I'll wait to see which one gets the anvil dropped on their head." She sat back, her smile making it clear she was pleased with her deductive reasoning. "Usually happens to the cat."

"I think you're confusing a cat with a coyote."

Avery shrugged. "Whatever." She leaned in. "Tell Dr. Preston why you invited her here tonight."

"I need to talk to you about those hideous skirts of yours."

"Millie."

Regardless of her opinions on Avery's style choices, the woman could switch on the stern-professor stare when she needed to. And Millie felt compelled to tap her inner adolescent. "What?"

"Stop talking about my clothes, and tell me what crawled up your ass." Avery frowned. "Or maybe the problem isn't something has, but rather someone hasn't?" Before Millie could confirm or deny her friend's theorizing, Avery plowed ahead. "Has he cut you off?" She stared at Millie in wide-eyed wonder. "I mean, we assumed after he tossed you over his shoulder and took you back to his man cave you two were doing it like minks, but maybe not. Is that the trouble? You're not doing it?"

"First of all, stop saying 'doing it' like you're fifteen or something. Second, yes, we are."

Avery pounced. "But the trouble is sex." She leaned in closer. "Am I right?"

Millie didn't answer. Instead, she stoppered the end of her straw with her fingertip, trapping some of the icy concoction in a vacuum seal.

"Don't make me take your slushie away from you," Avery warned.

"The sex is fine. Good. Great," Millie amended, pulling the straw from the drink. "More than great. It's sex like I haven't sexed in…well, ever." She moved her finger, and the contents of the straw slithered back into the glass.

"I'm sensing a big 'but' here." Avery held up a hand to stave off any rejoinder. "Not that you or Ty have big butts. As a matter of fact, I think we could safely say you make one of the most tight-assed couples ever."

Millie smirked, amused by her friend's wordplay. "Thanks."

"What's the issue?"

Sucking in a breath, Millie tried to compose her jangled nerves before she answered. "Me."

Avery snorted. "Oh, well, yeah. Shocker."

She smiled as she lifted her drink, but it was a grim smile of acknowledgment. "I just… He's all over me."

"The horror!"

Her friend's shocked gasp made Millie chuckle, but there was no stopping her now that the wheels were in motion. "He wants to go to dinner. Stay the night. Sit on the couch and watch movies in sweatpants, for cripes' sake," she complained.

"The bastard. How can a monster like this be running loose out in the world?"

"And he's all presumptuous about us. Like I'm supposed to be waiting around until I can see him."

"Well, you know I don't approve of the waiting on a man thing, but in all honesty, Mil, it's not like you've got something else going on right now."

Avery's switch from mockery to logic revved Millie's indignation. "He probably only has about five condoms left. Six tops. Add those to my eleven, and at the rate we're going, we're going to burn through them all by next week, and everything will be over!"

The barroom hubbub hummed all around them, but in the few seconds following her outburst, Millie could only hear the low whoosh of her own blood in her ears.

Clearly taken aback, Avery sat up straighter on her stool. She tipped her head to the side like an inquisitive bird. "Pardon me?"

Mortified, Millie snatched her glass from the table and took a long, brain-numbing hit of the frozen concoction. "Never mind," she rasped, pressing the heel of her hand to her forehead to quell the ache in her frontal lobe.

"Millie, are you trying to play by those idiotic dating rules or something? Because if you are, I think you messed up one of the crucial bits when you fucked him."

Blinking her way through the ebb of the brain freeze, Millie gave her head a subtle shake. "I'm not playing any stupid games."

"But you are keeping track of the number of condoms you've used?" When Millie didn't answer, Avery searched her face as if she might find the answer to all Millie's anxieties in her pores. But rather than teasing her, Avery pitched her voice low and soft. "If you're worried about exhausting your supply, I could always lift a couple dozen on my next run through the health services building."

To her horror, Millie nearly burst into tears at the offer. Though she managed to hold back, she did reach across the table to give Avery's hand a squeeze. On the surface, they were as similar as chalk and cheese, but a good friend was a good friend. And a great friend was one who was willing to steal government-subsidized rubbers for you without batting an eyelash.

"No. Thank you," she said, adding another squeeze of gratitude before taking her hand back. "The condom thing is just something I do." She looked away, a little ashamed of what she was about to admit. "I don't like to get too…involved. If I put a time limit on things or set up some kind of endgame—"

"The condom countdown is your out," Avery concluded. "Out of condoms, and you're out."

"I don't want to get too invested," Millie said in a rush. The need to explain herself both peeved and overwhelmed her. "He's younger than I am. He's newly divorced. One day, he's gonna want kids, and I can't give them to him." The justifications spilled out of her like milk from a tipped cup. "I see no point in either of us getting too attached—"

"In *you* getting too attached," Avery interrupted. "You're planning an out so you don't risk actually, you know, falling in love with the guy." She scoffed at the thought, then studied Millie narrowly. "I've got a thousand words to describe you, but I never thought 'coward' would be one of them."

"I'm not a coward," Millie retorted.

"Then be straight with the guy. Say, 'Hey, Ty, I really like you, and the sex is super awesome, but I don't want to have dinner with you because I'm scared you won't like the way I chew. I can't watch a movie with you because you might want to hold my hand. Oh, and mainly, I can't fall in love with you because I don't think I'm good enough for you.'"

"Bullshit." The word fired out of her like a cannonball. "It's not that I don't think I'm good enough."

"Then he's not good enough for you?" Avery challenged.

"I'm not saying anyone is undeserving. We're just two people at different places in their lives."

"I'll say." Avery picked up the tumbler of scotch and tossed back its contents. "He's in the dark, and you're in denial." She slid from the stool, plucked a wad of cash from a pocket hidden in the depth of her skirt, and tossed a few bills on the table. "You want my advice, Millie? Stop being a girl, and act like a woman. Tell the man what you are willing to give and what you want from him. If the two of you can't come to some rational agreement without counting condoms and pretending you prefer Lean Cuisines to having dinner with the man, then end it now. Not only is ignoring his feelings a shitty thing to do to him and demeaning to yourself, it's also an insult to everyone who is waiting for the chance at happiness you're too chickenshit to take."

Millie was struck by the flash of fury she saw in her friend's eyes. She reached out and caught her arm. "Avery, wait—"

A sad shadow of a smile curved her friend's lips. "We're okay, Millie. Or we will be." She pushed her wild mass of hair back with her free hand. "I just don't know if I can listen to you throw away a chance at the thing some of us have been waiting for our whole lives." She shook off Millie's grip and ducked into the thick of the Saturday night crowd.

"Avery!" Millie called, but her voice was muffled by the crowd. It was futile.

Settling back to the table, she eyed her mostly untouched drink morosely. The daiquiri was red and thick and sickeningly sweet, the fruit skewer sticking out of the top unappetizing. She spotted Avery's empty glass, and a coil of regret twisted inside her. Fishing a twenty from her wallet, she pursed her lips as she scanned the crowd for a likely looking lad. Spotting the boy who'd bumped into her earlier, she waved him over to the table.

The young man approached, his expression wary but disconcertingly hopeful. Stifling a sigh, Millie fixed him with a thoroughly patronizing smile. "Stand down, junior. I won't be teaching you the ways of the world tonight."

Hope and fear melted into utter confusion. "Ma'am."

She held up the twenty. "If you get the nice lady a double Dewar's straight up, you can keep the change for your piggy bank."

The boy ran off with her cash, and she slumped the slightest bit. Avery was right. She needed to grow up and be honest with Ty about what she wanted from their relationship and what he might expect from her. When they were done, they'd be done. No reason she shouldn't enjoy the ride until then.

She stared off into space, half wondering if Avery included herself in her statement about people waiting for a chance at happiness, and the other half worried her errand boy had made off with her twenty bucks, leaving her nothing but a fruity drink in which to drown her sorrows. She was reaching for the tall glass when someone slammed a highball down on the table beside her hand.

"Here you go!" her personal waiter exclaimed, clearly proud to have accomplished his mission.

"Thanks, sugar." Taking the glass, she toasted him with it as he hurried back to his friends. Staring hard at the pungent liquor, she muttered, "Look me up when your beard fills in," and downed the drink with a flick of her wrist.

Chapter 15

TY HADN'T CALLED MILLIE. HE DIDN'T TEXT, OR EMAIL, OR send up a smoke signal. He'd switched his phone off, both to save himself from temptation and because his ex-wife kept calling but hanging up without leaving a message. As much as he wanted to call Millie, he felt absolutely no compulsion to call Mari back. They'd said everything they needed to say to each other weeks ago, and what they'd said had been pitifully little. If whatever she had to say was important, she'd eventually give him a hint.

The fact that he had such an easy time ignoring the girl he'd married but couldn't trust himself not to prostrate himself at Millie's feet spoke volumes. He didn't allow himself to drive past Millie's house, even if the little bungalow was sort of on his way home.

She'd set up pick after pick, using one lame excuse after another to stop their relationship from progressing past square one. Fine. He'd wait her out. Riding a big, fat pile of mad, he showered, changed into a pair of the baggy shorts Millie hated so much, and went to the fridge to rustle up something to eat.

The only things he found were cartons of leftover Thai food.

Letting the door slam shut, he dug his phone from the pocket of his shorts, powered up, and ignored the series of alerts flashing across the screen. Barely paying attention, he scrolled to the number for his favorite pizza joint. Thanks to the magic of caller ID, his pal Mickey was making up a large coach's special before Ty disconnected.

Almost immediately, the damn thing rang. Blowing out a sigh, he stared at Mari's smiling face. The phone buzzed and bleated, but he didn't take the call. A few seconds later, the persistent noise stopped. Eyes locked on the Warrior logo on his wallpaper, he waited for a voicemail alert. The chime never came. Neither did a text, which was odd. If Mari was truly intent on speaking to him, she'd have no compunction about pulling out all the stops. When they were married, she'd had no problem upgrading a toilet paper run into the mobile equivalent of an all-points bulletin.

Restless and reluctant to stray too close to the wet bar, he stayed in the kitchen. He hopped up on the counter, because he had no woman around to tell him not to. To pass the time, he scrolled through the headlines on his tablet. He'd worked his way down to the entertainment section and resorted to tapping on a quiz designed to reveal which *Full House* character he was when the doorbell rang.

"Oh, thank God." He hopped down, grabbed his wallet, and beat a path toward the front door. "Man, you have no idea how close I came to being Uncle Jes—"

He stopped when he found Millie standing on his welcome mat. Sadly, without a pizza. Gripping the edge of the door, he took a half step back before he caught himself. His ears burned, but he tried to pretend he answered the door shirtless every damn day.

"Hey."

"So here's the thing," she said, pushing past him without further preamble. "I'm not a 'we' kind of person. I don't like other people making plans for me. I don't...function as a unit." She spun on her heel, lost her balance, but corrected before he could even get the door closed. "This is not a long-term thing for either of us. I like you. You like me. I'd like us to still like each other after all this is done." She waved a hand in an all-encompassing gesture. "We probably won't like each other much if we let things get all messy and emotional, so here's what I'm proposing..."

She paused, and he crossed his arms over his chest. Her eyes gleamed in the light from the chandelier. "Are you with me so far?"

"I'm riveted."

And he was. No power in heaven or on earth could distract him from hearing this mysterious "proposal" of hers. Not even the roar of a muffler-less motor pulling to a stop in his driveway. He made an impatient gesture for her to continue.

"How many condoms do you have?" she asked.

Within seconds of showing up, she threw him completely off his game. Letting his arms fall to his sides, he moved toward her right as the doorbell rang. "What?"

Millie glanced from him to the door, then back again. "Oh. You had plans." Holding up both hands as if to indicate a foul, she tried to shrug the strap of her bag back up to her shoulder. When she started for the door, he shifted to block her path. "Ah! Right. Sorry." She swung around and took off into the house. "I'll go out through the back. We'll talk tomorrow."

He caught her arm. "That's the pizza guy."

She looked up, her eyes wide but brightening. "Pizza guy?"

Ty was ninety-nine percent sure that if she could see the flash of hope in her own face, she'd have bolted for the door and never come back. The woman had no idea how much she gave away by working so hard to conceal even the smallest hint of emotion.

"Pizza guy," he repeated as the bell rang again. "Stay. We'll have pizza—" A mulish frown tugged at the corners of her mouth, and he backpedaled. "*I'll* have pizza, and you can tell me all about your proposed safe-sex campaign." She huffed a laugh, and he gently unfurled his hand, relaxing his hold on her millimeter by millimeter. "Okay?"

His phone started blaring. He cast an exasperated look at his pocket as the delivery driver resorted to pounding on the door with his fist.

Millie took pity on him and nodded. "Go ahead."

Frazzled and more than a little cranky, he groped through the fabric of his shorts for the mute button as he rushed for the door. The delivery man was two steps down the front walk and spewing a string of obscenities into his own cell by the time Ty flew out the door calling, "Sorry, man. Sorry."

He gave the frizzy-haired Dungeons and Dragons–type a conciliatory pat on the arm as he caught up to him. The kid ended his call without another word, his jaw falling slack as he tilted his head farther back to look him in the eye.

"No problem," he mumbled.

Flipping open his wallet, Ty extracted two twenties and extended them. "Here. Keep the change."

"Oh. Well, cool. Thanks." He almost tore the Velcro flap off the thermal bag in his haste to exchange his burden for a hefty tip. "Have a good night," he called as he headed for the beater parked in the drive.

Ty nodded to the kid's back and muttered, "Yeah, could go either way," under his breath as he returned to the house.

He found Millie perched on one of the tall bar stools lined up at the island. Ty gave his head a shake, then nodded toward the farmhouse table in what Mari liked to call the breakfast nook. "Let's go to the table. You can lay it all out for me."

He tucked a roll of paper towels under his arm and carried everything over to the table. Millie hadn't budged from the stool. Raising a challenging eyebrow, he gestured to the refrigerator. "Help yourself to whatever you want. I'm gonna grab a shirt."

He was halfway down the hall when he heard her call out, "Don't bother on my account," in a soft singsong.

Smiling, he ducked his head as he dodged into his bedroom. Afraid she might change her mind and bolt, he didn't waste time indulging his vanity. He yanked a clean T-shirt from his drawer and pulled the comforting cotton over his head as he walked back toward the kitchen.

She sat at the table, rolling an unopened bottle of water between her hands. He paused, taking the opportunity to drink her in. Her brow was furrowed. Faint lines radiated from the corners of her eyes. Her hair blazed like a bonfire, but her skin was so fair he could see the shadowy blue lines of her veins at her temple. As if sensing his stare, she set the bottle on the table abruptly and wiped all traces of pensiveness from her expression.

"I probably should have called first." She twisted her lips into an apologetic smile, but her eyes didn't light. "Talk about making assumptions, huh?"

"No problem. I don't have the hang-ups about it some people do."

Ty grabbed a bottle of water for himself, then joined her at the table. Straddling a chair, he flipped back the lid on the box, and the heady aroma of spicy sauce and melted cheese came rushing out. He took a deep hit, then beamed as he reached for the roll of towels and tore one free. Being a gentleman and all, he offered the rectangle to Millie, but she shook her head, her nose wrinkling as she stared into the box.

"Is that chicken?" she asked.

"Fra diavolo sauce, three cheeses, pepperoncini, spicy chicken, peppers, and onions." He raised his eyebrows and fixed her with a pointed look. "I wasn't expecting company."

She blinked and took a cautious sniff. "I guess not. Trying to hold people off for the next week or so, or practicing to become a dragon?"

"It's good. You should try a slice."

She snorted at his earnest encouragement. "Not without a truckload of antacids on hand." She nudged the box toward him with her index finger. "What's the white stuff?"

Ty smiled as he lifted a slice from the box. "A drizzle of ranch dressing to offset the spiciness." He toasted her with the pizza. "Mind if I...?"

"No, go right ahead." She laughed, shaking her head in what looked like amused wonder as he took a big bite.

The five-alarm flavors burst into fire on his tongue, but the taste explosion was nothing compared to the slow burn of curiosity snaking through him. "So…" He chewed around the word but waited until he swallowed to follow up. "How many condoms do I have?"

A peachy blush rose up her throat and stained her cheeks, but Millie didn't look away. "Yes. How many?"

He surveyed the slice in his hand as if he might have the exact figure stashed under a bit of pepperoncini. "Why?"

"Because I think we need a way to measure what would be a reasonable amount of time for this…relationship to carry on. I figured we could gauge it in condoms."

He gaped at her, amazed she actually managed to vocalize the last bit with an air of assurance that suggested her scheme was completely reasonable. But what truly rankled him was her insistence on taking the end of their relationship as a foregone conclusion.

"Why aren't we a long-term thing?"

"What?"

"You said earlier we weren't a long-term thing and we wouldn't want our relationship to get all messy and emotional." Ty forced himself to take another bite even though his appetite had taken a swift nosedive. He knew the fire burning in his chest and gut had nothing to do with the combination of toppings he'd ordered and everything to do with her, but he'd be damned if he let her think he couldn't take the heat. "Why not?"

Her eyes widened, and she gave her head one of those little shakes meant to make him feel like he was the crazy one, but he wasn't buying in.

"How come you get to walk in here and tell me the relationship I'm in isn't long-term?" He used the half-eaten slice of pizza to point to his chest. "I'm in this too. I get a say." He fixed her with an unwavering stare. "And I say it sounds like you're the one making plans and assumptions."

Those vibrant eyes narrowed. "Don't try to spin me."

"Stop trying to run the clock out."

Millie sniffed, plucked a loose pepperoncini from the box, and popped the spicy tidbit into her mouth. He watched as she chewed the tiny morsel. Of course he watched. She knew he would. But being aware he'd stepped into quicksand wouldn't give him any leverage when he had to pull himself out. Ty stared at her lips, recalling exactly how soft and pliant they could be, imagining them parting, picturing them as they closed around his dick.

Tearing his gaze away was almost physically painful, but he did what he had to do. "Six," he answered tersely.

Millie nodded. "I knew we'd gone through a few. I wasn't sure how many you had to start."

"Buying anything more than one box seemed like tempting fate, but you know I can get more."

"I was hoping we could go by the honor system."

He shook his head. "I have no issue with playing dirty."

"Ty, please."

Appetite completely gone, Ty tossed the uneaten pizza into the box. "I don't get this. What is your issue with seeing where things go?"

"Seeing where things go?" She repeated his words back to him as if he'd asked the most ridiculous question in the world. "My *issue* is it's messy." She tore a section of towel from the roll and wiped the tips of her fingers with meticulous care. "I deal with messes all day long. The last thing I want is a mess when I go home. That's why I pay for a cleaning service, a guy who mows my lawn, and have a standing appointment to get my color done every four weeks." She waved a hand toward her hair. "I like order in *my* world. I like to know what's going to happen when."

He shoved his chair back with enough force to make the legs squeal against the tile. Millie flinched a little but recovered quickly, of course. By the time he came to his feet, her face was a mask of polite interest.

"So basically, you want to schedule a fuck with me every Tuesday, Thursday, and Saturday, but you don't want any kind of real intimacy." He crumpled the towel he'd been using as a napkin and threw the wad into the open pizza box. "You gonna pay me?"

Her eyes widened, and he caught her soft intake of breath. Good. He'd shocked her. Pissed and tired of being jerked around, he crossed his arms over his chest.

"I assume you pay to get your toilets scrubbed and your roots dyed." He paused and pursed his lips as if giving the matter real thought. "I think a hundred a night seems fair enough, since I'm gonna get my kicks too. For that, you get oral, textbook sex, and, of course, as much finger-banging as you want—"

"Ty." Millie rose from her chair and placed a conciliatory hand on his arm, but he wasn't buying.

His phone began to vibrate in his pocket. He ignored the call but didn't bother to silence the alert. Instead, he shook her hand from his arm and flashed an insincere smile. "Unlimited orgasms. Tell you what, I'll even throw in an option for anal for free." He shrugged. "You can kick me out whenever you want, but I want cash, no checks accepted. I'd have to ask for two forms of ID, and we don't want to get too personal."

"Stop," she snapped.

He couldn't. He clenched his fists at his sides and tried to take a calming breath. It was no good. He had no capacity for holding back on anything else. "I've licked you, Millie. I've licked and kissed and sucked every inch of you. I've been inside you. My dick, my tongue, my fingers... I've felt you come and come inside you. There aren't enough condoms in the world to keep this from getting messy."

"Then we need to end this now," she said in a rush.

"Too late. I'm in love with you."

The admission surprised him as much as it did her. Not because he hadn't known, but because he figured it was way too early in the game to let her see his clutch play. But he had told her, and now the truth was out there, and he didn't want to take the declaration back.

"No."

The gleam in her eyes was the only thing that helped him believe her denial was an automatic response rather than a rejection. Millie Jensen wore the lean and hungry look of a woman who'd given up trusting in love but hadn't quite let go of believing in it.

He let one shoulder rise and drop as if the bomb he'd dropped wasn't atomic. Nothing to do but own his feelings for her now. "I love you, Mil. Started falling the day we met and have been ever since."

When she didn't take off for the door, he reached

for her. His hands closed around the lean muscle of her upper arms, and he drew her closer. But not too close. He wanted her to have all the space she needed to absorb what he was telling her.

"The night you showed up at my door…" He looked up at the ceiling, trying to find exactly the right words to say. "God, I was happy to see you. So happy I should be ashamed, but I'm not. I felt like…" He hesitated to put his true feelings on the line, lest she misconstrue his meaning, but he was in this far already. No point in pulling up short of the goal. "Like I deserved you. I'd done my time. I tried, honestly tried, to make my marriage work, even though I knew there was no hope. It would have imploded one way or another. I didn't want to be the bad guy." He pressed his hand to his chest. "I was the one who asked her to marry me. I made the mistake. I was the one who was old enough to know better."

Something in his speech seemed to plod her out of her shock. "But you married her anyway."

"Mari was pregnant when we got married."

"Oh."

The word came out of her so soft and small he almost didn't hear her. "She miscarried the week after we got back from Las Vegas."

"Oh."

"By that time…" He shrugged. "But I wanted a baby. I figured we'd try again, but Mari…"

"Right."

Millie took a breath so deep it rattled through her. Then her whole body convulsed, and she wrenched herself from his grip. He thought she was bolting and started after her, but the second she hit the hall, she took a sharp right and headed toward the bedrooms rather than the door.

"Millie?"

She didn't answer. Instead, she clamped one hand to her mouth and the other to her stomach, curling into herself as she race-walked toward the guest bath. Seconds later, he heard the lid hit the back of the tank, and the unmistakable sound of retching carried down the hall. Concerned, Ty rushed to the doorway. He arrived in time to see her groping for the toilet paper holder, tears streaming from her eyes as she wiped her mouth with the back of her hand.

Eager to be of some real assistance, he yanked the hand towel from the ring by the sink and pressed the soft cloth into her hand. "I'll grab some water."

He rushed to the kitchen to retrieve the bottle she'd never opened, but when he heard her vomiting again, he slowed his steps. As much as he wanted to be helpful, he knew no one liked an audience in these situations. Hanging back in the hall, he listened, his heart in his throat as she sniffled and blew her nose. He heard the flush and counted to three before swinging into the doorway.

"Here." His knees popped as he squatted beside her, extending the bottle out to her.

She uncapped the water and took a sip without meeting his eyes. She drained half before lowering the bottle, but her gaze remained locked on the tile floor.

Needing to look into her eyes, he hooked his forefinger beneath her chin and gently tipped her face up. When she met his eyes at last, he forced a shaky smile. "Better?"

"Can't hold my scotch," she said solemnly.

Matching her somber tone, he nodded. "We all have that trouble at some point."

Unable to restrain himself any longer, he wiped the mascara trails from her damp cheeks with the pad of his thumb. He'd never thought someone could still look beautiful when they cried, but Millie was proving to be the exception in so many areas of his life.

Her skin was the rich, velvety white of fresh cream. A rosy blush tinged her cheeks, and the tips of her ears were so pink they glowed. The contrast between the ripe, natural beauty of her face and the over-the-top shock of her hair suited her to perfection. Her eyes shone bright with banked tears, but the sheen only highlighted the sharp inquisitiveness in her all-seeing stare. This was the woman he'd started falling for years before he ought to.

"Was it the stuff about Mari that upset you or me saying I love you?" he asked quietly.

"Might have been the pizza," she challenged.

Ty dipped his head, then gave it a slow shake. "Nope, can't blame the food. You didn't eat any."

"Apparently, scotch doesn't mix well with strawberry daiquiri."

"What *does*?"

She sighed and scooted away enough to rest her back against the wall. Her eyes slid shut, and she let her head loll to the side, but still she answered. "Sunny days and warm sand."

"Well, the sun has been out, but we're pretty land-locked. Unless you count Lake Mason," he added. "There's a swimming beach." He ran his hand through her tousled hair. "I'd take you."

Though her eyes were already closed, she squeezed them tighter. "Please don't."

"Don't what? Take you to the beach?"

"Touch me," she whispered. "This will be so much harder if you touch me."

He cupped her cheek in his palm. The pad of his ring finger traced the stubborn line of her jaw. "I don't intend to make it easy for you to dump me, Millie."

"You're a good man, Ty. A nice man who always tries to do the right thing." Her eyelashes fluttered, and she opened her eyes, blinking a couple of times to bring him into focus. "But I can't give you what you want."

"So you say, but I believe in you."

"No, I literally can't." She knocked his hand away with a jerky wave of her arm. Before he could react, she scrambled to her feet using the wall as leverage. "You said you liked being married. Well, I didn't." Her hands clenched at her sides. "I'm not trying to be a jerk or to mess you around. I really like my life. I'm selfish. I don't want to have to share my space or let someone make decisions for me."

She stepped sideways, sliding along the wall, making it clear she wanted to get out of the room without any part of her touching any part of him. Ty stood up but otherwise didn't move from his spot.

"I like sleeping all over the bed if I want. Sometimes I eat a bowl of cereal for dinner. Standing at the sink," she added. As if her questionable meal choices might be a deal breaker. "I'm a crappy housekeeper." He must have looked surprised by the revelation, because she rushed on, eager to convince him. "Seriously, I can live with my own filth for a long time." She wrinkled her nose as she groped for the doorway. "I can't tell you how long some of the salad dressings have been in my fridge. Do I throw them out?" She gave her head an adamant shake. "No, I toss a new bottle in with the old. They keep each other company."

"I'm not looking for a maid, Millie."

She waved him off. "I'm not anyone's idea of a domestic partner."

"I didn't ask you to be mine."

Millie threw her arms up as she backed into the hall. "You said you were in love with me."

"I am." He took a single step toward her, and she reeled back, holding her palms out to ward him off. He halted, but the panic in her eyes gave him all the confirmation he needed. She was as scared as he was. "I think you might fall for me too if you give yourself a chance. Maybe that's why you're freaking out."

As expected, she planted her feet, squared her shoulders, and rose to the challenge. "I'm not freaking out."

"You keep putting me off, then calling me back. You refuse to see me, then show up at my door." He closed the distance between them but was careful not to touch her. "You keep saying no, but you keep doing things that say yes. You want to say yes. I know you do." He lowered his head until he could feel the hot, moist puffs of her breath on his lips. His voice broke when he spoke. "I can almost taste your yes, Millie."

"No." She whispered the denial, but there was no heat behind it.

"I have to tell you, when you say it like that, it sounds more like a 'yes, please.' But I know what no means." He took a half step back but no more.

A breathless laugh escaped her, but Millie only lifted her chin a millimeter more and said nothing.

"I wish you could see the expression on your face, Millie. Your eyes tell me everything."

"Do they?" She wet her lips. "And what do you think they're saying?"

"Please don't give up on me, Ty," he said in a low, taunting voice. "Please keep chasing me. Please kiss me. Fuck me. Love me." Her breath hitched on the last one. "And I want to." He took her hand and pressed her palm to the front of his shorts. He was hard as a rock and ready to roll here and now. Up against the wall. All she had to do was say the word. "All you have to do is tell me what you want, Millie. Say anything, and I'll give you everything."

"Ty, I can't give you a baby," she blurted, throwing her hands up in frustration.

He opened his mouth, but whatever he was about to say was chased clear out of his head by a jarring blast from his cell phone.

"Goddamn it!" he growled, pushing away from the wall and yanking the offending instrument from his pocket with every intention of smashing the phone into a thousand pieces. He almost did when he saw his ex-wife's smiling face beaming out from the screen.

Millie saw the photo too and took the opportunity to put some space between them. Sidling a couple of steps down the hall, she gestured to the phone. "She's been calling and calling. Why don't you find out what she wants?"

Steaming with anger and pent-up frustration, he leveled a finger at her. "Stay."

She flipped an entirely different finger back at him, but she didn't make a break for the door.

Keeping a wary eye on her, he swiped his thumb across the display to accept the call and snapped a gruff, "What?"

"Ty?"

He rolled his eyes, the sound of Mari's voice screeching down his spine like fingernails on a chalkboard. "Yeah. What? What do you want, Mari?"

"I want to talk to you. I need to talk to you."

"There's nothing more to say."

"But it's important," she insisted. "Can we meet somewhere?"

He blinked, confused by the request. The last he'd heard, his ex was shacked up in Los Angeles with her boy toy. "Meet? How? Aren't you in California?"

"I'm here. In town, I mean."

Millie took a step back, her eyes narrowing enough to let him know she'd heard Mari's answer and was wary too. Annoyed by both the intrusion and the stricken look on Millie's face, he hit the button to send the call to speaker. He had nothing to hide, and he'd be damned if he'd let the stubborn woman standing outside of arm's reach slip away because she imagined something might be going on between him and his ex.

"Sorry if you came all this way to talk to me, but I really don't have anything more to say. You got what you wanted, Mari. Now I'm trying to move on with my life."

"But this isn't what I wanted," she wailed. Impatient and unwilling to be drawn into whatever melodrama Mari had created for herself, his thumb hovered over the button to disconnect. He was about to say goodbye when she hissed, "You're the one who wanted a baby."

"A baby?" The question popped out of his mouth, but he stared at the glossy screen as if the image might tell him he'd misunderstood what she'd said. His head jerked up, and he spotted Millie standing at almost military attention.

"I'm pregnant," Mari snapped.

Her announcement startled him so much the phone spurted from his hand and clattered to the floor, but they both still heard her last words clear as a bell. "And the baby is yours."

Chapter 16

MILLIE KNEW HEARING MARI CLAIM SHE WAS PREGNANT should have sent her running for the door. But it didn't. She should be clocking record time booking it to her car. But she wasn't. Because this was what she was made for—crisis control.

She remained standing in Ty's house, her eyes locked on him. He was shocked into stillness, his fingers frozen in a classic horror movie curl. His stillness scared her. This wasn't the calm, happy Ty she'd come to know. This stillness had a sinister feel.

She needed to break the spell, do something, anything, to disrupt the horrible tableau they seemed to be trapped in. Stark panic drew Ty's handsome features tight. Every line and groove screamed the need for help. Her help.

"Ty," she whispered urgently enough to jolt him into looking at her.

His eyes met hers, but they were clouded with confusion. Raising her hand to eye level, she ignored the wheedling calls for attention coming from the now-forgotten phone. Taking a cautious step toward him, she popped up one finger. Then another. At the third, she raised an inquiring eyebrow.

"Is it possible?" she asked with a quiet calm that was the polar opposite of the upheaval roiling inside her.

"Huh?"

She closed the rest of the space between them, gently resting her hand on his chest to reassure him. His heart thrummed against her palm. Holding his gaze, she leaned in close. "Think back. You haven't seen her in more than two months, right?"

He blinked, and she decided to take his nonanswer as a yes. His blank expression set hope and wariness to war in her chest.

"Ask her how far along she is," she prompted.

Ty cocked his head as if she'd suddenly started speaking Hungarian. "What?"

This was her turf—a problem. Something that could be spun, if not fixed. "How pregnant is she? People don't have to wait three months or more to find out if they are anymore." Anyone who watched daytime programming knew medical testing had advanced enough that she could pee on a stick within days of missing her period. "If you haven't been with her since things blew up, then we're looking at more than two months. Three if things were rocky between the two of you before she actually left."

"Tyrell!" Mari's shrill demand burst the bubble.

They both looked at the abandoned phone. Mari's contact picture beamed up at them from the floor.

Millie lunged past him to retrieve the phone. "Ask her."

She gripped the case tightly enough to disguise the tremors running through her. Adrenaline. Fear. And yes, a spark. Millie loved a challenge. If Mari thought she could get Ty back by playing the pregnancy card again, she'd have a bigger fight on her hands this time.

Ty took the phone from her and held it in his palm between them. "How pregnant?"

"Who is that? Who's there? What do you mean, how?" Mari asked, exasperated. "The usual way."

Millie rolled her eyes, then nodded and circled her hand, prompting him to press her.

"How many months?" he clarified.

"Three," Mari answered without hesitation.

Her heart somersaulted in her chest, but Millie held steady. For her own sake as much as his. She couldn't fall apart. Wouldn't. At least not as long as she could focus on fixing him. She stared hard into his eyes, searching for the truth. All she found was a man who appeared to be completely lost. And more than a bit worried.

Choking down her pride, she tapped the screen to mute the phone. "Don't say anything now. Tell her you need to think and you'll call her back."

"Call her back?"

"Give yourself a few minutes to process. She's trying to psych you out. Hit you hard and knock you off-kilter."

"Psych me out?"

"Get you to admit something, agree to anything." She gave his arm a gentle squeeze, then shook him to be sure she had his attention. "Take some time. Think it through."

"Ty, we need to get some things settled," Mari insisted.

"No. Not now," Millie said firmly. He gazed down at her, his heart in his eyes. "You'll call her back." She relieved him of the phone and ended the call without allowing one more word.

They stood facing one another, eyes locked, breathing perfectly in sync, their bodies swaying in the maelstrom of emotion swirling around them.

"You're okay." The words came to her reflexively. Ty blinked, then swallowed as if they were precisely the medicine he needed. Smiling a reassuring smile, she slipped the phone into his pocket and gave it a pat. "These shorts are a crime against mankind."

"Millie—"

She pressed a fingertip to his lips to silence him. "Shh. Stop. Breathe. We're okay."

He gave his head an incredulous shake. "How can we be okay?" The crack in his voice put a pretty good-sized one in the shell around her heart. "She can't be… She can't do this."

Taking his hand, she started back toward the kitchen. Hard to believe that a few minutes ago, this man seemed like the biggest threat to her happiness. Now, she knew better. Adding presumption to the list of lessons learned, she swore off scotch chasers for the foreseeable forever and vowed to herself she'd get her head and her heart straight. No more messing around. The push-me-pull-you game was over. From this point on, she needed to choose. In or out. And if she wanted to be in, she'd have to go all in.

When they reached the table, she gave him a gentle shove, and he dropped into the seat he'd abandoned to go after her. "First, it takes two," she said firmly. "And I know you can do anything you choose to do." Regaining her seat, she sighed. "Second, you can't react emotionally now. You need to stop and think. Start with possible. Then we'll deal with probable and go from there. You have choices too. Not the same kind Mari has, but you do have some."

He massaged the vertical lines between his knitted

brows with the side of his index finger, and Millie found herself transfixed. "Three months," he mumbled. "So, yeah, possible. I guess."

"You and Mari were still sleeping together when she was…seeing Dante."

He lifted his hand enough to shoot her a look. "You're cute when you get all euphemistic. I seem to remember you being more blunt than this."

She reached across to pat his forearm. "Yes, well, I'm afraid you might cry."

He let his hand fall palm up on the table. Unable to resist the invitation, she slipped hers into his, sighing as those long fingers closed around hers. He squeezed once, then relaxed his grip. "I'm afraid I might too."

"We've got possible. Let's talk about probable." She took a bracing breath, then plunged in with the tough questions. "Were you guys still pretty…regular?"

He pulled back as if he'd been scalded. "Oh, for God's sake."

Millie wanted to smile when she spotted the blush darkening his skin, but she settled for a simple lift of her eyebrows. This wasn't the time for needling him about delicate sensibilities. Still, she liked that he had them. He had an honorable streak a mile wide. One strong enough to overcome the very natural and human impulse to seek revenge, validation, or solace in a woman's arms when his marriage imploded. No matter how hard the woman in question tried to lure him into temptation. Of course he'd be reluctant to discuss his marital relations with the woman who was now his lover.

"It's okay, Ty."

"Not one fucking bit of this is okay," he snapped, launching himself from the chair. "I don't want to talk about this with you."

Millie nodded once, then pulled her phone from the bag she'd abandoned in an empty chair. "Would you like me to contact Danny? Or Mike Samlin?"

Ty whirled on her. "What? Why?"

She shrugged. "Because they're men? Because you're not sleeping with them?"

"You think I can't do the math on my own?"

"I think you're upset—which is totally reasonable," she hastened to add when his lip curled into a sneer. "And maybe you'd have an easier time telling them things you might not want to tell me."

He tilted his head. "And why wouldn't I want to tell you?"

"Because we *are* sleeping together. Maybe you're afraid you'll hurt my feelings?"

He pounced on the hint of vulnerability. "Are you telling me you have feelings?"

"Good Lord, Ty," she blurted, exasperation overcoming her. "Of course I have feelings. I'm not a robot."

"For me."

He skirted the end of the table and came to a stop beside her chair. He stood unmoving, waiting for her to expound, but she didn't. He was a ballplayer, used to intimidating opponents with his superior height and strength, but he didn't scare her. She found him…breathtaking.

"Do you have feelings for me?" he asked, enunciating each word with precision. Before she could suck in a little oxygen, he leaned down, effectively caging her in with one hand planted on the table, the other gripping the back of her chair. "And if so, what are those feelings? Specifically?"

The intensity of his stare held her in thrall. She didn't try to bolt or slither from the seat. The truth was, she didn't want to elude him or them or what they might be able to carve out together. The only part she wanted to avoid was the bit where her heart ended up broken into a million pieces. She'd spent years reinventing herself after her marriage fell apart. If she Humpty-Dumptied again, there might not be enough horses, men, or superglue to make her whole once more.

She started to shake her head but stopped when he leaned in closer. "You know," she whispered at last, taking the coward's way out.

"Tell me."

But she couldn't. Verbalizing her feelings would make them actual information. Information was knowledge. Knowledge equaled power. This man had enough power over her already. She couldn't give him carte blanche. So she'd start with a few basic truths. Maybe those would be enough to placate him.

"I don't want Mari to be pregnant with your baby." He stiffened enough to tell her this was not the confession he wanted or expected. She needed to give him a little more. Enough to let him infer but not enough to confirm. "I wish you'd never slept with her, but given the circumstances, pretending would be fairly ridiculous."

His eyes narrowed. "Is this a feeling?"

"Jealousy," she replied with a jerky nod. "I'm jealous." When his brows rose, Millie felt the need to spin the confession. "Not 'I'm gonna put sugar in your gas tank' jealous, but yes, jealous."

Ty nodded, compressing his mouth into a thin line as he digested. "Jealous is a good start. What else?"

"Angry."

An emotion easy to own. She'd been pissed off since this whole mess started. Pissed at Ty for marrying the nitwit. At the nitwit for being too blind to know what she had. At Dante Harris's ingratitude and the vicious glee the press exhibited in taking what should have been a private matter and whipping it into a story concocted for consumption. She couldn't even think about the morons who sat like lumps in front of their computers and television screens gobbling personal pain like handfuls of mixed nuts.

She was angry he kissed like he did. Sweet, sensual, drugging kisses that burned hotter than one of those fire-starter logs. The feel of his big, rough hands on her body stoked the flames higher and higher. She didn't want to love him. Never asked him to love her. But now that she'd had him, she didn't want to share one bit of him with anyone else. Not even a baby.

"You're angry?" he clarified.

"Yes." She bit the word off hard, incensed that he seemed to be questioning her right to feel this way. "Yes, I'm angry." She tipped her chin up a notch. "What of it?"

Ty smiled as he pushed away and rose to his full height. But not a happy smile. The gleam of it glinted with a steely, sharp edge. "Nothing. I'm glad I'm not the only one."

Once she had some breathing room, Millie sucked in a deep hit and went straight to the heart of the matter. "When was the last time you slept with Mari?" He blinked, then started to recover, but before he could say a word, she held up a hand to stop him. "Not slept, had sex. And not oral or anything else. Full intercourse, including ejaculation. The kind of sex that gets a woman knocked up."

"A perverse part of me loves it when you get explicit."

She acknowledged the comment but didn't let the playful gambit deter her. "Great. We'll get to perversions later, but right now, we're talking about the probability of baby making."

"A week or so before she left." He raised a hand in a gesture of futility, then let it fall away. "I don't remember exactly. I thought about what went wrong a lot... after. I can't pin it on any trouble in bed, but I let a lot of other things go. Things I didn't want to admit to seeing."

Millie wet her lips, her mind clicking through various options as she tried to figure out how best to approach her next question. "And before you discovered the affair with Dante, did you suspect anything?"

He shook his head a split second too early for his denial to be anything but a knee-jerk reaction.

"Ty, anything?"

Something must have pinged, because he stopped on a dime. "Why? What did you hear?"

Despite years of speaking with caution and diplomacy, Millie couldn't think of a single gentle way to break it to a man that his trophy wife had been making a chump out of him behind his back long before he'd copped a clue. "I'd seen some things posted on social media sites—"

"You saw them?"

Millie nodded, a guilty grimace twisting her lips. "A

couple of pictures of Mari on PicturSpam with some of the football players." *Mari half-dressed and commanding the players' full attention*, she clarified for her own edification. "Maybe one or two with Dante." *Or ten*, she amended in her head. She firmly believed that in cases such as these, it was better not to quantify matters any more than one absolutely had to. "I'd seen a few but didn't want to make something out of nothing, so I didn't think to say anything."

Okay, that was mostly a lie. She had wanted to tell Ty about the photos but decided not to after talking the conundrum over with Avery and Kate. When her friends advised against getting involved, she had been relieved. Millie had been far too interested in Ty to risk being the one he forever associated with discovering his wife's infidelity.

Fire flared in his eyes. His jaw tightened, but he relaxed it with obvious effort. Inclining his head in silent acknowledgment, he averted his face. She watched his chest rise and fall, wishing she could touch him, comfort him, remind him that he was a thousand times the man those boys would ever hope to be. But she couldn't. Not now. Not if she wanted to hang on to any shred of her own sanity as well as preserve his.

"It's possible you are the father," she said at last.

"But I'm probably not," he added hastily.

The seconds ticked silently between them, but she couldn't *not* ask the question. "Does that make you happy or sad?"

"This whole mess makes me...mad." But rather than ranting and raving, he threw himself back into his chair, propped his elbows on his knees, and dropped his head into his hands. "I don't want any of this. I mean, I would have been happy to have a baby when I thought we were happy, but now?" He scrubbed his face with his hands. "Why do I ever think I'm going to get to be happy?"

The despair in his voice cut her to the quick. Needing to do something, Millie flipped the lid on the pizza box and closed it. "Whoa. Pretty nihilistic attitude you've got, fella." She rose, taking the box with her. "Should I bust out the tiny violin?"

"Christ, Millie, I get it. You're tough as nails, but do you think you can stop busting my balls for five minutes?"

She whirled back to face him, the box clutched in her hand. "No, because the second I do, you'll drop that fine ass of yours into your sulking chair and try to drown your sorrows in a bottle." Yanking open the refrigerator, she smirked at the nearly empty shelves, then shoved the box inside. "I can't let you. People like you and me, we suck at sulking. Pouting leads to nasty hangovers, extra housework, and"—she let the door swing shut as she searched for one more consequence for rampant self-indulgence—"pimples."

Dark brows rose. "Pimples?"

"Maybe only those of us who use chocolate as a crutch."

He rewarded her with a weak smile. "But we're not the type to sulk, you and me."

Drawing a deep breath, she steeled her spine and crossed the room to stand right in front of him. "No. We're the type to barrel right on through to the finish."

"I need to look into how paternity tests work."

She nodded and reached for one of his hands. He

gave it to her willingly. "I think a test would be the first logical step."

Ty looked up at her, his eyes dark and searching. "And if the baby is mine?"

"Then we figure out what to do next."

He blinked slowly, his jaw set. "Yeah. We figure it out."

"But first things first." She gave his hand a hard squeeze to command his full attention. "Admit nothing. Agree to nothing. Don't even talk to Mari." She crouched down until they were eye to eye. "Block her calls if you have to."

He started to say something, but she cut him off with a sharp shake of her head. "No. Call your attorney, and request the paternity test. I didn't say anything about this before because I wasn't sure if it was true or relevant, but the rumor mill has been saying she and Dante have been on the outs. If so, pregnant or not, she may be looking for a soft place to fall."

"And I'm a big, old softy," he said with more than a hint of bitterness.

Laying her hand along his jaw, she stroked the sharp slope of his cheekbone. "No. You are a good and honorable man." Giving him a wobbly smile, she leaned in and kissed him tenderly. "And if Jane Austen taught the world anything, it's that good and honorable men get screwed around a lot before they get their happy ending."

"And you think I'll get a happy ending?"

She forced a smile, but she knew the result was weak. "I know you deserve one."

"People don't always get what they deserve."

"Not if they leave everything up to destiny." She

kissed him again, this time with gusto, but pulled back before he could wrap her up and pull her against him. "People make their own luck."

Catching his forearms, she stepped out of the circle of his reach. A slick side step brought her back to the seat across from him. Plunging her hand into her bag, she groped until she got hold of her tablet, then yanked the pad free. "Call your lawyer," she instructed. "I'm going to do a little research."

Ty shifted his weight to one hip and dug in his shorts pocket for his phone. "What are you doing?"

Not looking up, Millie tapped an icon on the screen. "Doing what I do best—managing facts."

She smiled as she scanned her files, but it wasn't a happy smile. She'd come here tonight hopped up on Dutch courage and expecting to be in his bed by now. Instead, they'd bickered, played true confessions, and continued the crazy tango she'd hoped to end by scattering all her cards out on the dance floor. Then she'd barfed, and his phone rang, and the world went wonky. But now she had a mission: Protect Ty. Get Ty everything he wanted.

Replaying the events in her head, she tried not to react to the growing urgency in Ty's deep voice as he dumped all the evening's revelations into his attorney's lap. She had her own mission. A swipe, two taps, and a little scrolling later, she had new ammunition. Thanks to Mari's addiction to hashtagging every occasion in her life, Millie captured screenshots of a few less-than-flattering photos.

Under #MerryMari, she found several pictures of Ty's ex-wife partying with men who were not her husband, some dating back as far as a year prior. They proved nothing, but one didn't need proof to convict someone in the court of public opinion. All she needed was enough leverage to hold Mari in check until this mess could be settled one way or another.

She switched her search to the more incriminating #RecruitingTrip hashtag she'd stumbled across in the months before Ty's marriage imploded. It didn't take a genius to piece the string of events together. The Warriors' season had ended before the tournament. Ty and his assistants had made a round of visits to shore up their relationships with players who'd already committed to Wolcott and possibly sway a few who may have been on the fence.

Mari Ransom had used the same opportunity to get in good with Ty's star player. The pictures of Mari and Dante left little room for hoping their relationship was strictly platonic. Some had been dug up when the news of the affair went public. Mari had then deleted most of them, but Millie had grabbed screenshots before the posts disappeared. She'd started a file of them long before the story broke, just in case things got ugly. Uglier.

Tearing her gaze from the screen, she found Ty prowling the kitchen as he listened to his attorney. It boggled her mind to think any woman would choose an amped-up puppy like Dante Harris over Ty's sleek, smooth grace. He moved like a big cat. A leopard or panther. Each step deliberate. The play of muscle under satiny skin mesmerizing. His focus compelling and utterly unwavering. As if sensing her stare, he turned. Their gazes met and held. Her stomach twisted into a knot, but then he smiled. A rough, grim attempt. Wary and weary. A bit ragged around the edges. But a smile nonetheless, and meant only for her.

Hell, maybe he'd already caught her and she didn't realize. Or want to admit to being too far gone over him. Still murmuring yeses and nos into the phone, he closed the distance between them. His long toes bumped her shoes, then he covered her foot lightly with his, holding her in place as he bent to brush a bone-melting kiss to the top of her head. She put a hand on his chest, not quite sure if she meant to hold him or push him away. Either way, she had to touch him.

Straightening, he mumbled, "Yeah, she says three months," as her hand trailed oh-so-innocently over his abs. She curled her fingers into a small fist when she hit the waistband of his shorts but allowed her knuckles to graze his crotch when her hand fell away. Ty raised his eyebrows, his face a mask of mild shock. But the light in his eyes said her playful advances were always welcome.

"Right, I know," he said into the phone. He closed his eyes, snapping the connection between them like a thread. "I want to get started on whatever I need to do, so I can figure out where to go from here."

Millie stared at the rigid line of his back as he listened. He nodded twice, but the movements were jerky. He ended the call with a few brusque words of thanks, then lowered the phone to his side. He stood still—loose-limbed and unmoving—for a long beat. Then he went into a windup worthy of a major league pitcher and hurled the phone at the stainless-steel face of the refrigerator.

It hit with a *thunk* that jolted through her, then clattered to the floor, bits and pieces of metal, glass, and plastic shooting out like shrapnel. Millie stared at the dent in the fridge's gleaming facade and sighed. She couldn't blame the man for wanting to rid himself of the instrument, but it hurt her heart to see a hapless appliance caught up as collateral damage.

"Feel better now?" she asked softly.

Ty pivoted on his heel, his lips drawn into a flat line but his eyes blazing. "He says he thinks she can refuse DNA testing until after the baby is born."

Millie nodded as she processed that tidbit. Then she sighed. She and Ty had been coworkers and friends before they became lovers. As a coworker, she'd done her best to see him through the media shitstorm. As his friend, she'd tried to shield him from more hurt than he'd already endured. Now, as his lover, she'd have to show him the photos that would hurt him but provide the ammunition he needed to force Mari's hand if push came to shove.

Tearing her gaze from his, she went back to her tablet. Three taps later, she had the first screenshot open. It was a photo of Mari straddling Dante's lap, her skirt hiked up to her waist and her bare ass showing. The hashtags included #MakinIt, #MillionDollarBaby, and #IfAtFirstYouDontSucceed.

"I'd say it's possible but not probable you're the baby daddy. We can force her to play along if needed." Handing him the screen, she rose from her chair in hopes of outpacing the fresh surge of bile rushing up from her gut and ran for the powder room.

Chapter 17

KATE FLOPPED DOWN IN MILLIE'S GUEST CHAIR AND FOLDED her hands over her stomach. "Do you want the scoop, or do you want to call your boyfriend in to hear the unvarnished version?"

Millie peered over the top of pink polka dot–rimmed readers. "Do we need varnish?"

"Gallons. I tapped the sorority-girl network." Kate scrunched her nose. "I was in a sorority once upon a time, but I sure as hell don't remember college life being so…X-rated."

Snickering, Millie abandoned all pretense of typing the press release she'd been composing about sweeping changes the baseball coach was making in his program. "That's because we remember the days before MTV started airing spring break festivities."

Kate waved the explanation away. "I was no virgin as an undergrad, but I swear, I didn't learn about half the things they talk about until I was in my thirties."

Lacing her fingers together, Millie gave her friend a sympathetic stare. Which wasn't very good. These days, she had a hard time finding sympathy for anyone. "Do you need a glass of whisky or something before we can get to the point?"

"Mari's been partying with the kids on the sly for the last year or so." Kate wrung her hands together, then flattened her palms on the tops of her thighs. "She was involved with one of the boys on the football team over the winter, but he apparently broke up with her."

"Too clingy?"

"Too kinky." Kate shuddered, then laughed at herself. "Sorry, it's just… Can you imagine how freaky you'd have to be to turn some nineteen-year-old boy off? Guys are walking boners at his age."

Millie forced herself to lower her eyebrows. She'd be damned if she'd let Mari Ransom and her antics force her to become reliant on injectable fillers. "I don't even know what to say."

Wearing a grim smile of determination, Kate plunged ahead. "The girls said all she did was brag about how she liked to try new things and complain about how boring Coach Ransom was in bed." She grimaced. "Their words."

"Her opinion," Millie added.

Kate sat up straight in the chair. "Her loss. Ty's a good man, Mil. I wouldn't have let him come within five miles of you if he wasn't."

Her friend's proclamation startled a laugh from her. "You're my gatekeeper?"

"I'm your friend." Kate rose from the chair and strode to the door. "And I'm a goddamn giantess. It's my job to protect you mere mortals," she said with a grin that glinted. "He never woulda gotten past me if I didn't want him to."

"Katie—"

Kate made a slicing motion with her hand, effectively cutting off any protest. "No. She's not going to keep pulling this crap. Not on him, and definitely not on you."

"This has nothing to do with me."

"Right, because you aren't in love with the guy or anything," Kate snarked.

"I'm not." The denial landed so far short of the truth it burst like a water balloon. The seconds ticked by as every lie Millie had ever told herself or anyone else concerning her relationship with Ty splattered all over the floor. "I don't want to be."

Kate's answering smile was sympathetic. "Oh, I know."

Desperate for a subject change, Millie waved her hand in dismissal. "First things first."

"I have the names, but I'd rather not write them down." Kate wrinkled her nose in distaste. "We have tons of photographic evidence, thanks to her selfie addiction. Let's give Ty's lawyer a chance to reason with her like she's a grown-up before we drag students into the mix. I think the fewer people who know what's going on, the better."

"I agree."

Kate stopped when she reached the door. "But someone better clue the AD in before any of this caca goes kablooey." She smirked. "We both know Mike isn't a real big fan of surprises."

"No, he's not" came a deep voice from the hall. As if conjured, the athletic director stopped in the doorway just behind Kate.

"M-Mike. I didn't... You were—" Kate stopped short, took a huffy breath, then concluded with a brisk, "Hi."

Millie chuckled as she watched her friend's cheeks flush bright red. Nothing better than seeing her kick-ass giantess reduced to a stammering kid caught in the hall without a pass. Their athletic director seemed to enjoy her discomfiture too. Millie couldn't blame him, really. Kate and Danny's power play last spring had wedged the man solidly between a rock and a hard place. Mike and Danny had been good friends since their college playing days. Their interwoven personal and professional lives meant Kate, not a socially adept woman to start, had to navigate a whole minefield of awkward each time she encountered her boss.

"Hi, Kate," Director Samlin replied mildly. Poking his head around her guardian, he nodded to Millie. "Hey, Mil."

She gave him a regal nod. "Mike."

Smirking, he nudged Kate, demanding a more equal share of the narrow doorway. "I wanted to let you know Ty came by my office this morning." Seemingly enjoying their uneasy interest, he let the announcement hang. "He gave me the lowdown on the situation with his ex-wife." He paused, then heaved a long-suffering sigh. Mike clearly hadn't forgotten the trouble Kate's relationship with Danny had given him or the role Millie played in their escapades. "Also, he told me you two are…involved."

Millie sat up straighter. "I'm—"

He held up a preemptory hand. "I really don't want to know the details." Kate snorted, and he manufactured another one of those forbidding stares. "It's nice to be informed about what's going on in my programs."

Millie sighed and pushed back from her desk. "Listen, I don't want—"

Tilting her head toward Mike, Kate spoke out of the side of her mouth but loud enough to be sure she was heard. "She's totally in denial about the relationship thing."

"I am not," Millie retorted hotly.

Kate grinned, then elbowed their boss in the ribs. "Ha! She admitted it! They're in a relationship," she crowed.

Growling her frustration, Millie thrust out an arm, pointing in the direction of Kate's office. "Go. Out. Bye!"

"So articulate," Kate murmured with mock admiration. "No wonder you hired her. She's a linguistic genius."

"Get!"

Kate blew her a kiss, then ducked out of the doorway, the sound of her throaty laughter lingering after she was gone. Letting out a breath, Millie reclaimed her chair, then gestured for the AD to take the seat her friend had abandoned. "She's a menace."

"Danny's influence. She was always so easygoing before."

Millie cocked an eyebrow. "Then you have no one to blame but yourself. If you hadn't hired him, he wouldn't have had the chance to come in here and warp my friend with his love juju."

"Love juju?"

"You're the one who said she hasn't been the same," Millie replied with a zing. "And you're right." She let her smile spread slowly. "She's better. But don't tell her I said so. Her ego is healthy enough already."

"Agreed." He strolled oh-so-casually to the guest chair Kate had vacated and took a seat.

The moment he looked up at her, Millie blurted, "Ty and I aren't in a relationship."

"All reports to the contrary?"

"Well, I mean, not a *relationship*-relationship."

"More of a relationship then," he commented mildly,

imbuing the word with a mysterious third meaning with a slight change in inflection.

"Shut up."

He laughed then, crossing one ankle over his knee and relaxing into the seat. "I couldn't care less, Millie." She started to say something, but he winced and held up both hands in surrender. "I mean, I care. You know, as a friend." Looking less relaxed by the second, he leaned forward slightly. "As your boss. And his. Whatever." He threw his hands up. "Tell me we can move past this point in the discussion."

"We can move on," she agreed with haste.

"Okay. Well, so you know, no big secret or anything. Other than the thing with Ty's wife." He cringed again. "Ex-wife." He glanced back at the now-empty doorway where Kate had stood. "The alumni are still touchy about Danny. Up until now, Ty has been a favorite, but the publicity around Dante's leaving school and Mari's involvement... None of this is Ty's fault, I know, but I don't have to explain to you the powers of perception."

"We're going to shut this thing down."

She must have said the words with enough conviction to convince Mike, because he uncrossed his legs and prepared to stand. "Good. Let me know what I can do to help."

"We're trying to keep everyone and everything related to the university out of the picture."

"Best plan of all," Mike said with an approving nod. "Keep me posted."

The minute he left, she sagged in her chair. Letting her eyes slide shut, she focused only on her breathing. Air in, air out. In, out. Then she took a mental status report. Her skin felt too tight. The realization brought a ghost of a smile to her lips. Normally, a woman her age would welcome the taut feeling. But this wasn't an "I feel pretty" kind of thing.

More like she was ready to burst at the seams. Stretched so tight she was tender. Parts of her felt bruised, even though she hadn't a mark on her. Like someone had loaded her into a tumble dryer and flipped the switch.

A small laugh escaped her, and she opened her eyes.

Denial. She had a reservoir of the stuff buried deep inside her. This was the reserve she tapped into at about the mile-twenty mark. The one that pushed her through the wall. Her ability to spin crap into gold was her magic elixir. Her superpower.

She rolled her shoulders back and wriggled until she sat straight in the chair. No matter what anyone said or thought, she had a heart. The organ itself might be battered and somewhat hardened, but apparently, it was in full working order. And right now, it ached.

She glanced at her watch. Ty had planned to meet his attorney at eleven. She'd planned to sit in her office and wait until he texted or called with a progress report. One more way of standing back. Pretending she wasn't in this. In love with him. And Kate was right. She wasn't fooling anyone. Not even herself.

Sitting on the bench, waiting for news wasn't enough anymore. Time to lace up her shoes and get into the game.

———

Millie found Ty slumped at a bus stop outside the lawyer's office, his head back and his eyes fixed on something in the middle distance. Not wanting to startle him, she cleared her throat, then placed her ever-present tote on the bench beside him. "Is this seat taken?"

He smiled as he lifted his head, but his eyes remained dull and lifeless. "Hey."

She dropped down on the bench, leaving the bag as a barrier in case she was tempted to crawl into his lap and wrap herself around him, though she knew any attempt at comfort could take a turn inappropriate for public consumption if she touched his sun-warmed skin. "So, did they kick you out?"

He tipped his face up to the sun. "I heard all I needed to hear."

"Care to share with the class?"

He didn't look at her. "Are you sure you want to get involved?"

The petulant challenge was weak, but she didn't hold his pique against him. She'd jerked him back and forth on the topic enough to grant him some leeway. Taking a breath, she let it out slowly, then said, "I am already."

Her assertion captured his full attention. "What if I find out I'm the father?"

She sucked in a sharp breath. The question was blunt enough to shake the pillar of denial she'd been building her hopes on. She forced a wobbly smile. "Well, I guess my answer depends on whether you intend to get back with your baby mama."

"No." He answered with such quick conviction the breath she'd been holding whooshed from her. "But I will be the baby's father." He paused. "I mean, if I am the father, I will be a real father to my child. I may be dealing with Mari. At least for the next twenty years or so."

"Of course you'll be a father to your child." Reaching over her bulky bag, she took his hand and laced her fingers though his. "And you'll be a great one."

He laughed then. Rough and low. The kind of laugh so laden with disbelief, he couldn't seem to get any air under it. He closed his eyes, but his grip on her hand tightened. When he looked at her again, his expression was pained. Millie ached to launch herself at him, public spectacles be damned. She wanted to smooth the lines away with her lips and fingers. She'd lock her lips on his and draw the bitterness out of him like snake venom. Which, in a way, it was.

"I dread telling my father. Is that pathetic?" His question pulled her out of her thoughts. He chuckled, but she heard little true happiness in the sound. "Christ, I'm forty-two years old, and I'm scared to tell my dad I might have gotten a girl in trouble."

"A girl in trouble," she repeated, his choice of phrasing making her smile. "Yes, you are quite the villain, aren't you?"

"I'm serious," he said, scowling at her.

"I know you are."

Unable to hold back one more second, she reached for him with her free hand. He nestled his cheek into her palm. Dark, curling lashes swept down to shield his eyes, but she didn't need to see them to know the caress helped.

"I gave up thinking about babies a long time ago. They weren't in the stars for me. I think maybe because I knew deep down I didn't want kids." The confession came out of the blue, but once she started, Millie found herself hard-pressed to stem the flow. "I suppose some people would think that makes me a horrible person. An unnatural woman. But I never felt the…tug or tick or whatever women are supposed to feel. But maybe I just didn't get that far." She pressed her hand to her belly. "Not that I don't like kids. I just never pictured myself having them. I always kind of thought I would make a good aunt. Like Auntie Mame." She smiled. "I think I'd be really good at the spoiling part. Unfortunately, no siblings, so the aunt thing didn't work out."

He returned the smile, his eyes warming. "I bet you would be an awesome auntie."

"Kate and Danny probably won't have kids at this point in their lives, but Avery's younger. She still has time." The smile widened into a grin as she pictured all the gaudy, glitzy presents she'd heap on her friend's imaginary children. After all, someone had to contradict the hippie-dippie granola influence in their lives. "And now, maybe you."

His expression sobered. "Maybe me." He raised their joined hands to his mouth and brushed feathery kisses across her knuckles. "I don't want to lose you over this."

"You won't," she whispered.

He raised his gaze to meet hers. "You mean that?"

"Yes."

He nodded, then lowered their hands to his thigh once more. "We got Mari to agree to a noninvasive prenatal test. That should at least give us some indicator. If we're not sure of the results, we can try a more invasive procedure, but they're riskier, and I don't know if I'd want to take the chance."

Millie nodded as she digested the information. "No. Right. That makes sense."

"Either way, paternity won't be legally determined until they do the testing after the baby is born."

"I see."

"Some claim the noninvasive testing is accurate, some say it's BS, but I think it's worth trying. I have to know something one way or another." His expression grew somber. "Either way, I'm in for another six months of limbo. And I thought waiting six weeks for a divorce was bad."

She gave him a wan smile. "Six weeks was bad."

He looked her straight in the eye. "I've got no right to ask you to go through this with me, but I want to."

A myriad of questions, answers, and commentary scrolled through her head, but like the crawl at the bottom of a television screen, she ignored them in favor of the headline. "I'll be here for you."

His eyes brightened, but his smile was sardonic. "You sure? Up until last night, you were singing a different tune."

She laughed. "You'd think you'd have learned by now not to listen to anything I say." Releasing his hand, she swung her bag to the ground and scooted closer until they sat hip to hip. Then she took his hand again. But instead of threading her fingers through his, she raised his arm up over her head and draped his bicep over her shoulder. Settling into the crook of his neck, she patted his chest. "Words are spin, Ty. I'm a woman of action. Pay attention to what I do, not what I say."

She felt his silent chuckle. "What you do?" he asked.

"I might talk a good game, but I haven't been able to back it up. No matter what I say, I keep running right back to you."

He nodded thoughtfully. "True."

"And not for the cuisine," she said, adding a wry little laugh. "That pizza you ordered should be registered as some kind of weapon of mass destruction."

"You didn't even taste it."

"And still I ended up worshipping the porcelain god."

He gave her arm a gentle squeeze. "Don't blame my pizza for your questionable choices in liquor consumption. I know undergrads who know better."

The knots in her stomach tightened. "If you stick with me, this could be your only chance to have a kid of your own."

He smirked. "You think I looked at you and thought, 'Now, she looks like a baby-making opportunity'?" Angling his body toward hers, he ran his palm over her messy mop of hair, then traced the curve of her cheek with his fingertips. "No, Millie, I didn't choose you because I thought you'd be good breeding stock."

"Are you saying I wouldn't be?" She tried to sound affronted, but it was hard with an avalanche of relief *shushing* through her veins.

He rolled his eyes. "Not at all." He curled his finger under her chin, and their gazes locked. "When I look at you, I see everything I never knew I needed. You're smart, funny, and resourceful." He gave a self-deprecating chuckle. "We won't even get into the sexy thing, because we're sitting on a public bench, and I have a hard enough time keeping my hands off you without discussing the finer points."

"We could discuss them later though."

He squinted, eyeing her closely. "I'm still reeling a bit. Between you running hot and cold and Mari jerking my chain, I think I might have some whiplash. You'll forgive me if I'm wary?"

Millie's cheeks burned, but she managed as much of a nod as his grip would allow. "I get you."

"You do," he replied quietly. "Another reason I'm crazy about you." He lowered his hand, then gently disentangled the other from her grasp. "But I have a whole plateful of crazy right now, so I can't let myself think too hard about you."

He sighed and rubbed his palms over his thighs, flattening the knife-edged crease in his trousers. "Now, I'm going to ask *you* for some space. Ironic, huh?" He laughed again, but the sound came out hollow. "I'm going with Mari for the initial test. Mainly to make sure she shows up. Once we have those results, I'll be able to think things through. Make up a plan."

"But until then, you don't need me around."

A bitter smirk twisted his lips. "Oh, I'm gonna need you, but I can't let myself. I need to sort this out on my own."

"But you know I'll be here if you need me."

He looked her full in the eye as he corrected her. "*When* I need you, Millie." He planted his hands on his knees and pushed to his feet. "I'll call you next week."

"Okay."

Without another look or touch, he walked away, his back straight, his head high.

Rooted to the spot, she watched him go. His height made him easy to track. The breadth of his shoulders would have made a sculptor weep. Millie watched as he nodded greetings to passersby, stopping occasionally to accept a handshake or a friendly pat on the back. When they were alone, it was easy to forget he was who he was. Easy to believe he belonged to her and only her. But out in the world, he was a person people thought they knew. Someone they believed to be a part of their lives.

And he was.

Each time he led his team onto the court, he took the expectations of thousands of fans with them. The university administration counted on them to represent the school well. The staff basked in the reflected glory the athletic teams brought home. The students' hopes and dreams lived and died with each basket, touchdown, and home run. Every practice was designed to bring them one step closer to greatness. With the exception of Kate's Warrior Women's basketball, the school's teams were notoriously mediocre. But the cellar dwellers of the country's toughest conference had more to count on than many top-tier schools.

Every season spawned new hope. Maybe this would be their year. Perhaps this was their chance to come out on top.

Biting her bottom lip, she stared in the direction of Ty's departure long after he'd disappeared around the corner. He had every right to put her off. She'd been trying to hold him at arm's length ever since he'd come back from Reno.

Come back to her.

For her.

Despite the gnawing, twisting pain in her gut, she knew she had to let him go for now. It was only right and fair. To both of them, really. For weeks, she'd been telling him to back off, not only because she was afraid of getting in too deep, but also because she was terrified of being his rebound girl. The intensity with which he'd grabbed and held on to her scared her, but it didn't worry her nearly as much as what he'd do when he found he had an open path to a new life.

He wouldn't need to settle for a woman who had nothing more to offer than one slightly worse-for-wear heart.

So the tables were turned. Drawing a deep breath, she reached for her tote and swung the bag up onto her lap. Pulling her tablet from its depths, she tapped on the calendar app and started making notations. If she didn't hear from him in one week's time, she'd go after him. Baby, no baby. Didn't matter. She loved him, and she had no doubt she'd love his baby too. Either way, they'd both fought through worse times and come out the other side.

Maybe this was their chance to come out on top.

Blowing the air out of her lungs, she tapped on the messaging application and brought up the string of texts she, Kate, and Avery kept running. She typed with one finger but with what she liked to think was impressive speed. After hearing the little whoosh of the message winging away, she tipped her glasses down onto her nose and waited for their replies.

Almost immediately, the ellipses indicating keyboard action appeared beneath the bubble where she'd typed, Help! I've fallen in love and I can't get up.

Seconds later, Kate's initials appeared with a simple, Where are you? What do you need?

Almost immediately, Avery chimed in with, Booze is the answer. Calhoun's?

Millie shook her head and began to type. I'm going

home to wallow for a while. My house tonight. Bring ice cream. She stared at the message, then in a new message added, And booze. Another second passed. She tapped out a few more vital letters. And chips.

On it, Kate replied.

I'll bring chocolate too. Just in case, Avery responded.

Tears filled her eyes, but Millie refused to let them fall. Not until she was safe in her cozy little cottage. Blinking faster than a hummingbird's wings, she tapped out one last missive. I love you girls.

As she was tucking the tablet back in her bag, it vibrated to indicate a new message arriving. She peeked at the notification and smiled when she saw Avery's response: Worse than I thought. See you ass app! Then a second later: Damn autocorrect.

Chapter 18

TY SAT MIDWAY UP THE GRANDSTAND AND OFF TO THE SIDE, tucked away behind the piles of backpacks, gym bags, and other gear left behind by the drill team. Ignoring the autumn breeze slicing through his hooded jacket, he kept his attention focused on the lithe form on the track circling the football field. He knew her routine by heart. A two-mile warm-up on the rubberized track would end with a sharp right. She'd crisscross the spokes of the campus quadrangle, then shoot off down University Avenue. It was five miles from the edge of campus to the city water tower. Millie would touch her palm to one of the thick metal support beams to mark her arrival at the halfway point, then double back.

He wanted to follow her. Partly to make sure she was safe but mostly just to be close to her, pathetic as he was. But he wouldn't follow. He'd keep his distance because he loved her. Sounded stupid, but in his mind, the best way he could prove the depth of his feelings for her was by staying away. From her running routine, from her office door, and from her. Period.

The past week had been hell. Mari alternated between threatening, wheedling, and torrential crying jags. Once upon a time, he would have given in to any of those if for no other reason than to make them stop. These days, he could hang up on her.

She was scared. He knew she was. Hell, he was too.

He always thought he would like being a dad, but he never planned on anything like this. When Mari had told him she was pregnant the first time, he'd been nervous about the prospect of impending fatherhood, but at least he knew what to do. He'd married her. Made plans to have a family with her. Dreamed about adding a sibling or two for the kid as the years passed. Both he and Mari had been only children, so he loved the idea of his kid having the siblings he'd always wanted.

But none of those dreams were meant to be.

Chafing his hands to warm them, he leaned forward as Millie approached the near side of the track. This was her last pass before she'd take off toward the quad and all points beyond. As soon as she was out of sight, he'd have to put her out of his mind and return to the athletic center. The regular season had started, and the Warriors had posted a win in their first game. No thanks to their coach, whose mind had been off in la-la land.

His thoughts wandered away again as he watched Millie veer off the all-weather track and start pounding pavement. The headband she wore made her red hair stand up like the guy from the Christmas cartoon. He ached to tease her about it. To run his fingers through the fiery tumult of her hair, his hands over her tight runner's body.

Her ass fit perfectly in his palms. She wore compression tights and a form-fitting jacket. He knew she would shed the jacket by the time she left campus. He'd seen her tie the sleeves around her trim waist without breaking stride. And what a stride it was.

Watching Millie run was almost as good as watching her come. Ty found the play of lean muscle under skintight spandex unspeakably erotic. He'd give his left nut to feel her thighs bunch and flex. To run his hands down taut hamstrings. Feel her heels digging into his ass.

"Hey."

Ty started, his head jerking up as the decidedly masculine voice cut his trip down fantasy lane short. He blinked to clear his vision and glanced up to find Danny McMillan looming over him. "Oh. Hey." Returning his attention to the track, he did a quick scan but knew in his gut Millie was already gone. Stifling a sigh, he forced a tight smile for the football coach. "How's it going?"

Without waiting for an invitation, Danny dropped down on the bleacher. "Not bad. With a little hard work and whole bucket of luck, we might actually end up bowl-eligible."

Ty frowned, trying to remember what he'd read about the football program's upcoming conference games. They had two home games and three away before the conference championship game, and if he recalled correctly, every one of those games would be against nationally ranked opponents. Unable to hide his skepticism, he cast Danny a sidelong glance. "Ya think?"

To his credit, Danny laughed and shook his head. "Not really, but there's always hope."

"Any given Saturday," Ty intoned like a television announcer.

"Could happen." Danny dug his phone out of his jacket pocket, checked a notification on the screen, then tucked it away again. "You taking a breather out here?"

Ty shrugged. "Sometimes the smell of sweat socks can get to a guy."

"I hear you." Danny glanced over at him. "You doin' okay?" When Ty cut him a sharp look, he had the grace to shrug and look abashed. "The girls talk, but not as much as Mike does."

"So my secret is safe with no one."

"Secrets, no. You, though… You're among friends, Ty."

Danny's softly spoken reassurance spawned a lump of emotion the size of a fist. Before Ty could get a handle on himself, the damn thing rose up and lodged in his throat, making any kind of verbal response impossible. Pressing his lips tightly together, he feigned undue interest in the marching band's intricate formations as he nodded an acknowledgment.

"Kate and Avery are slobbering to tell Mari off," Danny offered.

Ty chuckled and swallowed the knot. "The line of people wanting to do that is long and distinguished." He rubbed his palms together and was surprised to find them damp. "At least they wouldn't be throwing elbows."

The other man bobbed his head. "Kate would, if you needed her to."

This time, Ty's laugh rang out hearty and true. "God, could you imagine?"

"Wouldn't be a fair fight." Danny snickered too. "Just as well. Avery's probably a pacifist anyway."

Ty gave the theory some thought. "I'm betting she'd do a little harm on Kate's or Millie's behalf." He smirked. "She lit into me in the student center the other day, telling me to get my shit straight and fix this thing."

"Yeah, because you're the one fucking everything up," Danny commiserated.

"It takes two. That's what everyone keeps reminding me."

"Yeah, it does. But that doesn't mean the timing doesn't suck."

With that one bit of unadorned acceptance of his plight, Ty's self-control snapped. "It's mine." His voice cracked. "The baby. They did the test, and it came back a match."

"Ah, shit."

Danny's soft exhalation echoed everything Ty refused to let himself voice since the call had come an hour before. Slumping forward, he closed his eyes in a weak attempt to ward off reality and caught his face in his hands.

"Crap. Should I have said congratulations?" Danny asked. "I don't know which is right in this situation."

"Yes. No. Neither do I." He gave his face a rough scrub. "God, now she's considering an abortion, and I…" He let his hands fall limp between his knees and stared bleakly at the field below. "I know it's her decision, but I feel like my life is being held hostage, you know?"

"Yeah," Danny replied quietly.

"I didn't plan this, and I certainly didn't want it to happen like this. I mean, you're right about the timing… but as Millie pointed out, this might be the only chance I get to have a kid. She can't have any, says she never wanted any, and I…" He trailed off, using only a helpless shrug as punctuation. "I do."

"But you don't want to be with anyone else."

"Right."

"Does she know? About the test, I mean."

Ty shook his head, incapable of voicing any more denial.

"When are you going to tell her?"

Again, Ty had no words.

"You can't wait, man. The longer you wait, the worse it'll be. She's been on pins and needles too," Danny reminded him.

"I know." Ty wrung his hands, then chanced a look at the man beside him. "But how? How do I do this? How can I have a relationship with Millie and be a good father to my kid? Will she still even want a relationship with me? She didn't sign on for dealing with a kid…and Mari. Hell, she's hardly signed on for anything."

"It's a lot to think about, but you'll figure it out," Danny assured him.

"Do you really think so?" he asked bluntly.

Danny clapped him hard on the shoulder, then rose, grunting a bit as his knee popped audibly. "I think you're a good guy who tries to live a good life." He surveyed the band members scurrying around in what looked to be complete disarray. "You know, it's always like this." He waved a hand in the direction of the field. "On Wednesday, they look like a pack of blind ants scrambling around for the last crumb. By Saturday evening, that mess will be a tribute to David Bowie complete with rocket ship and guitar formations."

Ty raised his eyebrows, surprised the football coach paid any attention at all to the band director's plans. "Will it?"

Danny nodded. "I started having a couple of film and television students video band practice and the halftime shows. I make the team watch them every Monday before we review game film."

"You do?"

Stepping down a row, Danny chuckled. "They hate

being compared to the band kids, but I think they're starting to see the point."

Ty blinked up at him. "Which is?"

Danny gestured to the field, where chaos seemed to reign. "If they can play 'Heroes,' then the sad, sorry bunch of misfit jocks I inherited can try to be heroes."

"Just for one day?" Ty challenged.

Danny laughed and shook his head as he proceeded to step from bleacher to bleacher. "Hell no. I need five more Saturdays out of them."

"Don't forget the bowl game," Ty called out to him.

Raising both hands over his head, Danny held up six fingers. At the bottom, he squinted up at Ty, shielding his eyes from the lowering sun with one hand. "Hey, Ty?"

"Yeah?"

"Congratulations, man."

And the fist in his chest was back. Resisting the urge to cover the sore spot with his hand, he waved and called down a gruff, "Thanks."

Practice dragged past at a snail's pace. Ty hung back, letting his assistant coaches handle the ins and outs. His powers of concentration were for shit, and the last thing he needed was anyone getting a glimpse of the mess in his head. But once the intrasquad scrimmage and post-mortem were done, he found himself reluctant to leave the Warrior Center.

Once he walked through those doors, he'd have to tell Millie the worst good news he'd ever have in his life. Because, in essence, it *was* good news. Danny's congratulations drove the reminder home. He was going to be a father, and no matter what the circumstances, he couldn't help but be a little happy. Between divorcing Mari and falling for Millie, he'd abandoned any hope of ever having a kid of his own. Now the opportunity had come around again, and he couldn't let it slip by.

As he loaded some notes, a DVD, and his tablet into his gym bag, he marveled at the turn his day had taken. That morning, he'd been ninety-nine-point-nine percent certain he was not the father of Mari's baby. Over the past week, he'd latched on to the low probability and ignored the looming specter of possibility. The last thing he wanted was to be forever tied to his ex-wife. And a child…talk about your unbreakable bonds.

Ty shuddered as he recalled Mari's behavior at the lab facility where the test took place. He didn't blame her for being nervous or scared, but she'd acted affronted when they requested pre- and postnatal DNA testing. Like she hadn't done anything to make him question her word. Yes, she'd been scared. He had been too. And the part of him that had loved her enough to marry her still cared enough to hate hurting her, but he needed things between them to be as clear as possible.

She was hurting him. Again. And he wouldn't roll over and take it this time. Now, he had more to fight for. More to look forward to. He loved Millie, and Millie loved him, whether she'd admit it or not. The back-and-forth they'd been engaged in didn't even bother him. She was wary; so was he. He had faith they could work things out.

He and Millie built each other up. Or rather, she built him up. He hadn't done much for her other than some sex and a little takeout. If only he could get her to stop fighting against him, against them. He might not be able to train for marathons with her, but he meant to prove he was in for the long haul.

But this morning, possibility and probability came together to open up a can of whoop ass on him. He still hadn't completely recovered, but he didn't have the luxury of waiting to tell Millie. He'd spilled the beans to Danny McMillan, and no matter how sneaky the former quarterback thought he was, Ty knew it was only a matter of time before Kate put the full-court press on the poor man and forced him to spill his guts.

Hefting his duffel bag, he shut off the lights and wound his way through the warren of cubicles between his office and the trophy-lined corridors. The majority of them commemorated achievement in women's basketball, but if Ty was reading his team correctly, this could be the year the men started their climb.

He'd set their sights on making the NCAA tournament the following March, but truthfully, he'd settle for a bid to the National Invitational Tournament. Some form of postseason appearance was becoming an imperative. He had only two years left on his contract, and he needed some wins in the professional arena to counterbalance the mess his personal life had become. If he couldn't spark a winning tradition, the more conservative factions around these parts would start gunning for his job. Division I coaching salaries were too high for the results to be anything less than satisfactory. Sure, he'd turned out a top draft pick, but he couldn't convince the kid to stay and play out his eligibility. The prospect of losing talent to the draft was a double-edged sword all coaches had to swallow, but few could say they'd lost their marriage to it as well.

The drive to Millie's house was short. Too short. He sat parked at the curb, the engine off and his gaze glued to her front door before he'd even started to work out what he'd say.

Drumming his fingers on the steering wheel, he tried to think of a way to spin this latest whammy, but he couldn't. He was no Millie Jensen. It was getting damn hard to find slivers of hope in the muck his life had become. And it was only going to get worse. His gut was in knots.

His attorney assured him support, custody, and visitation would be simple enough to work out, but the man didn't see the trapped animal look in Mari's eyes. She was scared, and her fear terrified Ty.

Even as an undergrad, Mari had been too sure of herself. Calculating. At the time, he'd mistaken her ambition for confidence. Now, the blinders were off. His ex-wife was a woman accustomed to getting her way, but now her plans were being thwarted, and it was his fault. He didn't need his psych degree to know exactly how this game had played out.

She'd tried to convince Dante the child was his, but the kid had been an academic all-American. Dante's math skills were sharp. Terrified of being saddled with a kid at twenty, he nipped his relationship with Mari in the bud. Then, he sicced his team of fancy new lawyers on her to discourage any further pursuit.

That left Mari with two options: going home to her family in disgrace or reconciliation with him.

Ty laughed out loud when she broached the subject

in the lab waiting room. He had to admit, Mari was at the top of her game. Pregnancy seemed to suit her. She was all dewy skin and wide eyes. Her hair was glossy and sleek, a waterfall of spun gold cascading over her shoulders and flowing over her breasts. She wore the diamond he'd given her. Her nails were polished in pale, innocent pink. The tip of one fingernail was adorned with tiny rhinestones. As if a two-carat center stone surrounded by baguettes wasn't quite enough bling for her.

I want us to be a family.

The words rang every bit as false in his head as they had the first time he'd heard them. She didn't want a family; she needed a fallback. And she was so sure he'd fall into line. That rankled. She'd never asked how he was, what might be going on in his life, or even if he was seeing anyone. Like the spoiled woman she was, she assumed her once-favorite toy would be waiting for her whenever she felt like playing with him.

He'd told her no in the gentlest terms he could manage, though she didn't really deserve the consideration. Lord knew she hadn't thought twice about his feelings when she'd run off with Dante. But he wanted to be the bigger man. A better man. He didn't want to hang on to grudges or let what happened between them taint any relationship he might have with the child she carried. So he'd been firm but as kind as he could manage, promising to be supportive of the pregnancy and the baby if the child was indeed his, but nothing more. When she pressed him, began asking questions she no longer had any right to ask, he shut down.

When the technician—who would explain the test results, the margin for error, and provide them each with a copy of the findings to give to their respective lawyers—called them into his office, Ty saw the flash of fear in Mari's eyes. But by the time they took their seats, Mari's shields were back in place, her eyes narrowed and focused on the file folder on the man's desk.

Ty would never forget that folder. Plain manila. Crisp, not yet dog-eared from use. The name printed on the label. Mari Ransom. Divorced or not, she still had the legal right to that part of him.

"The tests show a high probability that you are indeed the father of Ms. Ransom's child," the man began in a voice totally devoid of emotion.

It hardly mattered if the guy had any feeling on the subject or not, because in that moment, Ty was experiencing every possible reaction a human could manage. Gut-sinking disappointment. Heart-pounding excitement. Fear, elation, anxiety, and more than a little resentment. But…a baby. His baby. A son or a daughter. The prospect of holding his child, his father's grandchild, brought a rush of tears to his eyes.

The lab tech rambled on about percentages and likelihoods, but Ty couldn't tear his gaze from the small smile that curved Mari's lips. And his blood ran cold. He didn't know exactly what Mari would do when he failed to pony up whatever it was she expected from him, but he was fairly sure he'd never know peace as long as he was shackled to her. And neither would anyone else in his life.

He bit his lip and leaned on the steering wheel as he refocused his attention on the neat, little cottage where Millie lived. The lawn was barely bigger than a postage stamp. The oversized flowerpots boasted a few hearty stragglers but served mainly as repositories for clumps of fallen leaves. She'd painted the shutters a bright cranberry color. He smiled when he realized they were almost the exact same red as her hair.

Knowing he'd delayed long enough, he opened the car door and stepped out. His gaze was drawn to those jarringly red shutters like a pyro to fire. He was half-way up the brick walk before he realized the front door had opened.

First he saw her only in silhouette. Tousled hair. Slender arms outstretched, one braced on the door, the other hand on the opposite frame. A shadow made womanly only by the subtle curve of her hip and dip of her waist. Her endless legs were covered in loose pants, but she wore something snug on the top. She shifted her weight to one foot and blocked enough of the light for him to make out red and pink lipstick kisses covering her pajama pants. He vaulted the shallow steps and drew to a breathless halt, summoning the last shreds of his inner strength to keep from staring at the way her taut nipples pressed against the ribbed fabric of her tank top.

Instead of feeling winded, a mantle of calm settled over him when he stepped into the stream of light spilling from her home. "Hey."

She didn't lower her arms and beckon him in, but her smile was warm and affectionate. "Hi, Ty."

Greetings exchanged, he found himself without the slightest clue how to proceed.

Thankfully, Millie was feeling merciful. "Would you like to come in?"

He nodded. "Thank you. Yes." Following her into the tiny entry, he had to duck to miss hitting a lower branch of the funky, sixties-style chandelier. "Oh. Uh, hey." He chuckled as he sidestepped a frosted glass square suspended by filament wire. "That's cool."

She smiled as she swung the door shut behind him. "I swiped it from my stepmom's house. She and my dad had one of those mid-century modern ranch houses that made you think Frank Sinatra and the Rat Pack might be dropping by for a stiff one at five o'clock."

Ty grinned, taken by the image her description evoked. "So it really is cool, then."

"The coolest, man." Her bare feet whispered over varnished oak hardwoods. She walked backward as she led him toward the kitchen. "You look like you could use a drink. Hard day at the office?"

"You could say."

"I can offer you premixed margarita, some wine that has been open a little too long, or some rum." She paused. "If you're lucky, I might have a Diet Coke to go with the rum."

"I'm okay, thanks."

A big, fat lie, but as much as he could have used a drink, he needed to be stone-cold sober to say what he needed to say. Bracing himself, he stepped into the kitchen and came to an abrupt stop.

The room was so perfectly Millie it made his chest hurt. The appliances were newer models made of sleek stainless steel. The countertops had been replaced with some kind of speckled solid-surface material. The walls were stucco plaster and painted rich, buttery yellow. But the cabinets looked to be original, the glass panes wavy on a couple, one sporting a clamshell chip out of the corner. Other people would have painted them a glossy white, but Millie wasn't other people. No, she'd gone with an aqua so vivid it reminded him of a tiny inlet on an even tinier Greek island.

The place where he thought he'd found peace.

Now, he knew his peace resided in the woman across from him. A woman so vivid he had a hard time tearing his gaze from her.

But he did.

There were things to be said, and he needed to get on with it.

Ty drew a steadying breath and continued his inspection of her place. After all, who knew if he'd ever be invited into her inner sanctum again?

In addition to the bold color choices, she'd finished the room off with the kind of homey touches he'd never think to make. A shallow glass bowl held fresh fruit. A Snoopy cookie jar. The fridge was peppered with whimsical magnets from a variety of destinations and print-outs of Wolcott Warrior team schedules. The lacrosse team had a match the following day. She had a number of the games on the football schedule highlighted in neon green. A photo of Kate Snyder in a bikini had been printed on plain copier paper. Someone wrote the words *money shot* across the top with a magic marker. The photo held a place of pride in the center of the melee.

Swallowing the dull ache in his throat, he tore himself away from his study of her natural habitat and forced himself to face the inevitable. "The baby is mine." He spoke the words bluntly but found himself unable to meet her eyes. "At least, that's what the prenatal test shows."

He pressed his lips together tightly, hell-bent on having this all out in the open now. Quickly. No point in prolonging the torture for either of them. Better to rip the bandage off this farce of a life he thought he could live and let the damn thing bleed out. "They tell me the odds are pretty much certain the testing they'll do on the umbilical cord will confirm paternity, so there you go." He jerked his head up, his gaze homing on her like a laser-guided missile. "I'm going to be a father."

The pause that followed was beyond pregnant. Her pulse throbbed, the delicate skin of her throat no match for the impact his announcement had on her. Part of him was elated to see the evidence of her jangled nerves. She loved him. He knew she did, even if she never said so.

"Congratulations."

Her soft-spoken response deserved an equally polite reply. "Thank you."

"And Mari is doing well? Healthy?"

"She's fine." A laugh escaped him. "A pain in my ass, but physically fine."

"And her plan?" she prompted, suddenly intent on retrieving a bottle of water from the fridge. She glanced back at him over her shoulder. "Is she going to stay here?"

He jerked, stunned to realize he'd never thought to ask the question himself. "I have no idea."

She nodded as she let the refrigerator door swing shut, uncapping her bottle as if they weren't discussing the demise of everything they'd been to each other. "Well, it would be nice to have the baby nearby. Are her folks from around here?"

"They're near DC."

She pursed her lips. "Not too far." He stared transfixed as she wrapped her lips around the mouth of the bottle and took a deep drink. "Maybe she'll end up living near them."

"So you know she and Dante broke up?"

Millie's grimace confirmed as much. "Yeah, well, I saw some stuff online."

"You know, there are days when I hate the internet. Actually, most days."

The grimace softened into a smile. "Every day, I thank God I made it through school in the predigital era. Some things were caught on film, but by now, no one knows where the negatives are, and only a handful are savvy enough to work a scanner."

Silence stretched between them, but this time, the familiar tension was missing. This quiet was weak. Resigned. After months of flirting, feinting, and some downright incredible fucking, they were over. Before he'd even convinced her to get started. No matter how much he loved her and wanted her, she didn't want what he had coming into his life. And he had to accept her life choices.

"So, yeah." He ran his hand over his hair, then drew back. "My life is going to be kind of…"

"Chaotic?" she supplied.

"To say the least."

He nearly seized when she set the bottle aside and started toward him. He didn't know what he'd do if she touched him. Shatter? Implode? Break down and blubber like a little boy? God, a part of him wanted to. He wanted to howl and yowl and throw a hissy fit the likes of which the world hadn't seen since Bob Knight left collegiate basketball.

He held his breath when she came to a stop in front of

him. Her body swayed. Ty wouldn't have been surprised if his had too. The first time he'd kissed her, he knew he'd found an essential element. A pick that would let him roll. She was the alley, and he was the oop. One incomplete without the other. Did she know? Would she feel the loss too?

So gently he barely felt the heat of her touch, she laid her palm over his heart. "I'm happy for you, Ty."

"Are you?"

"Always."

The single-word response sounded a lot like a good-bye. If he didn't want to do the breaking and blubbering, he had to man up, try to tip the conversation to his side, and send this relationship to the showers as soon as possible. "Okay, well…thank you." He gave a nod and then shrugged. "I'm gonna need a little time to… figure things out."

Her eyes were warm but sad. "Of course. I meant what I said before. I'm here if you need me."

If he needed her? He needed her all the time. Didn't she know?

Christ, he wanted to swoop her up. Kiss her. Beg her. Ask her to take him on anyway, complications and all, but he couldn't. Wouldn't. It wouldn't be fair. A woman like Millie would never live a life dictated by someone else's choices. She knew her own mind too well, and he knew enough about the tender heart she kept hidden under her sharp exterior to try to box her into a corner.

Swallowing the last of a long list of wants, Ty forced a tight smile. "I appreciate your…friendship."

"And you'll always have it." She gave him a tremulous smile. "Let me know if I can do anything to help."

Love me. That was all he wanted to say. *Love me anyway.* But he didn't. He couldn't.

"Goodbye, Millie."

She inclined her head like a queen allowing her man-servant to take his leave. "Bye, Ty."

He swallowed a bitter laugh as he walked out. As far as he could see, the roles weren't too far off. From the beginning, she'd been the one calling the plays. And for the first time in a long time, he'd been someone's go-to guy. The playmaker. He opened her front door and paused to take a breath of the crisp autumn air.

Then, without giving himself a chance to overthink what he was doing, he stepped out into the night and closed her door behind him.

Chapter 19

MILLIE SAT IN THE CENTER OF HER COUCH, A THROW TUCKED snuggly around her legs and the remote control in her hand. Though it would take a mere flick of her finger to power the television up, she didn't bother. The floor show taking place right in front of her was more enjoyable to watch than anything she'd seen in the past two weeks.

Every square inch of the coffee table in front of her was covered. Avery must have used every clean bowl, dish, plate, and platter in Millie's cupboards. She stared down at the array, trying to make heads or tails of the logic behind the arrangement. A dish of peanut M&M's in autumnal colors nestled against her hip. A bowl of puffy cheese curls tucked into the cushion on her other side. Pints of ice cream arced across the coffee table, lids off and spoons jabbed into them. She was surrounded by the love of her friends. An open box of Godiva truffles. A tub of buttery popcorn. Rainbows of candy. Every variety of salty snack. And in the center of the smorgasbord—a pizza.

Not some crazy, burn-the-lining-of-your-esophagus pizza, but a nice, plain cheese pizza. With extra cheese. Comfort pizza.

Kate walked into the room with a bottle of wine tucked under her arm. Millie smiled gratefully as she watched her friend work the cork from the bottle with a twist of her wrist and a hushed *thwunk*. Had she been left to her own devices, Millie would have yanked and pulled at the corkscrew until she broke the cork. Then she would have poked it down into the bottle and drank it anyway, claiming that a little flotsam never hurt anyone.

"I'm not helpless, you know," she said as Kate made room for the bottle among all the other offerings.

"We know." Without missing a beat, Kate pulled a bottle of water from each pocket of her track pants and wedged them into the couch cushions. "One bottle for every glass of wine," she instructed sternly.

"She's the booze monitor," Avery huffed as she came back into the room carrying the open case of bottled water. "I'm in charge of junk food. Anything you don't see, you tell me. I know a guy at the market," she added, waggling her eyebrows. "I get free delivery."

Kate slid down to the floor with an audible groan, then pushed back until she was propped against the sofa beside Millie's knees. "Avery, trading tit for taters isn't exactly free."

Their friend had the good grace to laugh at the crack as she fell into the tiny living room's only other piece of furniture, an overstuffed armchair that Ty would have made look like it belonged in a kindergarten classroom. Millie smiled at the two women. How lucky was she to have friends like these? Reaching down, she gave Kate's shoulder a pat. "Plenty of room up here."

Kate shook her head and stretched her long legs out in front of her. "Nah, I'm more comfortable down here." She reached for the remote, and seconds later, the television lit up with the logo of a movie-streaming website. "Are we going nostalgic with John Hughes, mildly bitter and blatantly satiric with Rob Reiner, or the comedic genius of Mel Brooks?"

"Or my personal favorite wallowing movie of all time: *Fatal Attraction*?" Avery chimed in.

"I told you, no bunny boilers," Kate retorted in a tone that said she'd make Avery run laps if she could.

"Fine." Avery pouted for a second, then brightened. "*Thelma and Louise*? *Heathers*? *The Women*?"

"Guys," Millie said, interrupting their banter.

Kate blinked. "Hmm?"

Avery's forehead puckered. She hated being interrupted midflow. "What?"

Millie inhaled through her nose, surveying the array of caloric comfort her friends had provided for the second time in her nonexistent menstrual cycle and gathering the courage to ask the question plaguing her since Ty walked out of her life. "Do you think I'd be a good mom?"

Both women did excellent owl imitations, but neither offered up an opinion. Their silence made her nervous.

"I mean, not like a real mom, but more like a…" She trailed off, unable to finish the presumptuous thought.

"Stepmom?" Kate ventured, her voice tinged with equal parts caution and optimism.

"Yeah." The second the confirmation was out of her mouth, Millie rushed to qualify the question. "Not that anyone has asked anyone to be one, but…in general."

"Depends," Avery said at last. "Are you worried you'll be a Disney-caliber stepmother?" She wagged her head, and the riot of curls flew all around her elfin face. "No. Not even close." She shrugged. "If you're shooting for June Cleaver—"

"Or Donna Reed," Kate chimed in.

Avery acknowledged the addition with a nod. "—or even Carol Brady, I'd say you're lacking a certain, I don't know, Stepford quality."

"You could definitely pull off Peggy Bundy," Kate assured her.

Avery snapped her fingers. "Marge Simpson."

"No, wait! Lorelai Gilmore," Kate crowed, sitting up straighter. "Smart, funny, the edgy-sarcasm thing, but totally hip and cool."

Beaming her agreement, Avery reached for a relish tray filled with licorice whips, Skittles, Hot Tamales, and a neatly stacked pyramid of unwrapped Rolos and snagged a handful of rainbow-colored candies. "Yes, you can definitely do a Lorelai Gilmore thing. She was really good with that little mutant Christopher had with the flaky chick."

Kate snorted. "And Luke's DNA dork of a daughter."

"Not to mention Rory. Duh." Avery pulled a grimace, then cocked her head. "You know, I liked Luke's daughter, April. I thought she was a nice kid. It's not her fault she had a schizophrenic mother."

"Schizophrenic mother?" Kate asked.

"Same actress played another part in an earlier season."

Millie watched the two of them go back and forth. If they weren't discussing her life with such blithe references to television characters, she would have been as enthralled as any spectator with center court seats for Wimbledon. But it *was* her life they were discussing. And she'd asked her two best friends what was possibly the most soul-bearing question she'd ever asked anyone.

"Hey!" Much to her gratification, both women

jumped. Avery even had the good grace to choke on a Skittle. Millie waited until the younger woman was done pounding her chest and doing a self-Heimlich. When her coughs downshifted into excessive throat clearing, Millie nodded to the bottle of wine. "Wash it down."

Not waiting to be asked twice, Avery grabbed the bottle and downed a healthy swig.

Millie counted to three as she fought for patience. "Can we leave fictional characters out of this discussion and try to stay somewhere in the vicinity of reality?"

Kate looked affronted, but only for a second. "You asked a question. We were trying to give a little context."

"I asked if you thought I'd be a good mom."

"And we said yes," Avery asserted.

Millie searched her friends' faces for confirmation. "That was a yes?"

"Well, yeah," Kate said.

"Of course," Avery concurred. "Remember? 'Definitely not Disney'?"

"And definitely not a Nick at Nite mom," Kate reminded her.

"But a real kind of mom." Avery shrugged as if the conclusion was obvious. "One who does her best. Loves fiercely. Sometimes you might screw up, but I bet you'd do the job right most days."

Without so much as a tingle of warning, an appalling rush of emotion engulfed Millie. Every doubt and worry she'd been wrestling with since Ty walked out of her house evaporated. Hot tears scalded her eyes and clogged her throat. The cold lump of ache lodged in her chest exploded, scattering fragments of raw need like shrapnel.

Her hand trembled as she clamped her fingers over

her mouth, trying to hold in a sob. It was no good. A shudder racked her body, and the low, keening moan seeped out from between shaky fingers.

In a heartbeat, the bowls and bottles surrounding her were displaced. Kate wrapped her long, strong arms around her tight. Avery scooted in close and Millie sighed as she sank into their comforting embraces. At last, sandwiched between the two best friends ever to walk the earth, she let go.

"Oh God." She gasped between bouts of hysterical, snotty sobbing.

"I know," Kate crooned.

She stroked Millie's hair clumsily, but with such tender affection Millie cried even harder. Kate squeezed tighter, and so did Avery. Millie might have protested on any other day, but today, she needed this. Wanted it. The second her harsh sobs subsided, Avery took advantage of her vulnerable state and pressed a hard, smacking kiss to her temple.

"This isn't a tragedy, Mil." Avery spoke the words with quiet conviction. As if this were a subject she knew she had to make clear for a final exam. "Tragedies don't allow for disorder. Their path is set from the beginning, and the end is inescapable. No one is going to die from this." She leaned her head against Millie's, as though she might get her point across via mind meld. "If anything, this is a comedy. The plot is sloppy and chock-full of errors. You and Ty have both been trying so hard to stay disengaged, but everyone watching this farce of yours play out knows you're not."

Millie tensed, offended by her friend's lighthearted choice of words. "Farce?"

But Avery didn't back down. "Yes, a farce. Right now, it's a little more Blake Edwards than Noël Coward, but you get what I mean." She squeezed harder. "It's not funny because it's happening to you. I understand, but try to take a step back."

Millie wanted to, but she couldn't move so much as an inch, much less take any kind of step.

"You want him, he wants you, but he's married to her. Then he's not married to her anymore, but you're all gun-shy because you can't call the shots, so you try to hold him off by making up all sorts of ridiculous rules. He chases you around, and you let him catch you. Of course, the poor audience doesn't get to see the frolicking and fucking taking place behind closed doors. Suckers should have paid for better seats." She drew a dramatic breath before plunging ahead. "Mari pops up with a super surprise baby, and everyone scatters, doors slamming all over the place." She chuckled. "Hell, we should try to get Neil Simon to write the script."

"Avery," Kate warned.

But Millie shook her head to stop her. Avery was right. This wasn't a tragedy. Ty was going to have the kid he always wanted. Maybe it wasn't happening in the way he'd imagined, but that didn't mean his plan for his life couldn't change. And so could hers. It would be different. Not simple. Definitely wackier. But maybe better.

"No, she's right," Millie whispered, lifting her head as the truth settled in. "This *is* a farce."

The three of them clung to one another for a second longer, then Avery released them. Kate's arms fell to her sides, but a deep furrow creased her brow. Out of habit,

Millie reached over and smoothed the wrinkle away with her thumb. "Keep that up, and Aunt Millie will be filling your Christmas stocking with botulism shots."

A faint smile curved Kate's lips, but it vanished almost as fast as it came. "Since when is a farce a good thing?"

Avery waved the question away. "Common misconception. A farce is a form of comedy. Broad comedy played for laughs, so it gets a bad rap. But comedies usually have happy endings." She smirked and fell back against the arm of the sofa, her gaze locked on Millie's profile. "All we need to do is figure out how to get past all the door slamming and get you to your happily ever after."

Millie resisted the urge to make a Drew Barrymore comment. One slip, and these two would be back to vomiting bits of pop culture. "Might be easier said than done."

Kate pursed her lips, then dismissed the notion with a brisk shake of her head. "Nah. This is a man we're dealing with. They are not complex creatures."

"Truer words were never spoken." Avery pushed into the armrest and practically catapulted herself from the sofa. "Come on. Might as well start with the big guns to show him we mean business." She looked down at Millie, her hands planted on rounded hips. "Show us the naughty underwear you bought."

"Naughty underwear?"

Kate nodded, approving Avery's opening salvo. "It really is amazing how weak a scrap of lace can make someone. Pathetic, actually." She rose and picked her way carefully through the elaborate array of junk food and adult beverages. "I try not to think about how weak men are when it comes to sex. I hate to admit I married such easy prey, you know?"

Avery followed her toward the short corridor leading to the bedrooms. "I understand. Anytime I find myself tethered to one of them for more than, say, an hour or so, I feel the IQ points eroding away."

Kate paused in the doorway and looked back at Millie. "You coming, or do you want me to let Gloria Vanderbilt Steinem here be your fashion consultant?" She tipped her head in Avery's direction and raised both eyebrows.

"If I get to choose, I'm burning all the bras… Do you have any macramé panties, by chance?" Avery asked on cue.

Fueled by fear, Millie launched herself from the nest she'd allowed them to build around her. "Oh no you don't," she warned. "Stay out of my underwear!"

Laughing, Avery plucked the open bottle of wine from the collection of goodies. "You'd better come supervise then." She nodded toward the bedrooms and speared the air ahead of them with the neck of the bottle. "Let Operation Bag a Moron begin!"

~~~

She was nervous, and the realization was enough to spur her on. Millie Jensen didn't get nervous. Not in front of cameras or under fire from dozens of rabid reporters. She had ice water in her veins. Even the coolest free throw shooters looked like basket cases next to her. She didn't get het up over anything short of a semiannual shoe sale. Certainly not over a man.

Squaring her shoulders, she tipped her chin up and

stepped cautiously around the corner of the house. The backyard was dark, but she knew from her previous sojourn that straying too far to the right would set off a series of motion-sensor lights. The last time she snuck up on him, the gate had been unlatched. Millie was praying she'd be lucky again. She picked her way across the flagstone patio toward the back of the house. Once again, the flat-screen TV mounted on the wall provided the only light on the ground floor. Like the last time, she could see the outline of his chair, but this time, she failed to spot the man himself.

Cupping her hands, she pressed her face to the glass and peered into the gloom. Then a voice came from behind her.

"If I didn't know better, I'd say you were casing the place."

Millie jumped and whirled, slapping one hand over her mouth to muffle her yelp of surprise and the other to her hammering heart. Ty lay stretched out on one of the patio lounges behind her, hooded sweatshirt zipped to his throat and his hands buried deep in the pockets.

She squinted into the darkness, waiting until her eyes adjusted to the dim glow coming from the pool lights. She clutched her own jacket—a black wool peacoat Kate insisted was a must for any covert operation—tighter and started toward the man in the shadows. "What are you doing out here? It's freezing."

Ty snorted but made no move to stand and greet her. "You are a true Southerner. It's over fifty degrees, Millie."

She looked down at the long legs crossed at the ankles. He wore track pants and a pair of white, low-cut athletic socks. The outfit shouldn't have been alluring, but to her, it was. This was Ty at home and relaxed. He wasn't a snappy-suit or silk-tie guy, though he wore them well. He wasn't even the jeans and tee type, even if he filled both out as if they were made expressly for him. No, he was a man who padded around in his socks and wore his T-shirts until the collars started to fray because he believed the breakdown made them feel softer. And she loved him more for his foibles.

And so much more.

More. A word she hadn't allowed herself to entertain for a long time, but now, more seemed to be right... there. All she had to do was reach out and grab the chance. Exchange her safe life of order and control for one of chaos and adventure. But to have more, she'd have to risk it all. Her whole heart. Not only the part she so desperately wanted to give to Ty, but the others too. The corners she'd closed off so long ago, she'd almost forgotten they existed.

Her knees trembled and threatened to give way, so she beat them to the punch. Sinking to the side of his chaise, she looked Ty straight in the eye. "I never thought I'd be a very good mom." She saw surprise register on his face but didn't wait for a response. Talking almost more to herself than him, she forged ahead. "Which is ridiculous, really. My mom was great. So was her mom. I had tons of good role models." She paused and drank in a deep draught of night air. "But my ex wasn't really an... encouraging man."

"He's the one who made you doubt yourself," Ty said, his voice gruff with anger he didn't bother to hide.

Millie smiled at the knee-jerk assessment, then

ducked her head. "For a little while, yeah. But then he became the guy who made me want to prove myself." She wet her lips. "The more he belittled me, the more I wanted to show him what I really was." Her smile faded into the barest curve of her mouth. "Did I tell you my daddy taught me to play poker?"

"No."

Notching her chin up, she looked him straight in the eye. "I'm good."

"I have no doubt."

"I waited. I let him deal hand after hand, but then I had a miscarriage, and he announced to God and the world we'd try again as soon as possible, and I knew I could not let that happen. If we had a baby, I'd never leave him. I'd never get out." This time, she didn't bother masking her true feelings with a smile. "I made an appointment at a nearby clinic as soon as I had recovered. I had an implant done. Then I told him Dr. Watkins said the miscarriage caused irreparable damage," she enunciated the last two words with extra relish. "I was a dee-vor-say before Christmas. Best present I ever gave myself."

His eyes widened, then narrowed. "He was an ass."

Millie nodded. "Ancient history." She brushed the subject of her brief stint as wife and possible mother away with an impatient flick of her fingers. "Karma kicked in not long after. I tried not to get pregnant, but instead, I got cancer. At least I beat it. I'm grateful for that." She forced a quick smile, but it felt like a grimace. "I wish I could say I regret the choices I've made, but I don't. Not really. Cancer or no, I can honestly say I don't think I ever wanted to have a baby."

"There's no law saying you have to want kids."

A bitter little laugh popped out. "Yeah right. Maybe not for men, but women…" She trailed off, her gaze fixed on the gently undulating water in the pool. "Anyhow. I like kids." She flashed a wary smile. "I mean, I'm not an ogre."

"Not at all green."

Gathering her courage, she dragged her attention from the pool and met his gaze. "I may not have wanted to have a baby, but I do think I'd make a fairly decent stepmother." He looked so taken aback by the assertion, she rushed into the breach. Unfortunately, the only words she could conjure were the debates still echoing in her head. "Not like Carol Brady good, but maybe like Julia Roberts in the movie with Susan Sarandon."

"Stepmother?" He sat up so fast she would have toppled off the edge of the chair if he hadn't grabbed her. Incredulity etched into every line in his handsome face, he searched her eyes. "Did you just propose to me?"

"Well, no," she said, her mind reeling. "I mean, yes. Maybe." Frustrated, she stopped searching for the right thing to say and let her thoughts run loose. "I'm not proposing we get married so much as you let me do this with you. Be with you." He didn't respond, which did nothing to stem the flow of babble. "That is, if you and Mari—"

"There will never be a 'me and Mari' again," he said gruffly. Then he gave her a little shake as if testing to see if she was real. "I'm only interested in me and you. Haven't I been telling you from the start?"

A tremulous smile quirked her lips, but she wasn't exactly positive if they were running on the same track. "So you think we can still have a you and me?"

He huffed a laugh of disbelief. "Are you kidding? As

long as you're okay with you and me and baby making three, then yes. Hell yes." He gave her one more shake, then hauled her against his chest like she were no more than a rag doll. "Yes. God yes," he murmured as he rained kisses on her neck, jaw, and cheek.

"I don't know how to do this parenthood thing, Millie. To tell the truth, I'd pretty much given up on it ever happening and made my peace." He took a shaky breath, then pressed his cheek against hers so his lips were at her ear. "I sure as hell never wanted to do it this way, but if this way is the only way, then I want you with me. I need you."

A shudder ran through her, but it wasn't fear or dread. No, the adrenaline pulsing through her veins was laced with anticipation. "I need you too."

"Yes, I'll marry you, Millie," he whispered in her ear. "But you're going to have to buy me a big, fat ring."

She laughed, all the worry and tension flowing out of her on a shiver once his lips found the pulse in her throat. "I really wasn't proposing."

"Then maybe I'll have to do the honors." She heard his deep inhale as he forced himself to pull away. "Millie, will you—"

She silenced him with a single finger pressed to his lips. "Always pushing," she chided. "Let's table the marriage talk for one day soon and figure out how we're going to handle the other stuff first."

A stubborn frown stole over his features. "Nuh-uh. Answer me now. We can set a date later."

She pursed her lips as she took his measure and reviewed her options. Ty knew what she was doing and called her out.

"Oh, come on. All I'm asking for is a simple yes or no. Everything else we can negotiate, but you have to give me this much now."

Tickled by the determinedly mulish set of his jaw, she leaned in and pressed a tender kiss to the muscle ticking below his ear. "Yes," she whispered. "Good press or bad. Babies or no babies, yes. But I get to choose my own pizza toppings."

"Deal." He kissed her hard and fast to seal the bargain.

"And *you* proposed, so *I* get the big, fat ring."

He nodded once. "Done."

Resting her head against his chest, Millie smiled as she listened to the steady thud of his heart. She loved the constancy of the beat. Strong. Unhesitating. If any man embodied the term *wholehearted*, it was Tyrell Ransom. And he loved her. That oh-so-dependable heart was hers. And it came wrapped up in the pretty package of one utterly delectable man.

She smiled at him. Every inch of her body was trembling with cold and excitement, but her grin never faltered. He was looking at her as if she'd swished the winning basket in a national championship. She needed to tell him she loved him. She wanted him to know how much having him in her life had changed her. More than anything, she ached to ask him to take her to bed.

But when she opened her mouth, none of those things came out.

"I'm scared shitless."

He barked a laugh. The sound of it carried out into the night beyond the patio lights. "Me too."

She made no move to pull away. For once in her life,

she wasn't trying to finagle a little space or planning an exit strategy. Staying put felt good. Damn good. "Tomorrow, we'll figure out the angle and plan our attack on life."

"Okay."

Realization struck. Angling her head back, she peered up at him, squinting to make out his features in the dim light. "You know I love you, right?" The declaration came fast and breathy, but at least she got the words out. At last.

His lips twitched, but he didn't smile. "Took you a damn long time to figure it out."

Unperturbed by his cockiness, she burrowed back into his embrace. "You love me too."

"I guess we're even."

Reassured, she hugged him harder, hoping to steal some of his body heat. "I'm also cold."

"Me too," he whispered, brushing a kiss over the top of her head.

"I wonder if we can be clueless and scared but warm in your bed."

"Maybe."

Heaving a reluctant sigh, she peeled herself away and stood, offering her hand to him. His fingers were cool but still warmer than hers. She heard the pop in his knees and Ty's quiet groan of pain as he rose from the low-slung chair and made a mental note to kiss those creaky knees once she had him at her mercy.

"Let's get inside." Ty allowed her to pull him toward the sliding doors but stopped short. When she slid him a questioning glance, he only ducked his head and shuffled his ginormous feet.

"What?"

"I locked myself out," he confessed in a low voice.

Not sure she'd heard him right, she cocked an ear in his direction. "What?"

"The door. I must have accidentally hit the thumb lock when I came out here. Mike has a spare set of keys. I was going to call him to come let me in, but..." He let the rest trail off, then stepped forward to cup a hand to the glass. "My phone's inside."

Shaking her head in disbelief, Millie moved to the door and peered through the treated glass into the darkened great room. The television flickered, casting its eerie, blue-white glow over the empty armchair. Sure enough, she picked out the rectangular shape of a cell phone perched on the arm.

"Why did you come out here?"

He shrugged. "Chambers was yammering on NSN. The house was empty. I'm having a kid with a woman I don't love, and I couldn't even call the woman I do love." He pursed his lips as if deciding if he'd covered everything. "I guess I needed some air."

She studied him. "Have you had enough?"

"Enough what?"

"Air? Sulking? Self-flagellation?"

"Can anyone ever get enough self-flagellation?"

His quick response made her grin. "Nope."

"But I would like to go inside. With you," he said, his expression earnest. "If you'll let me borrow your phone, Mike isn't too far from here."

Millie snorted derisively. "We don't need Mike."

"We don't?"

She gestured to her feet. "I have the perfect footwear

geared to breaking and entering. Sturdy but stylish." She pursed her lips and studied the house before heading toward the slope along the side. "You never close the bedroom window, but it's too high for me to reach. I'm gonna need something, or someone, tall to climb, but I can get in."

Ty chuckled as he followed her to the side of the house. Stopping under the partially open bedroom window, he stooped and made a cradle out of his hands. "Never thought I'd be helping someone break into my own house."

"Yeah, well, I never thought I'd be so hard up as to seduce an innocent single dad, but here we are." She placed her hands on his shoulders for balance and looked him straight in the eye. "Thank God the alarm is disarmed. I'm in no mood to play spin doctor tonight."

"How about plain old doctor?" he asked as she took a practice bounce on the ball of her foot.

"Okay, but I hope you're up for a super-invasive examination. Possibly stirrups."

He snickered but held steady. "Who said *you* get to be the doctor?"

"Because I'll be the one controlling the locks." She pressed a quick smacking kiss to his lips, then flexed her knee. "Ready? Here we go."

Millie pinwheeled her arms as she flew into the air like a circus acrobat. Grabbing hold of the windowsill, she yanked at the screen one handed. "This looks so much easier on TV."

Ty pivoted to position himself under her. Seconds later, she felt him pressing up on the soles of her boots. She glanced down as the pressure on her straining arm muscles eased. He had her. And together, they could handle anything. Even custom windows with screens that fit like a glove.

The corner of the window screen popped free from its frame. Millie wrested the remainder from the tracks with a growl of triumph. Ty's voice floated up to her.

"This is turning me on. Is that wrong?"

"Not at all. I'm the hottest cat burglar in town." With another grunt, she leveraged the window up as far as it would go. "Doing okay?"

He peered straight up her legs. "Best view ever."

Millie chuckled as she adjusted her hold on the sill. "And I'm not even wearing a skirt."

"In my mind, you are."

"Get ready to push, big guy. I can see the bed, and I want in."

"Tell me you love me, Millie."

She scoffed. "Now is not the—"

"Tell me."

"God, you play dirty," she hissed down at him.

"I play for keeps. Now, tell me you love me, Millie, then crawl your fine ass through my bedroom window. I have sixteen fantasies playing out," he said through gritted teeth. "They all start the same."

Millie couldn't help but smile. His stubborn streak was almost as wide as hers. They were going to have a damn good time together. "I love you, Ty."

"And you're in."

He thrust her up and through his window with a growl that seemed to come straight from his soul. Her palms hit hardwood. She tucked her head and rolled, coming up into a neat little crouch worthy of a

Hollywood stunt double. "Damn, I'm good at this," she whispered to herself.

As if he could read her mind, Ty shouted up from the grass below. "Stop plotting your life of crime and let me in."

Millie casually strolled through the main floor, then sauntered down the steps to the lower level. She could see his shadow looming beyond the wall of glass. He rapped impatiently on the slider, but she took her time, stalking toward him like a cat picking out her every step.

"Hurry up."

"So impatient," she murmured, then blew him a kiss through the smoked glass. "What's the password?"

"Headline News," he retorted.

"Nope."

"TMX," he said, giving the glass another sharp tap.

"Z," she corrected. "It's TMZ, and no. That's not the password."

Ty's chest heaved as he let his curled hands fall helpless to his sides. "I love you?"

Millie unlatched the lock but slid the door open only enough to show her face. "Try again. This time like you mean it."

"I love you," he repeated, his gaze unwavering. "Now, if you don't let me take you to bed, we're going to give the world something really newsworthy."

She smirked. "I like a man who thinks highly of himself." He pushed through the door, slid it shut behind him, and flipped the lock. "Ooh! So forceful and commanding."

Ty snickered as he dipped a shoulder and threw her over his back in a firefighter's hold. "And I like a woman who knows when to be quiet."

Millie laughed as he started for the stairs. "Well, maybe one day, you'll meet a nice girl."

"One can always hope. Until then, I guess I'm stuck with you."

"You are." Millie spread greedy hands over the ridged muscles in his back. "And I plan on holding you hostage for a while, my handsome Coach Ransom."

Keep reading for an excerpt of

WITH HER FEET SPREAD WIDE AND HER LUCKY CLIPBOARD clutched tight to her chest, Coach Kate Snyder tipped her head back and gazed at the scoreboard suspended over center court. She didn't need to check the display to know they were up a mere three points in these final seconds, but superstition kept her chin up and her eyes locked on the garish display.

She never watched the last play of the game.

The LED display exhorted the crowd to "MAKE SOME NOISE." The timer switched over from minutes and seconds to seconds split down to hundredths. Her heart beat as hard as the sneakers pounding hardwood.

Without looking, she knew the opposing team's point guard was driving the ball down court with little impediment. Kate's players wouldn't risk a foul at this point. The Wolcott University Women Warriors played smart. They weren't about to give up any free shots. She'd made it clear she'd prefer to play it out in over-time rather than witness her Warriors exhibiting any self-defeating behavior.

Guard the perimeter. Make them shoot for the tie. Keep it out of the hot hands of the other team's lethal power forward. These were the key points she'd driven home in their final time-out. Now, she had to trust her team to execute. The increase in noise level told her their defensive strategy was working.

A collective gasp signaled the Huskies had finally succeeded in getting the ball to their shooter. The roar of blood in her ears muffled the mixture of cheers and groans. Two and three-tenths seconds left on the clock.

Then, a sharp slap shattered the preternatural calm. Cheers erupted into unchecked screams. Kate heard the lazy *thump-thump-thump* of a loose ball and tuned in just in time to see the basketball bounce to a roll, heading for the other end of the court.

The buzzer sounded and the bench emptied.

Staring up at the screen, hoping for a replay, Kate allowed herself to be carried along on a swell of people. Assistants and trainers pummeled her shoulders and back. Three of her senior starters enveloped her in sweaty, tearful hugs. Reporters tried to muscle their way into the throng, but her Warrior Women formed a wall around her.

A stepladder was set up under the home team's basket. They moved toward it in a clump of jubilation. Someone plunked a hat atop her head. One persistent reporter snaked a microphone through the mass of bodies, but the question was lost in the shuffle. Kate kicked her pumps off at the foot of the ladder and started to climb. One step, two. She'd been able to touch the cool, smooth iron of an orange-painted rim since she was fifteen, but the sensation never grew old. Perching a hip on the highest step, she reached for the gleaming gold-plated scissors her boss, Wolcott University Athletic Director Mike Samlin, passed up to her.

Security tried in vain to herd the players toward center court, but it was no use. They weren't moving until the net came down. Reporters continued to thrust their microphones in her direction, though how they'd isolate her answers in the cacophony of celebration, she'd never know. Still, she answered one inane question for each loop of nylon she cut through.

Snip. How big a role did strategy play in their victory?

She bit back the first sarcastic answer that sprang to mind. Her friend and university public relations guru, Millie Jensen, would be so proud. "Like flattery, strategy will get you everywhere," she called down to the milling crowd. "You can't win if you don't know how you're going to play."

Snip. "Yes, I am incredibly proud of these young women."

Snip, snip. "God yes, I'll miss these seniors. We've been through a lot of battles together."

Already impatient to move on to the trophy ceremony, she started hacking at the loops on the far side of the hoop. *Snip, snip, snip.*

"Of course we expected a fight out of the Huskies," she answered, trying to hide her irritation with a wide smile. "This is the championship game. We wanted a fight."

She pretended not to hear the garbled questions coming at her as she worked her way around the rim. There'd be a press conference immediately following the presentation of the trophy. They could wait until then to pepper her.

Mike Samlin beamed at her from his spot at the foot of the ladder. As he should. They'd done it. The Wolcott Warriors were the NCAA Women's Basketball champions again. Their boosters would be ecstatic. Alumni donations would roll in fast and furious. At least, for a little while. They'd gain a smidge more respect in the conference and leverage within the NCAA as a whole.

Millie gave her a squinty-eyed glare, but Kate knew her old friend well enough to be certain she was doing mental backflips behind that mask of imperturbability. The other member of their unholy triumvirate, Professor Avery Preston, was most likely scamming leftover nachos from one of the snack bars. Athletics weren't her thing, but Avery was a good friend. She accepted her ticket to the game with only a few grumbling words about the possibility of bleacher butt.

Kate skimmed over the crowd of reporters, looking for one familiar face, but came up empty. Tamping down a sharp pang of disappointment, she sliced through the final strands, then waved the net high over her head.

Mike took the severed net from her as he handed her down from the ladder. Kate wriggled her feet into her pumps, then started toward the hastily stretched-out red carpet at the center of the arena to accept her prize.

There'd be no denying her legacy now. Kate Snyder was the winningest coach in the history of Wolcott athletics. Period. No need to add any pesky sport or gender qualification to the accolade.

Anxious to score good positions, the reporters scurried off to the press room while the NCAA commissioner took his spot next to the table holding the trophy. Her players slipped championship T-shirts over their heads and snapped selfies. Unlike the endless hoopla surrounding the men's tournament, this celebration was already winding down. Only a few die-hard fans would stick around for the presentation.

"You ready, Coach?" Director Samlin asked, taking his place beside her.

Kate smiled, then plucked her net from his hand. She liked Mike, but winning this tournament meant she had the balance of power firmly in her grasp. This particular battle was over, but the war wasn't won. Yet.

"I'm more than ready, Mike," she said as she draped the net over the corner of the trophy. "More than ready."

***

"I can't tell you how proud the entire Wolcott Warrior nation is at this moment…"

The athletic director's words faded to background noise as Kate surveyed the crowd crammed into the too-tiny conference room. Never in all her days as a player or a coach had she seen so many media outlets assembled in one spot. Well, maybe when she played in the Olympics, but certainly not here in America.

She didn't see Musburger or Costas in the crowd, but National Sports Network had sent their golden boy, Greg Chambers. She hadn't seen him live and in person in years. Something was up. Something juicer than an NCAA Women's title.

A lump of apprehension formed in her stomach. Cameras whirred and flashes blinked like strobes. She shifted on the utilitarian metal folding chair and squinted into the glare of the portable lights set up on either side of the stage. Needing something to ground her, she reached out to touch the severed net dangling off the edge of the trophy. Ironic that something that usually hung nine feet off the floor should make her feel more secure.

"...Coach Snyder's unwavering dedication to the Warrior athletic program is an inspiration to me and everyone who has known her as a player, leader, mentor, and role model."

Kate plastered a gracious smile back on her face and promptly zoned out as Mike launched into the usual spiel. She didn't need to be reminded of her accomplishments. The proof of her hard work and determination sat front and center on the table.

The Wolcott University Warrior Women were the national champions, and she, Kate Snyder—Wolcott alumna, WNBA all-star, and Olympic gold medalist— was the one who'd led them there. Again.

This was her moment. The net-draped trophy was her third Division I championship as a women's basketball head coach. A stat that placed her a half dozen wins behind the current king—Geno Auriemma, from the University of Connecticut—but next in line after her idol, the late, great Pat Summitt, in the record books.

A banner achievement. One more personal milestone. She just never imagined it would garner this much press attention. Kate drew a deep breath, trying to calm the nerves making her heart stutter-step, and tuned back into what the AD was saying.

"Kate Snyder is the personification of the title 'Coach.' Grace under pressure and the instincts of a born champion..."

His voice held a slightly too-enthusiastic edge. Kate

shot him a curious glance. Mike was a former NFL player turned collegiate program builder. Women's basketball probably wouldn't have even registered on his radar if his first gig as athletic director had landed him anywhere but Wolcott. But the Warrior Women held the only bragging rights the university had reaped in decades. That meant it was time for Mr. Former Football Star to suck it up and sing the praises of women's hoops.

"We are honored that Coach Snyder continues to call Wolcott University home…"

Ah, a shot across the bow. Her contract was up this year. He knew it, she knew it, and the handful of people in this room who actually cared about women's basketball did too. Kate Snyder was no longer willing to be treated like the protégé she'd once been.

No more jokes about the salary differential between her and her male counterparts being her contribution to the alumni fund. If Mike thought he could bamboozle her with a charming smile and a hefty dose of sentiment, he had another think coming. She was done shooting from the outside. He'd better be prepared to pay her what she was worth or be ready to take a charge, because she was coming at him straight down the middle.

"Kate Snyder is the epitome of a warrior, and I, for one, am damn glad to have her on my team." He turned his smooth-operator smile on her. "Coach, on behalf of the Warrior nation, I congratulate you on another fantastic season and thank you for doing us proud."

The two of them exchanged smiles and nods. She reached out to touch the net again, and a barrage of flashes nearly blinded her. Kate hoped the cameras captured every morsel of Mike's sincerity. Her agent was most likely recording the press conference, but Kate wanted to be sure they had a good record of the depth of his gratitude. Those things were easy to forget once contract negotiations began.

"Thank you, Director Samlin."

Squashing the rising tide of nervousness building inside her, she scanned the crowd, looking for a friendly face to focus on while she gave her statement. She didn't need to look any farther than the front row.

Jim Davenport from the *Sentinel* held his micro recorder pointed directly at her. She stifled a smirk when she noted the grim expression on his face. It seemed out of place. Jim was Wolcott's hometown sports reporter and a die-hard basketball junkie. You'd think that would make him the friendliest face of all, but no. He frowned every bit as fiercely as he glared at the other reporters, clearly peeved by the additional media coverage. Why hadn't he been out on the court?

A hot flash of annoyance fired in her gut. Jim ought to be happy. He was the guy with the inside track after all. He should have been the first clamoring for a quote. Pushing through her irritation, she ignored Jim's snit and scanned the room until she landed on the familiar face of Steve Bishop from one of the Nashville news affiliates. When their gazes locked, she turned on her brightest smile and dredged up a little of the drawl she'd never quite shed.

"And thanks, y'all. My, I never imagined a turnout like this. I thought I'd just let y'all catch a couple of pictures of the new hardware and then hop on the bus."

Her comment was met with a low rumble of chuckles. Though she'd been dealing with the press for years, it still took her some time to get her feet under her at media events. She zoomed in on Jim for a moment, allowing herself to dally in her comfort zone before making eye contact with the bigger sharks in the tank.

"I appreciate Director Samlin's praise, and trust me, I'll be playing that sound bite over and over on my DVR," she added, flashing her boss a cheeky grin. "But I'm not the one who won the game, am I?"

Lifting a challenging eyebrow, she turned her attention to Greg Chambers. She hadn't had the pleasure of seeing the National Sports Network's lead basketball commentator since she'd been in the WNBA and he'd been hanging around the sidelines hoping for a quote. Well, she had one for him now.

"Most of y'all didn't expect much out of us this year, and I want to thank you personally for giving these twelve phenomenal young women the kick in the long baggies they needed to get the job done. Just imagine: if we'd believed our own press, we could have been watchin' the game from home."

The press corps gave another appreciative chuckle, and she plowed ahead, confidence growing. "Then again, if we were watching from home, we would have had snacks." She pressed a hand to her stomach and grinned at the assemblage. "I don't suppose anyone thought to bring us any Ro-Tel dip? Maybe one of those six-foot sub sandwiches?"

That earned her a heartier round of laughter, but it was laced with discomfort she couldn't quite identify.

"Of course, it's also nice to be able to wrap this one up so close to home. The Music City has been awful good to us, but I hope that the good people of Nashville won't be offended when I say I think we all look forward to sleeping in our own beds tonight."

She went on to praise a few individual players for outstanding performances and heaped the usual load of "I couldn't do it without you" on her assistant coach, but still an undercurrent of impatience hummed through the room. Reporters tapped pens and repositioned equipment. Onlookers gathered along the walls shifted their weight from foot to foot. Her words came slower, but her mind raced.

Was she missing something? Forgetting to thank someone critical to the process? Was her blouse buttoned correctly? Or maybe she was committing the kind of unwitting gaffe that would turn her into an internet GIF before the evening was out?

Watching the crowd warily, she wound down with a self-deprecating chuckle. "I guess that's all I have to say."

She glanced at Mike and found the athletic director sitting rigid in his seat, his eyes fixed on someone at the very back of the room. She squinted, but like ninety percent of the guys in the room, the object of Mike's attention was dressed in the off-duty jock uniform of khakis and a knit polo shirt. He wore a ball cap pulled low over his eyes, but it didn't bear the Wolcott Warrior logo or the logo of any media outlet. No, his hat had what looked like a coiled snake appliquéd just above the bill.

A jolt of unease fired through her belly as every reporter's hand shot up, but she kept her smile firmly in place. Director Samlin gave his head the tiniest shake, but she wasn't about to be waved off. They'd won. This was her night, and damn it, she could alley-oop any question the jackals threw at her. Her team had played strong and clean. She had nothing to hide.

So she went straight to the biggest jackal of them all. "Yes, Greg?" she said, giving NSN their due by nodding to Chambers first.

To her surprise, he didn't direct his question to her but spoke to the man sitting next to her.

"Director Samlin, at five forty-three this evening, a private plane owned by Richard Donner, one of Wolcott University's biggest boosters, touched down at Nashville International. Witnesses at the airport confirmed that the plane was carrying former Northern University football coach Danny McMillan."

Kate's gaze immediately flew to the mystery man at the back of the crowd, but the snake charmer was gone. Everyone in the room seemed to be waiting for Mike's reply. Turning to look at the AD, she found Mike wearing a mildly curious expression. But the man's eyes were sharp.

He offered an apologetic but confused smile. "I'm sorry, was there a question I missed?"

"What is he doing here?" Chambers asked. "Are you thinking of hiring him to replace Coach Morton when he retires?"

"Coach Morton has not informed me of any retirement plans, so I think it would be a bit presumptuous to start looking for candidates to fill his job," Mike answered smoothly.

"Then what is Coach McMillan doing here?"

The smile Mike turned on the reporter probably got him laid back in his playing days based on wattage alone. "Perhaps he wanted to come watch the game."

"But you and Coach McMillan played together—"

Mike held up a hand to stop the reporter. "People, I can honestly tell you that no one employed by the Wolcott athletic department is thinking about anything but basketball tonight. This is Coach Snyder's and her team's night, and if you don't have any further questions pertaining to tonight's stellar championship victory, I'm going to thank Coach for doing us all proud once again and let her get back to the celebration she so richly deserves."

The room exploded with shouts and calls, but Mike ignored them all as he pushed his chair back and rose. She stood too, and the moment their eyes met, she knew every word he'd just said was complete bullshit.

Acknowledgments

Special thanks to Cat Clyne, Laura Costello, Rachel Gilmer, and the Sourcebooks team for their unflagging dedication to making the Love Games series shine. I appreciate your willingness to share your expertise and your continued enthusiasm for these characters. I'm so happy to be a part of the Sourcebooks family!

Thanks to my agent, Sara Megibow, for her encouragement, support, and exclamation points. Your passion for what you do is as infectious as your smile.

I want to give a shout-out to my Super Cool Party People, DSRA Diamonds, and the assemblage of awesome authors and rad readers I've collected over the years. I have the most fabulous friends, everybody says so.

I could not do what I do without my critique partner, Julie Doner. She's my best bud, pesky little sister, and everyday inspiration. She keeps me motivated and curbs my comma abuse, all while working for peanuts. Literally. The PayDay bars are in the mail.

As the youngest of seven, I learned early what the phrase "No blood, no foul" meant. I like to think that early training toughened me up, but I admit to being a bit of a softy where my family is concerned. I mostly forgive you for the scrapes and scars.

And last but not least, thanks to Bill, the man who makes me feel like a champion every single day.

About the Author

By day, Maggie Wells is buried in spreadsheets. At night, she pens tales of people tangling up the sheets. The product of a charming rogue and a shameless flirt, you only have to scratch the surface of this mild-mannered married lady to find a naughty streak a mile wide. She has a passion for college football, processed cheese foods, and happy endings. Not necessarily in that order.